THE

TRIBUTARIES

of

ALEX

BECKHAM

ROBERT BECKSTEDT

TABLE OF CONTENTS

I wish to thank the following:

Phyl Good – Copy Editor
Ashley Quick – Illustrator
Molly Beckstedt – Illustrator
Murphy Rae – Cover Designer
Alyssa Garcia – Formatter
Carla Bradshaw – Proof Reader

I dedicate this book to my family and ancestors and to my youngest grandson, Cooper Battle Randall, who at age four has no idea the understanding he has brought into my life. I would have never fully comprehended as I do now so many events in my existence without him and his mother.

I believe the world is one big family, and we need to help each other.

Jet Li

In every conceivable manner, the family is link to our past, bridge to our future.

Alex Haley

Youth cannot know how age thinks and feels. But old men are guilty if they forget what it was to be young.

J.K. Rowling , <u>Harry Potter and the Order of the Phoenix</u>

PRELUDE

The Tributaries of Alex Beckham consists of six novellas which weave their way through a young boy's life until one tragic day, at the age of sixteen, he goes to bed a child and wakes up on the first rung of the next stage of his life. Threads of ancestry flow through the story as far back as nineteenth century Prussia. His feelings of being loved by his family, as well as doubting the love of others in his clan, become a lifelong quest for the truth. And as he grows, the very question of his emotional stability is challenged, bringing him to the brink of an unfulfilling future that would have failed to touch people all around the globe and benefitted so many.

These six episodes intertwine as Alex begins his life with an abstract blueprint taken from his grandmother's aging and crumbling plaster ceiling. For most of his youth, he was forced to use his imagination, as it was his only source of entertainment since those early days of his childhood found his family financially unable to afford a television, and the invention of electronic toys was still years away. But that necessity to use his own interpretations of the people and things around him to develop his own philosophies became a blessing and the key to his adult life as a writer.

Alex Beckham, like most all of humanity, struggled through those first years of life with the fears of love, hate and empathy as well as the emotionally heightened feelings stemming from the brilliance of the new discoveries that surrounded him. I hope Alex will allow you to feel those days of your own childhood, both good and bad, in which we all trudged our way to self-reliance and gained the ability to make healthy decisions for ourselves and our own young offspring.

INTRODUCTIONS

Hi, my name is Alex, Alexander Raymond Beckham, to be exact, and I just turned five years old. I'm so skinny I can count all my ribs, and I'm smart as a whip most of the time, but unfortunately, not all. Obviously, I'm not well-read, since at this age, I'm still illiterate. But I can gladly say I am "well-read-to" by my father. I also find myself uncommonly curious when it comes to social relationships, I mean, observing how people treat one another. But to be candid, at this age, I don't ponder them much; I just listen, watch, and store them somewhere in my brain for future reference. It'll only be in my young adulthood that I'll realize these observations have become the fundamentals of my personality, then go deeper and widen the love in my very soul.

I began my toddler era as an only child, cute as a button, according to some of my family anyway, attracting lots of hugs and attention, so much so that my grandmother entered me in numerous local baby contests. She became maternally agitated when I didn't get blue ribbons, and frankly, I never won any color ribbon at all. I did win a Popsicle once, and it made my lips turn blue. I would have rather played with my trucks in a mud puddle full of worms and toads than be in another one of those contests and listen to Grandma complain about "nepotism," whatever that meant.

But eventually, time ran out on Grandma as I evolved into my awkward schoolboy years, growing less and less adorable as time progressed. I was as bony as the skeleton on our front door during Trick or Treat, my head was shaped like a lopsided peanut and accentuated by my burr haircut, my front teeth had a gap like a seven-ten split in a bowling alley, and my mother began my social life on my first half-day session of kindergarten by dressing me like a 1950s Lilliputian business executive at some General Motors plant. And as I observed others in my classroom, I perceived their feelings were equally as awkward as my own, especially the ones dressed in rags and no socks. We were both on the opposite ends of abnormal, feeling the holes staring through us like we were Martians or something. It was too early for me to understand anything about prejudgment, but I sensed a misled attitude toward us, mostly from the teachers.

Consequently, being as I'm unable to read or write at all at this stage, and realizing by the time this era of my early youth concludes that I'll still not be talented enough to write a sophisticated novel or short story worthy of being read by anyone, except maybe my dad (maybe)—therefore, we hired Dad's adult friend, Robert Beckstedt, to be my ghost writer for these formative years. And he has done such a beautiful job of expressing my feelings and emotions, I'll wind up hiring him later in life as my mentor. He will go on to teach me how to write on higher and more varied platforms as I mature. So please, let him and me take it from here. I hope we can touch your hearts, as I hold these episodes dear and depict a life with assuredly abstract similarities to many of yours. Our goal is to instill some kind of enjoyment in you while observing the foundations of our culture and the choices and the attitudes we have all adopted subjectively and individually because of them.

A WORD FROM THE AUTHOR

It was 1955, and the alternatives available to occupy Alex's curious mind prior to the commencement of his formal education and literacy didn't include television, primarily due to his family's financial situation as well as the technology of the times. Radios existed, but the crackling reception caused the baseball games and 1950s music to be indiscernible and of no value to Alex. Neither computer games, cell phones, nor movies were available for preschoolers of any intelligence. These were all at least a decade into the future. The remaining options for any sort of mental stimuli were nursery rhymes, fairy tales, and other children's books read to him by his father. Also, Alex enjoyed comic books dominated by illustrations in which he quite enjoyed imagining the storyline himself, or listening to scratchy, thick vinyl records on his phonograph, which resembled his dad's briefcase. The sound created was truly just as bad as the radio, but at least they told stories.

So with the lack of formal, humanly developed entertainment, Alex was forced to create his own unlimited sources of informal amusement: the subliminal exploration of people and things surrounding him every day, a busy anthill, catching lightning bugs, a colorful gasoline spill after a rain storm, or the thrill of observing and attempting to understand unusual adult behaviors (especially when they didn't realize he was paying attention). But enough of this groundwork. Allow me to begin his memoirs here in the days of his initial memories, as expressed in my prose, with his observations and experiences of the adult world in which he would eventually find himself submerged.

A lot of memories linger for all of us. The brain is an amazing sponge of factual knowledge, blended with emotions, then intermingled with social interactions. No matter how insignificant or intensely penetrating they may be at the time, it's this combination, not simply the plot lines of our experiences, that create far more detail that buries itself into our own subconscious as well as that of our supporting players. Let Alex and me continue primarily with the highlights of his life and those of his ancestors that influenced him and many others. Then we will fill in the rest of the story with my omniscient narration to make them more enjoyable to you, our audience.

This collection of short novellas known as *The Tributaries of Alex Beckham* are fictional; however, each story has a foundation of abstract truth based on the earliest experiences and recollections of a young boy in the 1950s and into the 1960s.

As most all psychoanalysis begins on a couch with a person jotting notes on a pad as they ask about one's childhood, one's parents, one's friends, and one's family, I have attempted to delve into the core of Alex Beckham and discover what people and events were like rivers and streams, emptying lessons into and creating wisdom and personality for this young man as he matured and entered the adult world.

Some of you readers will recognize antiquities similar to those in your childhood, while others will be too young to have experienced things like the days before television and computers. Either way, I hope you find the development of this boy's character and soul to have similarities among all generations.

EPISODE I

NOVEMBER 1954
THE STORY OF ALEX BECKHAM ALMOST ENDS
BEFORE IT BEGINS

Mary and Randall catapulted from their peaceful sleep, both with stunned looks of terror, staring piercingly into each other's eyes through the semi-darkness. The streetlights and car headlights invaded their bedroom from the truck route that constantly rumbled past their windows like thunder on a hot summer evening.

"Oh my God, what was that? Randall, no, it can't be!" Mary heaved the covers across the bed, rocketing from her slumber as any lioness would do to protect her endangered cub. She flipped on the hall light, and the nightmare she had feared all her life, or at least since the day she realized her son had inherited the contaminated gene that afflicted many of her ancestors, lay limply at the bottom of the stairs below her bare feet, unconscious. His body was distorted, with blood splattered on the walls and gushing onto the bottom step of the uncarpeted stairway.

"Randall, it's him, it's Alex. He's fallen down the steps! Oh my God!" She raced down the steps without a thought for her own safety. Alex was hemorrhaging from his forehead, right between his eyes. Not considering any other injury to his spine or limbs, she scooped him up into her arms and embraced him as she sat on the bottom step, holding him tightly to her impassioned bosom. "Randall, his eyes are rolling back in his head. He's breathing but not crying. Get me some ice in a towel, and then get the car. We must get him to the hospital right now. We've no time to call an ambulance. He's never had a head injury. Oh, Randall, this is exactly the thing we've all been fearing."

Randall stepped over his wife's back and darted straight to the kitchen. Mary's pajamas, like Alex's, were instantly soaked in blood; the gash lay open deep and wide, as if he had been attacked with a meat cleaver. Mary held the thick chunk of skin tightly back in the wound with two of her fingers as the blood ran down Alex's face and the underside of Mary's forearm.

"Let's go, Randall, what's taking you so long?" screamed Mary in a panic.

"These damned cheap-ass ice cube trays won't let me get the ice out." Mary heard Randall slamming the trays violently on the sink as he swore profusely, something extremely rare for Alex's father. Alex still had not cried. Mary held him tightly and rocked him in her arms, her heart pounding and her face filled with terror.

"Here, Mary, here's the ice. How do you think this happened?" asked Randall.

"Go get the car, and we'll talk about it on the way to the ER. I'm scared, Randall, I think he's unconscious, and if he has a concussion, he needs to stay awake. Randall, where are you going? I said, 'Go get the car!'"

Randall squeezed past Alex and Mary, climbed the steps on all fours like an animal, and was back in seconds. "Let me get to his nose, honey." Mary pulled Alex's head from her bloody bosom, and Randall held the smelling salts under his toddler's nostrils. Alex's head jerked backwards as if in a seizure, but his eyes opened, and they flip-flopped around like jelly as he attempted to focus on his mother and father standing over him. Slowly, he regained consciousness, and as he did, he began to cry horribly from the pain. It was a pitiful sound, but one that gave Mary and Randall the first slim hope of Alex's survival. He was not in a coma, not yet, anyway. But a slow bleed inside his skull was the number one danger to their little love's survival.

Randall gave the salts to Mary and dashed for the garage. Again, within seconds, he came running to the bottom of the steps, where the blood-soaked mother and child held tightly to each other. "Give him to me, Mary, and get in the car. I'll carry him out to the driveway and place him on your lap."

As both were still in their pajamas and no shoes, Mary handed Alex to her husband and made a quick scamper upstairs and grabbed their slippers. As she glanced into Alex's room, she noticed his one-eyed scraggly teddy bear laying alone on his floor. She grabbed him as well. She knew Alex would need him, and the bear would need Alex. As she hurried down the steps, she made one more agile aside to grab her purse and Randall's wallet from the telephone stand in the hallway. She then hurried to the car; both of their feet ached from the cold concrete, as Randall followed her with Alex. "Did you lock the front door, Randall?" Mary was reacting out of pure habit.

"Forget the door, Mary, get in and let's go," responded Randall with no emotion. Mary realized at that point anyone could take anything they wanted from her home, but nothing was of any value except the life of her son, who she held passionately and protectively in her arms. Now that Alex was regaining conscious-ness, he was fighting her as she placed the ice on his wound; it hurt. But it would only take a few minutes until he would become passive once more as numbness set in.

It was four o'clock in the morning on a cool November night. The streets were empty except for an occasional truck deliver-ing newspapers or donuts or fresh bread, or a garbage truck emp-tying the cans of rotting food and liquor bottles from the closed bars and restaurants. A stray rat looking for an unemptied trash can attempted to cut across Randall's path, but a swerve wasn't even considered as the squish of its skull was felt under the front tire. Randall would slow down somewhat at intersections, but he treated stop signs and traffic lights as only suggestions, as he sped to save his son's life.

"Randall, be careful! What if you get stopped for running these red lights? We have to get Alex to the hospital now. We don't have time…" Mary scolded.

"Best thing that could happen, honey. The police would un-doubtedly escort us or put you and Alex in their cruiser and get you there even faster. How is he?" Randall gripped the wheel so tightly his hands were cramping and his knuckles were white.

"I can tell by his sobbing he's awake, and he's actually calmer than I would expect him to be, too calm. That scares me, Randall. I'm scared his brain isn't really with us, if you know what I mean," responded Mary.

"Maybe he's just a tough little kid, honey. Don't worry, we're almost there." Randall could now see the top of the hospital in the distance just a few blocks away.

Alex had stopped his arduous crying, which came as much from the confusion and panic of his parents as his external injury. His pain was gradually changing from sharp to dull, and his confu-sion over the chaos of getting him to the car had calmed. But blood still ran steadily down his cheek onto his mother's breast, and his eyes were distant. He stuck his thumb in his mouth and sniffed a sob or a whimper from time to time. He knew his mother would keep him safe, but he was too young to understand the situation that might be about to challenge his short life. This was the first, and unfortunately not the last, test of the true seriousness of his condition. Medicine had not come far enough to either diagnose the severity of his infirmity or discover any treatment for it whatsoever.

"So, what happened, Mary? Could you tell?" Randall didn't look at his wife and son, as he was bent over the steering wheel, concentrating fiercely, like a race car driver in a European Grand Prix.

"He had to have tumbled down the steps, then hit the corner of the windowsill at the bottom with full force. When I got there, his forehead right between his eyes was split wide open and, oh my God, Randall, it's deep. The chunk of skin was dangling, holding on by just a thread. That's what I keep pressing back into the contusion." Mary was able to picture every detail of that horrifying moment in her memory, and would be able to forever.

"But how do you think he fell down the steps in the first place," asked Randall, "and does he have any other injuries?"

"While you were fighting with and cussing at the ice cube trays, I squeezed his arms and legs, and I didn't feel any breaks. But he does jerk away when I touch his ankle." Mary was strangely calm, but that wasn't obvious by the quiver in her voice and the shivering of her body. "Randall could tell she was on the cliff's edge of breaking down. "But that's not what I'm terrified of. It's the internal bleeding inside his brain. Please, God, please let him live!"

Inside, Randall was terrified as well but needed to keep Mary calm so her serenity would be felt by Alex. "But how did he fall down the steps, Mary?" asked Randall. "We've never seen him sleepwalk before. When he climbs in bed with us during storms or when he has a bad dream, he's always awake."

"Randall, when I reached him at the bottom of the stairs, his pajama bottoms were around his knees. My guess is, since we still put a diaper on him at night, he was trying to be a big boy and go to the bathroom for the first time in the night. He must have lost his balance trying to take his pajamas and diaper off. Oh, bless his heart, he was trying to please us. Oh, Randall, this is all my fault. This gene came from my side of the family. I should have never had children. I've seen what my brother's gone through. Randall, I should have never brought Alex into this situation, or you. I'm so sorry. Please forgive me. Oh Randall, if he doesn't pull through…!" Mary finally broke into tears. "No more children, Randall, I won't take the chance of having another Alex." Alex was beginning to get his brain back and could hear the conversation, but it was like two people talking with buckets on their heads.

"Stop that right now, Mary. We did have him, and I was aware of the danger as much as you. He's been such a blessing to us and the whole family already." Mary held Alex tight as if to protect him from death itself. "He'll be fine, Mary. We both knew it wasn't going to be easy and there would be times like this, though I must say, the reality of the situation is way more frightening than what we imagined. I'll give you that. He's going to be fine though, I feel it."

Alex could hear them talking but didn't really understand what they were referring to. Alex thought, *What does 'pull through' mean? And what 'situation?' But especially, why doesn't Mommy want another me? Is something wrong with me? Doesn't Mommy love me? Anyway, I really don't want another me, either, I just want a sister!* He was starting to become cognizant of his surroundings but in a very foggy frame of mind, confused about what seemed to be the important pieces of their conversation.

"I think a gate at the top of the steps is a must," suggested Randall as he attempted to stay calm; using his brain to problem solve rather than his emotions. One of them had to do this, and in a hurry.

Randall pulled in behind an ambulance in the ER semicircle,

turned the car off, pulled the emergency brake, and rushed around to open Mary's door. He gripped her by the arm to help her from the front seat, but her adrenaline allowed her to stand by way of her own strength. She continued to press the chunk of skin firmly but somehow tenderly with her fingertips into Alex's wound.

As the three started towards the entrance, Randall heard a voice calling from a close distance. It was a security guard, an old man with gray scraggly hair, walking quite bent over. "Excuse me, sir, but you can't park there. That's for ambulances only. You need to move your car right away."

Without stopping his dash towards the ER, Randall turned his head in the direction of the approaching guard. "You move it, and bring me the keys inside. Keys are in the ignition."

'Sir, we aren't allowed to do that. It's against hospital rules!" yelled the old man as he followed Randall.

Randall rolled his eyes as he rushed to the glass doors and held one open for his wife and son. Without looking back, he yelled to the guard, "Then tow it!"

The doors entered directly into the ER waiting room. A dozen children or so populated the worn, uncomfortable plastic chairs as they sat on their mothers' laps being rocked lovingly, but there was an eerie silence of repose in the air. Randall placed his hand on the small of Mary's back and gently pushed her towards the registration window.

"May I help you?" asked an elderly woman in street clothes, with very tired eyes.

Mary spoke first. "My son fell down a flight of stairs and hit a windowsill at the bottom. He cut his head wide open and may have a concussion along with a possible brain bleed." She began to explain further but was abruptly interrupted.

"Oh, it does look like some stitches may be in order, doesn't it? But I'm sure he'll be fine. We see this every night, Mrs....?"

"Beckham, I'm Mary Beckham, my husband is Randall, and this is Alex."

"Mrs. Beckham, have a seat here in front of me, and we'll begin the registration process. Keep your fingers on his wound. This won't take long, fifteen, twenty minutes at the most," said the woman behind the desk. "I'll need you to fill out these forms, and all three of you will need to first meet with Social Services."

"Social Services? We have insurance, and we don't need any financial help," Randall said quickly.

"Oh no, sir, this isn't financial. They must ask you a few questions to be assured this was an accident and not a case of child abuse."

Mary and Randall couldn't help but feel insulted by the thought that someone was inferring they may have done this violently to their own child, but they understood. Still Mary blurted, "No, you don't understand the severity. My son needs to see a doctor right away. The paperwork can wait, not to mention your social workers. If you refuse, we'll burst through those doors and find one. And don't think we won't, because we will. A doctor now, please!"

As instructed in cases of confrontation, the elderly lady got up from her chair and disappeared into the back room. After a few long minutes, a nurse dressed in all white came through the doors. "I understand you are Mr. and Mrs. Beckham and you have a problem. We are getting to you as soon as we can, but first you must complete the registration forms and meet with Social Services. It's required and out of our control. Please have a seat with the other parents, Mrs. Beckham; he must be getting heavy."

"First, I'll continue to hold my son with his head elevated. He has a bleeding condition, hemophilia A, and—"

"Come now, Mrs. Beckham, do you know how many of you panicky mothers come in here claiming their children are bleeders to get to the front of the line? I hear it over and over. He'll be good as new by morning. But we must insist you follow protocol."

"Look here, Nursie, we don't have time—" Mary suddenly lost it, but Randall interrupted just in time.

"Honey, honey, let me explain to the nurse here. You just keep calm, so Alex stays calm. Don't scare him, love him. He's under-standing more than you think, right, Alex?" Alex gave his father a questionable glance from his mother's shoulder. "Your mommy has you tight. You'll be fine, Tiger." Randall brushed Alex's blond, angel-soft hair with his hand and modified his words with a confi-dent and reassuring smile.

Alex gave a faint smile back from the corners of his mouth around the serenity of his thumb. But he was unaware that this was all going to get worse before it got better, including stitches, IVs, ice, X-rays, and possibly major surgery if a brain bleed was present.

Randall looked at the nurse, who was taken aback by Mary's attitude. She suddenly appeared purposely noncooperative. Ran-dall picked up on the attitude, but cold hard facts, spoken in a straightforward tone of voice, were the only solution for proper care to save his son's life, he thought.

"I can see by your name tag that you are Nurse Spears," Ran-dall said calmly but forcefully.

"I am. I'm the head nurse on this shift in charge of triage, and I'm sorry if I upset your wife, but this is a routine injury, and judg-ing by your son's actions, if there is a concussion at all, it will be minor." The nurse addressed Randall, her voice quivering from the challenge to her authority. Randall knew Alex was not himself, and his eyes were still bloodshot and glossy. This nurse was just covering her buttocks by following "protocol."

"No, Nurse Spears, I assure you, this is not routine. We need you to page Dr. Anthony Shubert right away and tell him his pa-tient, Alex Beckham, is in the ER with an external wound and a possible brain bleed. He's the head pediatric hematologist here at Children's Hospital. He'll give you preliminary instructions as to what you and your staff need to do before he arrives. I'll give you his number. Please page him immediately." Randall could still sense a combative attitude from the nurse. He took his wallet from his back pocket and pulled out Dr. Shubert's card, with his emergency pager number as well as his office number.

"Sir, I'm sorry, but keep your card for now. We can call him in the morning when he's in his office. I'm sure our attending can do whatever is necessary," the nurse responded indignantly.

"Then get your attending right now and tell him you have a child with hemophilia A and a possible internal brain bleed, and I want you to tell him that you personally have made a unilateral decision to wait a few hours to call his hematologist. And if you refuse to go right now, I'll call Shubert myself, according to our instructed 'protocol' from him. But he will still need to talk to your attending." Randall's voice was no longer one of discussion or compromise with the nurse's opinion.

"You're positive he's a hemophiliac? You know these doctors need their sleep as much as any of us. You'd better not be conning us, sir," responded the nurse.

With that, Randall turned from the nurse and looked at Mary. "Wait here with Alex, Mary; I'll be right back." He spun around and burst through two swinging doors, down a short hallway, and into an area where sick and injured children lay quietly or whimpering in their beds, divided by dingy curtains. Randall walked through the maze as he began to yell over and over. "I need the attending right now! Where is he?" Nurses and parents poked their heads out from behind the curtains, attempting to understand the chaos taking place. "And I'll not lower my voice until he speaks with me. Is that understood, everyone? I need to see the attending now! Who understands that? I'll say it again. I need to see the attending right now! Where might I find him? Hello, people, someone needs to get the attending physician right now!"

The staff stood stunned at Randall's repetition. No one moved an inch, except Nurse Spears. She dashed in and raced to a phone. "Security, I need security right now. Come to the ER please. A parent is threatening one of our doctors and disrupting the ER."

Randall continued to yell for the attending physician as the nurse, hanging up the telephone, tried to calm him down by telling him Security was on its way. But suddenly, a doctor, looking like he'd just woken up, came out the door of a small side room.

"I'm Dr. Sanka, the attending physician. Please settle down, sir. You're disturbing the children and parents here. If you don't, I'll have you physically removed. Now, what's your problem? I know, your child is hurt, and it's an emergency. Every parent here thinks their child is our biggest emergency."

Randall calmed immediately, like a candle extinguished by two dampened fingers. He returned to his solid intensity and purpose. Although he was still frustrated, his actions of the last minute had been strictly an act to obtain the proper attention, and they had been successful. He finally had the ear of someone with power and authority.

"Dr. Sanka, I'll say this quickly. My son is diagnosed with hemophilia A, inherited from his mother. Her brother is also a hemophiliac, so there is no doubt. Your nurse isn't taking us seriously, thus, stepping it up a notch was my only remaining resource to get your attention. He's fallen down a flight of stairs, and there's a good possibility he has a brain bleed, the injury we all fear the most, as I'm sure you well know. I need you to page Anthony Shubert right away, as this is his instruction to us. He'll give you emergency treatment orders. He'll arrive as soon as he can. Here is his number." Randall was getting tired of repeating himself. He again pulled Shubert's card from his wallet. Sanka put it in the pocket of his white coat.

"Sir, I assure you, you now have my full attention," he said in an intensely deliberate tone. "Why didn't you tell us that right away?" The nurse looked at the floor. Randall stared at her so brutally, she could actually feel it in her bones.

"We tried, but your head nurse over there didn't feel it was anything out of the ordinary and questioned our credibility. She said you all needed your sleep. My son is still in the waiting room with my wife, for God's sake," Randall said with a frown that meant trouble for someone.

"Let's all go get him." Sanka moved quickly and spoke as he walked. "Nurse Spears, you left a head wound in the waiting room, one with hemophilia no less, and didn't get me right away?" Dr. Sanka was more than upset. It wasn't the first time she had ruffled his stethoscope.

Nurse Spears shuffled to keep up. "You were asleep, doctor, and you're on a thirty-six-hour shift. You need your rest. Dr. Shubert would be asleep as well, and frankly, sir, we don't have an open bed, with this influenza epidemic, not to mention it's a holiday weekend and we're short-staffed. I have others to attend to," answered the nurse, as if that was a reasonable answer. "I mean, I was just doing my job, doctor. I'm in charge of triage. Is that not correct?"

The doctor started to come back at Nurse Spears when Randall interrupted and raised his voice in anger, for real this time. "Can the two of you discuss your bureaucratic bullshit later and treat my son immediately? We have wasted too much time already."

The three reached the waiting room where Mary still held Alex close to her breast. "Spears, get this child to one of the ORs right away. Keep his head elevated, and I want ice on both his wound and the back of his neck." Sanka had finally taken the reigns from his nurse.

"And his right ankle, doctor," interjected Randall.

Sanka reached in his pocket and handed Shubert's card to the nurse. "Spears, here is Shubert's number. Page him and get him on the phone for me, stat!" he barked as he quickly checked Alex's pupils.

"Well, doctor, I can't do both, get him to the OR and page Shubert, now, can I?" Nurse Spears had just crossed a line that would affect her career for the rest of her life.

Randall got things moving from staff too tied up in their own set of rules to care about Alex. Without hesitation, the doctor snatched the card back from Nurse Spears' grip and called Shubert himself. The staff in the "understaffed" ER was now flying around like bees whose hive had just been attacked by a mean papa bear, though it had actually been attacked by one of humankind's worst enemies, a lack of accountability. Randall and Mary would, from that day forward, realize that Alex's medical treatment was in their hands and not in those of the health care providers. Being polite wasn't going to be in the best interests of their endangered son. And many times, and for many years to come, Alex would hear the story of this night, so he would realize that when the time came and he was an adult, he would have to guard his own life all by himself.

Randall took Alex from Mary's aching arms as they passed through the swinging doors, pressing one hand against the boy's hemorrhaging forehead, the other pressing Alex's bloody cheek to his own. Blood was now smeared on both parent's faces.

Mary scampered behind to keep up with Randall. "Is everything okay, Randall? I could hear your voice all the way out here. Is everyone angry with us now?" Mary felt she was about to be scorned as they entered the ER.

"No one is angry except the head nurse, but things are moving. Let's go." And as Randall, Mary, and Alex walked through the double doors, Nurse Spears appeared and stopped them with a young man in a blue jump suit and a gurney.

"Here, lay him down, and I'll get ice for his neck after we wheel him to the OR," said the nurse. She had a very worried but still indignant look on her face.

Randall lost it. He'd had enough of this woman. "What are you, just freakin' stupid, woman? Didn't you listen? The doctor said to keep his head elevated. You know what that means, like upright, like don't lay him flat? Now go, and I'll follow you to the OR if you don't get us all lost! And hey, Gurney Boy, bring a bucket of ice and some towels to the OR for my son! And get us a bed that cranks upright; move!" Randall was pulling no punches.

Gurney Boy looked at the nurse with a puzzled glance, as if he were thinking, *Should I really do that, that's not my job, you know? And he's not my boss!*

"Grab the first nurse you see and tell her to bring lots of ice packs to the OR, stat!" yelled Nurse Spears at Gurney Boy. "And yes, find a proper bed." She was ready to make a quick turnabout and quit right on the spot. She was truly exasperated. She felt she'd taken enough abuse and disrespect from this man over his kid, and her boss was going to hear about it in the morning! (Turned out she would walk out the next day, but not of her own accord. Sanka's recount trumped Nurse Spear's; done.)

Randall and Mary, with Alex held tight in Randall's grasp, followed the nurse expeditiously down a dimly lit hallway, the hallway to the emergency OR. Blood covered Mary's torso, and tears were running down her cheeks. Randall was all business, and Alex could sense the safety and strength of his father's embrace. *But why is Mommy crying? I'm the one that's hurt. I'm the one that should be crying,* Alex wondered.

Alex looked over his father's shoulder while he carried him. He could see three people, two nurses and a man in a white coat, behind them. The nurse, the one his daddy didn't seem to like, was in front, leading the way to somewhere. His head still hurt, and he was unable to stop whimpering. He then became aware of the cold sterile walls, and he could hear children and adults crying off in the distance. He was slowly becoming aware of his surroundings, and his memory was slowly returning. *What is this place? It's familiar, but I've never been here before. It's the smell, a smell somewhere between the odor of clean sheets and cough medicine. This must be the hospital place where my mother told Daddy to drive me.*

It was all starting to come back to him now, but he was still unable to talk. *I remember waking up, and I had to pee. Usually I don't wake up for that. I thought Mommy and Daddy would be so happy if I peed in the night in the toilet and not in my pants. So, OK, I remember, I got out of bed and went to the bathroom. I was gonna wake them, but I wanted to surprise them after I peed.*

They'd be so proud of me. But as I got to the bathroom door, I realized they had put a diaper and rubber pants on me, since I was still wetting the bed at night. I went to take my pajama bottoms off when I lost my balance and fell backwards down the steps, my body flopping everywhere. Next thing I remember, and not very well, are a few words in the car, Mommy holding me in that room back there, hearing Daddy's voice yelling at someone behind the doors, and now here I am in my daddy's arms being led down a hallway to somewhere; and everyone's in a hurry. I can feel a trickle of blood being wiped from my face with a tissue from time to time. Wow, my head hurts! And my ankle!

• • •

Dr. Shubert confirmed Dr. Sanka's preliminary instructions during their call. The staff had already started the procedures, thank goodness. He also told Sanka to get hold of the neurologist on call and have them all meet in the OR before any stitching was performed. Alex was to be kept awake and calm, preferably with a caffeinated drink of some sort, such as a Coca Cola or coffee. Mary knew Alex would have no part of coffee, so Coke it was.

In about thirty minutes, as Alex sat up in the hospital bed, which had been cranked up to near ninety degrees, he drank his Coca Cola through a bendy straw. The physician team of Sanka and Shubert joined the family in the OR. Sanka began, "Dr. Shubert, while we awaited your arrival, I examined the boy's joints, but only by touch. It appears his ankle is either sprained or fractured, and we have it iced as well."

"Thank you, Dr. Sanka." Dr. Shubert glanced at Alex's foot but didn't seem too concerned about his ankle. Sanka had the indignant Nurse Spears replaced by a male nurse named Rex Leatherwood, a tall, young and strong black gentlemen exuding an aura of tranquility. "Nurse Leatherwood, hold the boy's leg still with ice packs until the numbness penetrated his joint." Alex was in pain and wanted to pull away, but the new man continued to look at him with a soothing stare and a caring smile. Sanka knew some physical strength was going to be needed for what Alex was about to undergo in the next hour or so.

Nurse Leatherwood looked Alex straight in the eye. "I know, Cowboy, ice always hurts at first, like a bee sting or when you make a snowball without mittens. But it'll get better in a jiffy. I hate it too when I get hurt. But you have to take it like a man for just a few more minutes, until your foot turns into a Popsicle, okay? But I won't let anybody eat your foot, I promise!" Alex smiled for the first time since the accident. He liked this man, he was funny, and Alex trusted he knew what was best for him. When Alex's foot got numb, the nurse wrapped it tight in an ACE bandage, then continued the ice.

The last to arrive was the neurologist, Dr. Jwala Prasad. Shubert pulled him into the hallway, dark and cold, and explained the accident, Alex's hemophilia, and his concern for a possible fatal bleeding of the brain. The neurologist, a forty-something Indian physician, understood the need for his specialty immediately. They returned to the brightly lit OR, where introductions were made.

"I'm assuming the child is about four, more or less, by his size and demeanor? How did this happen?" Prasad asked Randall.

"Yes, he turned four two weeks ago. And we're not exactly sure how he fell down the stairs, but we're unaware of any sleepwalking issues in the past," Randall answered.

Mary's guilt for passing on the gene was overwhelming as she looked at blood still running slowly down Alex's nose and into his mouth. Randall and Mary both understood that the delay in treating the wound was necessary, and they were deeply appreciative of the attention now being given to Alex. Still, the fear and tension of what they didn't know was growing anxiously inside them. It was barely controllable.

"How intelligent is your son, Mrs. Beckham?" began Dr.

Prasad. "Is he autistic? What I mean by autistic, is he mentally slow in any way? Are his behaviors behind those of other children his age? Does he show signs of rage, or did he begin talking or walking late? Does he know his ABCs, colors, sounds? If I show him an object, will he know what it is?" Prasad was asking in such a rapid fashion that Mary was unable to answer each question individually, but she did comprehend the general purpose of the doctor's questioning.

"Yes, he's exceptionally familiar with all of those things. My husband reads to him most every night, and he and I do puzzles. And he helps me bake cookies and such, but mainly so he can lick the bowl." Mary spoke now in a monotone, ever so proud of Alex, as she held the ice on his head and kissed him on the cheek. Randall was on the other side, making sure the ice stayed on the back of Alex's neck, as the boy squirmed from the discomfort. Finally, the numbness set in just like Nurse Leatherwood had said it would and Alex settled down, still taking small sips of Coca Cola. There were no hints of him dozing off.

"His pupils were dilating properly about thirty minutes ago on my first examination," Sanka said to Prasad.

"Yes, they're not perfect, but they're dilating close to normal. Mr. Beckham, do you have your car keys on you?" Prasad was starting his examination.

"I don't, sir. I left them in the car and told the security guard to move it or tow it when we arrived. Do I need to move my car?" asked Randall.

"I have them in my purse, Randall. The guard brought them in when you were back in the ER." Mary and Randall smiled at each other like two children who won another battle against an unreasonable adult.

"No, no, Mr. Beckham. I just need your keys for a moment. May I have them please?" Randall reached into Mary's purse where she had put them and gave Prasad his keys, a disgusting soiled rabbit's foot attached to the ring. Prasad wasn't too fond of touching the foot, so he just held the ring by the keys themselves.

"Hello, Alex, I'm Dr. Prasad."

Alex had never heard anyone sounding quite like that, and he was having a slight problem understanding the doctor. "Dr. Prasad, you talk kind of funny, and I understand some of the words you're saying, but not all of them, especially when you're talking really fast," Alex interjected.

Those in the room smiled at the innocence, and Dr. Prasad told Alex to simply tell him if he ever needed him to repeat anything.

"Nothing I'm about to do is going to hurt you, son. I just want you to play some games with me. I'm going to ask you some questions, and you're going to give me your answers. Is that okay with you?" Alex nodded yes as he continued to periodically grimace in pain.

Alex didn't know what to say; he was again becoming confused by his surroundings. He thought, *All these people, Mommy's looking serious. Daddy has a strange smile on his face. And now this brown man who talks kind of funny asking me if we can play games together?*

"Alex, what do you remember about tonight?" asked Prasad.

"I remember wanting to go to the potty and trying to take my pajama bottoms and my diaper off. That's when I lost my balance and fell backwards down the steps. But I didn't remember that until I was out there in the chair with my mommy and heard Daddy yelling at somebody back here."

"Your daddy was yelling at somebody?" Prasad looked up at Sanka with a cold, questioning stare.

"That situation will be addressed with my staff later, I assure you," said Sanka.

Prasad continued, realizing that it really had nothing to do with what was happening right now or with him at all. "Mrs. Beckham, four years old is a bit late for a child to still be in diapers," he said.

"Doctor, he's fine during the day, but he still has a bed-wetting problem. That's why the diaper and rubber pants at night," responded Mary in a somewhat embarrassed tone.

"Oh, Mrs. Beckham, bed-wetting is very common, especially among boys of his age. Just needed to ask." Mary sighed in relief, and Prasad continued. "Do you know who these people are in the room with us, Alex?"

"Not everybody. I know my Mommy and Daddy, and that man over there." He pointed to Dr. Schubert. "I've seen him before, but I don't really remember his name." Alex's speech was clear; no slurring.

Prasad held Randall's keys in front of Alex and jiggled them. "Do you know what these are, Jimmy?" Prasad was testing Alex's attentiveness.

"My name's not Jimmy, it's Alex, and they're my daddy's keys."

Prasad looked around quickly at everyone with a promising smile. Alex did know his name, and he'd made sure the doctor did as well. "Okay, Alex, follow these keys with your eyes wherever they go and tell me if they disappear like magic at any time." Prasad moved them up and down and back and forth and in and out, each time getting a "yes" from Alex when asked if he saw them. Then Prasad held up one to three fingers, and Alex passed with flying colors.

"Do you have a dog?" Prasad then asked.

"Not anymore. She knocked me down the steps once when we were playing, and I never saw her again," answered Alex.

"What was her name?"

"Dixie!"

"Alex, if we help you, can you get out of bed and stand up by yourself?"

"I think so. Where are you taking me?" Alex looked at his mother with terror in his eyes. "Mommy?"

"Nowhere, son, you're staying right here with us. I just want to see if you can stand up nice and tall." Prasad had not paid attention to Alex's ankle.

Nurse Leatherwood held Alex by the waist and placed him on the cold marble floor. "This floor is freezing!" Alex squealed in shock as Nurse Leatherwood continued to steady him. "And my ankle really hurts to stand on. I mean, a lot!"

"All right, Alex, don't stand on your hurt foot very much. Nurse, let go of him slowly, so your hands just barely touch his waist," said Prasad. "Can you stand on your own, Alex?"

"Yes, sort of. But I'm starting to get dizzy, and I feel like I'm cold but sweaty. Aren't I supposed to sweat when I'm hot?" Alex was about to faint. It was obvious. His face was losing color quickly.

"Nurse, lift the boy back into his bed," said Prasad. "Let's give him a little time to recoup from that, since we can't lower his head."

Shubert interjected, "He's probably a bit anemic from the contusion, but that's still something we need to watch closely. We'll start some plasma when you're done, Prasad, and test his stability again in a few hours."

Alex had never heard those words before, but they sounded okay coming from Dr. Shubert. His mom and dad were nodding their heads calmly, so he figured it must be fine.

After a couple of minutes, the color returned to Alex's face. "You did good, son. I have just a few more questions for you. Are you able to talk again?" Prasad asked patiently.

"Yes, but that was weird, that cold but sweaty thing," responded Alex.

"I bet your head hurts, but does it hurt all over, like someone is squeezing it like a basketball ball, or just where you hit it on the windowsill?" All in the room, except Alex, knew how critical this answer would be.

"Well, it hurts a little all over, but mostly in the front where it's bleeding. But not like someone is squeezing it."

Good answer, thought Mary and Randall.

"Hear any ringing or buzzing in your ears?"

"Not now, but a little when you had me stand up."

"And my last question. Son, do you feel sick or like you're going to throw up?"

"No, not at all. Well, maybe a little when I stood up. Actually, I'm a little hungry, and Animal Crackers sound good right now. I like to eat the rhinos best." Alex looked at his mother. She usually carried a box in her purse.

"Good. Just sit up here in bed for a while, but Mom, nothing for him to eat right now, please. Mr. and Mrs. Beckham, the signs of a brain bleed or concussion seem remote, except for his eyes and his balance. His eyes are a bit red and bloodshot, but he's been crying and had the hemorrhage from the contusion flowing into them. That he doesn't remember his trip to the hospital is my only concern."

"I do remember some of it, doctor," Alex blurted.

Prasad continued, "Stay here with him and let us talk about our next step." Prasad, Shubert, and Sanka all left the room.

"Mommy, Daddy, I'm scared. I really don't remember much about getting here, but I do remember some."

Mary gave Randall a concerned glance. She knew Alex picked up on everything, obviously even when he was semiconscious. They both were thinking the same thing. *What did he remember?*

"Am I going to die like that cat in the street last week?" Alex asked. He thought, *'If I do, will they just throw me in a garbage can like Dad did with the cat? What's anemia, and what's plasma?*

Mary still held ice on Alex's forehead, while Randall still held Alex's hand and held ice on the back of his neck. They peered at each other, wondering how honest to be with the boy.

"Anemia is like when our car is low on gas and we say 'Fill 'er up' to the gas station attendant," explained Randall.

"Then we get all those green stamps, and I lick 'em and put 'em in the book so we can get a swimming pool someday?" Alex was reestablishing his ability to pull up detailed memories.

"Exactly, my boy, and when our bodies get low on blood, the

plasma is sort of like 'Fill 'er up, Leo'," Randall continued.

"Do we get those green stamps for plasma?" Mary smiled for the first time since she had found Alex at the bottom of the steps.

"No stamps for plasma, but maybe some cookies," Randall said with a grin as well. "And are you going to die like the cat? That's silly, my boy. You might if you ever run out into the street in front of a car like that cat, so don't do that. But the answer is no, you're not going to die. You just got a good knock on that little noggin of yours! The bleeding is slowing down already." Though Randall and Mary knew nothing was for certain yet.

Nurse Leatherwood suddenly added, "Your dad's right! You're too tough a kid for that. I can see it in your face. You're being one brave little boy, sort of like when Peter Pan fights Captain Hook!" He spoke with a big grin on his face, speculating that Alex knew who Peter Pan was. "While the doctors talk, let's get those bloody PJs off you, and let me clean you up. Looks like you've been in a boxing match."

Alex smiled. "What's a boxing match, Nurse Leatherwood? Never heard of that."

"You will soon! Who knows, someday you may be the Champion of the World!" Then Nurse Leatherwood, having forgotten the situation, looked at Mary and Randall with apology written all over his face. "Or maybe not. And kid, just call me Rex. We're buddies now."

"Is it okay to call a grown-up by his first name, Daddy?" asked Alex.

"It's okay if they ask you to, son, but this man is important and smart. Can we compromise and allow him to call you Nurse Rex?" Randall asked the nurse.

"Mr. Beckham, that is very respectful of you. I think that's a great compromise." Rex felt grateful that he was being treated with respect. Not many people held a male nurse of color in high esteem back in those days.

"Did they call you a nurse, mister, I mean Rex, I mean Nurse

Rex? I thought only girls were allowed to be nurses and boys were doctors?" asked Alex with a puzzled look on his face.

"There are a few of us male nurses around, as they call us, but not many. We do it because we like to help people. My dad's a doctor, and I hope someday I can be one as well." Alex thought that was pretty cool.

Mary helped Nurse Rex clean Alex, as the blood had already begun to dry and cake on his face. It took quite a bit of scrubbing, leaving Alex with cuddly, chafed cheeks. Nurse Rex also brought hot towels and a small water bowl, so Mary and Randall could clean off as well. After removing Alex's pajamas, the nurse suited him up into a worn hospital gown with bunny rabbits printed all over. The back was open, and Alex's little butt hung out. He looked so sadly innocent and so adorable Mary had to turn around to keep Alex from seeing her tears again.

It was obvious to Randall and Mary that Alex was not going home for a while and that pain from needles and stitches was close at hand. But except for a blunt headache, Alex felt fine, for now.

● ● ●

After thirty minutes, the doctors came back from their conference with a treatment plan. "Alex, can you stay here with Nurse Rex while we talk to your mom and dad?" Dr. Shubert asked. "We'll not be long."

"Sure," said Alex with a tentative smile, his brown eyes open wide, looking at his father.

Nurse Rex smiled, "I gotcha, Cowboy. Don't you go worrin' about nothin', partner. They'll be back quicker than you can say 'toady-frog.'" He coaxed a "safe from danger" smile from Alex's fearful face.

As the five all went into the hallway, Dr. Shubert said, "Randall, Mary, I don't want to get your hopes up, but we're seeing no signs of any brain bleeding. However, we want him to stay here with us for about a week. Sometimes, there are what we call 'slow bleeds' when the skull is fractured, even a hairline fracture. As long as he's not vomiting, dizzy, or drowsy or has bad headaches, he'll be fine and can go home after that. But you'll still have to watch him for about another week, possibly longer. If these things do appear, well, I must be blunt; the worst case is surgery on his brain and skull, drilling through the bone to relieve the pressure. But we're so far from that now, I need you to stay calm and hopeful. Don't show the boy you're scared of anything at all."

Mary did everything to keep herself from breaking down but couldn't. She fell into Randall's arms, and he held her to his chest, giving her the fortitude she needed to continue.

"Mary, Mary, I'm scared of the worst as well, but all three of these doctors see that as remote. He's already better than two hours ago. Be strong for Alex's sake, please. We can see he's a strong kid when it comes to pain, but oddly, he picks up on people's emotions and feels them himself." Randall stayed calm as the doctors finished.

Shubert laid out the treatment plan. "If there are no more questions, we'll need to start an IV and infuse him with two units of plasma until he's no longer anemic. He'll be poked with needles often for blood draws and labs, and he'll get tired of that quickly. But be aware, the most painful part of this will be when we reenter the OR; the first invasive catheter in his little veins will need to be done immediately. He's not going to like it, and neither will either of you. It's going to break your hearts. Then, stitches in his head, which will not be as bad, because we'll give him a local anesthetic, then finally X-rays, which will seem tame after the first two procedures. The X-rays will check his skull and brain for any bleeding, and we'll also take pictures of his ankle to be sure it's just a sprain and that he has no joint bleeding. Keep him awake with nothing to eat for a few more hours until I get the radiology reports. And continue the ice, and I mean ice, ice, and more ice!"

Randall tried to explain to Alex what was going to happen in the next few hours, but he lost Alex very quickly.

Alex looked at his new best friend, "Nurse Rex, can you do all that stuff my daddy's talking about?"

"Cowboy, I can only do one of the things, and it is the one that will hurt pretty bad for a minute or so. Are you going to hate me if I hurt you? I'm not going to hurt you on purpose, and you can cry or scream or yell all you want. You just can't pull your arm away from me. But it has to happen to get the plasma in and make you feel better. I'll bring you three boxes of Animal Crackers tomorrow if you'll be brave. But kid, it's going to hurt, no matter who does it. Will we still be buddies?"

Nurse Rex was not used to getting so close to a kid this quick. As a matter of fact, getting close was not a good thing for an ER nurse. But oddly, he really did want to be friends with Alex. There was some strange bond between them that had grown very quickly.

"Nurse Rex, if it's going to hurt anyway, I want you to do it. And no, I could never be mad at you. And I get Animal Crackers—three boxes, right?"

Spontaneously, Randall gave the nurse a hug. "I assume you'll need help holding him down. I would rather do it than have Nurse Spears do it or anyone out there. Mary, you must hold his head and talk to him. This is going to be hard on all of us."

Nurse Rex gathered the necessary supplies and called in one more nurse to hold Alex's lower body and other arm, while Randall held the arm where the stick was going to occur. Mary held her precious son's head and whispered reassuring thoughts to him, with her lips placed sweetly on her little man's cheek.

As Nurse Rex began, Alex's face turned blue. The first cry was so deep, he couldn't breathe. Mary blew in his face as she had when he was an infant, and the burst of pain became vocal.

"Go ahead, Cowboy, cry and scream as loud as you want. I'm almost done. Don't move your arm, kid! Please, just don't move your arm!"

It only took two sticks to insert the catheter into Alex's forearm, thank goodness. Mary was in tears, and so was Alex. Nurse Rex was close. He put a splint on the boy's arm to secure the position of the catheter. And when he had finished, he got right into Alex's face, and they both looked each other directly in the eyes.

"Still buddies, Cowboy?" asked Nurse Rex, his eyes slightly tearful.

"Still buddies, Nurse Rex!" Alex said through his sobs. "And that did hurt, and I mean a lot!" The nurse smiled as Alex managed a tiny smile of his own, the best the kid could muster at the time.

"It gets easier from here, Cowboy, and I'll come visit you upstairs every day." Nurse Rex smiled again. "I'm sorry, I have to work down here, but I promise, I'll be up to visit after I'm done every morning. We can have some breakfast. And I heard your mother say you like puzzles. Let's do some together!"

Alex was stitched up, and the X-rays, though still inconclusive, showed no sign of any internal bleeding. The injury to his ankle was just a mild sprain. Alex was taken to a room on the sixth floor. Even though he was in pain, no pain medication could be given so as not to induce drowsiness. But he could have breakfast, and afterwards, he was so worn out from the night's events, he fell asleep anyway. The docs were okay about everything, since he was clear of a concussion.

Mary slept in a recliner by her son's bed, touching her hand to his as they both napped. Randall went home to get Mary a couple of changes of clothes and some toiletries. He brought them back, then went to work for half a day, as he would all week.

When Alex and Mary awoke in late morning, Alex was in a foggy state of mind, like the weather outside, not sure where he was. Then he suddenly realized it was the hospital, and he slowly began to remember the events of the painful night eight hours before. Then, as he stretched his legs, he felt something at the bottom of his bed with his feet. There were three boxes of Animal Crackers and a toy cowboy laid out on the sheets. Alex thought it was the best present anyone ever gave him, other than Santa Claus!

EPILOGUE

As time went on, Alex's injuries were routine for a young boy, including bike wrecks, split lips, bloody noses, and nasty bruises. These would all render his diagnosis of hemophilia to be considered mild and not life-threatening. It would be almost twenty years later that a treatment other than ice and plasma would be discovered, and with that discovery, the "mild" diagnosis was confirmed. But in the first thirty years of his life, his parents and the whole family held their breath as Mary and Randall allowed him to be a normal little boy, fully realizing the dangers he encountered in everyday normal life. Alex was never truly cognizant of the danger he put himself in so many times. Randall and Mary's only restrictions on their son included no fighting, no football, and by the rules of the government, no entrance into the military.

Basketball, baseball, snow skiing, and normal roughhousing with his cousins were allowed, even though the whole family, again, held their breath. Alex refused his entire life to accept the doctors' overprotective wishes, until his youngest grandson inherited the gene. Then he held his breath for him as well and realized the stress his own parents must have endured. This was probably why the statement, "I don't want another Alex," spoken by his mother in the car that night, speeding to the emergency room, finally now made sense. And it was probably why Alex would have an adopted sister when he was six years old.

Finally, the scariest situation for Alex was not an injury or surgery. It was something unknown to anyone at the time. Had Alex been hurt between 1984 and 1987, he would have had to rely on a blood supply that had been sporadically contaminated with HIV. More than likely, he would not have survived to see the age of forty. But God had a purpose for him, and in the future, that purpose would present itself. His influence would come to impact many lives in many parts of the world.

Next in the Series:
Alex has the first glimpse of the blueprint of his future as well as experiencing the realities of social stigmas and the mortality of his elders as he spends time with his grandparents.

EPISODE II

HANGIN' WITH THE GRANDPARENTS BEFORE THE DAYS OF ELECTRONIC BABY-SITTERS

(This Episode II of *The Tributaries of Alex Beckham,* begins the cultivation of his creativity as he lay in boredom on a cold wooden floor studying the cracks and crevices of the aging and deteriorating living room ceiling in his grandparents' home. It is the first time he experiences the unreasonable righteousness of an adult, the warm respect of a friendly store owner, the contemplation of death, and the observation of his grandfather's swing in emotions from love to apathy then to hate all within a matter of hours.

As we grow and mature, we can all trace back to that source of the first tributary that entered our river of life, causing those small eddies to swirl around in our heads until our lives became deeper and deeper and the new experiences reached a consistent conclusion. Unfortunately, not all of those experiences form positive results. Some become the root of our cultural problems, which are hard to reverse and push back upstream.

Enjoy the innocence of Alex as he continues his journey of unending questions with never ending answers as his best friend becomes his imagination.)

Let us begin the story.

A cold, slate-colored sky blanketed the neighborhood early in this month of December 1955, the streets and sidewalks still slightly moist from the light mist of this quintessential autumn morning. A clammy dampness filled the air, reminding Alex of the night he had tumbled brutally down the stairs a year earlier, smashing his forehead solidly into the corner of that windowsill at the bottom. Then, the ammonia under his nostrils, causing his head to jerk violently, as if he was experiencing an abrupt seizure. And finally, the blood splattered onto the walls and bottom steps that was never able to be completely removed. Alex remembered the breasts of his mother's blood-soaked pajamas as she held him tightly to protect him from an early, forlorn death. And how that possibility was beautifully discarded even before they left the hospital. But the most obvious memory of that night was the brutally obvious scar between his eyes every time he gazed at himself in the mirror. He would carry that with him as a reminder of the danger nature had placed with him, and he would carry that burden the rest of his life.

Alex's memories of that night were sketchy at best; however, he did remember his mother saying she didn't want another "him," which would make no sense to Alex for decades, until his grandson was born with the hemophilia gene. He had survived a plethora of bumps and bruises since that night, and his parents had learned to live with it, albeit in a tentative and uncomfortable way. But as his life approached the end, he learned the effect he had on so many who loved him.

• • •

Outside, a few dry patches were beginning to checker the side-walks. Only the cracks were exhibiting the muddy remanence of the early morning shower. On days like this, both inside and out-side, regardless of what Alex's mother placed neatly on his bed for him to wear that day, a chill continued to crawl through every cell in his body. Lying face-down on his grandmother's faded "magic carpet" (as he called it) with his pillow and his thumb, he fidgeted with the worn/torn threads surrounding the faint flowery pattern in its center.

The carpet put forth its best effort to cover a large portion of the scratched and heel-stained hardwood floor in her living room, but no matter how hard the carpet tried, it just couldn't succeed. With an ear directly and contiguously aimed at the hot air duct of the furnace, he awaited the click of the thermostat, followed by a boom which ignited the flames in the gas furnace situated below him in the basement. It was then, and only then, that Alex felt warm, as the uncomfortable chill in his grandmother's drafty house was replaced by that make-believe warm summer breeze the furnace forced into his face.

As he waited patiently, he rolled onto his back, gazing upward at Grandma's aging plaster ceiling, his head resting on his pillow of tranquility. It was a feather pillow sporting a disgustingly soiled pillowcase, doubtless the result of his dragging it around the house on the floor all day like a dust mop.

Where most kids had blankets, or couchies, or woobies, or whatever pet name they were christened with because of most kids' early inability to pronounce the words properly, Alex had adopted a dirty feather pillow, which would remain nameless. To

Alex, it seemed to make logical sense. In the beginning, he did possess a blanket with frayed satin edges to tickle his face as he sucked his natural pacifier, his thumb. He knew his parents could never take away his pacifier, like he saw his aunt do to his cousin; duh, his thumb was attached. Plus, he also felt like a blanket was such a two-step process. Due to his inherited problem of bed-wetting at an early age, his naps were prohibited on sofas or chairs and were limited to his bed or the floor in the rest of the house. In other words, he wasn't allowed on the furniture, just like the dog.

But he found that his thumb still left a gap of emptiness in his security, so some additional modifier to his yearning for serenity was needed. After much thought, he decided a pillow to be the logical and functional answer. Since, by parental decree, his naps were to be on the floor, having that disgusting thing in tow, his pillow made it possible for him to nap anywhere, at any time. But like most good ideas, such as medications and cookies, his pillow had side effects.

Alex had developed a strange habit (or maybe it could even be categorized as an addiction) of pulling and pushing feathers out of the striped blue-and-white ticking covering his pillow. The technique resembled the doctor's actions when Alex had received his dose of the recently discovered polio vaccine injections. Reaching into the pillowcase and positioning his thumb opposite the feather's point, then pushing the pointed stem forward with the same motion as the polio vaccination in his butt, the feather could penetrate the surface and escape into the world. Usually, Alex used his fingernails to finish the job of pulling the feather into the universe, but for those real beauties, he needed his teeth! The bigger the feather, the better, sort of like fishing.

And as addictions always do, they leave enablers to clean up the messes. Therefore, his mother and grandmother had quite a different view of his daunting success since, once the feathers were out of the pillow, sort of like a baby leaving the womb, they couldn't be forced back in. It then became necessary, since Alex was scolded in a mild fashion every cleaning day, for him either to stuff them under his bed or to hide them in between the cushions of the closest piece of furniture at the time. That way, sweeping and vacuuming were required only on a regularly scheduled basis, and the feathers were unseen.

Oddly enough, this would be a habit Alex would retain all of his life, even as an old man. It was soothing and therapeutic, which, frankly, made no sense. Only one problem became apparent as Alex reached adulthood. He was forced to ignore the embarrassing question asked by his cleaning lady: "Where do all of these feathers come from, Mr. Beckham?"

Still waiting for that warm air to be blasted into his face, and due to the lack of technical stimuli for children at this point in history, he began to fixate on his grandmother's dingy plaster ceiling, stained heavily by the nicotine exuded by most everyone in the family. He imagined the cracks of varying lengths and widths to be either flowing rivers or cascading streams. Scattered across the landscape, small chunks of plaster had completely let go of their hold, and in Alex's head, had created ponds and lakes, some deep enough to sustain the fishing boats he imagined.

Starting with any of these streams at random, Alex pretended to cruise up one of these small tributaries just to see where it would lead. He could almost smell the mixture of oil and gasoline exhaust exuding from the outboard engine, one just like his grandfather had had when he took Alex and his mother fishing. And as he slowly cruised up the stream, he inevitably came to a fork, forcing him into a decision for his next adventure.

Alex loved to explore anything new, whether real or imaginary: the urban woods overgrown on the vacant lots in his neighborhood, the junkyard of cars a couple blocks away, unlocked so he could get in and pretend he was driving, or, if stuck in the house like today, the imaginary places up these rivers and streams on the ceiling. Subconsciously, he was learning that forks in life always arise and can be chosen voluntarily or involuntarily or may not be chosen at all, depending on an individual's tolerance for change. But at his stage of life and from the boredom creeping in each day as his brain evolved, settling on some motionless bank and just fishing every day was not an option.

So, picking a fork and setting his uncharted course deeper into this plaster labyrinth, he perceived some cracks to be wide and slow flowing, some boringly straight, some curiously squiggly like an earthworm, and some, just some, only tiny, fine hairlines faintly seen by his youthful 20/20 eyesight. Looking down his chosen path, multiple tributaries connected and attacked from each side, some appearing to flow endlessly in one specific direction, while others started, then stopped abruptly, like when his mom told him not to run into the street. At times, he would follow one as far as he could see across the room into the shadows. Sometimes, he decided to navigate a turn if he sensed it to be of some wild interest, and sometimes, the tributary just ended, boom, done, forcing him to backtrack to where he had made the decision that had gone awry.

However, Alex learned to look closely at every impasse he faced, and sometimes, just sometimes, if he squinted really hard, he might see a crack so small it had been ignored by him on his last journey. Or maybe that crack had just happened in a recent earthquake, forming a new avenue altogether for him to explore. That's when he imagined lifting the motor into the boat, climbing out and very possibly, no, probably, into alligator-infested waters, not to mention slimy leeches that would suck his blood from his legs as he pulled the boat by the rope on the front. He knew he had to get through this dark, dense swamp water, topped with green algae, as soon as he could. And, like always, he made it through unharmed.

Although in his head he could change the animals and jungles he encountered, ultimately, no matter what path he chose, he realized at one point that he was always confined to the walls and doorjambs of this one small room, his grandmother's living room.

This being the day of the week when both his mother and father worked and due to the weather, he was stuck, terribly bored in the house. But suddenly a thought hit him, like when his parakeet flew headfirst into the wall. All this time, his mind had only traveled in one room. It was then that an epiphany rushed over him that would literally change his life forever. He realized he wasn't dreadfully confined to one room. He wasn't even confined to one country or one continent or one planet, or perhaps even one lifetime. As long as he could get up and drag himself and his pillow to another room with a different type of ceiling, a whole new galaxy of cracks and adventures awaited him. He was free to choose and free to travel, not only now, but someday in his future to real places!

As he pondered the idea of moving to another room, he arched his back and gazed upside down and backward over his head into the next room, checking for new clusters of cracks. But in so doing, for a moment anyway, Alex became distracted from his purpose. He thought, *What would happen if the whole world was suddenly turned upside down, and the ceilings became the floors and all the floors became the ceilings?* If that were true, Alex saw himself climbing over the doorjambs in order to get to the other rooms, then how careful he would need to be so he didn't step on a ceiling light, or how he would have to duck and weave through each room to keep from hitting his head on the floor lamps.

But after a while, following ceiling cracks and turning the world upside down became really old. When he stayed overnight at his grandmother's, they had no toys for him to play with, and like most of the world at that time, no TV to watch. Alex could have brought his record player, but that was not permitted to be played when his grandfather was home, so he decided not to lug it around. Nobody, not his grandparents or his aunt or uncle, ever read to him like his father. (Alex found out later that his grandmother couldn't read at all, and his grandfather, well, he wasn't very good at it even when he tried.)

However, his uncle, who was sixteen, gave him a pile of old comic books the uncle had outgrown. Alex did have fun for a while creating his own stories from those little blocks of illustrations on each page. But like the ceiling, and like most writers, you can only make up a limited number of plot lines from the same catalyst, inside or outside of your brain.

Suddenly, Alex's grandmother entered the room. "Alex, want to do Grandma a big, big favor?" she asked, as though the question could possibly be answered with a "no."

"Sure, Grandma, anything," Alex answered excitedly. He was so ready to break the solitary monotony that surrounded his day, at least to this point.

THE WICKED WITCH OF THE WEST LIVES RIGHT ACROSS THE STREET, BUT TO THE EAST?

"Now that you just turned five and you've gotten bigger and stronger, I need you to run down to Mr. Thomas's and get something for me before it gets too dark," Alex's grandmother asked in a sweet but somewhat baby talk tone. Alex didn't care to be spoken to with baby talk, but he left it alone.

"Sure, what do you want me to get, Grandma?" He smiled as he answered with enthusiasm.

"I'm going to give you this note. Just hand it to Mr. Thomas, and he'll give you what I need. And take Tuffy with you, but don't let him pee or poop in the store." Alex thought his grandmother's instructions seemed pretty simple.

Tuffy was his grandmother's dog, a medium-sized purebred mutt, multicolored, soft, and furry, and he shed a lot, a streetwise Benji, of sorts. He was one of those dogs that always seemed to have a smile on his face, huffing and panting with his tongue out the side of his mouth. Tuffy and Alex's parakeet were Alex's first loyal and unconditional friends, and since he was an only child, he didn't have many kids to play with. Tuffy went everywhere with Alex—the store, the park; anywhere Alex went to play in the neighborhood, Tuffy followed. Not only that, but he used to show up on Alex's doorstep six blocks away after dodging traffic and crossing busy intersections. And his only reason for facing that danger was to hang out with Alex! Alex figured Tuffy was as bored as he himself was in that house.

He'd stand at the gate of the fence and bark until Alex or his mother came out. The dog was rarely bathed or brushed, so Alex was instructed by his mother to brush his dirty fur on the back porch before she'd let him come inside. She'd then proceed to call Alex's grandmother, who in turn called Alex's grandfather at work, who in turn, picked Tuffy up on his way home. This went on almost every day. And the dog was fed well, mostly from the decent chunk of Alex's sandwich secretly handed to him under the table at lunchtime.

Getting back to the errand at hand, Alex stood at the front door. His grandmother pulled the arms of his coat right side out, helped him put his arms in his sleeves, and zipped it all the way up, slightly pinching Alex's chin with the zipper. She held his mittens out as Alex slipped his hands in. She pulled his beanie down on his head and, finally, stuffed the note in his coat pocket.

"Wanna go with me, Tuffy?" Tuffy had been standing in the hallway, watching Alex getting bundled, wagging his tail, not taking his eyes off Alex for a second. He was so ready! With that question, his nose got right to the crack of the door, so close that Alex's grandmother had no choice but to gently nudge him with her foot to open it. As the heavy wooden door opened, Tuffy pushed the aluminum storm door with his paw and stood on the porch, looking back over his shoulder.

Alex followed him, not vice versa. How the dog knew where they were going was a mystery, but he did. They both bounced down the steps, and Tuffy made a side trip into the grass to relieve himself. Thank goodness, Alex thought, so it didn't happen in the store. Tuffy then skirted to the sidewalk and headed down the street to the corner, occasionally looking back to be sure Alex was following and was safe. Tuffy was fully aware he was taking Alex for a walk, not the other way around. It had turned much colder than earlier in the day, and as Grandma had predicted, nighttime was quickly approaching. There was only an old, paint-chipped four-car garage belonging to the dirty three-story brick apartment building between Alex's grandmother's house and the corner.

Mr. Thomas's store was actually on the first floor of that apartment building. Alex knew almost everyone living in the houses on his grandmother's street, adults and kids of all ages. The men mostly all worked in the factories close by. And there were no colored people, as they were called then, living in any of the houses or apartments; Alex only saw an occasional woman getting on the bus at the corner, wearing a uniform that made her resemble that woman on the pancake box.

Everybody acted quite neighborly to one another in those days. Yes, all quite neighborly, with the exception of one. Thanks to her, Alex had his first feelings of disdain toward any individual in his life to this point. She was volatile, and the world needed to be run according to her judgments and her rules. She was an elderly, skinny lady always seen in a light robe and slippers. Alex never saw her leave her house, except when she felt the need to display her unreasonable acts of despotism towards the children in the neighborhood.

Her name was Mrs. Grogan, deservedly earning her nickname "Old Lady Grogan." When Alex and the other kids in the neighborhood played stick ball in the street, Alex could see her peering at them through her sheer curtains, anxiously waiting for their ball to roll into her yard. When that happened, she would burst out her front door, scamper down her steps like a squirrel (impressively agile for an old lady), snatch the ball, and return to her porch. Then, continuing her routine, she would wag her pointer finger like a death tool, scolding everyone en masse in her righteous, high-pitched whine. She warned Alex and his little friends how playing in the street damages and destroys people's property and that someday, someone would be hit by a car and die. She never gave one ball back, not one! Alex figured she must have bushel baskets full of rubber balls somewhere in her house. She certainly wouldn't throw away a good ten-cent ball!

However, one day a confrontation arose from a place Alex could not have imagined. It was a hot summer afternoon in July; must have been ten kids playing stickball that day in the street. Alex was the runt of the neighborhood, but they let him play any-way. Mrs. Grogan was perched at her window like a warden in a prison, watching the delinquents defy her desires. This day was a lucky day; the bat came from a mop handle one kid had found in a garbage can. Some days, it came from a short broomstick, which was okay, but on the bad days, Alex and his buddies had to use a fallen tree branch, bent and crooked.

Everybody who played contributed to buying a rubber ball for ten cents at Mr. Thomas's, getting the money by either asking their parents for a penny or two or by finding pop bottles by rummaging through trash cans on garbage day. In those days, people got their two-cent deposit back on glass bottles. (In the name of progress, plastic bottles, instead of glass, would someday plague the earth and its oceans. But I'm the narrator and probably should not have brought my opinions into Alex's story. Sorry, but I couldn't help it.) So rarely did any one child possess a ball of his own, which was a good thing. You know the saying, "Then I'm gonna take my ball and go home?" Never give any kid too much power in a stick-ball game by allowing him to own the ball, or he'll always wind up the self-appointed umpire, one with whom you cannot argue, or it will be "Bye bye, ball!"

The kids would determine their own bases, the length between them depending on the age of whoever was playing, but it would always be to the advantage of the larger, more powerful boys. Mr. Wiegle's driveway curb was first (Mr. Wiegle was the oldest man Alex had ever met at that point, and his wife had recently died. Alex would visit him on his porch, but he always picked up the deep sense of sadness in Mr. Wiegle's eyes), the sewer lid in the middle of the street was second base, the fire hydrant, third base, and a piece of a cardboard box with a rock on it so it wouldn't blow away, home plate.

Alex's grandmother lived on a quiet side street. Maybe once every five minutes or so, a car would creep up, and one of the boys would yell "CAR!" Everyone then moved to the curb and waited until it passed; no big deal. That routine happened every day in every part of the world with either a baseball, a football, or a soccer ball. But one very peculiar day, Alex was playing in the street while his mother and grandmother sat on his grandmother's front porch, drinking beers, smoking cigarettes, and just talking about stuff, when the ball skirted into Mrs. Grogan's bushes. And as expected, Old Lady Grogan did her thing: out the door, scampering down the steps, grabbing the ball; game over.

Well, that was the first time Alex's mother had actually watched it happen. She'd heard about it, but this time, she saw it.

"That's a bunch of bull, Mom," Mary said to her mother. "What kind of damage did that cause? It's a ten-cent rubber ball. I'd rather have my kid in the neighborhood here than walking six blocks and crossing streets to play in the park. That's enough! I've had enough!"

Like a bat out of Hades, Mary came off the porch and charged across the street. As Mrs. Grogan was about to start her finger a'wagging, Mary yelled, "Hey, give those little boys their ball back! Who do you think you are? It's not yours! Give it back right now, and the rest of the balls you've taken from them."

Mrs. Grogan was startled somebody had the nerve to address her in that fashion. *Does this woman know my dead husband used to be an accountant?* she thought. Almost immediately, Ethel, Alex's grandmother, was standing shoulder-to-shoulder with Mary, both staring daggers at Old Lady Grogan. All the kids watched intently, eyes bugging out of their heads, but they all kept quiet. Alex and his buddies had never seen grown women fight before, and Alex was stunned.

Mrs. Grogan pointed at the kids, wagging "The Finger," and proceeded to educate Mary on how unsafe it was for children to play in the street. "Those kids damage cars, ruin people's bushes, and make too much noise!" (All not true, except the noise when they would argue "out or safe" after just about every play.) Then Mrs. Grogan, having never had children of her own, did it. She challenged the maternal monster. She couldn't even begin to comprehend the maternal insult she was about to let fly out of her mouth. Like stepping off a curb looking the wrong way, she was about to get hit by a Mac truck.

"And if you were good parents around here, you'd teach your children to respect people's property, and most important of all, protect them from getting hurt in the street. Or maybe you're just those irresponsible types who couldn't care less about your little brats. They'll probably all wind up in prison, anyway," she said in a smug tone, staring straight at Mary and Ethel.

That was a bad move, Mrs. Grogan, Alex thought, having seen that look on his mother's face many times when she was treated with way more disrespect than that.

Alex never heard his mother or his father, or for that matter, any of his family members use "foul language." At least, not in front of him. But all of a sudden, out of nowhere, Mary launched, "Oh fiddlesticks!"

Alex was puzzled. Not until first grade did Alex learn actual curse words, and that was from a chubby third-grader named Jimmy Douglas, who lived next door. So Alex wouldn't have known a curse word even if he heard one, but the tone of his mother's voice and the way she launched it caused him to conclude that "fiddlesticks" most certainly must be a curse word—but it came from his mother.

Since Alex had been taught that grownups were always right and kids were always wrong, he was both surprised and proud of his mother for that and would remember it his entire life. *My mother stood up for all of us kids,* he thought. But in the end, Mrs. Grogan still didn't give the boys their ball back nor any of the past balls that must have filled her basement to the brim. She would remain the infamous "Old Lady Grogan" forever.

ALEX TAKES A TRIP TO MR. THOMAS'S GROCERY MADE FAMOUS BY NORMAN ROCKWELL AND HIS BIG DILL PICKLES

Getting back to his grandma's boredom-breaking errand (since, as you've learned, both Alex and I have a way of getting side-tracked), Alex crept cautiously past the eerie brick apartment building, three stories high and covering the entire corner. As pointed out earlier, he knew most everyone who lived in the houses surrounding his grandmother's home, but he realized he never knew anyone who lived in that apartment building. Not only didn't he know them, he couldn't ever remember anybody coming and going. On occasion, a police car would be parked outside the main entrance, some-times with, sometimes without its lights flashing. The apartment building seemed like a different world, a little spooky, detached from the neighborhood, detached from the rest of the world.

On the bottom floor of this mysterious building was a Norman Rockwell replica of a grocery store, homogeneously designed like the other three stores within a three-block radius of each other but all owned by separate people. This one dangled a weather-beaten sign over the door that read "Thomas's Corner Grocery."

Alex pressed down on the rusty handle with his thumb to open one of the two glass doors. He and Tuffy bounced right in, scaring Mr. Thomas out of a light slumber as he sat on a stool behind his counter, guarding his cash register from being robbed again. "Hi, Mr. Thomas," Alex said in his perky little voice, so glad to be out of the house and doing something, anything, interesting.

"Hello, Alex," answered Mr. Thomas with a kind smile. Alex never knew his first name, ever, but he wouldn't have been allowed to call him by his first name anyway. (Kids never called adults by their first names back in those days unless approved by their parents.) Mr. Thomas was a medium-sized man with a stout belly that spread the buttons of his shirt right above his belt. Sometimes his hairy belly button would show, but Alex knew Mr. Thomas never realized that, since he couldn't see over his own tummy. He was around Alex's grandfather's age, with really nothing interesting or unusual looking about him, other than that hairy belly button. He was very respectful to Alex and treated him almost like he would treat an adult. Alex liked that, and therefore, Alex liked him.

"Can Tuffy come in, Mr. Thomas? He won't pee on anything. He just peed three times on the way down here and pooped once. I'll watch him real close, I promise. But he really never pees inside anywhere, Mr. Thomas, really. Well, except for the time he ate Grandma's bread dough before it rose, and his stomach almost exploded. That dog was fat as a blimp that day."

Mr. Thomas smiled and with a tiny giggle, shook his head. "Sure, if he wants, and hey kid, thanks for caring. I know he won't pee in here. He never has before. And anyway, I'm the only one here."

Thanks, Mr. Thomas," Alex said with a smile.

"I heard you just had a birthday, my boy! How old are you now, twelve? You married yet?" Mr. Thomas always, every time, asked Alex if he was married yet. It made Alex wonder about how smart Mr. Thomas really was.

"Shoot, Mr. Thomas, I just turned five. Mom and Grandma had a really fun party for me last Saturday. I got a new record player! My old one broke. Mom said I used it too much, and it just wore out. But I think she accidently dropped it down the steps and didn't want to tell me." Mr. Thomas snickered again. "And I got hit in the eye with one of those things you blow and it makes a noise like a horn and unrolls with a feather on the end. You know what I mean, Mr. Thomas?"

"Yes, I do know what you mean, Alex. They were around even

when I was a kid."

"Wow, that must have been a long time ago, Mr. Thomas. Did they have record players or even have music at all back then?" Alex inquired innocently.

"Yes, I guess it does seem like a long time for you, in kid years, anyway. And we did have music and record players back then, my boy. The speaker on our phonograph looked like a tuba horn to me. I bet that really hurt, getting poked in the eye. Let me see. Yes, your eye still looks a little red," as Mr. Thomas leaned over to get a better look at Alex's eye. "Now, what can I do for you, little guy? Or should I say 'big guy' now that you're five?" He smiled at Alex with another wink of his eye from behind the counter. Alex grinned from ear to ear.

"I have a note from my grandma here in my pocket. She said she needs a few things. So here I am!" Alex rummaged around in his coat pocket, the note being mixed in with some bubble gum wrappers.

"What does she need?" asked Mr. Thomas.

"I don't know. Here's the note. I still can't read yet." Alex handed the note to him across the counter.

"Oh, that's right," he chuckled. "You don't start kindergarten until next year, do you? By the way, is your grandpa bowling tonight? I hear he's really good, like a champion!"

"No, not tonight. My grandma says he and his buddies all want to stay home and listen to two men fight on the radio or something. I don't know why anybody would want to hear people fight and yell at each other on a radio. Do you like to hear people fight, Mr. Thomas?" Mr. Thomas gave a slight grin so as not to make Alex feel silly. "It scares me when I hear it from some of my neighbor's houses. Then sometimes, the police come, and they stop fighting for a few days. But they always do it again."

Mr. Thomas had been just as bored as Alex all afternoon, so Alex's naïve humor was refreshing. A small smile came to him once again. "No, I don't like to hear people fight either, Alex. I

can hear people fighting upstairs in their apartments, and sometimes it's really nasty. The police come here a lot late at night. But
I don't think that's what your grandpa means. He means there are
two men having a boxing match tonight to see who'll be world
champion; they just call it a fight. Nobody yells at anybody. Actually, they wear mouthpieces to protect their teeth, and they can't
say anything at all. But they do punch each other. Haven't you
ever seen a boxing match on TV?"

"Shoot, Mr. Thomas. I've never even seen a TV, except in a
store window once. Nobody I know has one, just radios and record
players. I do have my new record player, and a View-Master, and
a bunch of picture books, and comic books, but no TV. I think I
like the records with the story books best, especially *Johnny App-
leseed*! You know, the man that made friends with the Indians and
planted apple trees a long time ago?"

"Yes, I think I do remember that story. He was a brave little
man, sort of like you, I bet. Well, anyway, you'll have a TV someday. Everybody's getting one. Now, let's see, the note says two
six-packs of beer, four packs of cigarettes, two packs of Ches-
terfield Kings, two packs of Camels, and two bags of fried pork
rinds. I can't read this one part. I think it says 'Hudepohl.' Yes,
I'm pretty sure that's what they drink. Can you carry the beer all
the way home? Are you strong enough, or do you need my help?"
By the quality of the note, Mr. Thomas could tell Ethel had done
the best she could copying letters from the cigarette packs onto the
note. It was obvious she couldn't read or write.

"Oh yeah, I carry it in from the car for Grandma and my mom
all the time. But how about the bag?" asked Alex. "I can't carry
that too."

"It doesn't weigh much. I can stuff that in the hood of your
coat, okay? But walk slowly, no running. I don't want you to fall
and cut yourself. You promise, right, Alex?"

"I promise, I don't want to cut myself either, Mr. Thomas,"
Alex already realized he had some sort of bleeding problem.

Mr. Thomas began to gather the items, bagged them, then stuffed them into Alex's hood. They fit perfectly. He couldn't, of course, bag the beer. Alex would have to carry those by the handles, one in each hand.

"Well, happy birthday, little—I mean, big guy! Here you go. And tell Art and Ethel, I mean, your grandparents, I'll just put it on their bill, and she can pay me later. And, hey, hey, no running with those bottles!"

With the bag in Alex's hood and a six-pack in each hand, Mr. Thomas started towards the door to open it for him, Tuffy running ahead of both of them. But suddenly, Mr. Thomas stopped and turned. "Hey, candy bar for your birthday? On me. Or chips?" he asked.

"Uh, no, but how about a pickle from that jar over there on the meat counter? They're the best! My mouth is watering just looking at 'em."

"How about that really big fat one in the front, Alex?" Mr. Thomas suggested. His mouth was watering as well. He went to the counter, pulled the pickle out with a set of tongs, wrapped it in a piece of wax paper, and stuffed it in Alex's coat pocket. Alex could smell the juice leaking into his pocket. It smelled great.

Mr. Thomas again escorted Alex and Tuffy to the door and held it open as Alex exited the store and headed down the three worn steps to the sidewalk.

"See you soon, Mr. Thomas. And thanks for the pickle! C'mon, Tuffy." They headed up the street for home with Tuffy leading the way, a six-pack in each of Alex's hands, four packs of cigarettes, pork rinds and a big fat juicy pickle. (If it had been 2019, Alex's grandmother and Mr. Thomas would be on the national news in handcuffs for letting a kid do that. America has too many rules!)

Mr. Thomas picked up the telephone. "Ethel, Alex just left. He has a load. You might want to help him up the steps with those beer bottles, so he doesn't trip and hurt himself. Every time I see that big scar on his forehead, I worry about him, Ethel."

"Thank you, Bill. We all do. I'll go to the sidewalk right now. Have a good night," said Ethel.

Alex made it home in thirty-six steps. He counted them, because his dad was teaching him to count to a hundred, and he now counted everything he could find just for fun. He loved to learn anything new!

It was getting dark, and the streetlights had already touched the streets with their dull, dingy shadows. The sky had turned a soft mixture of purple and pink, touching the thin lofty clouds in the western sunset. As Alex reached the steps, Ethel was waiting to carry the beer into the house, as Alex held the door open for her and Tuffy.

"Wow, Grandma, my hands hurt! I didn't have my mittens on, because they wouldn't fit through the beer handles," said Alex. Grandma emptied the cigarettes and pork rinds from his hood, and that fat, mouth-watering pickle went straight into the fridge for later.

"Thank you so much, honey!" she said as she bent over and gave Alex a kiss on the cheek along with a warm hug. (Funny how the smell of cigarette smoke on a person's breath, on clothes, or in a room became very unpleasant to Alex later in life when he quit smoking, but in those days, most everyone smoked. Alex assumed that odor to be normal on everyone but kids.) Her lips were rough and chapped, making her kisses kind of prickly, but they still always lifted Alex's spirits. And even though she drank beer almost all day, every day, Alex never knew, and never would know, any woman who truly loved him more than his grandma. She treated him with such kindness and respect.

The thought of ever doing something wrong or being mean to her never entered his mind. Alex loved being around her, but then out of nowhere, a thought entered his mind in a panic, like when he awoke from a bad dream. He thought, *What would happen if she was gone, like forever, like Great-Grandma?*

SOME THINGS IN LIFE START OFF VERY CONFUSING, BUT IN THE END, THEY ARE STILL VERY CONFUSING

"You're not going to die like Great-Grandma did, are you, Grandma?" The question came so quickly from Alex's mouth, like a bolt of lightning striking a tree in the backyard. He thought immediately, *Why did I say that? I don't think I really want to hear the answer!*

As one's mind has a way of recalling entire abstract episodes in an instant, Alex only recalled visiting his great-grandmother on Easter and on her birthday, and he saw her once a year at his grandmother's house on Christmas Day. Alex remembered visiting her third-floor apartment, climbing up the black metal fire-escape steps, the ones he was terrified to climb, as he gazed through the slats all the way to the ground. It was Alex's first realization of his dislike for heights, which would grow into an extreme, almost unbearable abhorrence of the position.

Great-Grandma's apartment was poorly lit and carried with it the unique odor of the elderly. Seated deep in a deteriorating chair, the cushion swallowed her like quicksand into the earth, more and more with each visit. Alex was feeling scared, but why, he couldn't grasp. With the chair covered by a quilt becoming quickly thread-barren, she had given a fragile but loving smile to Alex as he approached. Alex returned the love. She was wrinkled and skinny with totally unbrushed meager white hair. Alex thought she must be at least a million years old, but until he learned to count that high, he wasn't sure how much that was, so he just went along with the figure of speech he heard others say when talking about something old. Alex was instructed by his mother to always give her an easy hug and a soft kiss on the cheek, but never, ever to sit on her lap, only on the arm of her chair, even if she asked. Alex was okay with that, because she did seem like she might break. And the salty odor in her apartment was definitely radiating from her.

She lived with her daughter, Alex's great-aunt Ruth, who was the sister of Alex's grandmother, Ethel. All that "who's related to who" thing was confusing to Alex back then, like it is to all kids at the beginning. And the "He (or she) died before you were born" was even worse. Alex was really glad his mother and grandmother didn't die before he was born, or he wouldn't have gotten to know them.

Alex's Aunt Ruth was a sickly looking woman, always hugging him and giving him terrible, sloppy kisses. He hated it—not her, just the sloppy kisses. Those kisses were disquieting and stinky. Alex so wanted to wipe them off, but his mother said that was impolite. That's when Alex learned to excuse himself to the bathroom, giving his mother the satisfaction that he was still being obedient to her.

At this stage, all Alex knew about his Aunt Ruth was that she wasn't particularly pleasant to be around. But as he progressed into his teens, Aunt Ruth would be committed to a mental institution for alcoholism, where she would die. Only at her funeral would her story be revealed to him. Alex was told Aunt Ruth used to take Great-Grandma's Social Security checks from the mail, cash them, and spend the money at the Cozy Corner Café, half a block away. It was her alcohol addiction that drove her to such dire actions, and it was probably the reason Alex's great-grandma was so sickly.

Alex's mother also revealed to him at an early age that his great-grandma was a Sioux Indian from Montana. This meant nothing to him at the time since the Beckhams possessed no TV and Alex was too young and fidgety for a movie theatre. However, that changed in 1958 when the family purchased their first T.V. Other than 'The Mickey Mouse Club', Westerns became Alex's favorites: *The Lone Ranger, Gene Autry, Roy Rogers*, and on and on. However, they always portrayed the Indians as the bad guys. They were referred to as "savages."

A final twist came, though, when Hollywood began to respect the Indians, changing their social label from Indian to "Native American." And as their ethnic group went from a national enemy to a wrongfully treated and a highly revered part of our culture, Alex's pride level in his heritage went from low to high. In his early life, he kept this to himself, but in his later life, well after that pendulum had swung, he performed an internet search to confirm his mother's story. He found that his great-grandfather, whom he had never met, had been in the US army and was stationed in Montana around 1880. That placed his great-grandfather and great-grandmother in the same territory at the same time, confirming, at least to Alex's fascination, that he did contain some Native American blood. And it made sense why his facial and body hair was sparse, and he could walk through the woods without breaking a twig. (Well, at least, that's what Alex liked to claim.)

Great-Grandma was the first person who forced Alex into the contemplation of death, a topic for which, since the beginning of mankind, many theories had been concocted for the purpose of immortality. His recollection was seeing her in this bed kind of thing, with this creepy white satin lining and a white satin pillow to prop up her head. There were two lids to the bed; one was closed, covering her lower body, and the other was open, so everyone could see her from her hands to the top of her head. She was still as wrinkled as ever, but her face and skin were as white as vanilla ice cream. Her hands were skinny and wrinkled, folded on top of each other. She almost looked like a rubber doll from the store. Her fingernails were so blanched, it caused Alex to feel nauseous. Between her fingernails and the color of her skin, Alex was unable to eat vanilla ice cream for a long, long, time, unless it was a butterscotch sundae. His mother had an ardent stare as she hugged Alex's grandmother, and she wept profusely. His father and grandfather stood quietly by the entrance to the room.

After his grandmother's grief settled a notch down to sadness, Alex saw his mother walking towards him with an emotion-free look about her. She took Alex by the hand, led him to his grand-mother, and all three stood hand-in hand. "Let's go say goodbye to your great-grandma, Alex." They led Alex to her dead body.

I so don't want to be this close Alex thought. He stood in be-tween his two matriarchs, so close to his great-grandma he could touch her if he wanted. He swore she was still breathing. Her chest was, without a doubt, going up and down, and at any moment, she was going to sit up and say "Hello, Alex." *Maybe dying just means you can't wake up for a while,* Alex told himself as total confusion set in. Alex's mother and grandmother kissed her on the forehead. His heart started to pound out of his chest, and he wanted to run back to his dad. O*h no, no, please, please, please don't make me do that! Please don't make me kiss her,* he thought in a panic. They didn't. They could see the fear and bewilderment clearly on his four-year-old face. His mom just calmly told him to tell her good-bye and tell her he would see her again someday in heaven. *Now I'm really confused,* thought Alex.

His mother and grandmother stood at the bed and hugged oth-er relatives and friends who came to say goodbye. His grandpa still stood by the door. He was not the hugging kind. As Mary and Ethel became involved in embracing their friends and relatives while crying, Alex slowly crept to the back of the room to stand with his dad once more. He stood in front of his father, as his fa-ther rubbed Alex's shoulders.

Alex studied the people. A lot of hugs to his mom and grand-ma, none to his grandfather, and a lot of "I'm so sorry(s)," but for what? Alex couldn't figure that one out. *What did these people have to apologize for?* Then, out of nowhere, a person in a black suit and a white collar that everyone called "Father" appeared in front of Great-Grandma's bed. *Now it's getting really weird,* Alex thought. Most of the people in the room dropped to their knees, holding necklaces of beads in their hands. They all began to say this one prayer over and over as fast as they could, and not at all together. It didn't make sense to Alex why they all didn't say it once all at the same time and be finished, like in school when they said the Pledge of Allegiance in the morning. Alex thought, *This has to be a race for something, for sure. That must be it. I bet the first one done wins all the flowers.* But they did what they did, and it seemed to go on forever, and no one was announced as the winner.

At the end of the race, they closed the lid to Great-Grandma's bed, and Alex's grandpa, uncle, and dad, along with three other men, carried Great-Grandma to a long black station wagon in the parking lot and slid her in the trunk. Everyone hopped in their cars, and everyone was given a cool little flag on their roof. Then, like a parade, they followed the station wagon with a policeman in front of them riding a motorcycle. (Alex thought how it was cool, because the policeman let them run all the stop lights and stop signs. They didn't have to stop once!) The parade went to a place where they put his great-grandma in a deep hole in the ground. He kept looking at his grandmother, wondering if that would happen to everyone someday, especially her. The whole day was strange and quite disturbing for Alex. From that day forward, he had nightmares about being caught and crushed and ground through huge metal gears. To this day, he doesn't know what those dreams meant, but they would haunt him over and over for years to come, and he always woke up crying in terror.

As they all drove home, it dawned on Alex that he really only saw his great-grandmother two or three times a year, and that was always a bit disturbing, due to those wrinkles, her odor, and her fragile hugs. He could sense she was going to "break" someday, like the skeleton they placed on their front door on Halloween. But more than that, what he would remember most about her was the excitement he felt when he received in the mail her Christmas, Easter, and birthday cards without fail every year, addressed to, "Alex Beckham," his name right there on the envelope. Inside the card, a quarter was taped, with a scribbled "I love you, Alex! *signed* Great-Grandma Foster." *That's a lot of money*, thought

Alex. That would buy him four pickles and a pack of baseball cards with a piece of bubble gum inside each.

But now those days were over, and that was a sadness he must learn to deal with from this day forward. But with the next holiday and no card, he realized it wasn't really the quarter at all, though that was fun. Those cards meant she thought about him and loved him. He began to cry inside, so no one thought he was a baby, but he hoped she would always be thinking of him in heaven, wherever that was, and he promised in his bedtime prayers that night never to forget her.

ALEX THINKS HIS GRANDPA MIGHT LIKE HIM, AT LEAST A LITTLE BIT, BUT NOT MUCH AND CERTAINLY NOT OFTEN

"Alex, what kind of question is that? I'm not going to die. I'm too young to die," his grandmother said as she tilted his chin up towards her face with her knuckle, staring into his questioning eyes, which were slowly filling with tears. "Great-Grandma was very, very old, and very, very sick. She was my mother, you know. I'm not ever going to get old like her, so everything is fine; no worries. Now here, take this bottle of beer and these cigarettes into the living room for your grandpa. We don't want him to get cranky, now, do we?" Alex seemed to feel like it was his fault, because whenever he was around his grandpa, Grandpa got kind of cold to his grandma. And he rarely showed Alex much attention, unless he wanted another beer.

As Ethel opened Grandpa's beer and obtained his fresh pack of Camels to be carried to the living room, Alex became perplexed. *Okay, Great-Grandma was Grandma's mother? No, I never knew that. And Uncle Harry and Aunt Estelle are who? And Great-Grandma Bachelor then is what to whom? And why do I have two great-grandmothers?* As Alex got older, it would become clearer, but again, like every young child his age, he thought it confusing trying to figure out who was whom to whom. But Tuffy was easy.

Alex's grandfather, Art, was sitting on his ugly brown sofa, his legs spread open, forearms on top of his thighs, drinking a beer and reading *Popular Mechanics*, all topped off with his Camel burning in the ashtray. Ethel, unlike Tuffy and Alex, allowed Art to sit on the furniture, but Ethel made him remove his dirty work pants, and he could sit either in a pair of pajama bottoms or, when it was warm, just his striped boxers. He also wore a pair of high-top leather slippers and a white sleeveless undershirt.

Alex was always told by his mother that his grandfather was a hard-working man, a foreman in a factory that made the machines that made the machines. Alex didn't know what that meant, but it sounded important.

Alex could easily pick up that rough factory odor as soon as his grandfather walked in the door. Then Grandpa would apply this liquid called "Heet," which caused his arthritic shoulders and calves to get really hot, and it relieved some of his pain. He rarely said anything to Alex except "Hey kid, get me another beer" or "Be quiet." But the "Be quiet" wasn't always verbal; sometimes it was only the glance from the corner of his eye along with a clearing of his nicotine-coated throat.

That's probably why Alex was convinced his grandpa didn't like him much. When Alex was around him, he experienced the same feeling as when a dog would growl at him on the street or when his mother scolded, spanked him, then sent him to his room. His stomach burned, his throat tightened, and most of the time he cried when his mother got angry with him. But he never cried in front of his grandpa, except when the fishing hook went through his finger. His grandpa was never mean or hurtful in any way towards Alex, but crying seemed just so babyish in front of this big, tough man.

"Here, Grandpa. Grandma told me to bring these to you so you won't get cranky," Alex said along with his bouncy smile.

"Oh, she did, did she? Cranky, she says. Thanks, Alex, but I'll show you cranky," Art said loud enough so Ethel could, without a doubt, hear him in the kitchen. He put down the beer and the fresh pack of cigarettes on the coffee table, then out of nowhere, he grabbed Alex, pulled him into his stinky body like an attacking papa bear, and started rubbing his face on Alex's cheek. "Like my whiskers, kid?" he said with a smile. "Someday you'll have whiskers and hair on your chest like your old grandpa!" Neither of them realized at the time that with the Native American thing going on, "hairy" was not going to be Alex's middle name.

Alex squiggled and squirmed, giggling the entire time. His grandpa's whiskers were as rough as sandpaper. As he hopelessly attempted to escape the papa bear's hug and get loose, his grandpa made growling noises in his ear, like two wolves in a fight, as he scuffed the boy's tender face. Then he let Alex go, and that quick, just ignored him again. He did things like that a lot: "mixed signals" Alex heard said by his dad to his mom a lot, especially at bedtime. But that attack was the only reason Alex ever thought, in some strange way, his grandpa did kind of like him.

Alex went to the chair where his grandmother always sat, grabbed his soiled pillow, and laid back down on the hardwood floor next to the heat register.

"Aren't you chilly after your trip to the store, Alex?" asked Grandma. But before he could answer, she covered him with a drab brown quilt that smelled like musty dust. Then Tuffy came over and lay right up against him on the blanket.

"Since you did me a favor, my precious, it's time we blow some heat right into you and Tuffy's faces. That'll warm up the both of you!" Ethel kissed Alex on top of the head.

"Ethel, it costs money to fire up that furnace just to please the kid," blurted Art.

"It costs money, Art? That's funny. What about your bowling three nights a week and that bottle of whiskey you keep in the closet?" Ethel said without even looking at Art as she just went back to her task of pleasing her boys.

"Yeah, give Tuffy and me a second to get ready!" They both rolled onto their tummies. "Ok, Grandma, on your mark, get set, now!"

She went to a circular dial on the wall and turned it ever so slightly. Alex laid his ear directly on the register and heard that faint click deep down in the belly of the duct. Then there it was. The gentle boom he had been waiting for all day. They were both only seconds away from a state of childhood and puppy bliss. There was a small metal half-hooded deflector on the register, directing the warm air to the center of the room. He and Tuffy stuck their faces smack dab in front of the deflector. Within moments, a blast of hot air arose from the basement, into their faces and under the blanket. Tuffy was lying on his stomach, paws stretched in front of him, legs stretched behind him, his shaggy face taking in the warm gust as well. It was sort of like what he did when he rode in the car, sticking his face out the window. (Alex told me he never knew a dog that didn't like to do that, and he also never figured out why they got such a kick out of it. He didn't realize how lucky dogs were back then, before A/C and interstates. As he moved into the future, people would drive with their windows up, and their cars would go 70 MPH on interstates. Imagine what that would do to a dog's tongue, nose, and eyeballs!)

Anyway, Alex so loved that blast, feeling warm and cozy on the floor with Tuffy, even though it only lasted a few minutes. Then the cold drafts would invade the house once more like ghosts—down the steps, off the windows, under the doors. He would then need to bundle up once more.

IF IT'S SQUARE, WHY DO THEY CALL IT A RING? AND IF THEY HAVE NO FINGERS, WHY NOT CALL THEM MITTENS? AND WHY IS GRANDPA ANGRY?

They all ate dinner, and while Grandma cleaned the kitchen, Art went back to his sofa and sat quietly, drinking more beers and smoking more cigarettes.

"It's almost 7:30, Art," Grandma called from the kitchen. "Want me to dial the radio into the fight? What channel?"

"We only get three good channels on that old thing, Ethel," said Grandpa gruffly. "Just start turning the big knob. You'll find it." Art was not patient with Ethel at all.

It was hard to imagine, as Alex looked back on those days, that it would still be another three years before he saw a television, not until he was eight. All the kids played outside until dark whenever they could. Alex listened to his dad read books to him until he learned to read for himself. A creative imagination was a must: puzzles, Lincoln Logs, Tinker Toys, Erector sets, and Bill Dings. And Alex never grew too old to help his mother in the kitchen, but really only when she baked cookies or brownies, because she, even into his teen years, saved the batter on the spoons and mixer blades for him, not his dad nor his sister.

Alex's family's first TV was a massive hunk of wood, with a tiny, disproportionate screen and lots of tubes. That TV single-handedly broke Alex of whining about having to take a bath every day. The reason? In the early days, TV didn't come on until 5:00 in the afternoon, and it started with *The Mickey Mouse Club*. So, as Mom put it so succinctly "No bath, no TV." Or as Alex heard it, "No TV, no *Mickey Mouse Club*." Mom had him right where she wanted him. She wouldn't have this kind of power over him again until the day he got his driver's license. TV became a parental dream. It was a built-in babysitter, a major disciplinary tool, and an educational and entertainment tool. And it cut Alex's father's boring lectures in half, thank goodness!

(For the record, remember, I am the narrator and his ghost writer. As you've experienced, Alex loves going off on tangents, but they're his memories, and that's what I'm here for, to write his story and the most influential parts of his youth.)

So, back to the radio. That thing was a wooden monster with tubes as well, as tall as Alex, an old round-topped apparatus perched right inside the front hallway. Why? Because that was the only place it would fit and be heard, not only over the entire first floor of the house but onto the outside porch in the summertime as well. Alex's grandmother began turning the one huge circular knob right in the middle. Alex had no idea what the little knobs did. The speakers made a noise like nothing else, sounds going up and down, loud and soft, high-pitched squeals, always a constant static in the background, and faint voices every so often, some in languages Alex had never heard before. It was known as a ham radio, able to pick up signals from all over the world. But Alex was only allowed to play with it when his grandfather wasn't home. "Ethel, don't let the boy play around with that radio. It's annoying!" Art yelled one day to Ethel in the kitchen. Alex only needed to hear that once.

Still, those faint voices tweaked his curiosity. They made him wonder where these funny speaking people lived and what they were saying. Occasionally, he heard people speaking like his grandpa and his two elderly aunts, Mayme and Carrie, spoke to each other. Sometimes he would hit on a channel that came out so loud it would stun him, knocking him backwards into the steps while Tuffy scratched his ear with his back paw.

"Art, I can't find it! I'm trying, but I can't find the stupid channel!" Ethel and Alex knew Grandpa was not going to take this well. Ethel was frightened. Art was frustrated.

"Never mind, Ethel, I'll get it." Art stood up slowly, grimacing in obvious pain. Ethel scampered immediately back to the kitchen. With a sigh, the man limped gingerly to the radio and tuned in the channel within seconds. Then, without a word or a glance at anyone, he shuffled back to his sofa, his beer, and his cigarettes.

"Grandpa, what's a boxing match? Mr. Thomas told me that's what you meant when you told Grandma you wanted to listen to a fight on the radio tonight. I thought you meant people were going to yell at each other like Mom and Mrs. Grogan did that day."

"You've never seen two men box, Alex?" Grandpa asked without looking up. Then he looked at Alex as he cocked his head to the side. "No, I guess you wouldn't have seen one, since we don't have a TV, and your daddy would never take you to see one. He's such a college boy."

"What's a college boy, Grandpa?" asked Alex.

"Art!" Ethel called from the kitchen. "Not necessary. Leave it alone."

Alex didn't know what they meant at the time, but they did refer to his dad as "the college boy" when he wasn't around, and it never felt to Alex like they said it in a good way.

"Dad took me to a basketball game once! That was fun. And to a Redleg's game once. And I watch him play softball where he works!" Alex was excited his Grandpa was talking to him.

"Well, that's a little different," responded Art. "Boxing is where two men get into this ring, then they each go to their corners and…"

"Wait, Grandpa, wait," Alex interrupted. "You said the men get in a ring and go to their corners. Rings don't have corners, Grandpa, they're round," he blurted with a puzzled look on his face.

"Well, you're right, I guess. Rings don't have corners. But it's not really shaped like a ring, it's not round. It's square, really, with ropes around it to keep the men close to each other when they fight."

"So, if it's square, then why do they call it a ring, Grandpa? Why don't they call it a square? I'm sorry, but that doesn't make any sense. Does it to you, Grandpa?"

Art didn't know how to answer the boy. He had a point. "Well, they call it a ring because, uh, I guess, well, it's because…" Art was stumped by Alex's question, and he could hear Ethel giggling in the kitchen. "Look, kid, you want me to teach you about boxing or not?" He answered Alex's question with a Socratic answer, a question with a question.

"Sure, tell me. I wanna hear! You know just about everything, don't you, Grandpa?" Art could hear Ethel giggle again.

"Well, the two men get into the ring, okay, this square ring, and sit on stools in opposite corners. Then when the bell rings, they go to the middle and try to knock each other out by punching each other as much and as hard as they can in the face and in the stomach. But they can't hit each other below their belts."

"Why not, Grandpa? Why not below their belts? And what does knocked out mean? You mean knocked out of the square?"

"No, no, boy. First, forget the below-the-belt thing for now. Ask your dad about that one, or now that you're riding a bicycle, you'll find out for yourself soon enough. And again, it's not the square, it's the ring. It's called a ring, remember? And knocked out is where you, well, kind of go to sleep for a while, and you can't wake up. And nobody can wake you up for a while, either."

"Sort of like when no one could wake up Great-Grandma?"

Art was going to blow right past that question. "No, that was different. These men do wake up after a few minutes of being knocked out. Okay, got that so far?" Art knew he could never explain Great-Grandma in any terms that would make sense to a boy that age.

"Sounds like it would hurt a lot, especially being hit in the face and stuff. And that must hurt their hands a lot, too."

"They do get bloody noses and cuts over their eyes, but they wear what they call 'boxing gloves.' They have padding inside them, so it doesn't hurt their hands as much when they punch. And they also tape their hands before they put them in the gloves. As a matter of fact—"

"Remember when I had a bloody forehead right here between my eyes where the scar is when I fell down the steps last year? Mom told me I was knocked out for a minute or two, but I didn't remember being knocked out. Now I get it. That hurt a lot, Grandpa."

"Yes, yes, I do. You were a mess; lots of blood. Yes, it's sort of like that. But, Alex, don't ever interrupt me again when I'm talking. You should never interrupt any adult when they're talking, even when you grow up. Understand?" Art stared seriously into Alex's eyes.

"Yes, Grandpa. I'm sorry. I understand, and I won't ever do it again. I promise!"

That was the first time Alex's grandfather ever corrected or scolded him. His grandfather wasn't mean or mad, but he was scary. Alex wanted to cry, but he held it in. His grandfather didn't talk to him much, if at all, and Alex certainly didn't want to give him a reason to stop now.

It was such an intense moment for Alex that "don't interrupt" was a phrase he never forgot. His grandfather was right in so many ways. Alex would take that into his adulthood, respecting conversations between two people, as well as facts and opinions expressed by others. The lesson Grandpa taught Alex was so powerful. And as he became an adult, Alex found himself judging people who did interrupt a conversation. He became so aware and amazed at the number of adults who interrupted conversations with no idea how inconsiderate and disrespectful they were being. He would never interrupt him again, or any adult or peer in the future.

"Good," Art nodded with a faint smile. "Now, what I was going to say about the boxing gloves before being interrupted? Your Uncle Jimmy has a pair of gloves hanging on his wall next to his bed upstairs. Run up and get them, and I'll put them on you, and your old grandpa will teach you how to box. Well, go ahead, boy, what are you waiting for? Run up and get the gloves. They're hanging on a nail on his wall."

Alex didn't really want to run upstairs to his Uncle Jimmy's room. The truth was, he was terrified to step foot into Uncle Jimmy's room. Jimmy was sixteen and was always good to Alex, when he paid any attention at all, but Alex always slept in his aunt's room; she was thirteen. The reason for his unease was that Alex was scared of this coconut painted like an ugly, mean pirate with a red bandana on its head and a bloody gash painted on its cheek. It was right there on the wall over his dresser, and no one could miss it whenever they entered. It was like Uncle Jimmy wanted to be like it. But now, Alex had to go in there, alone. And although he did realize it was just a coconut with a face painted on it and not a real pirate skull, it still really, really scared him.

Alex scampered up the stairs as he was told, but then crept cautiously to the end of the hallway, entered the room, and snatched the gloves off the wall as fast as he could. But even though he tried not to, he still took a quick glance at the coconut head before he bounced down the steps to safety.

"Alex, walk, honey. You know what happened last year. No falling down the stairs again," his grandma yelled to Alex, her own fear swelling up inside. But Alex really didn't care. He just needed to escape that bloody pirate!

"Ok, Alex, give me the gloves," his grandpa said as he reached, taking them from Alex's hand.

"Grandpa, these aren't gloves, these are mittens. They've got no fingers. They should call them boxing mittens?"

Art wasn't about to go another round with Alex after the square and the ring thing, so he ignored the question. Ethel giggled again. Art loosened the gloves a bit and decided to play along with Alex's technically accurate question. "Now, push your hands inside like you do your mittens." They slid easily onto Alex's small fists. His grandfather tried to lace them tighter, but even at their tightest, they were way too big and baggy on him. His grandfather raised his own hands up, one on each side of his face.

"Okay, kid, punch my hands. Go ahead, you won't hurt me." Alex took an unexpected and uncontrollable roundhouse swing at his grandfather's hand. As his grandfather tried to grab Alex's arm, he didn't stop it at all, and the punch glanced off Art's face.

"Holy crap, boy. That's called a 'roundhouse' and I didn't see that coming." Art was smiling, and Ethel laughed aloud.

"Oh Grandpa, are you okay? I didn't mean to hurt you. Really, I didn't." Alex was waiting for a spanking over his grandpa's knee, but instead, his grandpa started laughing. That was the first and one of the few times he ever heard his grandpa laugh.

"Okay, kid, let's start over," Alex's grandpa said, still with a smile on his face. He took a swig of his beer and put out his cigarette, as it was about to fall out of the ashtray and onto the carpet. "No, no, this time, forget the big roundhouse, champ. You might knock me out next time. Just punch straight at my hands this time, like when you're handing me a beer. It's called a jab."

Alex jabbed at his grandpa's hand, and his grandpa jerked his head backward as if Alex had hit him again.

"Grandpa, did I hit you again? I'm sorry." Alex wasn't liking this boxing thing if he was hurting his grandpa.

"No, no, boy, you didn't hit me. I was just pretending, so you could see what it looks like when you really do hit somebody." For the first time, Alex's grandpa was starting to see Alex in a different light, like maybe he could have some fun with the boy from time to time.

"Come on, kid, now punch with the other hand. That's it! That a boy! No one's gonna mess around with you when you get bigger with a punch like that! I can teach you jabs and hooks and uppercuts and how to move your feet. Hell, boy, I could make you a real boxer! I was a pretty tough kid when I was your age and got tougher as I got older. Nobody messed with Art. They used to call me a bad-ass!"

Alex was feeling pretty good about himself. It was the first time, other than the "whisker game," that Alex ever remembered his grandfather talking and truly playing with him. But after that night, for reasons unknown for many years, he never said much to Alex at all. He never asked Alex about school or his friends. A few times, he took Alex and his mom fishing with him, and a few times, he took Alex to the bowling alley with him, but even then, he remained quiet. The conversation was mostly one-sided: "Alex, get me another beer; Alex, get me some matches; Alex, go get the paper off the porch." And the day he died ten years later, "Alex, wheel me back to my bed; Alex, help me out of my wheelchair; Alex, tell your mom to call an ambulance." But that's a story for another day.

Alex's grandmother slowly walked into the living room and stood at the doorway, watching her boys laughing and playing together. She'd overheard their entire conversation from the kitchen.

"Art," she scolded, "you know they don't want him to fight. He has that same bleeding thing Jimmy has. He could die from a nosebleed, for God's sake. What are you thinking? Or aren't you?"

Art got defensive and didn't handle being scolded by Ethel well at all. Alex was confused, although he kind of knew what his grandma meant.

"Ethel, he isn't fighting. He's just punching my hands. We're just playing. He's a pretty tough little kid, and he's got a tough road ahead of him. He needs to be able to protect himself somehow." Art was right, but Alex would learn to protect himself in different ways.

Alex's grandpa lost some of his smile and seemed to have lost his enthusiasm to play with Alex. But he wasn't going to let Ethel "slap his hands" and make him stop.

"Okay, c'mon, kid. Hit me again. That's it. Now, that's what the boxers do, only they hit each other hard in the face and stomach, and their noses and eyebrows bleed. And like I said, the first man to fall down and not be able to get up before the referee counts to ten loses. Make sense?"

"Are the men on the radio fighting because they're mad at each other and don't like each other? Why are they mad at each other?" As usual, Alex was not running out of questions.

"They aren't mad at each other at all. It's a sport, like baseball and basketball. These two men tonight are fighting for the middleweight championship of the world," Art explained.

"What does that mean, Grandpa? Does that mean they're only fat around their stomachs in the middle?" Again, Alex never lacked the next question.

"No, no, Alex, it means they aren't the biggest and they're not the smallest boxers in the world. The winner gets a big belt made out of gold and a whole lot of money." Art was glad question time was about to end. He was getting frustrated. "Here we go, kid, fight's about to start. We want Bobo Olson to win," Art said quickly.

"Why, Grandpa, is he a friend of yours?" asked Alex even though he wasn't supposed to talk.

Art came back quickly again. "Never met him, Alex, but he's white, and Sugar Ray Leonard isn't. One more question, kid, and I'll make you leave the room." Alex looked at his grandma with a puzzled look, but she put her finger over her lips, motioning him to be quiet.

"Okay, now here we go. The fight's about to start, so let's just listen. Just sit and be quiet. No talking during the fight, none at all. That means you too, Ethel. Turn the sound up. And for God's sake, Ethel, take that phone off the hook. No talking to Mary or any of your friends until the fight's over. Got it?"

Alex's grandma turned the radio up, and Alex could hear a crowd of people mumbling in the background. It was a low mesh of voices, blending in such a way he couldn't make out anything anyone was saying, just voices like a hive of bumble bees. Then he heard the clang of a bell, and the voices got louder.

A man came on and started describing what was happening. Alex heard the words "punch," "jab," and "hook," and the man talked about the fighters "dancing around the ring." The vision of two grown men dancing together, like people at weddings, didn't make any sense, the way his grandpa described boxing, but again, Alex knew now was not the time to ask that question either. Spontaneously, loud cheers would go up, and his grandpa would get excited. Other times, he would have a terrible frown on his face. Then it would quiet back down for a while, before another wave of loud cheers, sort of like at a basketball game. Every so often, the announcer would get really, really excited, and everybody else did as well. And then the bell would clang a bunch of times, and some other man started talking about shaving cream and razor blades, and a group of girls sang a song about clean men. Then the bell would ring again, and Alex heard the announcer and the cheering resume once more.

Suddenly, the announcer started talking fast, almost out of control, and the crowd started cheering in a frenzy. He could hear someone counting faintly over the noise. When the man reached ten, the bell clanged violently over and over and over. Alex heard both cheers and boos from the radio.

Alex looked at his grandfather. "Can I talk now, Grandpa? What happened?" Art didn't say a word, didn't even look at Alex or acknowledge his question. He just got up slowly, limped to the radio, and turned it off abruptly. Returning to the coffee table, he rubbed some more Heet on his shoulder, grabbed his beer and cigarettes, and went through the kitchen and down the steps to his woodshop in the basement.

"What happened, Grandma? He's not mad at me, is he? I waited until the end to talk. I thought we were having fun!"

"No, no, Alex. He's not mad at you at all. That man, Bobo, the man he wanted to win, was knocked out and lost the fight." Ethel was not in the least upset and went to reconnect the phone.

"You mean like when the Reds lose? But he doesn't get upset like that when the Reds lose." Alex was so confused.

Grandma came over to Alex and pulled him tight to her apron. "No, he doesn't, but this is different. Your grandpa just wanted the white man to win."

"I don't understand. What does that matter? Why would that get him so upset? Was the colored man a bad man, like a murderer or something?"

"No, Alex, not at all. He's just not white," his Grandma replied calmly.

"Then that makes no sense to me, Grandma." Alex's confusion was growing, and Ethel thanked God Art was in the basement where Alex couldn't ask him these questions directly.

"Don't ever ask your grandpa that question. Don't ever say anything about the fight to him, not ever. You'll understand why someday, Alex, when you get older. Just the way things are in the world. Now, grab your pillow and the quilt, and you and Tuffy go lie down by the register. I'll make you both nice and toasty one more time." Alex ran from his grandmother's arms with Tuffy right on his heels.

Alex took the gloves off and lay back down on the floor by the register. Grandma turned the dial, and he heard the click, heard the boom, and then Alex and Tuffy waited. The warm air came rushing out and into their faces for a couple minutes; momentary bliss. As the warm air finally cooled, he rolled over on his back and looked at the ceiling, again following the rivers and streams and lakes, wondering where these waterways were going to take him next.

And as he was falling asleep, he was confused and was almost ready to cry about the unusual time he had spent that night with his grandpa. He wondered, *Does he love me like Grandma or not? He seemed to there, for a little while. He even laughed. But when the fight ended, he ignored me and Grandma. Then he stomped off to the basement. Grandma and my dad and Tuffy seem to be the only ones in the world that really love me. Maybe it's the scar on my head. Mom has never treated me the same since then. She hasn't treated Dad the same either. This kid thing can be real confusing at times. I guess I'll just have to go with what Grandma said, "You'll understand why someday." I want to grow up soon!*

Alex and Tuffy snuggled up together on the floor. Alex fell asleep for about an hour until his mom and dad picked him up and took him home, tucking him in bed as they always did. Alex was asleep again by the time he hit the sheets. He had no idea about the storm clouds gathering on his horizon, a storm, depending on which way the wind would blow, that would change his life forever.

Next in the series*:*

Alex and his family plod through the bureaucracy of child adoption as it almost tears the Beckham family apart forever and comes close to changing Alex's future into rubble.

EPISODE III

A SOFT MELODY FILLS THE BECKHAM HOME

This episode presents a series of events that cause doubt and confusion behind the complexity of the adoption of a female infant in the 1950s. Alex, never quite sure throughout his lifetime whether his parents made the decision to avoid a second child due to the possibility of Mary's hemophilia gene expressing itself in a newborn son or whether, as he was told, due to the inability of his mother and father to physically produce another offspring. No matter what the reason, the decision to adopt brings with it the need for an on-site inspection of the Beckham's household to determine the capability of this young family, including Alex, to raise a child in a healthy and loving environment. But an unfortunate event rears its head the day of the inspection causing deep sadness to affect the young boy's normal behavior. Therefore, Alex is put through a morning of psychoanalytic testing to assure the adopted child will not be exposed to unfavorable surroundings caused by an emotionally unstable sibling. Alex begins to wonder whether there just might really be something wrong with him.

But the story leaves itself open to the question of the deep inner consequences for each of us caused by questionable actions of people and things outside of our control. These tributaries entering all our lives can continue to carry us downstream and swirl around in our personalities like eddies throughout our entire lives, as well as influencing the lives of everyone they suck in.

September 1956

ALEX LOSES HIS BEST FRIEND AND ALMOST HIS TRUE IDENTITY

A loud, eerie scream resounded through the entire house, causing even the dog chained next door to begin howling. It was a scream Alex's mother had never heard from her little boy, one she would never hear again, and one she would never forget.

"Mommy...Mommy...Mommy!" With each summoning of his mother, Alex screamed louder and longer, each "Mommy" outcry rising to a higher pitch than the last. Mary was about to pour the first of her banana pancake batter for Alex and herself in her cast iron skillet. She turned off the stove, grabbed a towel, and wiped the batter from her hands. She darted to the living room as she flung the towel onto the floor behind her. In that infinitesimal moment of time, that panicked moment between first hearing the scream and getting to the reality behind the scream, Mary's maternal brain raced into numerous conclusions like a bolt of lightning followed by an immediate clap of thunder. *What could have happened? He fell down the steps again? Someone broke into the house and they have him? The house is on fire?* But she hadn't heard a tumble, certainly didn't smell smoke, and the front door, she was sure, was locked. But all those possible scenarios swarmed her mind as if they were simultaneously one thought.

As she burst through the doorway into the living room, Alex was still calling her name over and over, his eyes as wide open as fear could spread them. He couldn't catch his breath, and his feet wouldn't stop moving, as if he were running fast in little steps but going nowhere.

"Mommy, he's not moving. He's not moving. He just lays there even when I touch him. I pushed him a little, and he just lays there. He won't wake up! He won't wake up! Do something, Mommy! Wake him up! Do something!"

Pudgy was a blue parakeet with a bright, blue-feathered breast, a white head, and a subtle golden beak. And other than Tuffy, who really belonged to Alex's grandmother, Pudgy his first very own pet. They were mysteriously close for a human and a bird. Every morning, Alex would come down the stairs from his bedroom, take the small blue-checkered tablecloth off Pudgy's cage, open his cage door, and rub the bird's feathers a bit with the back of his fingers. He would voluntarily fill up Pudgy's seed feeder and change the water in his tube. And occasionally, Alex's mother would buy a special seed column for him that hung from the top of his cage. The bird wasted no time devouring that!

The bird loved being out of his cage (like we all do). He perched on anyone's finger and on Alex's head or shoulders. It was a tickly, prickly feeling like no other. Alex had taught him to say his name, "Pretty Pudgy" (at least it sounded close enough to Alex), and the bird would chirp whenever he was left in the room alone—thus, the cover at night. Alex loved that little bird so much, but the thing that made him really cool was when Alex and his mother and father would sit with Pudgy on the floor, all with bowls of ice cream. Pudgy would hop from rim to rim of the bowls, eating ice cream from each member of the family. It was those times, when all four of them were together, smiling, laughing, and chirping with each other, that were unforgettable and so special to Alex. But that morning, the peaceful routine of daybreak went terribly south.

The bird religiously rang his bell in the morning to let everyone know he was awake. But all was quiet, like no one was at home. When Alex removed the blanket resting on his cage, the bird wasn't on his perch. Alex wondered, *Did he get out in the night?* No, the cage door was still shut, and the blanket was still covering the cage. Then Alex glanced onto the floor of the cage, and that was when he saw the parakeet lying motionless on his side, eyes open but totally still, claws curled strangely up under his breast. As Alex opened the cage door, a tremor, like when he'd stuck his finger in an electrical socket once, ran through his body; something was really, really wrong. Confusion ravaged Alex's instincts. He was praying Pudgy was just still asleep or was fooling with him—yes, that was it, it was just a new trick! But then Alex touched him; he was cold and stiff. At that point, Alex confirmed what he already knew. And that was the moment his tremor transmuted from internal to external, and he began screaming for his mother. His best friend was dead.

When Mary entered the room and realized what had happened, she was so relieved Alex was okay. With her son's bleeding condition, she lived in constant fear for his very life. The bird meant nothing to her. As a matter of fact, Mary was so terrified for her son, she repeatedly refused Randall's pleas to have a second child. After Alex's tumble down the steps, Mary rebuffed the possibility of giving birth to another son, and this had caused the intimacy between Mary and Randall to slowly fade. Their relationship became more "brother and sister;" however, they did agree to attempt the adoption of a baby girl.

Mary was also less than affectionate to Alex than a mother should be. Subconsciously, she had put up walls around her heart. Therefore, it came to be that Alex and his father became closer and closer, causing Mary to form a resentful jealousy towards both of them and their delightful relationship.

As Mary contemplated the dead bird, she immediately knew this was going to be a tough one. It was terrible timing—the worst. Alex had always been a sensitive, emotional child. Not to the point of being psychotic or manic, but he cried over sad books and movies, like *Dumbo* or *Bambi*. And as he evolved into an artist later in life, he looked back to realize that not everyone had those heightened emotions. Mary and Randall were business types, very serious and very calculating. They weren't into literature, art, or theater of any kind. Randall enjoyed Big Band music, but Mary, not a bit.

Neither of them really knew how to handle Alex's heightened emotions. They wanted him to be "seen and not heard," as his mother used to tell him. He didn't become angry often, but when he did, look out. He would throw tantrums very much like those of his mother. He was extremely afraid of the pitch darkness of the basement and was suspiciously frightened of what was under his bed. He was so convinced something like an alligator or a monster was under there that he'd start a few steps away from his mattress, run, then leap onto it from a safe distance. There was no way that alligator was going to snag him. And he would never, ever let any part of his body, like a hand or a foot, hang over the edge, or it would surely be gnawed off by morning!

On the flip side, he was a delightful and unknowingly witty child, dancing and laughing much of the time. He giggled so much at times, his dad would threaten to lock him in the old coal bin in the basement until he settled down. His dad never went that far, but he was fully aware of how scared Alex was of the basement, so he used it on Alex as an emotional counterbalance. In the big picture, however, Alex was a well-behaved and loving kid. And love was probably Alex's strongest emotion.

Mary knew Alex's grief and sadness were going to be no easy task to overcome this morning, especially in this very short window of time. The child psychologist from the adoption agency was due to arrive in just a couple of hours. As Alex stood crying, sobbing, and yelling at her to do something, she had to figure out a solution and fast

Mary looked in the cage and, for what seemed like a long, long time, she just stared. "There's nothing we can do, Alex. God has decided to take Pudgy to heaven."

"Why? What does God need with Pudgy? He's my bird, not his." Alex snapped uncharacteristically at his mother.

"We don't always know why God does what he does, Alex, and we can't ever question God. God took him for a reason. We just have to trust God needed Pudgy. Or maybe because he was so special, God wanted him to be in a beautiful place with him and other birds, like heaven."

Well, that explanation wasn't comforting in the slightest. *Okay, I was taking care of him, feeding him special seed, cleaning his cage, feeding him ice cream; God can't do better than I can. Did he ever think to ask Pudgy what he wanted,* thought Alex, *or ask me?* But Alex knew better than to argue with his mother, or she would punish him with spankings or send him to his room or both. Alex then thought, *If that's what Mom does to me, what kind of punishment will I get if I argue with God?* Alex decided to just remain silent. He stared at Pudgy, dead on the rough gravel floor of the cage, unable to stop crying. But Alex wasn't buying that stuff about God needing Pudgy at all, not one bit!

To be frank, Alex's mother was not handling this crisis well, to say the least. Mary's only target was to chock-off Alex's severe sadness using the God justification. But in her defense, attempting an intellectual and philosophical conversation about the realities of life and death with a five-year-old who was flipping out would be just as fruitless. Plus, at that hour of the day, Alex didn't yet know why getting him under control was so important. All he knew was, his mom was letting him miss a day of school for some unknown reason.

THE TRIBUTARIES of ALEX BECKHAM

Alex looked up at his mother with a scowl of disappointment. He ran up to his room, slammed the door, and leapt onto his bed, crying and sobbing even harder than before.

After about fifteen minutes, Mary came upstairs to evaluate her predicament as Alex hung on the precipice. He was still sobbing. His pajama top was soaked with tears. She held an empty chocolate-powder Ovaltine tin in her left hand and held Pudgy by the tail with a napkin in her right.

"Alex, I've been thinking. I'll tell you what we're going to do. When your dad gets home from work tonight, we're going to have a funeral for Pudgy and give him a proper burial."

"You mean we put him in that tin can and then put him in a hole in the ground like you did with Great-Grandma?" Alex inquired as he continued to sob, his lower lip quivering.

"Well, yes, sort of like Great-Grandma. We need to put him in this tin first. The tin is now called his casket, and the hole we'll dig is called his grave. And we'll have a little ceremony called a funeral. We'll say some prayers, and we'll keep him in the backyard with us forever. And you can dig the grave yourself back by the garden when your dad comes home from work. Would you like to be the one that puts him in his casket?" Mary anxiously awaited Alex's response.

She's kidding me, right? Alex thought. *I take him and put him in there. I already touched him in his cage, and he was cold and stiff. I can't touch him again. What does she think this is all about? It's creepy! Yuk!*

"No, Mom, you go ahead and do it, I can't. I really can't," Alex said with watery eyes. The situation was going downhill like a landslide in multiple directions.

"Okay, I understand. I'll do it." And as she held Pudgy upside down by his tail feathers, she dropped him headfirst into the tin.

CLUNK! as his head hit the bottom. Then she snapped on the lid.

"Okay. Wait a minute, Mom. I'm not getting something here,"

Alex said as that *CLUNK* caused him to feel some anger over his mother's lack of respect for his friend. "I thought you said God was taking him? If God's taking him, what are we doing hiding him from God in that tin and putting him under the ground? Wouldn't it be easier to do what we do for Santa at Christmas, like the milk and cookies? We could just leave him out on a plate or something and let God take him while we're asleep!"

"Well, uh, uh, God doesn't take Pudgy's body. He takes his spirit, like he did with Great-Grandma. I know it must be really hard to understand right now, but it'll all make sense when you get older."

There's that 'Make sense when you get older' thing again. I hate that, thought Alex.

"Wow, that's a fantastic idea, Mom!" Alex said with innocent enthusiasm. "That means I can dig him up and see him every day if I want? Nice! I like that." Alex grinned for the first time all morning.

"Well uh, no, not quite, Alex. Umm, it doesn't really work like that either. Once there's a funeral, we say prayers and cover the grave with dirt. It's not a good idea to dig him back up. But does the funeral sound okay with you?" Mary was dodging Alex's logical questions like a bullfighter in the ring.

"So, we have a what and say prayers where, like we did when Great-Grandma died?" Alex had reached a point where he was getting all these new terms confused. And it wasn't helping his attitude.

"We say prayers at the funeral, which is the ceremony. Then we put Pudgy's casket down into his grave in the ground and cover him with dirt; that's called the burial," explained Mary once more.

"Okay. We put him in the hole and cover him with dirt, right?"

"Not exactly. The hole is called a grave, honey. It's a grave, not a hole."

"But they called it a hole and not a grave with Great-Grandma." Alex frowned.

"No, they didn't. Nobody called it a hole. I don't understand. What do you mean, Alex? Who called it a hole?" Mary was now becoming as confused as Alex.

"Well, at the end of the prayers, the man everyone called Father, but who really wasn't anybody's father, sprinkled water on the, uh, what's it called, Mommy?" Alex asked.

"The casket, honey. It's called the casket." Mary was following Alex so far.

"Okay, on the casket, and then he said, 'In the name of the Father, and the Son, and into the hole she goes.' He did! I heard him say it!"

His mother looked at Alex, trying hard to hold back her grin, the first smile on Mary's face so far that morning. "No Alex, he did say that, sort of, but you heard the very last part wrong. He said, 'In the name of the Father, and the Son, and the Holy Ghost.' Not 'into the hole she goes.' God's the Father, Jesus is his Son, and the Holy Ghost is what I was telling you about, with God taking Pudgy's spirit. 'Spirit' is just another word for 'ghost,' and it is what fills us all up, including Pudgy, so we can all love each other forever. I know it all sounds confusing, but I promise, you'll understand it all when you get older."

There's that 'You'll understand it when you get older' thing again. How many times? Alex had had enough of that line.

"Okay, I guess," Alex said as he looked away from his mother and agreed, experiencing his first feelings of hypocrisy, although at his age, he didn't know what that word meant. Alex thought, *It sure sounded like "in the hole she goes" to me.* But honestly, he was not buying a whole lot of anything coming from his mother that morning. *Now she tells me Pudgy is a ghost with holes in him, whatever!*

None of Mary's explanation or plans were helping Alex's pain in the least. *Pudgy is still dead, and I'm trying, but I still can't stop crying. I guess Mom did her best with what she came up with. And I can still visit Pudgy's hole whenever I want and maybe dig him up sometimes when no one is watching.*

(Just as an aside, Alex did dig Pudgy up about three months later. Whoa! Not what he expected to find. Alex never did tell anyone what he saw that day.)

"Now, honey, I need you to do Mommy a big, big favor. I know you took a bath last night before bed, but I need you to take another one this morning, brush your teeth, and put on these new clothes I bought for you. And Alex, I really need you to promise me you'll stop crying and be a big boy." Alex wasn't sure that was a promise he could keep, at least not yet.

"Why all the new stuff this morning, and why did you keep me from going to school today, Mommy?" he asked.

"There's a lady coming over this morning from the adoption agency. She wants to talk to us about getting you a sister. She'll ask all of us some questions and then look around the house. We don't want to look unhappy, now, do we?" Mary was trying to turn to the real issue.

"But I'm unhappy, Mommy, really unhappy!" Alex interjected.

"Well then, just pretend you're happy, like it's Christmas. Your daddy will be home before lunch today, so we can all talk with her together. Please, Alex, please stop crying, get cleaned up, and come downstairs for breakfast. I've already made you some special banana pancakes. How does that sound?" Mary pleaded with her heartbroken son. But she really thought maybe a good spanking would get his attention much more than being nice to him.

"Can I eat now before my bath? I'm really hungry." Alex looked so sad, and he really was; nothing was fake this time in an attempt to con his parents into ice cream or something. What could Mary say? She needed him to pull himself together, and soon. The clock was ticking.

"If you want to eat now, Alex, I won't be able to make the pancakes that quickly, but if cereal and toast work, you can eat right now, with grape jelly! Would that cheer you up?" Mary gave him an obligatory smile.

"I guess—and chocolate milk?" asked Alex.

"Well, sorry, but no chocolate milk. Remember, Pudgy's in the Ovaltine tin. Just plain milk is the best I can do this morning," and with the thought of Pudgy in the Ovaltine tin, Alex's eyes turned red once more. His crying had evolved into a sob, and his sob settled into a whimper. He moped down the steps in his ugly, green-plaid flannel pajamas, his shoulders slumped in innocent and inexperienced grief. He sat at the table, his left cheek in the palm of his hand, propped up by his elbow. He scooped his cereal over the edge of his bowl straight into his mouth. The initial shock was starting to fade, but his eyes were still red and puffy and filled with tears. Occasionally, one eye would overflow, and a tear would roll down his cheek. His mom would dab his tear and wipe his runny nose with her apron.

TIME FOR ALEX TO PULL IT TOGETHER WITH ALL HIS HEART

As Alex was finishing his breakfast, drinking the sweet, sugary milk from the remainder of his cereal bowl, Mary went upstairs to draw his bath. She put toothpaste on his toothbrush and laid it on the sink, fully aware that if she didn't, Alex would skip that part and brush his teeth with the dry bristles. Mary laid his new clothes neatly on his bed, even new white socks!

Alex finished his bath quickly. He had no desire to play with his boats or his frogmen. Mary dried him with a scratchy towel and combed his hair, at least as much as she could comb his buzz of a haircut. Mary then helped him to dress. Alex had a habit of putting his t-shirts on inside-out and most always forgot to zip up. Gradually, his insides began to stop the nausea. Mary instructed him to sit on his bed, but he didn't know what to do. His mom told him to keep his room straightened up—no toys, books, or puzzles—just sit. And as peculiar as it seemed, he really didn't have any energy to do anything but stare, unfocused, into the empty world without Pudgy. The dead gray light from the misty skies seemed appropriate to him, like maybe the whole world was crying just a little. Every so often, a single snort of a sob would hit him, like a hiccup, only it came through his nose like the sound of a pig in a pen. He rose from his seat on the bed and looked out his bedroom window, searching for the best spot to dig Pudgy's hole. *Probably next to the tomato garden*, he thought, *away from the horseshoe pits, so people won't walk on him.*

Suddenly, as he peered out at the early autumn day where the leaves were just starting to change colors, he saw his father's car drive up the driveway and into the garage. Alex knew his dad was home to meet the lady. When he saw his dad exit the garage and walk to the back door, seemingly in a hurry, Alex lost it again. He ran down the steps, craving a powerful hug from his father. Tears were coming so fast, they were dripping onto his shirt as Randall opened the screen door. Alex charged his father, burying his face into his shirt and trousers. With his father's suit pants wet and a little snotty in the front, Randall looked at Mary with a baffled glance and knelt down to give Alex exactly what he was looking for: love and strength from his father.

"Whoa, whoa, what's going on here, Tiger?" Randall pushed Alex back slightly, so he could look at the boy's face, filled with sorrow. "What are those big crocodile tears all about? Are you hurt, sick? Tell me, little buddy!"

"Beck, we have to talk," Mary quite sternly interrupted before Alex could say a word. "Alex, run back up to your room and stop your crying. We'll call you when it's time for you to come down and talk to the lady."

Alex had not had enough love yet from his father, but he obeyed his mother and sluggishly mounted the stairs as if his legs weighed a hundred pounds. He felt so alone once more as he wept. His mother had not hugged him once all morning, but he felt so safe and secure on the lap and in the arms of his father. Randall at least listened when Alex had a problem. Mary would just tell Alex to stop crying or she'd give him something to cry about. So, as he had figured out, instead of going back to his room, Alex settled quietly out of sight on the top step, where he could overhear what his parents were about to say about him.

"Beck, we have a problem, and I mean a big problem. Alex came downstairs this morning and found Pudgy dead in the bottom of his cage. Beck, he flipped out. I mean, he literally flipped out. You know how crazy emotional he can get sometimes. Of all the mornings for this to happen," explained Mary.

"Oh, Mary, he must feel so hurt," Randall said as he went to hug her. She pulled away. "I must agree, Mary, the timing couldn't be worse."

Mary was tired of hearing Randall defend Alex. "The woman from the adoption agency will be arriving any minute now, and he's been all over the house crying and sobbing for over an hour. You think we could send him to a neighbor's or something while she's here?"

"And what do we tell this woman?" asked Randall.

"I don't know, but darn it, Beck, he's gonna blow it for all of us. I knew his emotional crap was going to be a problem someday. I've done my best, but you know how unstable he is. Oh my God, why did that stupid bird have to die today? Doesn't he realize, it was just a stupid bird?"

Alex's father was always the gentler and more empathetic of the two, and Alex knew his dad would at least listen to him when he had a problem. He knew his mother wouldn't and never would. She was a screamer, a spanker, and sometimes a shaker. Alex and his dad were buddies, playing ball in the backyard, reading books, going to the hardware store together. Alex stayed clear of his mother most of the time and for good reason.

Therefore, Mary wanted this baby girl for two reasons. One, so she didn't have to deal with another son who might also inherit the gene that caused Alex's bleeding condition, and secondly, because she wanted to have a daughter who would like her best. She couldn't imagine ever treating a little girl the way she thought she needed to treat Alex. Adoption became the only solution. But today, of all days, with the most heartfelt problem of Alex's young life springing upon him like an unexpected tree branch falling on his swing set, he needed his daddy more than ever, while his mother just wanted him out-of-sight, out-of-mind. Any appearance of instability in Alex just might dash any hopes of adoption and thus, of Mary's baby girl.

"Mary, settle down. All will be fine. We merely tell the agent exactly what happened. It's really normal that he's upset. It would be abnormal if he wasn't. He really loved that bird and took care of it, mostly by himself. It was like his best friend, that bird and your mother's dog, Tuffy. That's why he wants a sister. He wants to love and take care of something. That's beautiful! That's why we all do. Think about how you felt when you were told your grandmother died on the floor of her apartment. You telling me you weren't upset?"

Mary was ready to rip Randall's lecture to pieces. "Well, maybe a little, but not like that, and Pudgy was just a dumb bird," she said as she flung her hands in the air.

That's what she thought about Pudgy? He was just a dumb bird? Alex thought.

"And Mary, you're an adult, and your grandmother was old and sick, and you really weren't exactly the one to find her on the bottom of her cage, were you?" Randall tried to hug her again, but Mary walked around to the other side of the kitchen table, placing a barrier against his affection.

"Oh, Randall. You can be so ridiculous at times. This has nothing to do with my grandmother." Mary folded her arms and rolled her eyes to the ceiling.

"Let's pull ourselves together, honey. What we don't want is you and me mad at each other when this social worker gets here. We'll just tell her the straightforward truth if it becomes an issue.

I'm sure she'll understand. Let me talk to him for a minute. He's a smart kid, Mary, whether you think so or not. He'll understand how important this is to all of us." Randall wanted to give Mary a hug and a kiss but knew it was pointless.

"Fine, but he's going to blow it for us, Randall! I know he is. Maybe we shouldn't adopt. He's about all I can handle. What influence will he have on a baby, his sibling? A good one, or will he screw her up, too? Maybe you should try staying home with him, and I'll go back to work. You'll see what it's like all day!"

So Mom thinks I'm stupid, too. And I'm going to blow it for them, Alex thought. From his spy station on the top step, he was able to catch enough to know his mother was mad at him again and didn't love him. He then heard his dad walking on the creaky floor, so he quickly and quietly scampered back to his room and hopped onto his bed.

"Hey, hey, how you doing, Alex?" Randall waved both hands back and forth in different directions, as he always did when he was trying to cheer up his son. "Tough morning, buddy. Wow, what a good friend you lost. We'll all miss him. He was a great part of our family."

"Mom doesn't care about Pudgy or me. She just wants me to stop crying. That's all she cares about." With that, Alex's pain came from two directions, and he started crying again. Randall cared and understood. He sat on the bed next to Alex, put his arm around his shoulder, and tucked him tightly into his side. He kissed Alex on top of his blond little head.

"I want you to know that it's okay to be sad and cry. I had a dog named Teddy when I was your age. He got hit and killed by a car. I saw it happen. Oh Alex, it was terrible. I cried a whole lot! But the problem we have right now is that today is a very special day for all of us." Randall was so soothing.

"You mean the lady that's going to give me a sister?" asked Alex.

"Well, it's not that simple, Tiger," Randall responded.

"I don't understand," said Alex. "Will she have it with her?"

"No, she won't, not today. But what I want to say is, well, we never told you, but a few weeks ago, you confused your kindergarten teacher," Randall began.

"Miss Taylor, you mean? She's not as nice as Mrs. Lowe."

"It was Miss Taylor, and do you remember when she told your whole class to draw a picture of their families?"

"I do!" said Alex with a bit of a smile on his face. "That was fun!"

"Well, you drew yourself, Mom, and me, along with a little baby in the picture," said Randall.

"Right, my sister that's coming soon, not today, but soon, right?" responded Alex.

"Well, you see, your teacher met us and talked with us just a month or so ago, like they do with all the parents of new students. She could see your mom wasn't pregnant with a big belly, you know, like Aunt Estelle is now."

"Okay," responded Alex with confusion on his face.

"Well, Miss Taylor called us that night and thought you might be having a problem. She thought you might be make-believing you have a sister just because you want one so badly."

Alex let out a frustrating sigh. "How come everybody thinks I have a problem? We're going to adopt a sister, right, because you and Mom can't have any more babies, right? That's what you told me, right? So, what did you tell her? I don't get it." Alex was now really confused, and some anger was beginning to brew.

"We told her exactly that, and she laughed. She said she understood and was very happy for you and all of us. She said you were a very special little boy."

Alex needed to hear that from his father at the moment. "But Mom thinks I have a problem. I know she does. She really doesn't like me much." Alex was feeling quite scared of the people around him, especially his mother.

"Now, what makes you think your mother feels that way about

you? She loves you." But Randall knew she could be pretty hard on their son, just like she could be hard on him.

"People can love crazy people, too," said Alex, "like that funny looking boy down the street they call retarded. I see his mom hugging him all the time." Alex was not convinced, though, about his own mother's love for him.

"No, no, my boy. We both love you so much and are very proud of you. But adopting your sister is not for sure yet. We have to be approved by this lady first. That's why this lady is visiting us today. She wants to look around and make sure our home is good and safe, and she especially wants to be sure you'll make a good big brother." Randall felt Alex was beginning to understand.

"I'll be a great big brother. I'll love her and play with her and teach her how to play baseball and…" Alex was getting defensive.

"Whoa, whoa, slow down there, Tiger. Before any of that, even though it's up to all of us, it's especially up to you whether you get a sister, you know. I need you to stop crying while the lady's here. Be nice and say the least amount you can if she asks you any questions, okay? Then you can cry again later all you want."

Alex had calmed considerably until he heard "especially up to you." *This is all up to me?* he thought. *I'm just a kid! That's what Mom meant when she said I was going to blow it.*

Alex told his dad what he wanted to hear. "Sure, Dad, but I already really miss Pudgy a lot. He was so stiff and cold when I touched him; and his eyes! When I looked at his eyes, they didn't look back! Mom said we can bury him tonight by the garden when you get home, right? I'll dig the hole this afternoon before you get home from work, okay?"

"You betcha!" Randall agreed; however, he had no idea what he would find dug up when he came home. "But let's wait until I get home before you start digging, so we can do it together." Randall also didn't need Alex to hurt himself on top of all this. Mary would become manic if they had to make a trip to the hospital.

Just then, the doorbell rang. Alex heard his mother call from the bottom of the stairs for Randall to come down and greet the lady. "Beck, she's here!" She sounded scared. Randall gave Alex a big hug. "I'll bring home some chocolate ice cream tonight for dessert. How's that sound?"

"No thanks, Dad. I'm not ready to eat ice cream without Pudgy yet. But how about some Twinkies? Pudgy never cared for Twinkies."

"Okay, now just stay up here until we call you, and remember, try not to cry. And try not to say much." He kissed Alex again on top of the head and went downstairs. Alex folded his hands and took a deep breath.

HUMAN EVALUATION IS A SCIENCE, NOT AN ART FOR THE PSUEDO-INTELLECTUAL

When Alex heard the door open, he left his bed and moved like a stalking cat to the top step. This time, however, his curiosity bubbled over, and he peeked around the banister where he could observe everyone greeting and introducing themselves. The lady introduced herself as Miss Pendleton as she handed her card to Alex's father.

Katharine Pendleton, MA, LPC
Specialized in Child Assessments

She shook Randall's hand as he extended it, but when Mary extended her hand, Alex noticed she didn't respond. It was at that moment Alex clearly saw her glance up, catching him peeking around the banister. Their eyes connected, but the lady turned away quickly. Alex pulled back and out of sight.

The lady was close to the age of Alex's mother, mid-twenties maybe, but she exuded quite a different aura. She had donned a dark blue skirt with the same color jacket and a white blouse buttoned all the way to the top, her hair pulled back tightly into a bun. She didn't look very friendly at all, almost like the nurses in the hospital, only dressed different. She possessed a large black briefcase. Alex had never seen a woman with a briefcase before, only women with purses. His father wore suits to work every day and carried a briefcase, but again, Alex had never seen a woman carry one. Alex found that briefcase disturbing, with no indication of why. He observed that his mother was dressed nicely as well, better than what she usually wore around the house, but not as smart as this lady. Alex began to anticipate something very serious and very scary was about to happen.

Mary most graciously offered the lady a seat in the somewhat worn and oversized chair in the living room. With a disgusted review of the upholstery, Miss Pendleton slowly descended into its quaggy cushion, appearing quite uncomfortable in a variety of ways.

"May I offer you something to drink, Miss Pendleton, coffee, tea, water?" Mary was being most hospitable. Miss Pendleton squirmed to position herself so she would be able to sit like a lady.

"No, thank you, Mrs. Beckham," replied Miss Pendleton without looking up and with no pleasantry whatsoever in her monotone voice, suggesting total apathy. As Mary's politeness was being rudely ignored, Miss Pendleton opened her briefcase, pulled out a file, attached her forms to a clipboard, then clicked open her ball-point pen. When all was in place, she finally looked up.

Mary took a seat on the sofa next to Randall as Miss Pendleton began her interrogation in the way a lawyer performs a deposition in a custody hearing. (And in reality, it was a custody hearing.)

"I must confirm some basic information from your application to the agency, both past and present. Do each of you have siblings, how many, and are they still alive? Are your parents still alive? If not, what was their cause of death? Do you have nieces and/or nephews and how many? Do all of your siblings and parents work for a living? Are any of them on government assistance? Has anyone in your families been convicted of a felony or any type of domestic violence?" Mary and Randall, between each question, confirmed the information they had submitted to the adoption agency a few months prior. They both felt proud and confident about the wonderful family in which they would be raising the child.

Then Miss Pendleton asked if they all spoke English and how long the families had been in the US. Alex, overhearing that question, thought, *What kind of a stupid question is that? Everybody speaks English.* But then again, he thought, *Aunt Mamie and Aunt Carrie and Grandfather do speak German to each other from time to time. And those people on my grandfather's radio speak really weird sometimes, too.*

"And what religion are you, and what church do you all attend and how regularly?" asked Miss Pendleton.

Mary and Randall had studied this requirement quite diligently a few years prior and knew both spouses must be of the same religion in order to adopt. Mary had been raised Roman Catholic and Randall, Protestant, Lutheran to be exact. Different religions, and even sects of the same religion, were unacceptable for adoption in the 1950s. So, to satisfy society, Mary had converted to Lutheran well over a year ago, and Alex had been placed in the preschool Sunday school class.

"We attend the United English Lutheran Church, located about a mile from here, with my husband's mother, his brother, and our son's cousins. It's quite a friendly church, with a wonderful children's program." Mary finally felt reconciled that she had agreed to leave the church in which she was raised. She could answer that question with complete confidence and honesty. Her family hadn't been pleased with Mary's decision and thought Randall and Alex should become Catholic, but then again, Mary's family only went to church on Easter Sunday, funerals and weddings. Oh yes, and for Alex's baptism.

"Mr. and Mrs. Beckham, it says here you have a five-year-old son named Alexander. Is that correct?" Miss Pendleton stared intently at Mary and Randall. Why so intently was a mystery.

It was here, the moment Alex was dreading as he lurked like a shadow in the darkness. He knew all the other answers so far, no big deal. But now the questioning had just turned to him. Bouncing around his brain like a hard rubber ball were his father's words on his bed, "it's especially up to you whether you get a sister." And his mother's words, "he's gonna blow it for us." Alex was petrified. He wanted to cry and throw up, or both at the same time.

"And where might your son be at the moment? Is he in school today?" Miss Pendleton inquired as her voice raised slightly. She knew Alex was home and listening on the stairs. And Alex knew she knew he was there as well.

Something wasn't right. She knew he wasn't in school. She knew exactly where he was. She and Alex had made eye contact when she entered the door. Alex got a strange premonition mixed with confusion. He actually felt a twinge of anger, but he didn't know why, at least not yet.

"He's usually in kindergarten in the morning, but we kept him home today due to our meeting," answered Alex's mother. "Dr. Johnson told us you wanted to meet him. He's upstairs right now waiting in his room. I thought it best, so we could talk down here for a while without interruption."

"Do you find him disruptive when around adults, Mrs. Beckham? And you say he's missing a day of school to meet with me? Doesn't the child go to school all day?" asked Miss Pendleton.

"No, the children only go half a day in the morning in their kindergarten year," replied Mary.

"Then why didn't you schedule me for this afternoon, Mrs. Beckham?" Mary was being forced into playing defense. "Do you allow him to miss school often? It seems as if we could have worked this timeframe so your son's educational priorities were considered. I don't understand, Mrs. Beckham. Is education important to you, or isn't it?" Miss Pendleton spoke quickly and with an impersonal and accusatory intonation.

Oh no, Alex thought. *Mom doesn't handle that tone of voice well at all.* He remembered the day of "Old Lady Grogan!"

Randall, sensing Mary's changing temper, quickly took over the conversation. "I'm so sorry, Miss Pendleton, but we were simply instructed by your office that you would arrive at eleven o'clock today and to have our son present. We didn't realize the time was flexible. We're so sorry for the miscommunication." Randall's interjection successfully avoided a possibly perilous response by Mary.

Miss Pendleton rolled her eyes. "Mr. Beckham, you might have been more forceful. But I guess the damage is done, so let's continue." Mary was beginning to turn red in the face. Randall squeezed her by the knee, so she realized that he too was finding this woman rather unreasonable and manipulative. Both Randall and Mary were beginning to question this woman's motives.

"Okay, back to Andrew's schooling," Miss Pendleton began.

"His name is Alexander, not Andrew, and we call him Alex," said Randall. Miss Pendleton was scribbling notes.

"Alex attends a very nice school, just about four blocks up the street. And no, Miss Pendleton, just to clear things up before we go on, he does not miss school unless he's ill," Mary interjected with a very subtle quiver in her voice.

"Is the school private or public, Mrs. Beckham?"

"Public, Miss Pendleton."

Miss Pendleton gave out a sigh, as suddenly Alex's parents felt guilty of something in some strange way.

"How does he get to school, Mrs. Beckham? I assume he rides the school bus or you drive him? There seems to be a lot of traffic on your street."

"Well, Miss Pendleton, he walks like all the other children in the neighborhood and in this entire city. Our street out in front is a state highway, a truck route through the city, actually. But as you can see, the road is very windy, and the speed limit is only twenty-five through this part. There are no buses in this school system, since the grade schools are so close and central to each neighborhood. So he walks with the rest of the children. There are lots of children around here." Mary pulled herself together and answered quite calmly and factually.

"Mrs. Beckham, isn't the school only two blocks from the large General Motors plant? Aren't you concerned about the possible actions of those men against young children?"

"What men are you referring to, Miss Pendleton?" Mary asked with a puzzled look on her face.

"The factory workers, of course. You feel safe with factory workers in close proximity to the school and the children? And a son is one thing; a daughter that close to 'those kind of men' is a whole other issue."

Suddenly, Randall felt he knew where she was going. She wasn't a young woman raised in the city. She felt superior to them. As he looked at her, his twinge of suspicion became more defined. She stared back at Randall and read his stone face perfectly. He then remembered the feeling one gets as a child when a bully continues their intimidation. Mary became outright insulted.

"I'm so sorry, Miss Pendleton, but I'm still not sure I know what you are insinuating?" Mary had rephrased her question making sure she understood what she just heard. *My father, his friends, and most of our neighbors are all factory workers. I know what she's inferring!* Mary thought to herself. "I feel totally safe," Mary replied with a deep anxiety welling up inside of her.

"Okay, then, Mrs. Beckham, between the trucks and the traffic and the factory workers, you feel your son is in no danger whatsoever, or at least not enough to be concerned about. Let's just leave it at that, then, and move on." The notes were jotted at breakneck speed after that conclusion.

But Mary couldn't "leave it at that," as was suggested. Her voice was starting to quiver, and the flames under her temper were rising quickly. Alex knew continuing to question his mother's parenting skills was a precarious path upon which Miss Pendleton was treading. And Alex also knew, if it continued, that his mother was going to blow like a pressure cooker. He had heard that tremble in her voice before. *Please Mom, please, please, please don't*, he thought.

Mary began to justify her position in the verbal pace of a race-horse. She explained about crossing guards and school patrol boys and official city police cruising around the schools before and after. Randall was about to stop her, because he felt it was useless. He could see that Miss Pendleton was bored and wasn't listening at all. She already had her mind made up. She was convinced it was simply a matter of child neglect by all of these blue-collar people in this blue-collar town. But Randall's decision to let Mary explain released that pressure valve in her brain. He knew his wife.

Good job, Mom, Alex thought, *you didn't get mad*. Miss Pendleton jotted nothing after Mary's explanation.

"If you're finished, Mrs. Beckham, I'd like to take a walk around your home and then meet your son. He'll be six in November, about three months from now? Is that correct?" She stood up first, followed by Mary and Randall.

"Yes, that's correct. He's a good boy and loves learning. He's doing well in school already," Randall boasted, feeling he had a lot to do with that.

"Mr. Beckham, truly, it's only kindergarten, and he just started." With that discounting of Alex's young personality, Randall's suspicions continued to expand, and his premonition was that her report was not going to be favorable.

"What I mean is, Miss Pendleton, we read to him a lot; do a lot of puzzles and games, as well as music. I'm sure he'll be proud to show you all his books and records. He especially has fun with his picture encyclopedias, since he cannot read yet," replied Randall.

"He's illiterate, Mr. Beckham? Is he a slow learner?" Miss Pendleton asked as she spun around to look Randall in the eyes.

"Miss Pendleton, like you just said, it's only kindergarten, and he just started," Randall replied. "They learn to read in the first grade."

"Mr. Beckham, I could read before I started kindergarten. My nanny taught me. But I assume education is not that important to people in this part of town. Let's continue the tour." Miss Pendleton looked at Mary and Mary began the tour.

Overhearing what his dad had just said was the first thing that made Alex feel good all morning. *But what's a nanny?* Alex thought. *I thought it was a goat. And should I be able to read already?*

The Beckham home was quite small but had everything necessary to raise a family. Alex wasn't cognizant of the size, because it was the same size as just about everyone else's in the neighborhood.

The house was simple. The first floor went in a circle: living room, dining room, kitchen. Upstairs included the master bedroom, Alex's room, and a bathroom with a claw-foot tub, toilet, sink, and a small towel closet. The basement was pretty dingy, with a stone, whitewashed foundation, worn red-painted floor, an obsolete coal bin used for storage, and a workbench. Randall usually had a one-page calendar of a sort of naked woman caught skinny dipping in a car's headlights over his workbench, but Mary had made sure it was down that morning, before the tour. As a matter of fact, she had thrown it away. The Beckhams also had a washing machine but no dryer; clothes were hung outside on a clothesline in the summer and inside in the winter. And there was a toilet in the basement with a cracked seat that pinched one's butt when sat upon.

Outside featured a front porch with a swing, quite cool on summer nights, since very few people had air conditioning. The front of the house had virtually no yard, only a steep bank up from the sidewalk; almost impossible to cut. But Alex loved the backyard! It was small, but not to Alex. It had a huge cottonwood tree right in the middle that, when it bloomed in the spring, made the yard look like it was snowing. The yard also contained a swing set and a pear tree. Alex could climb this and then hop onto the garage roof, and when he was caught by his parents, this would cause a scolding, and he would be sent to his room. The pears were delicious (the wasps thought so as well), as were the cherries from the cherry tree and grapes from a grape arbor on the fence. There was a vegetable garden containing mostly tomatoes as well as a horseshoe pit sprawling diagonally across the back half of the yard. It was all fenced for Alex's safety, with beautiful rose bushes blooming along the fence by the driveway.

Miss Pendleton started in the basement, where she spent little to no time. She found it rather dirty and disgusting, as if she had never been in an unfinished basement before. As they ascended the narrow stairway, it opened directly into the kitchen, where Mary then began her tour. They walked through the crowded kitchen to the back door, showing Miss Pendleton the safely fenced-in backyard, then the small dining room, then back into the living room, where the woman stopped to take notes.

"It's ample, I guess," Miss Pendleton said, barely loud enough for Mary and Randall to hear.

As they entered the living room and approached the stairs, Alex again crept quickly and quietly back to his room, sat on his bed Indian style, and waited. Now he was getting really scared. His throat was choking from the anxiety. He wanted to cry. But if he did, he might not get a sister! *I can do this!* Alex thought.

They first went into the master bedroom. Miss Pendleton looked at the bed and then briefly into the closets; made some more notes. Then the bathroom and more notes.

"Only two bedrooms?" asked Miss Pendleton. "Where will the baby sleep?"

"Well, in her infancy, she'll sleep in a bassinet in our room, so we may feed her and change her when necessary," Mary replied.

"And after that?"

"We'll place a crib in the other room until she's about two to three years old," Mary replied again.

"And then what? Where will the little girl sleep then?" Miss Pendleton was ready for her next round of degrading insinuations.

"Hopefully, since my husband has an executive position and is doing well, we plan to look for a bigger house." Mary thought this would satisfy Miss Pendleton. But Randall knew where she was going with this.

"Mrs. Beckham, if you're unable to buy a bigger home, do you think it to be appropriate for a little boy and girl to share a room?" asked Miss Pendleton. Randall had predicted that question.

"Excuse me, I don't understand," said Mary.

"Come now, Mrs. Beckham. Boys can cause problems with their, let's call it 'curiosity,' and that curiosity could leave an emotional scar on a little girl."

Miss Pendleton had gone over the line, especially with that insult and insinuations about Alex.

"Miss Pendleton, I'm confident with my earning potential, and I'm extremely confident in my son's mental stability. Coming this far into the process, we were never informed of the need for separate bedrooms. Is this a requirement by your agency, or just a personal concern of yours?" Randall was going to find out just who this woman was pretending to be.

"Well…"

"No, no, never mind. I'll call Dr. Johnson, who I assume is your boss, when we end your inspection and ask him that question directly." Randall could tell that she was, for the first time, shaken on her high horse.

"No, Mr. Beckham, that won't be necessary. I'll address it with him myself and let him decide if my concern is valid." Miss Pendleton turned away from Randall, knowing he was still going to call. And Miss Pendleton still had plans of her own.

"I appreciate that, but I'd still like to speak to him directly on that subject, Miss Pendleton." She then took some rather lengthy notes this time in the small hallway. Randall could tell she was scratching out something on her clipboard. She then moved quickly on to her next question.

"The gate here at the top of the stairs; it's here for what purpose?" she asked. "He's five, correct? Isn't that a little old to need a baby gate?"

Mary began her explanation quickly, but she could tell by the look on Miss Pendleton's face that she, like before, had already drawn her own conclusion. "Alex has a mild hereditary bleeding disorder. Not contagious, of course—genetic. My brother has the same disorder. One night, about a year ago, Alex was going to the potty in the middle of the night and was trying to take his diaper off and…"

"Wait, you say a year ago? That would make him almost four. Isn't that a bit late for a child to still be in diapers, Mrs. Beckham?" A few more notes were scribbled.

"Not at all," Mary replied. "Alex is fine during the day, but as our pediatrician tells us, it isn't unusual for children, especially boys, to have bed-wetting problems. So we put a diaper on him only at night. I'm assuming you don't have children, since you refer to yourself as 'Miss'."

"That's correct. But I'll be sure to research that explanation when I return to my office." Mary and Randall were confused. They were told this woman had her degree in child psychology. She should know these things. "But please continue with your story, Mrs. Beckham."

Mary resumed. "As I was saying, Alex got up in the night to please us and use his potty chair in the bathroom. You can see how close the steps are to our bathroom door. As he was taking off the diaper he still wore to bed, he lost his balance and fell backwards, tumbling down the steps. You see that windowsill at the bottom? He hit his forehead right on the corner of it, splitting it wide open, right between his eyes. He was actually knocked out for a minute or so. Scared us to death—you can imagine." Miss Pendleton was staring at Mary with a look of total indifference. "We rushed him straight to the emergency room, blood everywhere. He had numerous stitches, and it took a good week or more of ice and pressure for it to stop bleeding completely. When you meet him, you'll still see a pretty good-sized scar between his eyes. He's okay now; no concussion, thank God. But we bought that gate just to be safe in case he stumbles again going to the bathroom or if he needs us in the middle of the night. It has kept him safe as well as allowing us to sleep peacefully."

"Any brain damage or odd behavior on his part since?" she asked.

"No, nothing like that, nothing at all," Mary answered.

Miss Pendleton made a few more notes, only she took considerably longer this time.

Now it was time, the time Alex had been dreading for the last hour. When they all entered Alex's room, Alex could feel himself tense up and shake inside. No one was smiling, especially his mother.

She said, "Alex, this is Miss Pendleton. She works for the people who are helping us adopt a sister for you. She's here to talk to us, get to know us, and see if we would be a good family to adopt a baby. Say hello." She gave Alex what seemed to be a hollow, fake smile.

Alex knew what his mother was thinking. *"He's going to blow it."* His emotions were all scrambled like a skillet of corned beef hash. First, he thought, *She didn't have to tell me to say hello. I know how to be nice to adults.* In reality, Alex had been around more adults than kids at this point in his life—his relatives, his father's friends, his neighbors and their teenage girls who babysat him, the babysitters all little mothers in the making. His mother was acting way different than usual. Actually, she was being much calmer and much nicer than her usual self. *Weird!* he thought.

"Hello, Miss Pendleton," Alex said as he stood up, jumping slightly down off his bed. "Nice to meet you. Your clothes are really nice." Alex stuck his hand out as he had been taught to do with all adults.

"Alex, it looks like you've been crying. Your eyes are red and swollen," Miss Pendleton said with a frown and without saying hello or thank you or extending her hand to greet him in return. (Good thing Alex had always been taught to be polite to adults, but he didn't like this rude woman at all. He would learn a word for this kind of person someday.)

His mother and father looked at each other, and before they could say anything, Alex started to tear up, and boom, bam, crash, out came the explosion; a terrible mix of feelings and emotions. He couldn't hold it back. He began talking a mile a minute, one big long sentence with no periods and no pauses, exactly what as he'd been instructed not to do.

"Well, I got up this morning and went downstairs, and Pudgy was lying in the bottom of his cage, and he was cold and stiff and his eyes were all weird, and he wouldn't move when I poked him and Mommy couldn't do anything and he used to eat ice cream with us and sit on my head and he could say his name and…"

"Alex, that's enough," Mary scolded in an uncommonly sweet tone.

Miss Pendleton looked at Alex, her frown still there, but now her eyes were squinted. "Wait, wait, who's Pudgy?" she asked the room.

By now Alex was sobbing and hugging himself as he rocked back and forth. He couldn't catch his breath and therefore, now, couldn't speak.

"Pudgy is, well was, his parakeet." Randall knew it was time for him to do his best to salvage this moment and calm this chaos. "It really was an incredible bird. And it was Alex's first actual pet. He fed it and took care of it every morning like it was his child. They really did have some sort of special connection. We could truly sense they were both always glad to see each other. I can't really explain it. Well I can—he was like one of the family."

"You say it was just a bird, Mr. Beckham?" Miss Pendleton asked with a sarcastic giggle, its meaning grasped only by Randall.

"Yes, Miss Pendleton, it was a bird, and Alex loved it. Then about two hours ago, before you arrived, Alex came down for breakfast and stopped to feed Pudgy like he did every morning. But when he removed the sheet from over the cage, there laid Pudgy dead on the bottom of his cage. That's why he's upset."

Alex's mother stood quietly and stared into space, her arms crossed, biting the inside of her bottom lip. Randall wanted to make sure Miss Pendleton understood the situation clearly.

"Okay, I think I understand what's going on here. I'm finished now and have seen everything I need to see," she said as her head bounced up and down slightly. "I can finish my report back at my office, and I'll give it to my supervisor, Dr. Johnson. He'll get back to you very shortly, I'm sure."

Miss Pendleton left the room without saying goodbye to Alex as he sat sobbing on his bed. Alex's mother and father escorted the woman back to the living room, where she gathered her notes, placing them in her briefcase. Mary opened the door and held out her hand to say goodbye, but Miss Pendleton, without any response or common etiquette, walked out the door and to her car. Mary turned and rushed straight into the kitchen in such a rage Randall expected to hear crashing dishes at any moment.

He put his light raincoat over his arm and watched out the front door as Miss Pendleton drove away. He then walked through the kitchen and out the back door to his car in the garage; no goodbyes, no "see you later," no "be home late?" Mary sat at the kitchen table, her hands clenched in tight fists, her teeth grinding as her jaws tightened in anger. Mary said nothing to Alex all day except to call him for lunch. Alex was too scared to come out of his room. When she called him down, he found a sandwich and a glass of milk on the table, but when he sat down, she left the room and went to the basement. She made no eye contact whatsoever.

And for the rest of the day Alex thought about Pudgy just lying upside down, dead on his head in the Ovaltine tin, waiting to be put in the hole.

Finally, after the longest day of his life, Alex heard his dad pull up the driveway. He looked out his bedroom window, and as he did, he discovered his mother had thrown the tin off the back porch and that it lay on the wet grass in the misting rain. Alex was devastated.

THESE SHOULDERS ARE STARTING TO GET REALLY TIRED

Well, time moved slowly from that crazy day of Pudgy's demise and the judgmental young lady of questionable motivations. It had been a little over two weeks since Miss Pendleton had conducted her visit, and as far as Alex knew, no word of a decision had been received either way. Alex distinctly remembered her saying in his room, just before she stormed out, that she would submit her report and was sure her supervisor would get back to them very soon. Almost her exact words, he thought. But Alex wasn't old enough to pick up on that cruel woman's sarcasm that broke his parents' hearts.

Since that very, very ugly day, everyone's behavior seemed to be drifting slowly back to normal, but not entirely. Alex still had a heavy presage inside, like the cool breeze preceding a torrential thunderstorm gathering over his house. He couldn't help but think there was something his parents were keeping from him. He'd felt somewhat detached from them both since that day, like he wasn't really a part of the family, at least, not the way he used to be. And, of course, Pudgy was gone and buried in his hole in the backyard.

Alex began to think his parents had been contacted and the adoption denied, all because of him. He deduced that if they had been contacted, and the answer was yes, they would have told him right away, and they all would have been happy, hugged each other, and celebrated by eating ice cream. But on the other hand, if they had been contacted and the answer was no, they probably didn't want to tell him and have to listen to him cry, so they were just going to let it fade away. And because of Alex's strange talent, even in his youth, to see the big picture, he thought there was actually a third option. Maybe there really was no word; no phone call; no letter. Frankly, considering all the options, Alex was afraid to ask, so he didn't. He remained quiet.

With dinnertime approaching. Alex's father told him to go play outside for a bit longer, and he would call him when the time came. Alex made a beeline to his swing, playing his favorite game, getting the swing as high as it would go and jumping out. He felt like superman. Mary refused to watch. She knew she couldn't stop him and that someday he was going to hurt himself, and it would be hospital time again.

In the kitchen, Randall sat at the table as Mary was preparing dinner. "Any word from the agency yet, Mary?"

"No, Beck, when are you going to accept the truth? Alex blew it for us." Mary didn't turn around from the stove.

"Mary, we all had our part, not just Alex," responded Randall.

"When are you going to accept the fact that Alex isn't normal? You're so protective of that child, taking him places and reading to him all the time. He's not ready for that stuff yet. And he doesn't respect me at all," replied Mary.

"What does that mean? He always wants your attention. You just never give it to him. Try playing with him once in a while." Randall was getting defensive for both himself and Alex.

"I'm the one that disciplines that child, since you certainly don't do it. And the only thing that works is a good spanking, or I have to yell at him at the top of my lungs. I refuse to let him grow up disrespectful and such a crybaby." Mary was getting angrier and angrier.

"Maybe if you would lower your voice and talk to him instead of punishing him all the time, he might be different around you. But let's stop this. We're getting nowhere." Randall went to the back porch, leaned over the rail, and enjoyed watching his son have fun on his swing set.

"Time for dinner, Tiger." Alex took one more flying leap from his swing. "Nice jump, kid. But take off those muddy tennies and leave them on the porch, so you don't track dirt on your mother's clean floors."

"Sure, Dad!" and Alex scampered for the porch, giving his dad a big hug as he reached the screen door.

Alex removed his shoes and entered the kitchen. His dad parked himself in his chair at the wooden table just large enough for their plates and a few condiments. Alex's mom stood at the stove, her weight mostly on her right hip, with a metal spatula in her hand as she fried slices of Spam, little round potatoes, and cauliflower.

"Smells great, Mom. I'm so hungry I could eat a horse. Well not really, but that's what Grandpa says all the time. Are horses any good to eat?"

Mary poured browned butter on top of the cauliflower for flavor, and dinner was ready to be devoured by her two men. Alex was always asked to say grace, and he did. "Thank you for the world so sweet..." and he continued to the end. Then his dad divvied up food between himself and Alex and handed Mary the cauliflower, Spam and potatoes, so she could determine how hungry she was. Randall had noticed that Mary hadn't been eating a lot lately, and it was showing in her cheeks. Alex poured a lake of ketchup on his slice of Spam and his potatoes.

Dinner was concluding. This was "round potato night." With their forks, Alex and his dad fought for that last potato in the skillet. But even though Mary felt left out, she had to admit she loved watching them have fun over her last potato.

As they all began to clear the table, the phone was heard ringing in the living room, —the big black rotary phone that sat on a stand with a handset that could kill a bear.

"Awww, who's calling us at dinner time?" Mary said in frustration. "Beck, can you get that? My hands are wet. If it's my mother, tell her I'll call her back later. And if it's someone selling something, just slam the phone in their stupid ear."

Randall went to the telephone and answered it on the third ring, in a pleasant, professional tone. "Hello, this is the Beckhams' residence. May I ask who is calling?" There was silence, then the person on the other end finally responded.

"No, no, Dr. Johnson. Not a problem at all. We just finished and are cleaning up. Is there any news? Were we approved?" Mary and Alex heard Randall from the kitchen. Alex's question about the adoption had just been answered. Mary was nervously waiting for that one-hundred-pound shoe to drop and shake the entire foundation of her family's future like an earthquake. Randall was cool and collected.

There was a long pause where Alex's father said nothing. His mother turned off the faucet and sat back down in her chair as she dried her hands. Mary and Alex were both quiet as mice, neither looking at each other, neither able to hear what Dr. Johnson was saying on the other end of the telephone. They only knew it was the adoption agency.

Randall listened as Dr. Johnson spoke. Finally, he began to respond. "Well, I think there's a little more to it than that, Dr. Johnson. Did her report mention that the gate is there because our son has a mild bleeding condition and accidentally fell down the steps one night as he was trying to go to his potty chair? He was trying to please us and was unaware of the danger. He split his head open terribly on the windowsill at the bottom of the steps, with numerous stitches. It was actually life-threatening. He was hospitalized for a week. We felt it wise to keep that from happening again. So we bought the gate. I assure you, he does not and never has walked in his sleep."

His father was quiet again and listened for a moment before he said, "Well, that's not the case either. As I said before, and we told her, the gate's just in front of the stairway. It's never been placed in his bedroom doorway. We've never had a need to confine him."

Randall was again silent as he listened to Dr. Johnson.

"Emotionally unstable, really, she said that? Did she elaborate in her report that my son was the one who found his pet parakeet dead on the floor of its cage when he came down to feed it, less than two hours before she arrived? My son was crying when he couldn't hold back his tears any longer and quite accurately explained to Miss Pendleton the events of those last two hours." Randall listened again.

"No, Dr. Johnson, I'm positive she understood, because to make sure, I followed up with the story in my own terms. So no, she was not confused, and he was not making it up." Randall paused to listen.

"That's right, Dr. Johnson, emotional instability is not the term for what happened. I would say it seems normal for a child to cry when they lose a pet or someone they love. I did at his age, when my dog was hit by a car. How about you? Ever have a pet die, Dr. Johnson? And may I add one more thing, Miss Pendleton was quite rude and judgmental towards all three of us with a somewhat spoiled arrogance about where we live and the people who live around us."

Randall had spoken his piece to Dr. Johnson in a calm and controlled demeanor, defending his son and his wife. Alex and Mary listened intently, understanding quite easily what Dr. Johnson was stating to Randall on the other end of the telephone. But now came Randall's question to get to the real answer; yes or no.

"So, Dr. Johnson, what does all this mean? Were you going to tell us no without the full story? Can we have a second interview with Miss Pendleton and with you present as well? Can we appeal this somehow? Something isn't quite right here. Don't you agree, Dr. Johnson?"

Randall was quiet once more, listening to Dr. Johnson for what seemed like a very long time. Then Randall spoke once more. "Dr. Johnson, we'll be happy to have our son visit with your psychologist. If the doctor has hours on Saturdays, that would be best for me not missing work and Alex not missing school. And the sooner the better. This has been quite an ordeal for my entire family." More silence. Then Randall said, "Thank you, Dr. Johnson, for your reconsideration. I believe you're making a wise decision. We'll await your call tomorrow for the time of our appointment. Have a nice evening. Goodbye, sir."

His father came back into the kitchen, sat down in his chair, and looked at Alex with a smile. He kissed Mary on the cheek.

"Okay, any ice cream in the freezer? Let's add some chocolate syrup and a cherry to these babies tonight. What do you think, Tiger?"

Randall and Alex were smiling, but not Mary. Randall took quick notice. "Alex, can you go to your room for a few minutes until we make the dessert? I want to talk to your mother in private. Then we can all talk about the phone call over ice cream."

"Sure, Dad." Alex had stopped smiling, wondering why he couldn't be included in the conversation, but he went to his room as he was asked, without any argument.

From his room, Alex heard them go outside onto the front porch and close the door. They sat on the porch swing. It was smart of them to go outside where he couldn't hear them. They were getting wise to his "top-step" eavesdropping. Actually, they had suspected it for a long time but had just never caught him. The floors were creaky, but Alex was way too quick.

Alex had heard the telephone conversation and could easily deduce that the problem had to do with him. His parents' conversation, however, was much longer than a few minutes. It was at least half an hour. Then the door opened, and Randall came to the bottom of the steps.

"Alex, can you come down here please? Your mother and I need to talk to you." His voice seemed gentle, and Alex wasn't picking up any fear or anger from his father's intonation.

"Sure, Dad, be right down." Alex wanted to finish the puzzle he was working on, but he knew the answer would be "No, we need you right now," so he left it on the floor unfinished and scrambled down the steps. His stomach felt upset, but it had been feeling like that since the day of Pudgy and the lady. Alex was not sure if he was in trouble or if the answer was no for a sister, or both.

He bounced into the living room. His mother was sitting on the couch, and his father was in his oversized green chair. "Sit down, Alex, on the couch next to your mother, please."

Alex sat with apprehension on the end of the couch, to the right of his mother, and faced the side of the chair straight across from his father. Unable to relax, Alex sat on the edge of the cushion. He wanted to have his feet touching the floor. As he got settled, his father sat on the edge of his cushion as well, turning slightly sideways so he could look Alex in the eyes. His father began to speak. His mother stayed silent.

"Alex, as you probably figured out, that was Dr. Johnson from the adoption agency on the telephone after dinner," Randall began in a calming tone.

"Yes, I heard you say his name. What did he—?"

"Alex, I need you to be quiet now. Let me talk. I'm going to tell you exactly what he said," Randall said quickly, brows raised, looking straight into Alex's eyes. "He told us that he finally received the report from Miss Pendleton, the lady that was here a couple weeks ago, and everything was good on the report—our house, where we lived, my job—all except for you." Alex's heart dropped. "She reported the gate upstairs was because you walk in your sleep, and your crying was because you were, as she put it, 'emotionally unstable'."

Are those good or bad things? he thought. Alex was confused. "What does that mean, Dad?"

"That means you walk around the house at night in your sleep without realizing it, and 'emotionally unstable' means you can't control your crying or your feelings."

Well, that made Alex want to start crying again. He began to wonder whether Mom and the lady were right about him. Did other kids cry? Was he like Cheryl in his class, who cried all the time when she wet her pants? Were there only a few of them that cried? Really, a lot of the girls cried in school sometimes, but Alex couldn't remember many boys crying unless they were hurt. Alex couldn't remember ever crying at school, except for when he got spanked in front of the class for talking too much. And, of course, when Pudgy died, and when he fell down the steps, and when his Mom spanked him.

But now, as Alex thought about it, neither his mother or father cried when Pudgy died, and when he told his grandmas and grandpas and aunts and uncles and cousins about it, they didn't cry either. So other than when his cousins got hurt and when his Great-Grandma died, Alex thought, *Maybe other kids and grownups don't cry. Maybe it really is just me.*

Alex began to talk. "First, I don't walk around the house asleep, do I? I don't ever remember doing that. You put the gate up right after I fell down the steps, and you told me it was to keep me from falling again, right?" Alex's lack of confidence in himself was creating a crisis within his very being for the first time (though this wouldn't be the last time in his life).

"Actually, people who walk in their sleep don't know they're even doing it. But that doesn't really matter, because you don't; you never have. Miss Pendleton was wrong about you sleepwalking. She didn't report the whole story about the gate for some reason, and we can't figure out why. That's what your mom and I were discussing on the porch. Your mom told her very clearly, the reason was because of your occasional bed-wetting, and it was. We even pointed out your scar when we went into your room that day. As I said, we can't figure out why she didn't report the real reason for the gate. Maybe she didn't believe us, or we think she just didn't like any of us."

"Wait, wait, I don't understand. Why wouldn't she like us? And Mom was being really nice to her that day. I could hear her from the…" *Oops, I think I just goofed,* thought Alex.

His father looked over at his mother quickly, and she stared back into his eyes. Randall then looked back at Alex. "First of all, we know you listen to us from the top step. We can see your shadow on the wall. It's okay, Alex. And the answer to your question as to why she doesn't like us is, some people don't like other people for all kinds of reasons. Let's just leave it at that for now, okay?"

"And you said she said something, like I was 'emotionally in a stable' or something?" Alex had a perplexed expression on his face.

Randle chuckled, and Mary chimed in abruptly. "'Unstable,' son, not 'in a stable.' She reported you were 'emotionally unstable', because of all your crying and sobbing that day." Alex squinted at his mother in confusion, but she quickly turned away from him and toward Randall to answer the question, her arms crossed as if she were hiding something.

"Yeah, but Pudgy," he blurted as he slid off the cushion and onto his feet to defend himself.

"Okay, stop right there, Alex, and settle down," commanded his father in a peaceful and understanding tone. "We both know how hurt and baffled you were that morning. And you explained to Miss Pendleton exactly why you were crying, but Tiger, you talked faster than a bullet."

"I couldn't help it, Dad." Alex again defended himself.

"We understand. That's why I explained it to her a second time. You did the best you could through your tears. I wanted to make absolutely sure she followed what you told her. But she still put nothing in her report about Pudgy, nothing at all. Your mom and I have been talking about that for half an hour. It doesn't make any sense to either of us why she would leave all those details out of her report."

"So what does all this mean?" Alex asked, scared to hear the answer.

"Well, the way it stands right now, you can't have a sister because of the report. Everything is fine except for Miss Pendleton's description of you and your behavior that day," said Randall.

Alex covered his eyes with his forearm as he broke into tears, jumped off the cushion and began to make a mad dash for his room. He actually really wanted to bolt for the door and run away from home so his parents could have a baby, but he knew he wouldn't get far, at least not yet, not while they were awake. Nothing had ever crushed his heart that much, not even finding Pudgy dead. He couldn't utter a word. He just thought, *Mommy was right, I did blow it for everybody. Maybe they can trade me for her, but then who would want me?*

As Alex attempted to dart past his father, Randall grabbed him by his upper arm and pulled him into a hug. Alex spoke into his father's chest without looking at either of his parents. "I'm sorry. I'm really, really sorry," he stammered through his terrible lament.

"No, no, no, my boy. Let me hold you for a minute and finish what I was about to say." Randall held Alex tight. Alex looked over at his mother, who continued to sit without any emotion whatsoever on her face. She remained reticent.

"Okay, now it's time for all of us, as a family, to really talk and see what we can all do together. This isn't over yet, guys," said Randall. "We still have a chance, and I think a great chance, at getting this baby. But I must say, Alex, it's really all up to you now."

"What do you mean, Dad, it's all up to me?" Alex asked as his tears were beginning to subside.

"Well, Alex, when I talked to Dr. Johnson on the telephone earlier, I explained the real story about the gate and your fall down the steps and Pudgy."

"So everything is all right and I'm going to get a sister." Alex began to show signs of excitement.

"Son, don't interrupt me. Let me finish." Alex just listened as Randall continued. "As I was saying, I challenged Miss Pendleton's report, and Dr. Johnson truly sounded confused, the same way we are right now. He, too, had no idea why Miss Pendleton forgot to mention all those details in her report. He said when all the details were added to the report, it all made more sense; then her conclusions could surely be challenged." Alex listened intently. "Dr. Johnson went on to tell me that in some confusing cases like this, they have someone else, called a child psychologist, meet personally with the child involved to determine whether the agency representative's conclusions are correct. It'll then be this doctor's decision as to whether he feels you would make a good brother, Alex, as well as whether we are good parents." Randall wanted to look at Mary but knew he probably shouldn't have said that.

"A child psychostatis? What is that?" Alex quickly asked as a flush of fear went through his body.

"No, he's called a psychologist. He's a doctor that studies the way children behave, and if he thinks you do have a problem, he can help us with that problem."

"You mean I have a problem?" Alex timidly asked.

Unexpectedly, Mary chimed in for the first time. "No, you didn't listen. Your dad said *if* you have a problem! You need to pay closer attention, Alex!" She rolled her eyes.

"Sorry, Mom, I'll pay real close attention." Alex was always hurt when his mother scolded or corrected him. But at the moment, it hurt even worse. Even now, Mary was skeptical of Alex's ability to please the psychologist, and he knew it.

Ironically, Mary wasn't paying attention either. Randall's comment about "whether we are good parents" had gone unnoticed. Mary wasn't even considering the possibility that part of Alex's problem just might be the way she treated him.

Without looking at her, his father continued. "What we're saying is, we both think you're pretty special, and we love you so much. We both think Miss Pendleton was wrong in her report about you. We think your crying over Pudgy was what you should have been doing. It's what any kid would have done."

"Really, that was okay?" asked Alex in a surprised whimper.

"Yes, really, like when my dog was hit by a car and died when

THE TRIBUTARIES of ALEX BECKHAM

I was your age. It was terrible, and as I told you, I saw it happen. I cried for a whole day, just like you did." He gave Alex a big hug, and his mother came over, rubbed his stubbly buzz haircut, then held his cheeks in her hand and kissed him on the forehead. Tears ran down Alex's cheeks once again, yet not because he felt bad but because he was feeling good. They were backing him. He was feeling loved by both of them again, and at the same time. That certainly didn't happen very often.

"Okay, Dad, when do we go see the psychostatis? What do I have to do?" Alex was ready.

Randall laughed under his breath again, as he thought Alex's word for psychologist sounded more like a word for a dinosaur.

"We're going next Saturday, and we're to meet at the doctor's house in the country. Dr. Johnson gave me his address," Randall explained.

"Then what?" asked Alex curiously.

"He'll ask you some questions and have you play some games. All you have to do is just be you, my little man. You'll be alone with him, just you, not us. Tell him anything he wants to know. Sound easy?" Randall appeared upbeat and confident.

"Sounds easy-peasy, Dad! No hard questions? He knows I can't read yet, right? I'm only in kindergarten, but I heard Miss Pendleton say she could read by my age. He knows I can't read, right?" Alex wanted to be sure that was normal.

"Right! And, oh yes, they want a note from Miss Taylor, your teacher, as to your behavior at school. She'll send the note home with you before Friday."

Oh no. The spanking Miss Taylor gave me for talking too much. I'm done. I'm sunk!

"Can Miss Lowe write it, Dad? She knows me better. I'll ask her first thing tomorrow," blurted Alex.

"Either one is fine," Randall responded. "But be sure you ask her and don't forget. It's important."

"I promise, I won't forget." Alex felt relieved but knew he had to get to Miss Lowe first thing in the morning.

"Alex, your mother and I are still going to talk to her as well, so she knows what's happening and the purpose of her letter. And by the way, Miss Taylor already called us and told us about your excessive talking in class. She said it was no big deal. She actually chuckled a little about it, but she had to let you and the whole class know it's not okay to talk when she's talking."

"So you know about that, and I'm not in trouble?" asked Alex.

"Not unless you keep doing it. She actually called because she forgot about your bleeding, and she was concerned she might have hurt you. She felt bad."

Alex thought that maybe Miss Taylor wasn't as mean as he thought.

But his father continued, "Tell her you're sorry and you deserved the spanking. Also tell her you're fine, and you'll be quiet when you're supposed to be." Randall accepted the fact that Alex was an energetic little boy with many more lessons to learn.

"I will, but I was telling my friends about Pudgy, and…"

"Stop, Alex, stop," his dad said with a small smile on his face. "It's no big deal. We all do dumb stuff sometimes and get in trouble when we're kids. That's how we learn. She said you didn't hurt anybody; you were just disruptive. Other than that, you've been a pleasure. Now go upstairs and get your PJs on, grab an encyclopedia, and bring it back down so I can read it to you."

Alex ran upstairs, brushed his teeth real fast without toothpaste, put on his PJs, and grabbed an encyclopedia. He raced back down the stairs to the living room.

"What are we going to learn about tonight?" Randall asked Alex.

"Africa, and the rhinocosores and elephants and the natives with spears and stuff. I saw a picture on the wall at school today. Looked fun!" Alex was excited.

"Rhinoceros, Alex, but just call them rhinos for now. It's a big word." Randall chuckled again. *He does give things a try,* he thought.

So, after the second most confusing day of Alex's young life, Randall read to him, showing him where Africa was located on the globe in Alex's room and telling him about the strange animals and different kinds of people. Then Randall spoke of things not in the book. He told Alex about a man named Tarzan in the movies and in comic books. He told Alex he'd take him to see a Tarzan movie someday soon, and he did, very shortly after.

Frankly, Alex loved the animals, but he thought those natives were really scary looking, with faces all painted, and they killed people with spears and dart guns. And they beat on drums. But still, Alex thought it was kinda fun, as long as they didn't come into his backyard.

As Randall and Alex were finishing studying about Africa, Mary called them into the kitchen, and on the table were three chocolate sundaes, each with a cherry on top. "Okay, boys, let's eat up, and then it's time for bed." Alex had forgotten about the ice cream but Mary had not and was starting to feel some compassion for the tough position in which her son had been placed. After Alex gulped his down, Mary turned to him at the table. "Time to go up to bed, Alex. We'll come up and tuck you in in a couple of minutes," his mother said as she looked at him with a loving smile.

Alex ran up the stairs, took a running leap so the monster under the bed didn't grab him, and slid under the covers. Mary and Randall followed shortly after, and they said the "Now I lay me down to sleep" prayer, like every night, and they both kissed him and left the room.

Alex stared at the ceiling, picking feathers from his pillow and stuffing them under the bed. He thought, *So here I am again. It's all up to me for the second time whether I get a sister and they get a baby. I can do this. After all, I'm almost six. Okay, off to the psychostatis person.*

Winter of 1942

THE SAINT ALOYSIOUS ORPHANAGE FOR PARENTLESS CHILDREN AND UNWED MOTHERS

A damp chill permeated the chipped plaster walls in the long-ago established residence of children tragically without parents and young women hidden away to avoid embarrassment to their families. As most of the unwed teenagers spent their time in prayer and repentance, the sisters did their best raising the troubled children, educating them, feeding them, and attempting to show the right balance between love and discipline. Five Catholic parishes provided the primary support to this group of confused girls and lonesome orphans, as well as feeding and housing the nuns. But it was never enough to oust the sadness within the children, as they began to realize their lives had started with the sad disadvantage of no family. Their only hope was adoption into a loving and understanding household.

"Katharine, follow me, child. We need to speak immediately," commanded Sister McCormick, in charge of the orphanage and the principal of the school. She wielded unquestionable power over the orphans and nuns as well as all the administrative duties the parishes placed upon her. Katharine Pendleton was twelve years old and had been in the orphanage for just a bit over two years. She scurried behind as ordered and followed Sister McCormick into her dimly lit office, the gray skies attempting to add some happiness to the room. But the weather was failing.

Katharine stood across the desk from Sister McCormick with her head bowed and hands folded in front of her. There were no chairs on which to sit. "Yes, Sister, what do you want with me this time? I cleaned the bathrooms as you asked, and Margaret and I changed all the sheets in the toddler wing. They can still be quite messy. We are doing the best we can."

"Katharine, my child, you know perfectly well why you're

here. This is the third time I've had to speak to you. One more time, and I promise you I will lock you away whenever we have potential parents visiting our home." Sister McCormick scowled at Katharine.

"I don't know what you mean. I'm nice to those people and try to make them feel welcome. I'm confused, Sister." Katharine still looked at the floor.

"You know exactly what I speak of, young lady. Through adoption, we make most of the money to run this home. You don't believe the parishes alone give us what we need to operate, do you? Look around you, young lady." Katharine still acted as if she was confused.

"I'm just trying to make another sale for you, Sister."

"Don't refer to these children as 'a sale.' They are placements and giving both the parents and the children what they want. Everybody receives an advantage in this process." The sister stood up with intensity in her eyes.

"I don't, Sister. I get nothing. I'm just your maidservant, at my age. No one wants a daughter approaching puberty. They whisper and look at me with those pitiful stares. I know they what they think now. They wonder how a girl of my age could be with child. They think I must have been abused or I'm a loose one, or worse, that I was abandoned and must be damaged. I know they are thinking it, Sister, I know they are. And I know they're worried I'll have a baby and they'll be stuck with two children. That's why I talk to them. I want them to know my mother and father were killed in a car accident. That's all. I would make a wonderful daughter or sister. Please let me talk to them when they visit. Please, I beg you Sister McCormick, give me a chance." Katharine began to cry.

As silence filled the room for only a few moments, Sister McCormick began to speak. "Katharine, I don't know what they're thinking and neither do you, but they must be specific as to gender, age, and race when they apply. No one ever applies for a child over ten, especially a female." Katharine began to cry harder. The

Sister stared coldly across the desk. "You're almost thirteen, and you'll be released to live on your own in five years." Katharine was being pounded into reality like a square peg in a round hole. "You're correct; people want babies or toddlers, at the most, not teenagers. And most of them want boys, at least the fathers do. Let us do what we can to prepare you for the real world when you leave here. Understand?" It was the first time Katharine had heard the brutal truth, but she had already been aware of the facts shortly after she came to Saint Aloysious. That horrible time when she grieved for her parents, then had to grieve for the rejection by her only aunt.

"I must insist you remain silent when people from the adoption agency and potential parents tour our facility. If you do not, I'll be forced to keep you locked away while they are present. Do you understand? Now go." Sister McCormick sat back down in her chair and refused to look back at Katharine.

The girl turned and ran off, weeping. The simmering resentment against this system as well as God's betrayal by the death of her parents began to boil. This was her day of decision. She swore she would find a way to get even with all those kinds of people who rejected her and her teenage friends.

• • •

The year 1948 came quickly. Katharine, despite never being allowed to groom or dress well by the sisters, grew into an attractive young lady. The nuns taught all the girls, including the unwed mothers, typing, shorthand and essential bookkeeping skills. All the orphan girls were presented with high school diplomas and were set up with interviews for jobs offered by the parishioners. They were most kind and cooperative in their hiring, as they had worked with Saint Aloysious over the years to develop their vocational curriculum. They also offered inexpensive rental housing, also owned by parishioners, to house up to four of these girls at a time and share the rent. In turn, the girls all worked for minimum wage.

Katharine took a job in the secretarial pool of a large tool manufacturing company. The nuns had taught her proper grammar and writing skills. Once on the job, she studied the actions and observed the wardrobes of the "higher-ups" in order to simulate their behavior and increase the potential for growth in her job. Each day, she grew more and more competent, more and more professional, but more and more angry.

Miss Pendleton, as she was now referred to by her superiors, worked hard and was an ideal employee; however, raises and promotions were elusive, due to her age and experience. So she was told. But as far as Katharine was concerned, this was becoming a lame excuse as the months and years passed behind her.

• • •

It was now nearing the close of 1955. As the girls came home from work, they all took turns making dinner and doing dishes. Around the table, they all shared the events of their days. Girls had come and gone in this simple apartment, but Katharine and her roommate Emily were the only ones who had remained together since their concurrent release from Saint Aloysious. As dinnertime ended, it was Katharine and Emily's turn to wash dishes.

"I got passed over again for a promotion today," said Katharine.

"Why? I thought they liked you, and you've just turned twenty-five, so age can't be the reason. Did you do anything wrong? I mean, you dress well and look professional, at least more professional than the women where I work." Emily kept washing as Katharine dried.

"You know what I think it is, Emily? I'm an orphan, and they know that," said Katharine. "I'm not married and don't have any family working somewhere else in the company. That's it. It has to be." Katharine was getting angry. The thoughts of those days after her parents died, when her aunt rejected her and Sister Mc-Cormick let her know she was unwanted by anyone, came rushing back into her memory like a disturbed swarm of bees.

"Come on, Katharine. Give it some time. You're a pretty girl. A man will come along soon. But that will mean the end of us. And I like our nights together." Emily handed Katharine another dish, and as she did, Emily kissed her.

"Stop, Emily, not out here where the other two can see us. Wait until later. The last thing I need is for someone to find out about us, and we'll both be fired," said Katharine.

"You're right, you're always right. And these church people would never let two lesbians live in their apartment." They both finished the dishes, both with smiles on their faces.

As they went to their room that evening, they stripped down to their slips and climbed into bed together. Emily began to become playful.

"Stop, Emily, not yet. I have had enough of being the victim on this planet. There is a debt owed to me by the entire world as well as God himself. I'm going to get even, but I need your help."

"Sure, anything, my love," and the lights went out.

• • •

"Well, Miss Pendleton, your resume is impressive. You graduated with honors from your high school and received your undergrad and master's in child psychology from Duquesne. I'm very aware of your alma mater. I'm a devout Catholic as well." Mr. Johnson, actually William Johnson, PhD, was the President/CEO of the Holy Cross Adoption Agency. The agency had nearly twenty field psychologists whose job was to research the parental applicants and their families. This research would result in the approval or rejection of these applicants to adopt unborn infants from Holy Cross.

"Thank you, sir," responded Katharine, her hair up in a tight bun and dressed in a new blue suit exuding professionalism and confidence.

"I also see you have worked in the clinic at University Hospital for the last year; impressive. And this person is your reference at University? She can be reached at 673-6752, correct?" Dr. Johnson was excited.

"Yes, sir. I will inform her to expect your call, but this is her home phone. She asked that you call her in the evening around 6:30. She said she finds herself so busy during the day and wants to have time to do me justice. I have learned a lot from her. She has been my mentor." Katharine was pulling this off as if she was born to act.

"Thank you, Miss Pendleton. It has been a pleasure. And where do I reach you with my decision?" asked Dr. Johnson.

"I'm making rounds during the day and never know where I'll be. But I'm looking forward to your answer, so what number do you have where I can reach you during the day?" Katharine smiled with just an ever so slight twinge of flirtatiousness.

"You can call my assistant, Robert, at 513-3674. I'll leave word with him." Katharine thanked Dr. Johnson, smiled and left the room.

Dr. Johnson immediately sent word for his personnel director to come to his office immediately. When he entered, Dr. Johnson pushed the resume across the desk. "Robert, we have one. Now we're only down three, thank goodness. If we don't fill those positions soon, we'll lose more field agents. Call her reference at her home number tonight at 6:30. Her name is Emily Hanson."

"What about transcripts, sir?" asked Robert.

"No way. That'll take weeks. We don't have time for that. Just call the reference and get back to me tomorrow morning. If the reference is acceptable, tell her to have the applicant call me by noon tomorrow. Unless we're missing something, this is the type of employee we have been looking for. Maybe she has some other connections. What a break." Robert left the room, and Dr. Johnson went back to his busy schedule.

THE DAY HAS ARRIVED FOR THE RECKONING OF ALEX BECKHAM AND HIS BANANA

"Alex, wake up, honey, c'mon, wake up. It's eight o'clock. Time to get movin'. Big day today, kiddo," Mary said as she jostled her son gently on his shoulder. She then attempted to pull the covers off his skinny little body. Alex grunted, as he did every morning, while gripping his covers tightly under his chin. But on this day, even though the sunlight brilliantly covered his walls in addition to his room being snuggly warm, Mary was very cautious to awaken Alex slowly. Finally, he left his dreamland, his eyes opened, and he burst into daytime. It was at that point he became cognizant of the fact it was a Saturday.

"Aww, Mom, its Saturday. Why covers off on a Saturday?" He knew his mom rarely if ever woke him on a Saturday. Sure, she did it for school now during the week and for Sunday school on Sundays, but not on a Saturday. *Mom must be confused*, he thought. *She knows I love to sleep!*

"Mommy, why do I have to get up so early? It's Saturday," Alex whined the same way he did when he was forced to take a bath. He pulled the covers back up to his chin. "Let me sleep! Leave me alone!" Mary only allowed Alex to talk to her that way in the morning, and on this particular morning, she would be deeply tolerant of his morning crankiness.

"You're right, Alex, this is Saturday. But this is the day we're all going together to visit the doctor who wants to talk with you. Now, go brush your teeth with toothpaste, Alex, take your bath, and slip into those nice clothes we bought for you when the lady visited a few weeks ago. I'll lay them out here on your bed. And please, put on clean socks! When you're all cleaned up and dressed, come down to the kitchen. I'm making a special breakfast for the three of us: banana pancakes, bacon, and chocolate milk!"

For just a brief moment, chocolate milk reminded Alex of Pudgy, but the thought drifted away like a balloon floating to the clouds, leaving just a twinge of sadness in its wake.

Still not entirely ready to start his day, Alex rolled his little body out of bed, rubbed his half-opened eyes with his knuckles, and with hunched-over shoulders, he shuffled to the bathroom. The floor was not carpeted and was always cold. Alex sensed something inside his stomach as his mind began to grasp that this was the day of his visit to this "psychostatis" doctor. This wasn't the same feeling he felt when getting up for kindergarten or Sunday school or to play outside. It wasn't like going to his grandmother's or running errands with his dad or going to the grocery store with his mom. His stomach felt queasy, and his throat was tight. Alex was having trouble breathing deeply.

The more awake he became, the more thoughts began to run through his head. *What is this doctor going to do to me? A doctor is a doctor, right? Is this going to be like going to Dr. Ventress, who wore that big round mirror on his forehead while he looked inside my ears and up my nose? Will this doctor stick that big fat stick down my throat until I gag and almost throw up? Am I going to get shots in my butt? Sometimes those hurt and I cry, but I can't cry today, no matter what.*

As Alex's brain raced through all the possibilities of what might happen to him, he took a speedy bath, put on his new clothes, including clean socks, and even clean underwear, the ones with the teddy bears on them. It was time. The little gladiator was ready for battle.

Alex, ever so timorously, one step at a time and gripping the rail, descended from the upstairs, then into the kitchen. His mouth began to water when he caught his first whiff of bacon crackling in the skillet. He remembered his mom saying "banana pancakes." He hoped he'd heard it correctly, because you really couldn't ever smell pancakes cooking (unless his dad cooked, and then you could smell the burnt ones all over the house). And he hoped they were the kind with the colored lady on the box. Her name was Aunt Jemima, Alex was told.

His father was already at the table reading his newspaper, one leg crossed over the other, carefully sipping his hot coffee. His mother was at the stove, cooking.

Randall folded his newspaper neatly and placed it on the table. "Good morning, Alex. Your mom's making us a great breakfast. She's such a good cook! How do we both stay so skinny with her around?" Randall gave Alex a strong, confident hug with a big smile on his face. Alex's smile was forced and not very big. "Are you ready to meet the doctor? His name is Dr. Winston, I'm told."

"Uh, sure, I guess. Am I going to get any shots in my butt?" Alex blurted as he sat down, not smiling or looking up. "I need to know ahead of time, so I can try real hard not to cry. I promise, I won't cry no matter how bad it hurts!" He then looked up to see his parents' reaction, especially his mother's.

Randall chuckled, "No, no, Tiger, he's not that kind of doctor at all; no shots, I promise, unless you start jumping up and down on his desk like a monkey and scratching your armpits!" Alex looked puzzled. "I'm just joking, Tiger. He's called a child psychologist. First of all, he only works with children and studies their nature and their daily habits. He studies what they do every day when they get up." Mary looked worried, but Randall seemed tranquil and confident as he continued to educate Alex.

"Daily habits? Like going to school and brushing my teeth; stuff like that?" Alex wondered why anybody cared about him brushing his teeth. He decided, if asked, he would lie a little about not using toothpaste all the time.

"That's what I'm saying. It's no big deal. He'll have you put some puzzles together and play some games and tell some stories. And he'll probably show you some funny pictures made of ink, and you just tell him what you see! It'll be fun." Alex's stomach and throat were beginning to loosen, and he was feeling hungry.

As Randall mentioned the ink blots, Mary got scared.

"A child psyyyy…chologist, is that right, Dad? It's only taken me five days to get that one down; that was a tough one." Alex was proud of himself for finally learning such a big word.

"Perfect, my boy, very good! Remember Monday when you called him a 'psychostatist' or something like that? It sounded like a dinosaur to me. Your mom and I laughed all night over that." Even Mary turned to give Alex a little grin.

Oh great, now they think I not only have a crying issue but I'm stupid and can't say big words. But I never heard it before! Alex thought.

Randall sensed Alex was a little hurt by his last statement. "That's a big word for anybody, my boy, especially a kindergartener. I couldn't say spaghetti for a long time when I was a kid. I kept calling it 'basghetti.' Your grandma and grandpa and your uncle Jack used to laugh at me every time I'd say it." Randall smiled and affectionately slapped Alex on his shoulder, as men buddies do.

That made Alex feel a little better. Alex thought his dad seemed unusually relaxed, even owning a twinge of excitement about the day. He was sensing his dad had confidence in him; that was a good thing. But he was picking up something different from his mother. Her silence was transmitting tension and edgy vibes to Alex. And even with all the answers and explanations just given, those mixed emotions betwixt his mother and father still had Alex on the hesitant side of what was about to happen in the next few hours of discourse.

Mary placed the bacon and pancakes on the table, along with the maple syrup. She poured Alex a glass of white milk, stirring in a teaspoon of Hershey's chocolate syrup, no Ovaltine, and like magic—a new kind of chocolate milk! Mary knew what she was doing. An Ovaltine tin on the table was the last thing Alex needed to see this morning. She would never again allow one in the house.

"Stir it up really good, Alex," she said as she turned back to the stove.

He stirred it hard as the syrup settled to the bottom. Alex knew what his mother was doing; however, for the rest of his life, chocolate milk would remind him of that horrible day. Plain milk would become his drink of choice. And even though that morning, it was not Ovaltine, the thoughts of Pudgy came back. Alex jumped inside his own head at the table to stop those thoughts. *Come on! Not this morning, not now! Stop it up there, stop it, stop it! No crying. Not this morning. La, la, la, la, la!*

So even though pancakes, bacon, and especially chocolate milk were always his favorites, the chocolate milk ruined his typical ravenous appetite. His tummy returned to feeling funny, like it had when his mother had mentioned the doctor visit as she awakened him. His throat was still a bit tight, and he felt like he had to go "number two" but couldn't. His father noticed him picking at his pancakes but didn't say anything. Randall perceived and understood Alex's contemplation and apprehension. And Alex wouldn't die if he missed one breakfast.

"Alex, let's do it! Let's go! Stop picking at your food. Eat up! I made this especially for you," his mother said in a subtly scolding manner. "We don't know how long you'll be with the doctor. It could be a long time before we have lunch, and I don't want to hear you whining about how hungry you are later. Come on, eat up, right now, and I mean right now!"

With that, Randall knew what he had to do to break this spell being cast on Alex. He stood up and tucked his newspaper under his arm. "Time to go, Mary, grab our jackets and let's be on our way!" he said.

"Beck, he has to eat more than that, and we have to do the dishes," Mary argued.

"Mary, the last thing we want to do is be late. We're starting behind the eight ball already. We'll do the dishes when we get home. Ready, Alex?" Randall stated calmly but emphatically. He had no intention of caving to Mary's suggestion and had no intention of starting any kind of altercation whatsoever. Emotions were already close to eruption all around.

With a disgusted snarl, Mary snatched a banana off the table. "Here, Alex, at least eat this on the way. It'll tide you over until lunch. Eat it, or I promise you, I'll give you a good spankin'!"

Randall knew that was the last thing Alex needed to hear at the moment. He could sense that Alex's angst was swelling and had a hunch Alex wanted to cry and bolt straight to his room. That would be the end of any chance for an adoption. But after all, a boy his age should be scared, thought Randall. But Mary showed her fear in a different way. She transferred it so it became Alex's fault, as usual.

In a weak and quivering voice, Alex responded sheepishly, "But Mommy, my tummy feels kinda funny, and I'm not really hungry." Mary's scolding was escalating Alex's stage fright into a high-pitched fear of the unknown, like a dangerous ocean wave crashing on the beach inside his head.

"I said eat it, and I mean it! You can do it on the way. You're probably just hungry," said Mary as she gathered the jackets for her and Alex. Randall was wearing a well-tailored blue sports coat. The adults walked briskly to the car, while Alex trotted to keep up. His mom and dad sat in the front. Alex climbed into the back seat behind Mary, so she couldn't reach him if she did decide to spank him.

UH, WHAT'S UP, DOC?

The drive seemed as if it was taking forever. Alex felt carsick like he did whenever the family took a trip of any length, especially over country roads that went up and over hills. He also felt the same as when he went over the apex of a Ferris wheel or a roller coaster.

"Daddy, I feel like I'm going to be sick," Alex said as he leaned onto the front seat next to his father at the wheel.

"Sorry, Tiger, but no Dramamine on this trip. Can't have you falling asleep in the doctor's office, can we? Eat that banana like your mother suggested, and here, hold my pocketknife." Randall reached into his pants pocket and pulled out a small pocketknife.

"Why should I do that, Dad?" asked Alex.

"I used to feel funny in the car when I was your age too, and my dad said if you hold onto something metal, your tummy will feel better," answered Randall, looking at Mary out of the corner of his eye.

"I guess if Grandpa Beckham says it works, then it must work." Alex took the knife in hand, then peeled the banana and mushed it around in his mouth. After a few minutes, Alex thought, *I do feel kinda better. Grandpa Beckham knows everything.*

While Randall drove on, Mary read the directions and studied the map, telling Randall where and when to turn, until finally Randall slowed down and looked at the house numbers on a stone pillar. There were two tall pillars, one on each side of the driveway.

"This is the place," Randall confirmed, as now his heart started to pound as well. "Okay, Alex. This is it," he said as he looked at Alex in the rearview mirror. "Your sister's all up to you now. Just be yourself and answer the doctor's questions."

"And whatever you do, try not to cry," Mary blurted as she glanced at her terrified son quickly over her shoulder with one eye, shaking her head back and forth as if she knew he would cry at some point and again blow it for all of them.

Alex knew not to say a word, but the truth was, he was so scared, he couldn't say anything if he wanted to. Questions raced through his five-year-old mind. *What if he asks me if I cry a lot, or about Pudgy, or spankings, or he does give me a shot? Do I cry? Do I lie? I was taught at Sunday school never to lie! "Be Honest" was a sign I colored in Sunday school, and Dad taped it to my mirror over my dresser. I see it every day; it's one of the few words I can read. But if lying means we get the baby, Mom and Dad will be so happy, and Mom might stop being mean to me. Should I, or shouldn't I?*

His father turned into the entrance and drove between the pillars, then down a long tree-lined driveway. The grass was fresh and green and cut flawlessly. The trees were just beginning to turn into their autumn hues. At the end, the driveway curved into a semicircle in front of white marble steps leading up to what was way more of a mansion than someone's house. It was a massive structure: three-stories, red brick, with a steep roof made of slate, making the place look even larger. And finally, a large screened-in porch that spanned the entire left side of the structure.

"Randall, I thought you told me Dr. Johnson said we were going to this doctor's house." Mary threw out her question and became uncomfortably silent. Randall stayed silent as well, as his palms began to sweat, unbeknownst to Alex or Mary.

An older woman in an all-white nurse's outfit, white shoes, stockings, and nurse's cap came out onto the stoop at the top of the marble steps. She silently pointed to her right, and Randall easily understood her unspoken words. He advised Mary and Alex to get out of the car, and after they did, he drove to the parking lot. When he came back, the intimidated family climbed the steps together, all holding hands. The nurse stood in the large elongated doorway as she cordially invited the uneasy family inside.

The foyer was so clean, Alex was afraid he was going to track dirt in on his shoes. And to Alex, it smelled hauntingly familiar, like a ghost from his past. It reminded him of the hospital when he tumbled down the steps. He was confused, since he wasn't hurt anywhere. The woman in the nurse's uniform, who had directed Randall to the parking lot, greeted the family once more, this time introducing herself. "Mr. and Mrs. Beckham, I assume? My name is Nurse Read. I'm the good Dr. Winston's assistant. And you, young man, must be Alex." She greeted each member of the family with a pleasant handshake. "I want to welcome you all to the Longview State Children's Institution. Please have a seat. Can I get you anything? Coffee, tea, water?"

In a flash, Alex perceived her as peacefully kind and gentle. She had a beautiful, caring smile—sort of like his grandma's whenever she felt sorry for him as his mom scolded him for doing something wrong. For the first time since he realized this was the day of the doctor, Alex's anxiety began to subside. He returned the smile and held his hand out to greet her as well. He then glanced up at his mom and dad, expecting a smile from them, but they both had looks on their faces as if they were suspicious and apprehensive of their surroundings.

What Mary and Randall now realized, completely alien to Alex and his innocence, was that Longview was a state mental institution in the city, where only the truly troubled resided. And this was the specific branch of this state institution where children with mental illnesses were committed and treated. If Alex had known anything about this, he would have freaked.

"Please, have a seat, and I'll tell Dr. Winston you've arrived," said the nurse. But before they all could sit, the door opened to a room off to the side of the entrance foyer, and a white-haired man, teetering on the brink of elderly, with a white mustache and pale skin, entered the room. He was attired in a white doctor's coat with his name displayed in a cursive signature above his pocket full of pens. He wore a pair of baggy brown suit pants and a pair of brown wingtip shoes. Alex was enchanted by the design on the doctor's shoes.

"Mr. and Mrs. Beckham, I'm Dr. Winston. It's a pleasure to meet the both of you." He extended his hand to both of them, and they engaged. "And this must be Alex. How are you, my boy?" He leaned over and extended his hand to Alex as well.

"I'm fine, sir. And nice to meet you, too. I like your shoes, but I'm a little scared." Alex said as he shook the doctor's hand with a forced smile. "My mom and dad told me we're just going to talk and play games, Dr. Winston. No shots, right?"

"No shots, I promise, Alex, just talk and games." The doctor winked at Alex and rubbed the top of his head. He then glanced at the nurse with a compassionate smile. Alex felt like crying, but not because of fear this time, but from relief. He sighed, as if he had been holding his breath all morning.

"Mr. and Mrs. Beckham, I'm going to take your son into my office. He and I will talk for a while. We truly will play some games, and I'll get to know him, and he'll get to know and trust me as well. This will probably take about two hours. If you have any shopping or anything to do, feel free. He's completely safe here with us." The doctor smiled.

"Well, thank you so much, Dr. Winston, but I think we'll just wait out here. I see you have some interesting magazines. I can catch up on my reading," said Randall. Mary didn't know what she would do for two hours except worry and expect the worst.

"Yes, please, make yourself at home. We have water, tea, and coffee. Just ask Nurse Read if you need anything, anything at all. Alex and I will see you shortly. Are you ready, Alex?" He put his arm around Alex's shoulder and opened the door, and together they walked through the door to the porch.

Alex didn't remember a whole lot of specifics about those two hours. But he could recall it was a beautiful day on that screened-in porch. He felt peaceful and at ease, as the unique smell of autumn filled the gentle breeze. Alex remembered, at one point, he felt so tranquil he wanted to nap.

After Alex put some square pegs in square holes, round pegs in round holes, arranged pictures so they made a story, and looked at these funny spills of ink on pieces of paper and telling Dr. Winston what they looked like, the doctor asked him to sit in a big leather chair across from him at his desk.

"Gee, Dr. Winston, we did play games. That was fun. What next?" asked Alex enthusiastically, now totally past his anxiety. "Do you have 'Candyland'? You want to play that? I promise, I never cheat."

Dr. Winston smiled and graciously declined. He then began

to question Alex in an adult manner, and Alex perceived this was the important part. It felt good to Alex to talk with a grown-up in a grown-up way.

Dr. Winston asked him, "Other than when Miss Pendleton came to your house, and we'll get to that in a minute, are there other times you've cried or felt like crying in the last, let's say, few months?"

There weren't a lot of times, but Alex would go into such detail about the people and the surroundings and timelines that Dr. Winston would have to cut him off. Alex was a natural storyteller and very observant, but sometimes it was a little over the edge.

Dr. Winston then asked the question Alex knew he really wanted to ask. "Alex, that lady that came to your house a few weeks ago told the adoption agency a few things that are confusing to me. You are here because I want your side of the story." The anxiety began to creep in again, and the fear of crying came into Alex's head. "Tell me about the gate at the top of your stairs. Do you ever go to sleep and wake up somewhere, like in another room, not knowing how you got there?"

"No, never that I can remember." Alex chose to tell the truth, no matter what, to Dr. Winston.

"Well then, what is the purpose of the gate, Alex?" Dr. Winston took a pen from his coat.

Alex proudly showed the doctor his scar between his eyes, then began the story about his bleeding condition and the potty training and the fall and his stitches, and Rex his nurse, all in a perfectly logical train of facts.

Halfway through, Dr. Winston stopped Alex with a smile as he nodded his head. "Alex, thank you for your story. That was fascinating." He finished his notes.

"Now, Alex, Miss Pendleton said when she tried to talk to you, you started crying terribly for no reason. She assumed you were just too unstable to talk to grown-ups. Is that true?" asked Dr. Winston. "You're certainly talking with me just fine. What made you so scared of her? Was it maybe because she was a woman?"

"Oh, heck no, Dr. Winston, not at all. Actually, since I'm an only child, I talk to more adults than kids. I was crying because I found my pet bird Pudgy dead in the bottom of his cage a couple hours before she came, and when I touched him, he was stiff and cold. It was really weird." Then he continued on with the details of that horrible morning and the entire day. And as he went through the details, he didn't cry, but Dr. Winston could see his eyes were beginning to tear up.

Again, Dr. Winston had heard enough and stopped him. "Alex, my boy, that's a really sad story. I'm so sorry, and I see you're getting sad just thinking about it. Let's stop here."

"Dr. Winston, do you think I'm 'emotional a stable' like Miss Pendleton said?" asked Alex with one tear about to drip down his cheek.

Dr. Winston came over and sat in the other leather chair next to Alex. He put his hand on his forearm. "Alex, the word is 'unstable' and no, I think you're pretty normal. At least, as normal as any of us are. My dog died when I was your age, from being run over by a milk truck, and I cried for days; happens to all of us." Dr. Winston gave an understanding smile, tinged with a bit of sadness from his own memories in his eyes.

"My dad's dog died the same way, but it was a car, not a truck," Alex added.

"Well, Alex, it has been a pleasure being with you this morning. In my business, there aren't many kids I enjoy. Most of the time, it's hard work, and many times it's very, very, sad."

"What kind of work do you do, Dr. Winston? This was just playtime as far as I could see. How can this be sad?" asked Alex in his most innocent tone.

"It's complicated, Alex, but someday you'll understand," said Dr. Winston.

I wish I had a piece of bubble gum for every time I heard "Someday you'll understand," Alex thought again.

"Now, let's go and see your parents. Whatcha' say, my boy?" Dr. Winston helped Alex out of the big chair, tucked him into his side and they opened the door to the foyer where his parents were restlessly waiting. Alex broke from the doctor's grip and ran to hug both his mom and his dad.

"All right, folks, we're all finished. I must ask you, however, to wait here just a little bit longer. About fifteen minutes or so. I'll meet you right back here and discuss my conclusions." Dr. Winston turned and went back into his office, seemingly a bit upset.

"Well, how was it, Alex?" Randall asked. Mary showed no emotion as she sat silent.

"It was fun, Dad! We put some puzzles together, and he had me make up stories and look at these funny ink things. Then we talked about the day Miss Pendleton came over and the gate and Pudgy. It was really fun, and really easy, especially the ink things."

"Did you cry at all?" asked his mother with a very uneasy look on her face.

Alex didn't know whether to say no and make her happy or tell her yes and get her upset with him. "Well, I guess I did, but just a little bit, but not much at all, only like one tear." Mary sighed as she peered at Randall. Randall knew she was disappointed in Alex.

"Well Randall, that's that," she blurted.

"No Mom, it really was only when he asked me to tell him about Pudgy. And, Mom, it was just one—well, maybe two little tears. It was mostly because my eyes got a little watery and kinda overflowed, but no sobbing or anything. Dr. Winston gave me a tissue and told me about his dog that died when he was my age, and he said even he cried back then too, just like you, Dad. And look, he grew up to be a doctor, Mom. Maybe I can grow up to be a doctor like him. That'd be fun!" Alex studied his mom's face. She didn't look mad. But she didn't look happy either, just blankly staring.

"Okay, Alex," his dad responded. "Let's just all sit here quietly and wait for Dr. Winston to return." They all sat and waited without saying a word to each other, probably about twenty minutes; it seemed like an eternity. Eventually, the door opened, and Dr. Winston entered the room. The family all stood up to hear what they did or didn't want to hear.

"Please, please, don't get up. Stay seated," said Dr. Winston.

Alex and his parents sat back down. Dr. Winston pulled up a chair from across the room and positioned himself in front of the three of them.

"I'm so sorry to keep you waiting. I'm sure this must be a terribly stressful ordeal for all of you. Your anxiety levels must be soaring. The adoption process can be very trying for a family. So let me say, I can see how important this is to you. And from what Alex tells me, it's very important to him to have a sibling as well." Then Dr. Winston sighed, leaned forward with his forearms on his knees and folded his hands, as if he were going to tell them all a secret.

"I just got off the phone with Dr. Johnson at the agency. He wanted me to call him at home as soon as I finished. He told me the birth of the baby is expected to be at the beginning of November, and the birth mother and her family are anxious, as well, about our outcome here. That makes time of the essence, providing it's a girl." Randall was not able to read Dr. Winston's conclusion in any of doctor's mannerisms.

"I told Dr. Johnson I thought your son was one of the most well-behaved and pleasant children I have met in a long time. He's cooperative and very intelligent, and you have done a wonderful job with his social skills. And as the report states, he is emotional." With Dr. Winston's last observation, Mary almost got up from her seat to head for the car. The look on Randall's face changed from an expression of hope to one of tension, like the proverbial shoe that just dropped with a huge plop.

"Well, he told me about his pet bird, Pudgy. That's the name, correct?" asked Dr. Winston.

"Yes, that's right!" Alex answered with a smile, so glad the doctor remembered. Randall patted Alex on the knee, motioning for him to stay silent.

"He told me he cried a lot the morning Pudgy died. He told me he was scared today when he got up and had trouble eating breakfast. He told me he cries when he gets shots from the doctor. He also told me he cries sometimes when you read him sad books or you take him to see a sad movie. He specifically mentioned Disney's *Dumbo* movie, when they took Dumbo's mother away." Dr. Winston smiled at Mary. "And he told me about the night he tried to go to the bathroom and fell down the steps. I think he's actually pretty proud of his scar." Dr. Winston looked over at Alex, smiled, and squeezed Alex's shoulder.

"What I'm concluding, Mr. and Mrs. Beckham, is that your son's an emotional child, as the report states, but he's in no way 'emotionally unstable'. His logic skills, his chronological skills, and his ink blot interpretations are all totally normal, if not a little ahead of his age. If he wasn't scared this morning or sad reading books or watching movies, and especially if he was not sad over losing a pet he loved, he would be abnormal." Randall was feeling good. Mary was not quite sure what the conclusion of all this would reveal. "I could sense the pressure he has been put under for this adoption, and frankly, he thinks it's his sole responsibility for you all to be approved. Emotions are a good thing when they are appropriate. Then, when they are encouraged by families, teachers, and mentors, coupled with the cultivation of the consequences of those emotions, they become very powerful character traits. But if they are suppressed or criticized, that's where we find our children, and even adults, becoming emotionally unstable. I'd predict, even though you find it uncomfortable at times to see him sad, angry, scared, or even overly silly, if you accept his strong emotions and help him to channel them properly and not repress them, someday he's going to have an artistic, creative, and loving side that will be very beneficial to a lot of people, including you and his entire family."

"Okay," asked Randall in a questioning tone. "You just talked to Dr. Johnson, I assume, and what did he say? Does this mean we are approved?"

"I told him Alex was totally normal and would make a wonderful sibling to any child. Alex has my clearance." Dr. Winston rubbed Alex's stubby buzz haircut and gave Mary and Randall a loving smile.

Well, at that point, Mary and Randall hugged each other, and Alex was so happy he had finally pleased them, especially his mother. Alex smiled and began to tear up, first because he was told he wasn't crazy, and secondly, because he was finally going to be a big brother. Also, Alex found it a relief that crying and other feelings were okay. But what he didn't know was that his strong emotions would never really be totally okay with his parents, especially his mother. His life would be an internal struggle most of the time, but he would always return to that day Dr. Winston gave him permission to be himself.

As all of them rose from their chairs, Dr. Winston stopped them. "And, oh yes, one more thing I think you all should know before you leave," said Dr. Winston. Mary held her breath.

"I asked Dr. Johnson why he thought Miss Pendleton left out so much in her report. Or why she didn't come back a second time after hearing the extenuating circumstances of that day," said Dr. Winston.

"Yes sir, I must say, we talked extensively about that and couldn't find an answer. That's why I questioned the report with Dr. Johnson, and he sent us to you." Randall was anxious to finally hear a logical answer. "What did he say?"

He said he left a note on her desk last week to come see him about your case, but she never showed up," said Dr. Winston.

"What does that mean?" asked Randall.

"I assume it just means she doesn't work for the agency anymore, and none of us will ever have an answer to that question.

I'm sorry, Mr. Beckham." None of the group were satisfied with that void in the process, but it would have to do. At this point, it was completely irrelevant.

Then Dr. Winston squatted to his knees, so he was face-to-face with Alex. He enclosed Alex's checks in the palms of his hands and stared intensely into the boy's eyes. "And I am truly sorry about your bird, my little friend." Alex didn't answer, but threw his arms around Dr. Winston's neck and hugged him tightly. Dr. Winston hugged him back, then stood up.

"If you have no more questions, it was a pleasure to meet you all, and I wish your family love and happiness." With that, Dr. Winston turned and went back to his office. Mary gathered up the jackets, and they all headed out the front door.

As they made their way to the car, Randall put his arm around Alex's shoulder. "Proud of you, Tiger! I knew you could do it! That's my boy! Did you hear all those wonderful things he said about you? He thinks you're pretty special! But your mom and I already knew that, right Mary?" Randall had a spirited smile on his face while Mary still had not said a word. "Race you to the car, little man," said Randall. Alex skipped all the way to the car and beat his dad, no contest. Randall opened the door and gave Alex a playful swat on the butt as Alex climbed in the backseat.

Mary settled into her front seat as Randall positioned himself behind the wheel. All doors were closed, and Randall started the car. It was only then that Mary finally broke her silence, "Oh my God, Beck, that was close; too close." She peered straight ahead through the windshield. Then, looking over at Randall, she coldly uttered, "He must be completely different around other people than he is at home with me. I didn't think we had a chance, Beck. I thought sure he would blow it for us again."

Hearing that from his mother, Alex felt the same way he had when he saw that his mother had thrown Pudgy in his tin off the back porch, into the cold rainy mud in the backyard. *Whoa, that really hurts,* Alex thought. *I mean it really hurts! I thought she'd be happy and proud of me, like Dad is. She still thinks there's something wrong with me.*

As they drove down the long driveway to the street, Randall spoke up. "How about a big hamburger, French fries, and a milkshake at the Big Boy for our big boy? We're gonna have a baby girl soon, everybody!" Randall and Alex were bouncing like popcorn popping in a kettle. Mary was doing what she could to give a half-hearted smile. She was thinking, *At least now I'll have a child that loves me best and not have to deal with Alex 24/7.*

"That sounds great, Dad. I'm really, really hungry! Can I have a strawberry milkshake this time?" The thought of lunch at Big Boy made Alex forget about his mother's comments, for now, anyway.

Mary twisted halfway around in her seat and gave Alex a frown. "I told you at breakfast you would be complaining if you didn't finish your pancakes, didn't I? I don't want to hear any more of your complaining!"

Alex was finding it quite a formidable task to stay happy around his mother. He was also beginning to observe it was becoming more and more difficult for his dad to stay happy around her as well. But as usual, Randall kept quiet and drove. It was just what he did—stayed quiet.

The family was informed, providing the birth mother had a girl, that the baby could be delivered to them as soon as within the next five weeks. After the birth, there would be a nine-day waiting period for medical evaluation. If all was fine, they would be blessed with a nine-day-old baby girl. Alex was unaware of the changing role on which he was about to embark. The threesome days were over. The Pudgy and ice cream days were also gone forever. This was the last lunch the family would have as just the three of them. Alex's "only child" days were about to end. But still, those six years of total attention had had their effect on him. The spotlight that had been all his was now to be shared, and with his emotions, the sharing was not always going to be sufficient and acceptable to him. But ready or not, here she came! And Alex was going to be a very loving brother, most of the time.

• • •

Two years later, Randall sat at the breakfast table reading his newspaper. Alex sat across from him. Mary was cooking pancakes, and the baby was in her high chair.

"Well I'll be, Mary, read this headline, then the rest of the article when you join us." The headline read:

FORMER AGENT AT HOLY CROSS APOPTION AGENCY FOUND GUILTY OF FRAUD

Next in the Series:
As the Beckham family grows, Alex and his cousins grow tighter, however, his question as to whether his aunt loves him comes into question and the answer comes to him in a most unexpected way.

EPISODE IV

A TIGHT GROUP OF COUSINS TAKE THE PLAYING FIELD

This episode exposes Alex's confusion as he endures the testing of his growth from a late toddler to a young boy. 'Mommy' and 'Daddy' seem inappropriate for a boy now his age. He replaces the terms of endearment with the more mature terms of 'Mom' and 'Dad'. And now, as a young boy, he begins to ponder the relationships between himself and the sincere feelings of all his relatives towards him. These feelings would shadow him closely into his adult life. As we all take negative actions towards others or we interpret the rejections of others as a personal shun of our personalities, we many times conclude those actions have nothing to do with us. The actions arise due to unique combination of tributaries emptying into everyone's souls from their own very beginning. Love comes and goes in all of our lives. With these experiences, most of us take them as some flaw in our characters, when in fact, we all have behaviors judged differently by others. Life does not last forever. If you have love for someone, tell them sooner, not later. Your expression of love can change a person's life forever. And their love can change you.

November 1956

IT'S FUN TO HAVE VISITORS TO YOUR HOME FOR A WHILE. NOW GO AWAY AND LEAVE ME ALONE.

After a bureaucratic ordeal that became quite troubling to the entire family, especially Alex, the newest member of the Beckham family was delivered to the Beckham household at six o'clock p.m. on November 9, 1956. Although it was cold and the cars and trucks filled the air with the sound of the rainy road, the feelings for this newborn child could not have been warmer. Mary wept as she held her daughter in a loving bundle of soft cotton blankets, coddling her in her cozy new rocking chair. Randall, the new father, sat on the couch, his heart overflowing with happiness as he observed Mary's tears of contentment running down her cheeks. And Alex sported a proud grin from ear to ear as his dream of a baby sister to love in his life had ultimately come true. Alex leaned on the arm of the rocker, his feet dangling rhythmically off the floor, staring in awe at this ever so tiny baby in his mother's arms. He couldn't wait to hold her and show her all his toys, books and puzzles, as well as play ball and push her on the swing in the backyard. But within the next week, disappointment for Alex would sadly creep inside his dreams, like a nighttime in the summer, as the excitement and expectations of this sibling would be short-lived. Alex would come to quickly realize Melody would be unable to play with him for a long, long time; and not only would he find her boring but noisy beyond belief! *I think I may have been better off replacing my dead parakeet,* thought Alex. *At least Pudgy was quiet so I could sleep.*

That first week after the addition of Melody, the phone rang off the hook! Every night at the dinner table, Mary would report to Randall who called and what they asked. Over and over, Alex heard his mother answer the same questions from their friends and family: "How's the baby? What's her name? Named after someone? How much did she weigh? When can we come visit? What can I bring you? What can I do to help?" Alex's feelings were becoming jumbled more each day. He had a new feeling sliding in that he had never before experienced. No one was asking about him anymore. He was becoming scared to look in the mirror; he just might be invisible.

After the telephone calls, then came the revolving door of visitors. First the relatives, some of whom Alex had never even met. *Who is Uncle Frank and Aunt Dot? They smell like farm animals and Uncle Frank has a feather stuck in a drop of blood on his dirty boots.* Then came friends, neighbors, people from the church, fellow workers and almost Randall's entire softball team. Alex thought Melody could be the new Christ Child, except she was a girl and the three Kings never showed up. Randall hadn't read to Alex in weeks and Alex was feeling very ignored and beginning to feel unloved. But there was one positive—the cookies, cakes, and pies people brought. They were delicious. *But they can keep those fruit cake things. They look and taste disgusting.* Alex kept that comment to himself.

As people arrived in person, a whole new set of stock questions were launched over and over: "What's her actual birthday? How old was she when you got her?" Then the funny ones asked by people who really didn't know Alex's parents well. "Are you getting your strength back, dear? She looks like you, Mary?" Alex stayed silent but thought, *duh people maybe my dad should have a talk with you about what adoption means like he did me. Melody didn't come out of my Mom's tummy. She was adopted, remember? My mother's fine. She didn't go through labor, whatever that is exactly, and are you breast feeding, Mary? I'll ask Dad about those two later.* But the one question that caused Alex to struggle and bite his lip was, "Is the baby sleeping through the night?" Alex remained quiet but wanted to burst out with, *hey, people, asking the wrong person there. Ask me! That would be a huge NO, she's not! And that means another huge NO, I'm not sleeping through the night either because of her crying, you know. I'm a growing boy who needs his rest, big time! I have to go to kindergarten, you know! Don't any of you care about me anymore?*

But the question Alex remembered most was only asked once by his Aunt Sara, a well-dressed, beautifully classy woman with a soft, gentle voice supporting her deep 'Southern Belle' accent. She was married to Alex's Uncle Harry, a wealthy and distinguished businessman; well-dressed with classic white hair combed straight back. Harry was, instinctually, Alex's hero from the first time they met. Aunt Sara placed her hand on Mary's knee and asked in her aristocratic fashion, "Tell me now, precious, do you have a wet nurse? Harry and I would be delighted to pay for one if you wish. We have some servants that would be perfect." Now that questioned puzzled Alex to no end. He had no idea what that meant. Why would a nurse get herself all wet? His curiosity instantaneously blew out of him like a whistle from a boiling tea kettle on a hot stove!

"What's a wet nurse, Mom?" he asked his mother and Aunt Sara.

"Now, sweetheart, that doesn't need to be any of your concern. That's just saved for talk between mommas, not for young, handsome men, like yourself," said Aunt Sara. Alex always loved the way Aunt Sara talked to him. She was nature's rendition of ultimate charm.

But Alex couldn't forget that question. He couldn't get rid of the picture of a woman dripping water on the floors all over the house. So, after everyone left, Alex approached his mother with his burning question eating at him like a hungry hamster from his insides.

"Mom, what did Aunt Sara mean by a wet nurse?" And why would she want to be wet all the time?" Mary looked at Randall with an undecided tilt of her head. Randall smiled back with a nod of his own.

"Mary, tell him. Don't be afraid. Nothing wrong with it. It's natural and we always said we wanted him to know the truth about everything. Go ahead, explain to him one of the most divine natural process' of life." Mary wasn't sure how to tell him. She was quite timid when it came to talking about things like that to Alex.

"Well Alex, God made women with breasts, like mine on my chest, so we can feed milk to our babies," Mary explained.

"I always wondered why mothers have bigger chests than fathers." Alex just learned something brand new! Mary continued as Alex made his short little observation.

"Yes, Alex. God makes milk inside of mother's chests to keeps our babies from getting sick with colds and things like that. I breast feed you for about six months and look how big and strong you are now." Mary handled that beautifully.

"God's pretty smart to do that. But how does it get out?" Alex was puzzled and Mary glanced at Randall for help. "But somehow it comes out then you put it in a carton and keep it in the fridge. Then when it's time for Melody to eat, you pour it in one of the bottles you put in her mouth. Do you add chocolate to it sometimes? Is that what I'm still drinking, Mom? Is that what's in the carton?" It was all making sense to Alex until Mary spoke again. Mary, but especially Randall, were trying hard not to laugh.

"No Alex, the baby puts its mouth on the end of the breast and sucks the milk straight out." Alex rethought his questions with his perplexed imagination running wild.

"Yuk Mom! I did that to you when I was as big as Melody, until you say about six months?" Alex didn't really want to think about it too deeply, but it was what he did and it was his mom. "But I still don't know what Aunt Sara meant by a wet nurse."

"Alex, a woman can only produce milk for their babies if they're pregnant and give birth to the child themselves. Since Melody was born by another woman, I have no milk to give her." Mary, again, felt pretty comfortable with her answer.

"That still doesn't answer my question about a wet nurse," Alex came back in a hurry. "Why is she all wet?"

"A 'wet nurse' is a woman that has just had a baby and the baby was either adopted by another family, like Melody, or her baby may have died in childbirth. Wet means the woman has milk; she's not dry. They then go to work feeding other people's babies and the family pays them money." Mary could see the look on Alex's face. He was disturbed.

"So, we're going to have somebody come in and feed Melody from her breasts, not yours?" asked Alex. "I think that's a little weird. I don't have to watch, do I, Mom?"

"Not weird at all, Alex, and no you don't have to watch," interjected Randall. "That's been going on since the cave-man days. But no, we'll be feeding Melody, as you've seen, from a bottle with a mixture of powdered milk and vitamins. Don't worry. We're not having a 'wet nurse'." Alex was feeling a bit appalled at the thought of breast feeding anyway, but especially by a stranger. However, at the same time, he was also feeling satisfied over the answer of the natural way God makes babies survive. His dad would be sure to point out the next female dog he saw feeding her puppies and when he did, Alex felt more at ease.

But, getting back to the visitors, besides the questions repeated over and over to his parents, there were the questions thrown at Alex over and over as well. Alex liked the questions at first; well at least he liked the attention. But, after a few hours of this interrogation, Alex thought *C'mon people, your questions aren't cute anymore; enough already.* He would rather be outside on his swing set.

"Do you like having a little sister, Alex?" *(Like I'm going to say no, duh.)* How old are you now, Alex? What grade are you in now, Alex? Oh, Alex you're getting so big. I remember when you were just a baby like your sister. I'm so sorry about your bird, Alex." Alex thought *Thanks for reminding me!*

But there was one statement that agitated Alex to no end and caused him to realize these conversations were merely attempts at social pleasantry. He came to realize nobody really cared how old, or what grade, or how dead his bird was, but Alex did come to realize they were, at least, trying to be nice.

But the attempted compliment of "Oh my, Alex, you're getting so handsome, just like your daddy." Then they'd rub Alex's head as if they were petting a furry dog and Alex would just smile as they walked off to talk to an adult with something interesting to say.

But as they walked off, each time Alex would think the same thing. *Are you blind, people? Look at me. I'm skinny. You can see all my ribs even through my shirt. My arms look like strings hanging from my sleeves. I was cute at one time, but now, I'm not cute at all, or handsome; you're not even in the ballpark; not even in the parking lot. Hey, let me give you a big smile. Have you checked out these two colossal buck teeth in the front here with the chasm between them that look like a seven-ten bowling split? And my ears, have you gotten a load of these? I look like a two-door sedan from behind with both its doors wide open. How about this very flattering burr haircut atop a head shaped like a peanut? And look at how funny my mother dresses me. Mom says I look "keen" in these clothes, like a miniature Frank Sinatra, whoever he is. So please, somebody just say it, please.* "Alex, you were so adorable the last time I saw you, so absolutely adorable! What happened? Did you get hit in the face by a school bus or something?"

After a while, even if Alex really knew and liked the visitors, he performed his social graces as he was taught, took their well-intended stock compliments with a smile, then snuck away to his room, grabbing a handful of cookies and brownies on his trek upstairs.

After a week or so, visitations tapered off and the holidays were swiftly approaching. There was no better time for Alex: food, presents, no school so he could sleep-in, Christmas trees, cookies, lights on houses, and most of all, Santa Clause! However, now with Melody around, this would be the last Christmas Santa would consider Alex the king. But Alex didn't know that yet.

TWO COUSINS STRIKE A DEAL THAT WILL LAST A COUPLE OF LIFETIMES

Time plodded on after Melody's arrival. Alex was getting bigger, but certainly not any cuter. He was now seven and a half, and he made sure everyone knew about that 'half'. It was a beautiful summer Sunday afternoon, with puffs of white clouds contrasted against the hue of a crisp blue sky. Sunday afternoons at Grandma and Grandpa Beckham's home became the traditional gathering place after church for the entire Beckham clan; Alex, his parents and sister, Randall's brother, Uncle Joe, his wife and his three boys (with one more to come), Grandma and Grandpa Beckham and Great Grandma Beckham. The feast was always fantastic and after dinner was playtime in the backyard while Alex's mother and his Aunt Estelle finished the dishes and cleaned the kitchen.

The whiffle ball game was the height of the boy's week. Alex smacked a shot over his cousin Michael's head into the neighbor's yard. As he slid into second base, Alex permanently embedded grass stains into the seat and knees of his new beige khaki's; the new ones his mother made him wear to Sunday School that morning. Then, like any routine base hit in Grandma Beckham's back yard, his cousin, with the ball in his hand, dove on top of Alex.

"You're out, Alex. I tagged you out," Michael yelled as he pulled his thumb into the air and over his shoulder with an umpire 'out' sign. Alex and Michael were both seven (and a half), only one month apart, and about the same size. But Michael had the advantage of fighting a lot more than Alex since he had his brother Johnny, four years older, to beat on.

"Not even close, Michael. You're a big cheater," returned Alex as he popped to his feet. Michael responded by wailing the whiffle ball as hard as he could, hitting Alex square on the cheek. Alex retaliated by tackling Michael and the two of them wrestled to the ground, rolling around in the grass, but as usual, neither of them trying to get in a punch of any kind.

Johnny, laughing with his chuck-chuck laugh like his dad, pulled Michael off Alex by the tee-shirt and flung him a few feet to the base of the concrete birdbath. "Really, tough guys? Knock it off. You're both so stupid. Let's just make it a do-over."

Grandma Beckham, sitting in the backyard swing with Melody on her lap, yelled to the kitchen. "Mary, Estelle, get out here and break this up. Michael and Alex are fighting again."

Mary and Estelle were close to finishing the dishes, but both mothers exploded through the door of the screened-in porch. By the time they arrived, it was all over. Johnny had seen to that. Alex's cheek was bright red with some nasty welts from the whiffle ball and both were breathing hard, their sweaty faces covered in brown dead grass. "Michael," Estelle yelled, "We've told you about Alex. He's a bleeder and you can't play as rough with him as you do your brother."

"And Alex, I've told you no fighting, not even if it's just your cousin and even if it's not your fault," scolded Mary.

"What makes you think it was Michael's fault, Mary? You think your boy's just this sweet little angel, and because he's a bleeder, he's some sort of 'Golden Boy'," said Estelle." He knows he can hide behind your skirt and get away with murder." Not only the boys, but all the other adults knew what was coming. Estelle and Mary had got into it before over Alex and Michael play wrestling like lion cubs on the savannah, in the snow, in the living room; and they were way more like brothers than cousins. They liked it that way, especially Alex.

'C'mon Estelle, you never have been able to control your boys. They back-talk you and tell you to 'go to hell' and you do nothing. If Alex ever said that to me, I'd spank his bottom so hard," responded Mary.

"Oh, so you can hit your little bleeder son, but nobody else can. Is that what you're saying? Hogwash Mary, hogwash," said Estelle. She was livid! "Get your things boys, we're going home. Joe get the boys in the car. I'll get little Joey's diaper bag and meet you there."

Johnny took aim at his mother. "Aww Mom, why is it everything is all fun and games until Alex gets hurt, then we all have to go home? And shoot Mom, he's not even hurt."

At that point, Michael and Alex intervened. "Aww, c'mon Mom, we're just playing. We argue after every play. Nobody gets hurt."

"C'mon Aunt Estelle, don't leave. I'm fine," Alex blurted.

"Well Alex, your cheek is as red as an apple, but doesn't look too swollen other than the welts. But what if that was a croquet ball, Alex. You might be dead. And your mother thinks Johnny and Michael are animals. Nope Alex, we have to go until my boys learn not to hurt you no matter whose fault it is." Estelle was settling down, but Mary wasn't. The fathers, like the rest of the Beckham men, avoided any confrontation with their wives, especially when it involved the children. They just continued to sit around the picnic table, talking about baseball and ignoring the whole thing.

"Honest Mom, I was out. That's what started it. We aren't mad at each other. We really do argue after every play. Please Mom, let us keep playing. I won't start a fight again." Michael looked at Alex with a smile.

"Really Mom," Michael said to his mother as he walked over

and put his arm around Alex's shoulder. "I won't do it again even if he does call me a cheater."

"I called you a big cheater, Michael," Alex said with a big grin. Michael returned the smile and gave Alex an affectionate brotherly shove.

"And I won't ever throw anything at him again. Shoot, we weren't even really mad at each other. And since he's a bleeder, I know you've told me to be careful with him." Johnny knew Michael and Alex would be pretty equal in a fight, but Michael was way more likely to throw a punch since that's what he had to do to his older brother at times to stop Johnny from kicking his butt.

"You saying you're tougher than me, Michael?" Alex wasn't going to let that pass unchallenged.

"C'mon Cuz, you know what I mean. You have a problem and you know it. It's not your fault. I mean we can wrestle all the time, but I promise I'll never hit you, ever in my life, not like I do Johnny. But you can't hit me either." Michael knew Alex didn't want to be babied and to make matters worse, Alex and Michael both agreed that Mary dressed Alex like a sissy. Michael and Alex made a lifelong promise that day and sealed it by licking their hands and slapping them together. Mary and Estelle, both thought that was pretty disgusting, but without smiling, both felt better about their sons' friendship.

Well, the two mothers never did get along, even before and after that day. Estelle would continue to put more and more distance between herself and Mary, and as a natural result, Alex. However, the deep consequences of that antagonistic relationship between the two mothers went unnoticed as to its influence on Alex. It was beyond both mothers' comprehension to even consider the subconscious feelings of that young boy. He could only conclude his Aunt Estelle never did and never would love him.

Anyway, the game was allowed to continue that day, and for many. many Sundays to come. And the cousins continued to get closer as the years went on, despite their mother's feud.

ALEX, THE QUESTION ASKING PINBALL
MACHINE

That same summer as the infamous whiffle ball game, Alex and his dad climbed into the car, doing one of the things they both loved most in life; running errands together in the family's 1953 green Ford Crestline. They were turning into good buddies.

This hot sunny afternoon in July was a scorcher. Randall had the Red's game blaring on the radio to overcome the sounds of the wind and traffic noise entering the car. Like most cars in the 1950's, the Ford had no A/C, so everyone cruised the streets with their windows down. Even the cozy wings turning the breeze onto Alex and his dad only created an additional blast of hot summer heat, like an electric hair dryer.

"Where'd you say we're going, Dad?" asked Alex.

"As far as your mother knows, we're going to the hardware store to get wood and nails to fix the garage door she ran into last week," responded Randall shaking his head as his lips transitioned into a smirk.

"She broke it. She should fix it, right? That's what you both always tell me when I break something," asked Alex.

Randall smiled differently this time as he took a quick glance at Alex next to him in the front seat. "Doesn't work that way with your mother, kid. But you have to promise to keep our little trip a secret. You don't keep secrets really well, you know." Randall pulled his sunglasses down and peaked at Alex over top of them.

"I promise, Dad, what is it? Tell me! C'mon, tell me!" Alex said with an excited pout. It was always fun when his dad told him secrets. But his dad was right. Alex was a blabber-mouth when it came to secrets.

"We're going to stop at Sears and Roebuck after the lumber store. I want to learn more about television sets, like how they work and how much they cost." Randall knew what was coming next.

"Oh wow, Dad! We're getting a television set. I can't wait to tell my friend Chuckie."

"Alex stop, it's a secret, remember? I don't want you and your mother to get all excited because we may not be able to afford one yet. So, it's a secret, promise?" Randall looked at Alex and made the 'Zip your lips' sign across his face. In reality, Randall knew Alex would blurt it out to his mother the first chance he had.

Alex was so excited he sat on the edge of the front seat, his forearms propped up on the hot metal dashboard. (This was way before the days of seat belts or air-bags. The only restraint in those days was the parental arm across a kid's chest at a quick stop.)

After Randall and Alex bought the materials to fix the garage, it was a long ride, light after traffic light, turn after turn, to the appliance store that carried televisions. Not many stores did in the 1950's since not many people could afford them. And they were so big, people didn't have a place to put them. Alex started thinking about his Grandma and Grandpa Beckham who had the only television he had ever seen outside of a store. But that train of thought from televisions to Grandma Beckham's house hit a switch and took Alex's brain onto a totally different track.

"Dad, how come Aunt Estelle doesn't like me?" Alex blurted, completely unexpected to Randall.

Randall responded with a weak giggle as he patted Alex on the knee. "What makes you think that, Alex! She loves you. We're family."

"She hardly ever talks to me and really pays no attention to me at all, unless Michael and I start fighting. But then again, neither do Grandma and Grandpa Beckham. I understand Great-Grandma Beckham, being as old as she is. She probably doesn't even know who the heck I am. She calls me Michael most of the time. But Aunt Estelle and Grandma are always holding and hugging Melody and Joey." Alex, more every day, was hurting from the change of being little, cute and an only child. He was growing-up and a whole new regime of cuties were invading the space which had always belonged to him, his sacred ground.

"Alex, your Aunt Estelle loves you, I'm telling you. But I can also tell you, you and I both know she's not too fond of your mother," Randall responded, not knowing whether he should involve Alex in that complicated maternal mess.

"No kidding! They do go at each other sometimes, but it usually has to do with me." Alex knew that was it. He was causing his Aunt Estelle to dislike him and his mother somehow, but how?

Randall was tolerant of Alex's feelings of neglect since Melody had arrived. Mary was not. Randall wanted to be cautiously sympathetic to this question of love from his highly emotional and loving son. "Well, it does have to do with you kinda, but not really, Tiger. I know that sounds confusing to you right now. The odd thing is they both love you, but your mom gets scared when you and Michael and Johnny start wrestling. She's afraid somebody, especially you, is going to get hurt."

"But Dad, Michael and I promised with a spit-slap that we'd wrestle but never hit each other. And Johnny, shoot, I'd never punch him. He's bigger than me. He just laughs and holds me upside down by my feet whenever I even try to tackle him." Alex was confused. Randall laughed over the sight of Alex hanging upside down by his feet.

"No, no kid, You're still missin' it. Aunt Estelle's not afraid of you hurting her boys, she's afraid they'll hurt you and you'll bleed to death," Randall knew as soon as 'bleed to death' came out of his mouth that Alex was not going to take that well.

"Whoa, I know you all call me a bleeder, but did you just say I could 'bleed to death'? I've cut myself and fallin' down and bled before, a lot, but it always stops. Could I really die from it?" Alex was starting to understand a little more about death, but hadn't ever contemplated his own. "No way, Dad. I'm not going to die from it, am I?"

"Alex, anyone can bleed to death, even me if I got hurt bad enough, like a car accident or shot or something like that," Randall responded.

"You're not going to ever get in a car accident are you, Dad? And who would want to shoot you?" Alex was getting scared and going way too far in the wrong direction. His Dad needed to reel him in from this disturbing course of thought and back to Aunt Estelle, or really, back to the television sets they were going to explore.

"No, Alex, that's not the point and no, I'm not going to get in a car accident and no, no one is going to shoot me." Randall was getting firm with his son Alex, the little question machine, trying to put the brakes on this runaway bus of inquisition.

"Okay, if I'm not going to die, then I still don't understand why Aunt Estelle is so mean to me." Alex was clouding up from the thought of dying, his father dying and his Aunt Estelle hating him, all in the last minute or so.

"Alex, Aunt Estelle's so scared Johnny or Michael are going to hurt you as you're all just playing and rough-housing like normal boys, she and your mother are ready to blame each other if you do get hurt. Have you noticed, Aunt Estelle only scolds her own boys, and your mother only scolds you? Aunt Estelle loves you and doesn't want you to get hurt, but in so doing, she ignores you so she won't get close and feel bad if you do; or get your mother mad at her. I know it sounds bewildering. Just trust me on this one. Are you getting it yet?"

"No, well kind of, maybe. What if I talk to Aunt Estelle and tell her I'd never blame her or my cousins if I got hurt, would she hug me and talk to me then?" Randall was on the spot.

"Alex, your Aunt Estelle seems mean at times, especially when it comes to her boys, even Uncle Joe at times and, of course, your mother. She has three boys now and Joey is a baby the same age as Melody. Your Uncle Joe, my brother, was in World War II and survived not only the war and him being killed, but he almost died from malaria as well."

"What's malaria?" asked Alex. Randall knew Alex never ran out of questions. Probably why his favorite books would always be encyclopedias.

"It's caused by mosquito bites, but not the mosquitos around here, so no, don't worry, you won't get malaria. Uncle Joe was what they call 'a foot soldier' in the jungles of the Philippine Islands, a long, long way from here." Randall needed to add that in a hurry to avoid Alex's paranoia over another something new that could kill him.

"Is that when we fought the Japs?" asked Alex.

We'll yes, but we call them…" Randall began.

"Okay, you mean the 'gooks' then. That's what Michael and Johnny call them," Alex interrupted. In his heart, Randall knew he must excuse his nephews because he knew that term came from his brother. He knew it was a whole different thought process for his brother towards the Japanese since he fought ferociously against them in his youth and saw a lot of death and hate in that jungle warfare.

"No son, those aren't nice names to call them anymore. We now refer to them as Japanese. We kinda forgave each other and are now friends, so we don't call each other names. But it's sometimes hard for soldiers to forget what happened on the battlefield since they were there." Randall was doing his best to avoid the planting of any racial seeds in the psyche of Alex's developing sponge of a mind.

"So, is that why Uncle Joe goes crazy in the recliner sometimes when he takes a nap after dinner and snores really loud? That's scary and too creepy for me to watch!" Alex vented.

"That's the reason, son," replied Randall. Many soldiers come back with what they call 'Shell Shock.' They have memories that emerge when they're dreaming or if you've ever noticed, we're not allowed to set off firecrackers around him on the Fourth of July."

"Yea, and when somebody does set them off in the neighborhood, he turns the radio up really loud and Aunt Estelle holds his hand." Alex was beginning to understand. "So when Uncle Joe falls asleep after dinner sometimes and snores like a growling bear, he sometimes dreams about the war. That's when you and Johnny and Grandpa hold him down while Aunt Estelle shoves that needle through his pants and then he settles down. Grandma and Mom do get all us little kids out of the room in a hurry, thank goodness!" Alex's voice was bearing signs of fear just remembering those times he watched his Uncle Joe go crazy.

"Aunt Estelle gives him an injection called a sedative that settles him down. It helps Uncle Joe's terrible memories to go away, at least for a while." Alex was listening closely.

"Wow! Uncle Joe was a real war hero! I never knew a real hero that was still alive. Aunt Carrie told me I had a great great Grandfather a long time ago in someplace called Prussia who was a war hero, but Uncle Joe is too; that's neat!"

"Be proud of him, Alex," Randall said with an obvious look of pride on his face. "My brother fought hard for all of us and your Aunt Estelle takes good care of him."

"Wow, do you have any pictures of him in his soldier uniform, like with his guns and knives and stuff? That would be neat to put them on my wall." Alex knew just where he wanted to put them.

"We do, but most soldiers don't talk much about the wars they were in. I only asked him once and he told me in an angry voice to shut up and never ask him about it again and that was strange because he never got mad at me. I was his little brother and we were close friends," responded Randall.

"I'll be sure not to ask him then," responded Alex. "I don't want him not to like me too, like Aunt Estelle. I wish I had a big brother. Johnny's like the closest I'll ever have." Randall needed to avoid that whole other topic.

"Alex, I know we just took the long way around to answer your question, but I'm going to say it only one more time and then we move on." Randall had done all he could and was getting frustrated, maybe because he understood Alex's confusion. Estelle didn't treat him very lovingly and Randall knew that. "Aunt Estelle loves you, but like I said, she just has so much, with two older boys, a baby, and Uncle Joe to worry about, she just doesn't have a lot of time for you or Melody." With that Randall fluffed Alex's hair.

"I guess you're right. I heard her say to Grandma when she asked her if she wanted to hold Melody one time 'No, I don't know what to do with a little girl. You keep her'. (Melody told Alex later in life she thought the same, that Aunt Estelle was mean and always scared her.)

"Strange thing Alex, she never had a baby girl. None of the Beckham mothers have for three generations." Randall needed to sum it up.

"No girls, really?" Alex asked in another state of confusion.

"Nope, all boys, no girls. Now let's stop this and leave it at your Aunt Estelle loves you and she just doesn't show it well. And I'd suggest you not talk to her about it. I do have to agree with you though, she's not the warmest person I know, but then neither is your grandma or your mom. But they all love you."

So, Alex didn't really buy his Dad's logical reflection on the situation. He held tight to the conclusion that his Aunt Estelle didn't love him or care for him much. Only a few times, when Alex came through the kitchen to use the bathroom and Aunt Estelle and his grandma were preparing dessert did she show him any affection, and that wasn't a hug. She'd just shove an enormous spoonful of ice cream through his lips or squirt a shot of whipped cream from the aerosol can into his mouth, which sometimes, hilariously spewed out Alex's nose. "Don't tell your mother or anybody about this, it's our secret, Pumpkin." She would then smile, kiss Alex on the forehead, and go back to her preparation.

Now Alex was beginning to grasp the fact that his bleeding condition may have an impact on his life and his relationships. *I don't want to be treated differently because they call me a 'bleed-er.' I hate it. I don't want to be treated like a girl. They're not putting me in a bubble,* he thought to himself. And it was at this stage, Alex realized he was going to be the 'black sheep' of the family, needing to work and fight smart, not hard, and certainly not violent. And he lived most of his life with the remembrance that only his father, Melody, his Grandma Schaefer, and his great great aunts were the only people who ever truly loved him.

2008 – Fifty years later

A LOT OF WATER HAS FLOWED UNDER THAT BRIDGE

In 2008, Alex was now fifty-seven and had more than learned how to work and fight smart, protecting himself from critical injury without giving up his self-respect and the respect of others. His dream of being a successful businessman like his Uncle Harry had come true. His Uncle Joe, and all of his grandparents had died of heart attacks, strokes or cancer. All of them died by age seventy primarily due to diet, obesity, lack of exercise, and most of all, cigarettes. But Estelle died at age eighty, outliving all but Alex's father, despite the horrible self-inflicted damage inflicted on her lungs every day since her first cigarette at age fourteen.

It was a cold and uneventful morning approaching the end of winter. As Alex was preparing for a monthly board meeting, a call displaying no caller I.D. appeared on the private line in his office. The number appeared with a long-distance area code, unrecognized by Alex.

Rarely did an unidentified call come directly to his private line and when one did, Alex would immediately flip it to voicemail. But sometimes, in rare incidents, when he was in an arrogant or annoyed mood, Alex would answer the call just to play with the poor cold caller. "Alex Beckham, how can I help you?" Alex answered in his dignified voice as President/CEO of his company, attempting to foil any confident counter- attack from the salesperson.

"You sound all grown up, Cuz!" was the answer followed by an unmistakable chuck-chuck laugh.

"Oh my goodness, Johnny, how are you, big guy? It's great to hear your voice. Wish I could give you a hug and wrestle you to the ground right here on the floor. Tell me you're coming to Cincinnati for a visit!" Alex was so excited he could hardly talk as he chocked to hold back his tears. "We haven't hung out in ten years, not since your dad died. How are you? How's the family?"

"Alex, I so want to chat and catch-up, but right now, I have to get straight to my reason for calling. Mom was just admitted to the intensive care unit at Christ Hospital. Her lungs have finally giving out from her chain-smoking and she's in Stage IV emphysema. They're giving her only two to three days, Alex. She just can't absorb enough oxygen, even with a mechanical ventilator." Johnny was talking fast and his voice was quivering intensely.

"Aunt Estelle's at Christ Hospital? What can I do to help? Anything." Alex was now feeling the anxiety injected into his stomach by Johnny's voice.

"I can't get a flight out of Tampa until tomorrow morning, arriving tomorrow afternoon about 2:00. I need you to go over and check on her and get back to me as soon as you can," Johnny asked in a pleading manner, even though he knew he didn't have to with Alex.

"I'll leave right now. I only have one meeting and can easily push it back to whenever," responded Alex without hesitation. "What about your brothers?"

"Michael has some sort of family problem in Atlanta and he can't leave until later tonight, so he'll drive up and be there by morning," said Johnny.

"And Joey?" asked Alex.

"He's on some hunting trip in Michigan with his buddies and

the cabin doesn't have a telephone. But he calls his wife from a diner pay phone down the road every day or so, and she's going to tell him what's going on," Johnny explained.

"And Patrick?" asked Alex.

"Patrick? Really Alex. He'd probably suffocate her with her pillow to get the inheritance a couple days earlier. You think he was weird when Dad died; he's gotten worse." Johnny's voice had turned as a twinge of hate and disgust entering his tone.

"Oh, Johnny, that's terrible. I don't get it. He was always a bit strange, but not like that," Alex replied.

"Drugs, man, he gets high every day, pot, cocaine, acid. Mom told me he's getting worse, even finding a few syringes in the garbage from time to time. She's offered to pay for his rehab, but Patrick just steals her money and hops from job to job. His last job, he cashed his paycheck, told them he lost it, they issued him another one and he cashed it as well. That idiot really didn't think he'd get caught. Luckily, no charges were pressed, they just fired him because they knew Dad from a long time ago. Hope that doesn't hurt the Beckham name for you in any way." Johnny was getting angrier as the conversation lengthened.

"Don't worry about me. What can I do, Johnny? Tell me." Alex waited restlessly.

Johnny began his assumption. "Since Patrick lives with Mom, I'm sure he knows she's in the hospital. But if I know him, he's telling his new boss his mother is dying so he can go home and get high without Mom knowing it."

"Okay, but Johnny, I still don't know exactly what you want me to do?" asked Alex.

"Cuz, this is what I'm asking of you. I'm truly afraid he'd do whatever he could to end her life if he knew how. I'm sure he's plotting it right now. I need you to go to the hospital, guard Mom for me as long as you can and protect her from Patrick." Johnny expressed his instructions to Alex succinctly.

"I'll stay all night until Michael arrives in the morning, Johnny," replied Alex.

"No, probably just until visiting hours end tonight. But make sure you get there first thing in the morning when visiting hours start. By tomorrow morning sometime Michael will be there. But I also want you to talk to the head nurses, administrator, whoever you need to and tell them of this possible threat to Mom's life. Tell them no one can visit her outside of visiting hours and if Patrick sneaks in, have that son-of-a bitch arrested. Got it?" Johnny had now raised his anger level to life threatening; the life of Patrick that is.

"Got it Johnny. I'll call your wife with any news and you call her since we both may not be able to reach each other by telephone. Can Jill do that or is she out of town?" asked Alex.

"No, she's fine and we have an answering machine I can check remotely." Johnny and Alex had set the plan in motion.

"I'll call you in a few hours after I visit with her, Johnny. I'm so sorry for all of you! Trust that I'll take good care of Aunt Estelle. Be safe and see you tomorrow. Love you, my man!" Alex said goodbye and disconnected. He went for his suit coat and rushed to be with his aunt as soon as he could. Suddenly, on the way to his car in the parking lot, he began to cry, not only for Aunt Estelle, but because of all the wonderful memories they all had growing-up.

AND THEIR TEARS MELTED TOGETHER

Alex's contact with his aunt had been sparse over the last few decades. Johnny and Michael had moved away, and Alex, although still in the area, had a family of his own. The days of the Grandma Beckham Sundays had slowly faded into a sweet memory for the boys; only funerals brought them together. And even during those gatherings, like the old days, Alex's Aunt Estelle said few words to him. She was usually busy talking to everyone else, then cooking at the wakes. To Alex, even observing her fifty years later, the pain from her lack of love still hollowed the heart of that little boy from the 1950's.

Adversely, there was no lack of camaraderie and brotherly love among the cousins, especially, Alex, Johnny, and Michael. Joey and Melody had been six years younger in those golden years and not mutually involved in the same activities as the three older boys. And Patrick, eleven years younger than Alex, had truly turned to the black, if not the charred and damaged sheep of the family. His appearance manifested the look of a languid bum just leaving an opium den, checks indented, skin tone a cadaverous gray, and any discussions with him had only to do with carp fishing or the borrowing of money. Then Patrick topped it off by asking Alex's twenty-two-year old daughter, Patrick's second cousin, out on a date. Alex held his daughter's wrist to keep her from slapping him.

· · ·

Alex sped to the hospital and arrived within thirty minutes of Johnny's call. As he found his way up elevators and through a maze of hallways, he was immersed with emotions closing in from all directions. The smells reminded him of his numerous hospital stays as a child, a teenager and even into his adulthood. All having to do with some sort of injury and bleeding problem. There were some scary moments in Alex's life, but he learned to survive on his own from those first touches with death as a young boy.

Mixed with his own medical memories, he was still pleasantly obsessed with those days of his cousins and their crazy escapades, many remaining forever unknown to their parents. But the closer he came to his Aunt Estelle's room in the intensive care unit, the more he felt alone and unloved, that same feeling he had as a child around her. The only memory he cherished was the big bites of ice cream and squirts of whipped cream followed by a sweet Aunt

Estelle kiss, like a cherry on top of his little forehead.

Knocking on the door lightly with his knuckle, he gently inquired "Aunt Estelle?" as he moved slowly towards her bedside. Her eyes were closed. Her body, pale and frail. She wasn't the same woman Alex remembered telling his mother 'Hogwash' in Grandma Beckham's back yard fifty years ago" An IV was inserted into her left arm and multiple wires streamed out from under her worn hospital gown, all attached to electrodes pasted strategically over her torso. The critical sounds of clicks and beeps and the forced breathing machine filled this soothingly lit room, continually assuring the nurses she was still alive.

Inserted down her throat was an endotracheal tube hooked to a breathing apparatus, allowing her blackened lungs to absorb enough oxygen to keep her barely alive. Alex loathed the sound of that machine; the constant pulsating was the only thing keeping his Aunt from passing on in his presence. Obviously, she couldn't speak, not even a peep.

As her eyes remained closed, Alex just watched her and let her rest. She seemed beyond pain and at peace. Obviously, Patrick, even if he had visited, had not changed his Aunt Estelle's condition. Alex's eyes began to swell with sorrow. He wanted to cry right then and there, but he didn't. His emotions just choked his throat like a tight collar on a droopy hound dog. He was flashing back to those early days, when he would cry over something at Grandma Beckham's house (and Alex did cry more than the average kid) and his Aunt Estelle would say, "Alex is crying again. Get the bucket and put it around his neck to catch the tears." That, of course, didn't help back then, quite the opposite. His early masculinity was competing with his tough-guy cousins, not to mention crying in front of his Uncle Joe, the war hero. So Alex remained quiet as not to wake her, at least until he got control over this first blast of love and sentiment. He didn't want her to awaken to his tear-filled countenance.

After a few moments, Alex gathered himself. With love in

his heart, he gently approached her bedside and ever so softly squeezed her hand while giving her a delicate kiss on her forehead. He was sure she would be kind to him, but he also knew she would feel a touch of disappointment when it was him and not one of her sons. Her eyes-lids fluttered a few times before they opened wide enough for her to recognize her nephew who, although he had aged gracefully, his eyes were still the same innocent eyes she loved fifty years. Without hesitation, Estelle smiled and squeezed back with beautiful affection.

"How are you, Aunt Estelle? Aww, it's so good to see you. It's been a long time. Looks like they're taking good care of you." Alex was desperately at a loss for the proper thing to say. He felt what he said was trite but it was a beginning.

She nodded her head with a smile, and after a few excruciating coughs from deep in her lungs, she pointed to the tube and shook her head no. She was trying to tell Alex, of course, that the tube blocked her from talking to him at all. She looked directly into Alex's eyes with a benevolent stare, one he had never seen before. She then pressed the button for the nurse to join them.

For a split second when she pushed that button, a burst of panic cascaded with a shiver through Alex's body. "Are you okay, Aunt Estelle? Is there something wrong? Can I get you something?" She held one finger up in the air, motioning for him to be patient, then pointed to a pen and a pad of paper on her nightstand. "You want the pen and paper?" She nodded yes. Alex made his way to the other side of the bed, picked them up, and placed them in her jittery hands. She then pointed for the table that extended over the bed. He rolled it over and positioned it in front of her so she could write. Alex elevated the bed to a semi-sitting posture and with that she began jotting something on the note pad. The nurse came in and watched her as she finished writing down what she desired. She handed the note to the nurse.

The nurse looked at her. "This is your nephew, Alex?" Estelle nodded. The nurse glanced at Alex and smiled, then looked back at Estelle with a very serious and questioning look. "You're sure about this, Mrs. Beckham? This will be extremely painful, both in and out. You know that, right?" Estelle looked at Alex with a reassuring beam on her face and without hesitation, nodded her head yes, keeping her eyes on Alex the entire time.

The nurse proceeded to move the table, strategically positioning herself next to the bed. She then, quickly and rather violently, without a word, yanked the tube from Estelle's esophagus, all in one quick motion. The machines went crazy, making terrible beeps screeching and bells ringing. Another nurse came running in the door urgently, but quickly deduced what was happening and was given reassurance by the nurse removing the tube that everything was under control. Estelle was making frightful sounds of agony: her gagging was horrid; her body tensing in struggle, her lungs coughing tortuously from deep inside. But, thank goodness, the tube was removed so quickly Estelle was able to gather herself in a short period of time, taking deep breaths and trying to relax her body. Alex could hear the sound of her lungs gurgling viciously as she coughed up small amounts of blood into the gauze held to her mouth by the nurse. She pointed to a cup of water, and the nurse held the straw to her lips. She sipped slowly.

Alex held his Aunt's hand the whole time. She had squeezed tightly during the removal, at least as tightly as her feeble hand could squeeze, but now their grip was returning to placid. After what seemed like eternity, she finally spoke in a weak and raspy voice. "Come closer, Alex, please. Bring your ear close to my lips. I can't talk very loud." She clutched his hand tighter again as she pulled him close. He leaned down to an angle where now their cheeks were touching. Her hand went gentle again. "I never told you this when you were a little boy, but I loved you so much back then, and I'm so proud of you today, in so many ways." She reached up and held Alex's cheek with the palm of her hand, pressing it into her own. Alex did the same, pressing her cheek to his. They both kissed each other's faces with pure devotion.

Alex whispered in her ear, "I love you too, Aunt Estelle. You were one of the most important people in my life growing up. And you have no idea how important your love means to me." Tears rolled down both their cheeks and melted together in a single stream of affection. It was a moment both would cherish for the rest of their lives and beyond.

Alex's aunt asked a few more three-word questions like "How's your Dad? How's Melody? How're your children?" Alex did most of the talking, but it soon became obvious Estelle was appearing very pale and very weary. Alex pushed the button for the nurse without his Aunt Estelle realizing he had done so. It was time.

The nurse returned to the room with a controlled look of panic on her face. She could see clearly that her patient needed oxygen and right away. "Mr. Beckham, I think it would be wise to reinsert the tube for your aunt, then you can return and talk more if you wish." Alex nodded and the nurse knew he agreed. "This time, I must insist you leave the room. We have had people faint watching us reinsert, and frankly, we can't take care of you until we're finished with your aunt."

"I understand completely. Aunt Estelle. Your sons will be here within the next twenty-four hours," Estelle gazed over at the nurse with a frightened look. It was then she realized without a doubt her days were coming to an end. "I'll be back shortly. I need some lunch anyway. Get some rest, dear. I'll be around all day if you need me. I love you, Aunt Estelle!" It felt so good to say those words out loud after all those years. Alex kissed her one more time on the cheek and Estelle waved to Alex, but only with four weak fingers. She was unable to lift her feeble arm from the mattress top.

But Alex didn't go directly to the cafeteria. He needed to stand guard outside her room until he could address the situation of Patrick with the necessary authorities. The gagging and grunting from the tube being reinserted into Estelle's throat was over the edge of restraint for Alex. He began to weep again. He couldn't imagine the pain she was enduring all so she could finally express her love to him, her beloved nephew.

Within ten minutes, the agonizing chaos within the room quieted and Alex could hear all of the machines returning to their normal beeps and blips. As the nurse left the room, Alex stopped her. "Ma'am, may I speak with you for a few moments in regards to a very difficult and embarrassing subject for my family?" The nurse gave Alex a nod, expressing a puzzled look. She would soon be dealing with something neither of them could have ever imagined.

ALEX CONVINCES THE HOSPITAL OF DANGER HE PUTS A PROTECTION PLAN IN PLACE FOR HIS HELPLESS AUNT ESTELLE

The nurse led Alex to a small conference room at the entrance of the intensive care unit as he had asked to speak to the head nurse. He asked the nurse to block any visitors from his aunt's room until he returned. She curiously agreed.

He pensively pondered whether his need for discussion was being exaggerated. He had not spoken with Patrick in quite some time, and never anything connected with their relationship as cousins in any significant fashion during their youth. But Johnny had sounded as if the situation had the possibility of a grave and tumultuous outcome. Having remained in touch with his parents for years, Johnny was well aware of Patrick's ability to manipulate Estelle's enabling weakness. Alex promised Johnny he would make sure Estelle was safe until he and Michael arrived. As Alex sat in a chair around the conference table, retying his shoe string, a strong nurse with a cold stare entered the room, looking rather put out that she was being interrupted from her tasks on the floor.

"Sir, I understand you have something you feel is of grave importance in regards to your aunt. She's your aunt and not your mother, is that correct?" Alex put on his business face so he at least had a chance of matching her pomposity.

Alex quickly finished tying his shoe and stood as he greeted the nurse with dignity and respect. "Yes, that is correct. My name is Alex Beckham and I'm here to carry out a request from my cousin, John Beckham, Estelle Beckham's oldest son. And you are?"

With a slight sigh, the nurse responded, "My name is Cynthia Roseman, the head nurse of the intensive care unit on the daytime shift this week. If you're going to ask me to take special care of your aunt like every other relative of our patient's asks, I'll stop you right there and make this brief. We take special care of all our patient in this hospital, especially the intensive care unit. Your aunt's in wonderful hands."

Alex began to respond. "Oh, no, that's not it at all. It's---"

"Then what is it, sir? I really must get back to the floor," the nurse snapped.

"A possible, or should I say probable, attempt at euthanasia has been plotted towards Estelle Beckham," blurted Alex.

"Sir, we can stop right here. Euthanasia is considered murder in this state, and way beyond that, no matter how desperate a patient's condition may be, no one on this hospital staff would ever consider an action like that. If she has a 'Living Will' yes, euthanasia no. Your aunt is able to communicate, therefore the 'Living Will' is not applicable at this point in her condition." Ms. Roseman stood like a soldier at attention and was about to spin and leave the room.

"Wait please, Nurse Roseman. You're misunderstanding my intentions. There is a real possibility that my youngest cousin, her son, may make an attempt on her life. Please hear me out," Alex pleaded.

"Frankly sir, why would he do that? I'm sorry to say, truly, but we don't believe your aunt will survive the week. Her lungs are showing the first stages of shutting down, as well as the circulation in her legs. We have already put hospice on alert." Nurse

Roseman knew she was already overstepping her confidentiality limits, but at this stage, and with Alex's professional appearance, she felt safe.

"Nurse Roseman, my cousin Patrick, should we say, is not quite right. He may even be psychopathic. He's forty-seven, still lives with my aunt, has been in drug rehab three times, and is a convicted felon on numerous fraud charges." Alex was short and to the point.

"But why in the world do you think he wants to kill his mother? Any inheritance he'll receive will come to him soon. He must know her condition, Mr. Beckham." Nurse Roseman was not feeling truly concerned.

"Nurse Roseman, I've been thinking that same thing. Why doesn't he just wait?" Suddenly an idea popped into Alex's head. "Nurse Roseman, the last time my cousin was in rehab, his brother told me he almost OD'd on heroine laced with fentanyl. He still has that look of a crack-head. I'd assume he has access to those drugs through his circle of friends. He has, in no way, cleaned himself up." Alex looked at the puzzled nurse.

"I still don't … Oh wait a minute. Malpractice! You're thinking his motive is to over medicate her or somehow cause a machine to malfunction so she dies at our hands and at the very least, the family gets an extra chunk from the insurance company, in or out of court. Now that's possible." Nurse Roseman was now paying attention. If something did happen now, she would be blamed for ignoring Alex's warnings. And Alex knew that as well. The last thing she wanted was to cause the hospital to depose her and under oath she would need to admit she was aware of a threat to one of her patient's life. That would be at the least, and at worst, malpractice.

"Mr. Beckham, what do you suggest?" asked the suddenly cooperative nurse. "But remember, by the time a plan would get through our bureaucracy, I'm afraid it may be too late."

Nurse Roseman and Alex began a discussion that would not

compromise either Estelle's health or her desire to visit with all family, especially all her sons here in these final days of her life.

"Mr. Beckham, we do have the authority as nurses to declare limited visiting hours, even though generally, we don't. We can also limit the number allowed in the room at any one time," suggested Nurse Roseman.

"I promised her oldest son I would guard his mother until he arrived from Florida tomorrow afternoon or until his brother Michael arrived sometime tomorrow morning from Atlanta. What if, for now, we limit visiting hours to be say, eight a.m. to eight p.m.? That way you can turn Patrick away starting this evening at eight, and if he comes before eight p.m., I can be in the room with him during his entire visit." Alex had what seemed to be a viable plan.

"Yes, we can do that as well. If he arrives after eight tonight, security will be warned and instructed to turn him away." Nurse Roseman and Alex were both on the same page.

"But to be sure, even though we limited those visiting hours for tonight, please permit me to sleep in her room in a recliner or something. My cousins and I, except for Patrick, have always been more like brothers. I refuse to let them down. My Aunt Estelle must be protected. Patrick's rather devious. He could still find a way to sneak in and out without any of us knowing it. Then, bingo, malpractice suit." Alex was methodical and earnest with Nurse Roseman and she appreciated his dedication.

"Mr. Beckham, as embarrassed as I am to ask this, can I talk to one of your cousins to be sure you're not the one conning me?" Alex smiled.

"Absolutely, I'll give you both their numbers and you can call them now. That makes sense. You're correct. I could be the threat and not Patrick. Shoot, I could be Patrick!" Alex put his hand on top of Nurse Roseman's. "Let me write the numbers down for you and you can call both of them right away." Alex took out his wallet and showed the nurse his driver's license and credit cards to confirm his identity. "But in the meantime, allow me to return to my aunt's room to guard her, accompanied by one of your nurses, at least until you confirm my intentions with my cousins."

• • •

Nurse Roseman made the calls and all was confirmed. Johnny, Michael and Alex's stories jived. The plan was set in place. Alex explained to Estelle the concerns of her other boys and the need for him to stay with her until after her sons arrive. Estelle understood the reasoning, but Alex could see in her eyes, the sadness and motherly pain piercing her soul from the disappointment in her youngest boy.

The night reached eight and the only visitors were Estelle's younger sister and her husband. There was no sign of Patrick. The hospital brought dinner, a recliner and, at Estelle's request, a TV on rollers. Alex called Johnny and explained the plan and for the moment all was tranquil. Alex sat in the recliner next to her bed and held her hand most of the night. He wondered whether the recliner brought back memories of Uncle Joe's seizures for Estelle, because it certainly did for him.

THE NIGHT WENT WELL BUT THE MORNING, OH THE MORNING!

The next morning, the soft bluish-gray light of a cloudy day entered the room at dawn. Estelle was resting comfortably. Alex had had a surprisingly peaceful night as well, with the exception of the nurse's routine rounds which caused his heart to pound a few beats faster whenever the door opened. The floor nurse entered the room and asked Alex what she could bring him for breakfast. The entire nursing staff, as well as hospital security, were aware of the possible threat to Estelle's safety.

Suddenly, at eight thirty AM, before Alex's breakfast arrived, a somewhat anxious young nurse, slightly out of breath, briskly entered the room.

"Mr. Beckham, security at the front desk just informed us your cousin Patrick is on his way up to see his mother. I thought you might want to know," said the nurse. Estelle was still asleep and didn't hear her announcement.

Before Alex had time to mentally prepare for any possible confrontation, Patrick entered the room with a smile that combined both sympathy and concern. He was wearing a worn, dirty pair of jeans and what appeared to be motorcycle boots. He had a black "Metallica" tee-shirt covered by a wrinkled sports coat made of a putty-colored linen. Alex was stunned by Patrick's cheeks, which had been hollowed by his years of self-abuse, accentuated by his greasy scalp and ungroomed facial hair. It reminded him of a pirate's head made from a coconut, belonging to his uncle during his childhood. Alex was uncomfortable.

"Alex, I'm surprised to see you here so early. My brothers maybe, but not you." Patrick gave Alex a weak obligatory hug. As he did, Alex wondered how long it had been since Patrick had bathed, and the combination of body odor and the residue of pot smoke caused Alex to back off with a twinge of shock. He felt like he had just discovered a homeless man under newspapers in the park.

"Johnny called me yesterday. I was the only one that could get here right away. He said he tried your number, but he couldn't get ahold of you," replied Alex without emotion, knowing that was really not the case at all.

"Well, that's odd, but I was working on a project and finished it past visiting hours last night. You must have arrived right at eight o'clock this morning, Alex. Thank you for your dedication to my mother, but you can leave now. I have this under control. And I would like to spend some time alone with her." Patrick had an almost convincing look of genuine love on his face.

"No, that's okay Patrick, I can stick around for a while." Alex sounded nonchalant and sincere. The game was on.

"Alex, I want to spend time alone with her before my brothers arrive. She's my mother, not yours," Patrick said with a frown, upset over Alex's lack of cooperation. Alex felt the first confirmed pang of suspicion and danger for his aunt.

"No, that's okay, Patrick, really. Michael will be here sometime this morning, and I told him I would be here when he arrived," Alex said politely.

"What time did he say, Alex?" Patrick inquired.

"Oh, he's driving from Atlanta, so with traffic, like I said, I'd think sometime this morning, maybe anytime." Alex suspicion continued to swell within. *Why the question about Michael's arrival time and the need for alone time?*

"Is there anything else the two of you need?" asked the young nurse, who had delayed her departure to observe the initial arrival of Patrick. "If not, I need to attend to other patients, but just press the button and I'll be here right away. And Mr. Beckham, your breakfast will arrive shortly."

"Oh, thank you. You have been good to my aunt all night. It's so appreciated." With that, Patrick gave Alex a perplexed glare.

"I thought visiting hours started at eight o'clock. What do you mean 'all night'? And why are they bringing you breakfast? What's going on here, Alex? Something's a little fishy." Patrick stared Alex down with a dangerous squint of his brows.

"Nothing's going on, Patrick. I just meant they told me she rested well all night, and I was thanking her for it. And I got here a little early and they offered me breakfast, that's all." Patrick gave Alex one more ugly stare, then turned to his mother, squeezing her hand just gently enough to wake her.

Estelle opened her eyes and saw her youngest son standing over her with an unusual smile on his face, for Patrick. She squeezed his hand back, and he kissed her on the cheek. As he did, he whispered in her ear, "Everything's going to be alright, Mom. I'll make sure of it. You'll not be suffering much longer."

Alex was unable to hear the whisper, but Estelle looked at Alex, confirming Patrick was definitely up to something. And even though Estelle knew she had only a few days left in her life, her strong desire to survive revolved around seeing all of her sons to say her final goodbyes. But Patrick knew his task would need to be done before his brothers arrived.

Patrick proceeded to tell her he was taking good care of the house and he was feeding her dog regularly. He then turned to Alex and again asked for some alone time with his mother, but Alex refused. Patrick realized at that point that his brothers had instructed Alex to protect her from him.

As Patrick stood to the right side of his mother as she partially reclined in her bed, Alex stood at the foot. Patrick again whispered something in his mother's ear and simultaneously pulled a syringe from his right coat pocket.

"Patrick, what's that?" asked Alex, as Estelle saw the syringe as well. Her eyes widened in fear.

Patrick looked at his mother and said, "I told you, your suffering and pain will not be for much longer. I'm going to put you to rest."

"Patrick, no!" Alex yelled, as he moved quickly around the bedside. Patrick pulled the recliner instinctively between them, blocking Alex's attack.

"I told you, Alex, she's not your mother, she's mine. You're just her wussy, cry-baby nephew. You think you're going to stop me. How you think you're gonna to do that, old man? You gonna bleed all over me? I assume you're still a bleeder." Patrick was now worse than Alex ever imagined. Patrick's brothers were right. He was insane.

With his left hand, Alex lunged over the recliner and grabbed Patrick's sickly wrist with the hand holding the syringe. The struggle began. Estelle fumbled for the call button, but Patrick had conveniently knocked it off her bed and kicked it underneath. Patrick knew that Alex, though older, was stronger and had more stamina than him. Patrick also knew Alex was not going to allow him to force that nameless potion of his into his mother. But suddenly, Patrick pulled a switch blade out of his left pocket, opened it quickly and slit deeply across Alex's right shoulder blade, then painfully down into his one tricep. Alex's white shirt was immediately drenched in blood.

"How do you like that, bleeder boy? Never thought your little cousin would be the one who'd open you wide up, did you? C'mon, let's hear some crying, Alex. Let's get that bucket Mom always talked about and put it around your neck." Patrick had a demonic scowl in his sunken, drug-glazed eyes.

Still not releasing Patrick's wrist, Alex pulled him into the recliner, but as he did, Patrick twisted and put his knee into Alex's crotch. In pain, Alex helplessly loosened his grip on Patrick's hand that held the syringe, just enough to lose his leverage. "Here, Alex, I know the nurses will be here soon, and I'll never have time to get this into Mom, so why waste it? Why don't I present you with this little cocktail I made for her last night, fancy-man." With that, Patrick leaned into Alex and rammed the syringe into his abdomen. Alex was losing strength quickly on his right side where he had been sliced. Patrick dropped the empty syringe to the floor and lifted his fist to begin punching Alex in the face.

Estelle watched helplessly. She was shocked to see Alex in the state he was in. After all these years and all the worrying over her nephew's hemophilia, this was the first time she had ever seen him truly bleed.

"I've been wanting to see you bleed for years, rich boy. 'Alex this and Alex that.' I'm so tired of hearing Mom and Dad talk about you. Now you'll all be dead, and I don't have to hear it ever again." Patrick had gotten one punch into Alex's cheekbone when, like a rocket, Patrick was launched across the room, slamming into the wall at the end of Estelle's bed.

Estelle was paralyzed in fear over the violence she was witnessing. From her angle of her bed, she could see who was attacking Patrick, but Alex couldn't. She was no longer strong enough to break up the fights between her boys like she did in the old days, so she did the only thing she could. She reached for her ECG wires and ripped them off her chest. Alarms from the machines in her room resounded as well as the alarms in the nurses' station.

Still stunned by the punch, Alex was disoriented. All he could make out from his position in the recliner was that Patrick was being punched rapidly and repeatedly until he finally doubled over, whereupon he was kneed brutally in his ribcage. At that point, Patrick fell to the cold floor of his mother's chaotic room and lay there in a ball, gasping for air. At the same time, while Alex was getting weaker by the moment and his eyes were starting to blur, the door flew open and two security guards, two nurses and Nurse Roseman flooded the room like the whirlwind of a snowstorm. They all quickly evaluated this unusual battle ground.

The man standing over Patrick scurried to the recliner where Alex lay on his side, bleeding. He got right into Alex's face. "Just in time, Cuz. You were in some trouble there, bud. You still haven't learned to punch anybody, have you? Good thing you're the only one I ever promised not to punch." It was Michael, who had just arrived from Atlanta. Michael licked his hand and rubbed it on Alex's one bloodless palm, renewing his childhood promise. Alex, unable to return the gesture, could only smile, even though in agony.

With guns now drawn, one guard grabbed Michael by the collar and pulled him away from Alex while the other straddled Patrick with his gun pointed downward. They began to handcuff both brothers, while Alex lay bleeding in the recliner. Nurse Roseman spoke up and took charge. "Nurse, call the ER and tell them we have an emergency in ICU and explain it's a knife wound." She looked at the other nurse. "Get me scissors, large gauze pads and cold packs." She then looked at Estelle. "Mrs. Beckham, you're all right? Smart move, setting off those alarms." Estelle, weeping, nodded her head. She wasn't all right, not at all. The nursing crew scrambled.

Nurse Roseman knelt down to gaze into Alex's face. "Help is on the way, Mr. Beckham. Tell the officers which one of these men is Patrick, and who is this other man?"

"Patrick is the scrawny one in a ball on the floor. The other one is Estelle's son, Michael, my cousin, who just arrived from Atlanta. He saved my life as Patrick was attacking me, at least for now. Patrick was going to kill his mother, as we were warned." explained Alex.

"Mr. Beckham, you're hurt badly. You need to be silent now." The two nurses reentered the room. "Can you sit up straight for me, Mr. Beckham, just for a second?" When Alex sat up, he became faint, but as he did, Nurse Roseman put her hands inside his shirt and ripped it open; buttons flew everywhere. She then ripped it firmly down from the back where it had been sliced, then cut off the rest with the scissors. "Nurse, get those contacts back on Mrs. Beckham." Then the recliner was laid back in a flat position.

Alex was placed on his stomach, sliding in the blood that smeared the recliner. The nurses packed his back and down his tricep with gauze and ice. "Now relax and be calm, Mr. Beckham." The nurse could tell Alex was growing weaker, but she also knew he hadn't lost enough blood yet to be anemic. Something wasn't right. Alex looked over at Nurse Roseman. Everything was moving too fast.

"Nurse Roseman, stop for a moment and listen. I need to talk quickly. As I saw Patrick pull a syringe from his pocket..." Alex began.

"A syringe? What do you mean a syringe, Mr. Beckham?" Nurse Roseman was shocked.

"Nurse Roseman, quiet please. As I saw Patrick pull a syringe from his pocket, I firmly gripped him by the wrist. That's when he sliced me with his blade. The struggle gave him the opportunity to inject me with whatever is in that syringe instead of injecting my aunt. The syringe is somewhere on the floor."

"Nurse Roseman, should we arrest both of these men? It appears the bigger one assaulted this man on the floor," interrupted one of the guards, clueless of what was taking place.

"No!" Alex yelled. "I punched Patrick in the scuffle. It was my cousin, Michael, who just came in and broke it up."

"Liar!" yelled Patrick from the floor. "You're a big liar, Alex. You're the one that had the syringe, and you were going to kill my mother. You're setting me up. And you never hit anybody in your life, weeny boy. My brother hit me, officer. Don't let him protect my brother. He attacked me as well. Arrest him!"

Michael and Alex smiled, both knowing Patrick was right; Alex had never hit anybody in his entire life. He was just trying to free Michael from any involvement. Patrick was cuffed. Michael was not.

Michael again knelt down next to the recliner and ran his hands through Alex's hair. He then put his hand under Alex's cheek. "Thank you, Cuz. We owe you!" Michael kissed him on the forehead. "The ER squad is on its way." The love and compassion of these two now grown men had only strengthened over the years.

"Michael, in case I pass out, tell the ER team about my hemophilia and get them to call the Hematology Department at University Hospital. They'll take it from there. But at this point, this bleeding is the least of my worries. What was in that syringe?"

Soon the room was filled with paramedics getting Alex onto a gurney, starting an IV, and applying pressure to his back and tricep. While he was being prepared, Nurse Roseman found the syringe on the floor. She approached the cuffed Patrick as Michael watched. "What was in here, Mr. Beckham? What did you inject your cousin with? Nurse, get this to the lab, stat. Tell them it's a matter of life and death."

"What was in that syringe, you piece of crap little brother?" Michael angrily asked as he rushed Patrick, picking him up off the floor and slamming him against the wall by his grungy sports coat. One of the officers again grabbed Michael by the collar to restrain him.

"Nurse Roseman, I must interrupt this interrogation for now. We have to get this man to the ER right away. His eyes are beginning to roll back in his head," said one of the paramedics.

"Yes please, go, go now. The lab will run that syringe in a hurry. If they don't, we're all in trouble." But just as the paramedics started to roll Alex into the hallway, Estelle's alarm went off once more. As Michael and Nurse Roseman looked at Estelle, she had a wire in her left hand; all were confused. Looking Michael in the eyes, she pointed at Alex on the gurney. Michael knew what she wanted. He turned Alex's face towards his mother. She had a loving smile on her face, and with the four fingers of her feeble right hand, she waggled them goodbye to Alex for the last time. Alex smiled back. Then the paramedics took off, rumbling him down to the ER.

Now that Alex was gone, the confrontations continued. "Stick it up your butt hole, Michael. I hate you all. I just wish that was you on that gurney." Patrick was not making any friends. Just then, the city police arrived to arrest him. Nurse Roseman took them both back into the hallway, but only for a minute. As they reentered, Nurse Roseman began to talk. "Mr. Beckham, if you wish to keep your little secret about what was in that syringe, and your cousin dies before we can get the results, you do know what they call that, don't you?"

"Yea, a crying shame for that little wimp. Best thing that ever happened to this world." Patrick smirked. Michael was ready for another attack, like a bull in an arena, but Nurse Roseman stepped in front of him.

"Mr. Beckham," said a police officer, "at the station we will call it murder. Nurse, do you have a private room where we might ask this man some questions? He might be a little more cooperative with us asking, if you know what I mean." Nurse Roseman was so upset, she was ready to turn her back on whatever techniques the officers wanted to use. Patrick sensed it.

"All right assholes, it's no big deal. I planned on spending the last hours of my mother's life together with her high as a kite and in total peace. Out in the parking garage, I shot myself up with the same cocktail I mixed last night for her, and I'm starting to feel great! Fine. Well, maybe I did put a little more in Mom's syringe for her enjoyment, but not too much more. Hell, she's going to die anyway, look at her." Estelle had tears running down her face. She had not cried like this since her beloved husband Joe had died. "It's heroin with a touch of fentanyl, then mixed with some high-grade LSD; the best I could find. She was going to go out with a smile on her face!" Patrick began to laugh deeply from his demented soul. It was spooky.

"Nurse, call the lab and tell them heroin, fentanyl and LSD; have it confirmed. But first call the ER and tell them to inject Mr. Beckham with Narcan to be safe. Go, go!"

Michael looked at his brother, held tightly on each arm by the two men in uniform. "Get him out of my sight," Michael said in disgust. "Can I just punch my brother before he goes?" Estelle watched and listened in solemn grief. She felt guilty somehow for the tortured personality of her youngest. He had been bullied constantly by his older brothers, but never by Alex. Oddly enough, she realized Patrick's plan to inject her was his way, in the end, of telling her he loved her.

TRIBUTARIES CONTINUE TO CONTRACT IN WIDTH AS TIME FLOWS ON

Alex was stitched with up to three layers of fifty-nine sutures across his back and down his arm; no organ damage, just muscle. The Narcan was injected, and Alex survived any chance of overdose by his cousin. But that was the good news. To be on the precautionary side, the sutures would be placed with a local anesthetic and no pain medication for at least six hours.

Next came the second part of Patrick's concoction. It was obvious that the LSD included in his injection was strong and had been cut with some sort of potent amphetamine. It had been a number of years since Alex's brief stint with psychedelics in his academic days and it had been something he never had any intention of doing again, but here he was. He was unable to sleep or lie still. In case of any severe reactions of paranoia, he was taken to a private room in the psychiatric ward, where he would spend his next forty-eight hours under close observation.

But Alex didn't anticipate one strange complication from the LSD—the body pain caused by laughter. And he laughed a lot. When Estelle would sleep, Johnny and Michael would come down to visit. The stories among the three would go on and on for hours, each one causing belly laughter and each story embellished to the brink of reality. And, of course, there was the night Michael entered the dimly lit room with his head wrapped in gauze and dragging his foot like "The Mummy," knowing Alex had always been terrified by that movie as a kid. Alex did freak for a while, but the terror quickly turned to laughter once more.

So on the morning of the third day after the anarchy in Estelle's room, although ten pounds heavier from constant snacking and fatigued from lack of sleep, Alex was cleared to be released. Johnny and Michael came down to his room to help carry his suitcase. "Time to leave this loony bin, Cuz," said Michael. Let me help you to my car, and I'll drive you home," he offered with a gentle hug, avoiding any injuries to Alex's torso.

"No, Michael, I want to see Aunt Estelle before I go home today. Is anyone else upstairs?" Alex was fatigued but relaxed.

"Alex, no need. You've already said your final goodbye the day before I arrived; Mom wrote the story down for us, and you told us while you were in your trance."

Alex was unclear. "No, Michael, I want to see her again. How is she?"

"I said you've already said your final goodbye, Alex." The

stare in Michael's eyes now caused Alex to hug him and Johnny as they all wept together. The family of those early years was fading into fond memories as the new generations were growing like beautiful rose gardens.

"Mom left this for you, Alex."

Alex sat and began to read.

Dear Alex,

Thank you for sacrificing yourself and giving me two more days to say goodbye to all my loved ones. You are and have been a special person in all of our lives. Your courage to be a real boy and man as opposed to placing yourself in a bubble is way beyond what any of us ever imagined. I love you, and I am sure your Uncle Joe in heaven feels the same way. See you on the other side, my little love.

Aunt Estelle

P.S. Your cheek looked like Michael hit you with a wiffle ball.

Alex choked on his grief and couldn't speak. Tears silently ran down his blushing cheeks. Joey and Melody patiently waited outside outside the psych ward as Johnny and Michael escorted Alex through the guarded door. The cousins all left the hospital crying and hugging, that is, all except for Patrick.

EPILOGUE

Patrick was charged with assault and denied bail until after Estelle's funeral and Michael and Johnny left town. Patrick would never take the permanent exclusion from the family seriously. He thought it would all blow over; but it wouldn't.

The day of Estelle's visitation and funeral service, Patrick was granted a guarded visit to the funeral home, escorted by two armed police officers. He arrived in an orange jumpsuit, cuffed with his hands behind his back. The police were there, not only to keep Patrick in check, but to protect him from his brothers, especially Johnny. As Patrick passed Alex on his way to his mother's casket, he stopped and stared with a demonic smirk on his face. He then whispered, "Alex, check out my hands in these cuffs behind my back as I view Mom in the casket. I must leave you with my sincere sentiments, my beloved cousin." Alex was confused.

He watched Patrick at the casket, alone and unaccompanied by his brothers. His hands were dirty and displayed an obvious message. Both of Patrick's hands were fisted but with his middle fingers sticking out from the rest. As he passed Alex on the way out, he just smiled. "You haven't heard the last of me, Cuz!"

• • •

Johnny died of a heart attack ten years later. Joey died of a heart attack as well, only six months after Johnny. Michael and Alex remained close friends; however, they still only saw each other at funerals.

Patrick continued to weaken from heavy drugs and alcohol, but Alex still heard from him every so often. Alex would find a dead carp on his front porch with a syringe stuck in its belly. But that was it. Alex took out a restraining order on Patrick, and his brothers never talked to him again. Alex never knew why Patrick hated him so.

In the end, Alex took care of another childhood myth. His Aunt Estelle had loved him and as time went on, respected him more and more. But Alex learned an important lesson that he would pass on to his children and his grandchildren. It's never too early to express love to those you love. But sometimes, it can be too late.

Next in the Series:
An historical recount of Alex's elderly aunts and the history of their parent's migration to the United States from Prussia in the mid-nineteenth century.

EPISODE V

THE GREAT-GREAT AUNTS FROM PRUSSIA

This episode is one of love, courage, sadness and intrigue. It is a story of the history of the Wehmeyer family, starting in Prussia in the mid-nineteenth century and ending in a Midwest city of the United States in 1960. As the two elderly sisters deal with their individual problems of aging, Carrie, the younger sister by less than a year, shares with Alex, her five-year-old nephew, the heroic and loving past of the Wehmeyers. Alex is on the edge of his seat, proud and enthralled by the exciting history of this branch of his family tree. Then, five years later, as Mayme is approaching her mental and physical demise, Carrie shares with Mary, Alex's mother, the dark secrets of the family to be kept under wraps until the passing of both she and Mayme. This story reveals the reason for Mayme's eccentric personality, the life-long relationship of these two spinsters and the reason for Carrie's undying love and dedication to her sister.

The Summer of 1956

Cincinnati, Ohio

THE HOME OF TWO ELDERLY SPINSTERS MAYME AND CARRIE WEHMEYER

The dog days of summer spread heavy upon the city, so much so that even the nights granted no relief from the daytime energy drain upon the helpless population. The sheets of the two sisters shared double mattress were mildly soaked with their mutual faint perspiration. As each consistently rotated her pillows throughout the night in an attempt to preserve some similitude of coolness on their cheeks, constant sleep became impossible for either. The black oscillating fan in front of the screened windows caused a slight breeze, moving the humid air throughout the bedroom, occasionally drifting directly across the bodies of these two very distressed women. The saggy brassieres and panties worn by these two elderly sisters played a minor role in combating the minimal comfort of the night.

As daylight began to touch softly on the walls and floor, shaded by the awning over the bedroom windows, the phone rang loudly from the music room in the front of the house. As Mayme continued to snore right through the ring, Carrie grabbed her thin cotton robe, and before her legs began to loosen, she shuffled painfully to the phone. As she turned on the light, she lost her balance, causing one hand to crash upon the keyboard of the beautiful Baldwin upright, provoking a chaotic thunderclap of sharps and flats. Mayme, hearing the tangle of the piano's disharmony, confusingly arose to check on the cause.

Carrie made it to the telephone and in a voice still coated with the nighttime's gruffness, answered. "Uh, yes, good morning. Who may I ask is calling?"

"Mayme, this is Mary," the person on the other end replied, unable to tell the difference between the two elderly voices in this early birth of the day.

"No, Mary, this is Carrie. Is everything all right, honey?" Carrie was initially scared of a call coming this early in the morning. Perhaps Alex, her great-grand-nephew, had been injured in the night again.

"No, Carrie, everything is fine, and I'm so sorry to wake you this early. I know this is short notice, but can you keep Alex today? I was just called in to work. One of the girls went into labor last night, and they need me to cover for a while." Mary was being apologetic but knew Alex's Aunt Mayme and Aunt Carrie loved to hang with their five-year-old buddy.

"Mary, we'd love to. When will you drop him off?" asked Carrie.

"Well, like real soon, maybe?" Mary asked apologetically. "Randall and I are just going out the door and need to drop him off in, let's say, five minutes? Then Randall needs to drop me off on his way to work. Is that a problem?" asked Mary.

Carrie was fine, although she didn't feel comfortable exposing herself to Alex in her present attire, and Mayme was still unrobed. Alex had spent the night on their couch before, but he always slept well beyond the awakening time of his two aunts.

"Sure, you have a key to our front door. Just let yourself in and take him straight to the living room with his things. Mayme will probably go back to sleep after you leave, but I'm sure she'll want to jabber with you. I'll be ready in fifteen minutes. I'll feed him breakfast. He loves my pancakes!"

"Carrie, he already had some cereal, and—"

"Mary, that skinny little boy eats like a horse. I assure you, he'll not pass up my pancakes. And we just made a fresh batch of anise cookies!" Carrie added.

"You didn't make them strong with what you Germans call anise wine, right? We call it Sambuca, Carrie, and it could be a bit much for Alex if you used a lot." Mary trusted Carrie to tell her the truth, though Mayme, not so much. Mayme was not shy when it came to her daily allotment of anise wine. "If he's hungry, by all means, Carrie, feed him as much as he wants."

Carrie loved to cook for Alex. "Does he have his swimsuit? We can play in the sprinkler and take him to the pool in the park. It's going to be a hot one." Carrie had no intentions of going swimming with Alex, but Mayme, on the other hand, was unique at age seventy-five in a kids' pool. Mayme had always been and still was a kid herself. She loved to play and splash with Alex and to splash the other little kids in the pool as well. And all the other kids loved splashing her back and watching her giggle.

"He has his suit, Carrie, and some books. I'll bring him in and tell him to wait for you in the living room. Carrie, thank you so much. I'll pick him up about five o'clock. See you then."

Mary hung up and ran to the car. Randall and Alex were all packed up and ready to go.

"Let's get going, Mary. We're both going to be late as it is. Carrie said yes, I assume?" Randall began backing out of the driveway before hearing the answer.

"Yes, go to Mayme and Carrie's house. They can keep him all day, thank goodness," Mary replied.

"Those two love keeping him," said Randall. "Carrie, I trust. Mayme, well…"

"Aunt Mayme's really fun, Dad," Alex said. "She's the one that plays with me most. Aunt Carrie kinda just takes care of me, like feeds me and makes me take a bath and stuff like that. But Aunt Mayme gives me horsey rides, wrestles with me on the floor, and plays at the pool and in the sprinkler. She's like playing with one of my friends." Alex was always excited, at least at age five, to stay with Mayme and Carrie.

Randall glanced over at Mary from the corner of his eye. Mary knew what Randall was thinking, because they had discussed it before. Randall's concern was Mayme's behavior as a seventy-five-year-old woman. As Alex said, she played just like one of his friends. Although she had never put Alex in any danger and had shown him nothing but deep affection, Randall was concerned she had what some people called "bats in the belfry," so Randall always insisted she wasn't left alone with Alex.

The car approached the house of the two spinsters and parked in front on the street, temporarily blocking the fire hydrant. "Take him in and no chattering. You know how Mayme likes to talk. Remember, Mary, we're running late," Randall insisted.

"I get it, Randall," said Mary. "I have to hustle as well." Mary kept her promise, taking Alex inside and directly to the living room. And as expected, Mayme intercepted her in the hallway on the way out, this time with her robe tied at the waist, asking questions totally irrelevant to the day. "Have to run, Mayme. Love you, but I have to get to work, and I'm late already. We can visit tonight when I pick up Alex. Have fun and stay cool. His swimsuit's in the bag." Randall was both surprised and pleased when Mary came out the door so quickly. She'd kept it so short. Mayme followed her to the front door and held it open as she watched Mary hop in the car.

"Mayme looks a bit scary in the morning, especially with no false teeth," said Randall with a smile.

"Be nice, Randall. We'll look that way when we're in our seventies, only I'll still be cute. You'll be bald, fat and ugly," Mary said with an answering smile.

Randall leaned over and kissed Mary on the cheek. "But we do owe them one for today! I'll pick them up a bottle of Sambuca after work. They can make some more cookies," and they both laughed at the irony. Mary and Randall waved as they sped from the curb and off to work.

A NEW TRIBUTARY SPLITS OFF FOR ALEX BECKHAM AND INTO HIS MENTAL LIBRARY

As Alex sat quietly with his hands crossed on the timeworn sofa, upholstered with austere flowers, barns and farmhouses, Carrie was dressing behind the closed bathroom door. She combed her thinning white hair with her pearl-handled brush and inserted her false teeth from the glass she had taken with her from her night-stand to the sink. But Mayme wasn't as concerned about her appearance in front of Alex. Alex had been informed by his mother that Carrie would need a few minutes to get dressed and groomed, but Mayme felt no need to delay greeting her favorite little boy. She was obsessed with little boys around his age.

After watching Mary and Randall pull away, Mayme made her way to the living room to greet Alex with a big grin and all her love. "Oh, how's my little buddy?" She sat down next to Alex on the couch, giving him a hug around his shoulders and a tender kiss on his cheek. Mayme couldn't keep from hugging and kissing her little boy every chance she got. "We're going to have some fun today. Yes sir, we're gonna have some fun today! Want to go to the pool this afternoon? And we can play in the sprinkler until the park opens."

Alex was confused by his feelings. Mayme was so fun and so loving, but at the moment, her hair and her body were still a bit wet from the night's perspiration, which created a strange smell as she hugged him. Also, Alex had never seen her without teeth, and he didn't know whether to laugh at the way she talked or be a little freaked out at her looks.

"Hi, Aunt Mayme. Mom said we were getting you out of bed way too early, and she told me to tell you she was sorry." Alex gave Mayme a hug but really didn't want to, at least not until she got cleaned up and put in her teeth.

"Alex, no problem. Carrie's going to take care of you and cook breakfast. I think she said pancakes. So your old Aunt Mayme is going back to sleep for a little while. And after breakfast, you can take a nap on the couch if you'd wish. It's pretty early for you too, I'll bet." Mayme was yawning and already making her way back to her bed by way of the kitchen. She went to the counter and picked up the quarter full bottle of Sambuca.

"Making cookies last night, Aunt Mayme? Can I have some for breakfast?" Alex watched Mayme from the living room, not leaving the sofa, as he had been instructed to do by his mother.

"Uh, well, yes, we do have some anise cookies around, and certainly you can have some. We make them really for just you and your grandpa most of the time. Now I'm going to get a little more rest, my sweet." Mayme blocked Alex's view as she grabbed the bottle of Sambuca and slid it ever so gently inside her cotton robe, hiding a shot glass in her hand, situated behind her back. Mayme slowly made her way back to her bedroom. Sitting on the edge of her bed, she downed two glasses of the sweet liqueur. With that, she removed her robe and laid peacefully on her back as the Sambuca gently, but unfortunately temporarily, removed the aches and pains from her arthritic joints. She fell back asleep almost immediately, belting out snores so loud, Alex could hear them all the way to the living room. He was giggling as Carrie walked into the room. Carrie made snoring noises to mock Mayme, and they both giggled like school children.

"Come, my child, I've prepared you milk, pancakes and cookies. They're waiting for you in the dinette." Alex arose from the sofa and followed Carrie like a hungry puppy dog through the kitchen to the dinette table. "I think I have all you need, milk, butter, syrup. Can you think of anything else, Alex?"

"No, Aunt Carrie, the pancakes look perfect. My mom burns them most of the time." Carrie turned and smiled as she walked to the kitchen, poured herself a cup of coffee and joined Alex back at the table.

"Aunt Carrie, I have a question. I keep meaning to ask my mom, but I forget." Carrie was having problems understanding

Alex. His mouth was full and his cheeks packed with pancakes like a little squirrel.

"Alex, don't talk with your mouth full, honey. Take your time and chew it all up first." Carrie waited patiently, having no clue what Alex might be about to ask. She knew her little nephew was very inquisitive, and she thought it was going to be about Mayme's Sambuca bottle.

Alex swallowed and then, with another bite on his fork, held upright pointed at the ceiling, he asked, "I sometimes hear you and Aunt Mayme and my grandpa talk to each other in words I've never heard before. I sometimes hear people talk that way on Grandpa's huge radio, but never anybody in person. Sometimes I think my brain is weird or something. Is it?"

Carrie began to laugh as she stroked the soft bristles of Alex's burr haircut. "Oh honey, not at all. Your brain's not weird at all. We're just talking in a language called German. That's the language my parents spoke when Mayme and I were children. Then we learned English as well for when we started school." Alex wasn't clear as to why they ever spoke German.

"Why would you speak that German language when you live here? People can't understand you." Alex was still too young to understand the concept of immigration.

Carrie smiled again at Alex's naivete. "Germany is where your great-great grandparents were born, only it was called Prussia at that time."

"Wait, who were they again?" That kind of ancestry was way past confusing to a five-year-old boy.

"Okay, Alex, let me try to explain. Your Grandpa Schaefer's grandparents, you know, I mean those people that he called 'Grandma and Grandpa', were August and Maria Wehmeyer. They were born just over a hundred years ago in Prussia. They were mine and Mayme's mother and father, along with six other brothers and sisters." Carrie thought that might make more sense to an inquisitive young mind.

"You mean Russia, don't you, Aunt Carrie? I've never heard of Prussia, but I've heard of Russia. They're like the people that want to blow us up with those big bombs, right?"

"That's true, but Prussia was a country in Europe for a long time until there was a war and they took over a bunch of little countries. Then they changed the name to Germany soon after. As a matter of fact, your great-great grandfather, my father, was a war hero, and your great-great grandmother, my mother, was a nurse on battlefields. They both became quite famous and well-respected." Carrie was proud of her heritage and was honored to share that fact with young Alex. She thought he was old enough to appreciate and understand the big picture, but maybe not the details.

"Really, I had grandparents that were famous! I want to hear, Aunt Carrie, but you can tell it in English, right? I don't understand German." Alex was excited. This was like the stories his dad read him from the encyclopedias, only real.

"Alex, I won't be able to tell you all of it at once. It's a long story. But since your mother will be working for a couple weeks until the lady that had the baby comes back, I can tell you a little at a time over the next few weeks. Sound good?"

"Sounds great, Aunt Carrie. Can you write down some notes so I can write the story in a book someday?" Alex was ready to start school and was only about a year or two from being able to read and write.

"Okay, Alex, I'll tell you what I was told, but we'll need to stop when Mayme wakes up, so we can go play in the pool down the street." Carrie took the dishes to the kitchen sink and led Alex to the sofa in the living room. She was as excited to begin the story as Alex was to hear it.

September 16, 1866 — The Wehmeyer home in Berlin

PRIVATE AUGUST WEHMEYER'S LIFE CHANGES DRASTICALLY AFTER THE BATTLE OF LANGENSALZA

"Aww, kissy, kissy, another letter from your little sweetie, eh, August? I bet she writes ten of those a day to all them boys she met at Langensalza." August could see the faint shadow of his brother through the bandages still protecting his decimated eyes. But with the loss of one sense, his hearing was becoming more astute about what was moving around him. Henry playfully slapped August on the back and began to run around him like a neurotic puppy. As Henry teased his big brother with another slap, not being mature enough to realize they weren't little boys anymore, August prepared to attack. Seeing Henry's shadow, August grabbed him like a snake striking a field mouse. Life had grown up around these brothers like weeds in an unkept plot of land. August wasn't the same innocent and loving lad he had been before he'd joined the Prussian army three years prior, fighting brutally against the Danes in the Second Schleswig War and then the Hanoverians in the Austro-Prussian War.

Unlike August's gentle nature towards his teenage brother in the past, this time August had the front of his little brother Henry's white schoolboy shirt in a violent grip. He pulled Henry into his face with a vicious unseen stare. And even though Henry couldn't see August's eyes through the bandages, he could see August's jaw clenched tight with impatience. Henry was so scared; tears filled the innocent teen's eyes. He was speechless as he watched August's nostrils flare, as the older brother took a deep breath like a madman.

"I've warned you twice, you little asshole, and now there will be no more warnings. Got it, Henry?" Their mother, Hilda, was watching her two sons in the courtyard from her kitchen sink. She came running out the door, stunned to see her son of twenty-five handling his little brother of fifteen with such brutality.

"August, what's your problem? That's your baby brother. You've never treated him like that before. Shame on you. You're a grown man now, not a kid. No excuses, now let him go." With that, August pushed Henry onto the grass. Henry skidded on his behind, leaving a heavy grass stain and a rip in his woolen school knickers.

"I'm warning you, Mother, just like I'm warning Henry. My shoulder's still in terrible pain, and those pills I've been taking for months now aren't helping. I can't see, and I don't know if I ever will again. He hits my shoulder one more time, and he'll be flattened on his ass."

Hilda was shocked by the unexpected outrage of her oldest son, by far the most mature of her six children.

"Henry, did you really slap your brother on his wounded shoulder? My goodness, son, your brother had a bullet go all the way through him from front to back less than three months ago. What are you thinking, boy? You strike your brother again, and I promise you, your father will take care of you in the shed when he gets home from the factory, and your butt will be sore for a week." Hilda now understood. She was overwhelmed with happiness that her son had survived two battles but was bereaved by her son's blindness. She also knew the problem wasn't just his sight and his shoulder. There was something else causing his anger and frustration. Something else had happened out there, and it had something to do with those letters he received every couple of weeks.

"August, I'm sorry," said Hilda. "Henry, go in the house now, I want to talk to August—alone." Henry, still weeping a bit from his surprise over the extreme reaction of his brother and the severe scolding by his mother, got up off the lawn and ran inside, his head bowed in shame. August, ever since Henry could remember, had been his little brother's guardian. August treated his baby brother with such deep fraternal love, and in Henry's eyes, August was and would always be the hero of his life.

"It's not just your shoulder, is it, August?" asked Hilda. "You haven't been the same since you came back from Langensalza. You want to talk about it? Is it that girl that writes you all the time, or is there more to it than that?"

"NO!" August yelled, his nostrils flaring again like those of a vicious dog. "I don't want to talk about it, and that little twit keeps bringing it up every time I get a letter from my friend. I'm telling you, Mother, I never want to think or talk of that battlefield ever again. She's the only one who knows what happened during that godawful day, and it shall remain that way. So if any of you bring it up, I'll not stand for it."

"August, it must have been something terrible for you, if you are still this upset." His mother was trying to help.

"It was a war, Mother. No one ever gets over it, so stop it. Just stop it." August was not in the mood to be coddled and was certainly in no mood to be interrogated.

"What can I do to help you, my love? And these letters? May I ask what kind of friend is this? Henry assumes it's a girl, but none of us really know. Your father and I have talked, and our question is, when did you ever have time to meet a girl? You were in the ranks the whole time. Is it another soldier friend? Was he injured as well?" Hilda asked.

"I said leave it alone, Mother!" It was unusual for August to be indignant with his mother, but she wouldn't stop.

"But who reads these letters to you, August?" Hilda wanted to take that question back as soon as she said it. She knew it sounded invasive.

"That, Mother, is none of your business. If I wish to have a private life, then—"

"I'm so sorry, son. I have no right to interfere. You're right. I just love you, and I want to help." Hilda walked back into the kitchen, weeping. August couldn't see that through his bandaged eyes, but he could hear her faint whimper.

June 26, 1866 — The small village of Langensalza, Prussia

TENSION BUILDS AS AUGUST DOES NOT LIKE WHAT HE SEES HAPPENING ALL AROUND HIM IN THE ARMY'S ENCAMPMENT

From the hilltop, a dense fog sprawled as still as death in the grassy valley below the Prussian army's bivouac. Mildew-stained canvas tents pocked the wooded hillside, spread out so as to make it appear that the army was larger than it actually was. The air was filled with the begrimed smell of smoldering campfires brewing tea and cooking raw venison on the ends of sharpened tree branches. It was June 26, 1866, in the area outside Bad Langensalza, located in the Prussian province of Saxony. Nearly 9,000 Prussian troops had been ordered by King Wilhelm I to make haste into this remote area and, with their sheer presence, block the Hanoverian troops from marching westward and uniting with their provincial Bavarian allies. This would give King Wilhelm I a small window of time to gather the rest of his troops and attack Hanover from the north, trapping them with no escape.

In the conflict known as the Austro-Prussian War, Hanover's purpose in joining Bavaria was to defeat Prussia and bring the Austrian government to power over all German-speaking provinces, with the united power later to become known as the country of Germany. The Hanoverians were unaware that the Prussians had only half as many troops in their path as their spies, who crept unnoticed through the Prussian camp, had reported. But for the Prussian foot soldiers, their purpose on this hillside was unknown, and anything they spoke of was pure conjecture.

August sat under a beautifully seasoned pin oak, peering down at his army's camp below, his needle pin rifle laid with anticipation on the ground by his side. It was at these moments that those soldiers who had participated in previous battles for King Wilhelm attempted to quiet their minds and think about nothing at all.

August knew to always be prepared. He had learned from the war with the Danes two years earlier that an attack could come from anywhere and at any time, day or night; and who knew what might be lurking in that stagnant fog in the valley? As he sat alone, quietly waiting for his mundane breakfast of tea and oatmeal, he watched and listened for any movement from that seemingly dead cloud below. Suddenly, a young boy with the countenance and body of an adolescent and with soft, pale hands shaking as if in winter, stood over August, looking down at him with frightened baby blues. "What's your name, sir? Mine's Otto. May I sit down with you, sir?" The boy reminded August of a lost puppy dodging wagons in the muddy back streets of Berlin.

"My name is August, August Wehmeyer." That was August's quick and distant response. Otto was in grave need of someone who exuded the same confidence and ability to protect him as his big brothers had back home in Cologne.

"You look older than me, sir. I'm the youngest of four brothers at home," Otto responded, still standing. His abstruse request to sit had in no way been approved by August. He neither needed nor did he want some boy disturbing his peace.

"My name is August, not sir, kid. Call me sir, and you could get me picked off by a sniper or have one of these spies around here cut my throat from ear to ear." August was cold and seriously rude. Otto was embarrassed.

"Spies? What makes you think there are spies in camp?" asked Otto with eyes wide, glancing quickly in every direction like a fawn that had just smelled a wolf.

"Part of the battle, kid. The Hanoverians need to know what we have over here if and when they attack," responded August.

"What we have? Like what?"

August couldn't believe this kid was this naïve. "Like how many soldiers and artillery and horses. Come on kid, why else would they be creeping around?" August continued to scan uphill and downhill and then stare at the fog in the valley again.

"Yea, but they're just spies looking around, aren't they, sir? They don't hurt anybody, do they? It's not like they're soldiers or anything." Otto was starting to frustrate August.

"Okay, kid, I'm going to start calling you sir, and I'm going to get up and salute you a few times. Your throat will then be slit somewhere in the night as you go to take a piss. They do that to the officers for good reason. With no trained officers, we're in chaos over here. Shit, boy, most of the officers we have are idiots anyway. Those spies are probably watching us right now. That's why I stay by myself, so nobody thinks I'm of any importance. Get it?" August had had enough of Otto.

"Oh, I'm so sorry, sss—I mean August. I had no idea that could ever happen. Seems like cheating." Otto so talked like a schoolboy.

"It is cheating. And if a spy is caught, they're hung by their neck and they're left dangling, just to remind other spies what we'll do to them if we catch them. Look down there near the edge of camp." August pointed, and Otto eventually caught glimpse of the swaying body with two turkey vultures picking at the face of the carcass.

Otto lost his breath at his first sight of death. "I was just being respectful, really I was. It's just you remind me of my big brothers at home, that's all. One's name is Marcus. He's the oldest." He paused. "Maybe I should…" Otto felt he was doing and saying everything wrong, and maybe it would be better if he talked to a kid his own age.

At the same time, August was beginning to feel Otto really needed him. He remembered all the times he had protected his little brother, Henry, at home. August interrupted. "No, no, kid, wait. I'm sorry. But didn't they teach you anything in boot camp?" asked August.

"Boot camp? Shoot, two days after my draft letter, I had to

report to some military camp. They shaved my head, gave me a uniform, showed me once how to shoot this thing and the next day, I left Cologne." August was starting to understand what was happening around him. "Last Friday, I graduated from high school, and now this Friday, I'm here in these woods, wherever these woods are. Yes, they jammed us all in train cars with no seats. It was so tight, we would have to squeeze through each other to get between cars to take a shit or a piss or even vomit while the train rattled down the tracks. There was a lot of diarrhea from a lot of nerves, but here I am. It all started four days ago."

August rolled his eyes as he spit on the ground and threw a small rock at a tree ten feet away. To Otto, it felt like August was still a bit perturbed with him. "I'm sorry I got down on you kid, really. It's not your fault. But if we're about to go into battle, God help us. We're all assuming it's the Hanoverians on the other side of that valley marching this way. I heard they've just finished their summer training exercises not too far from here. We have spies too, you know." August had only overheard rumors, but the recent influx of these kids was starting to make sense.

"I'm still confused," said Otto. "They're really marching towards us right now?"

"No, no, I said I was assuming. I don't know that for sure, kid, but the Hanoverians know what we're doing with more than half of our troops arriving here in the last three days. And obviously, your training was a joke." The only thing August knew, with all these new untrained troops arriving and the Hanoverians not far away, was that this wasn't going to be a great Prussian victory. This was going to be a massacre of children, even if they did win.

"Okay, kid, fine, so first sit down and stop swinging that rifle all over the place. They go off accidently, you know, and I don't want to be shot by some dumb-ass new recruit. Now sit down and put your rifle next to you on the ground like I have mine, pointing away from the camp. And never let it or your ammunition be out of your arm's reach." August was beginning to take this boy under his wing.

"August, don't be worried about my gun going off. It's empty. I don't even remember them teaching me how to load it, really. Can you teach me?" August shook his head as he looked straight down to the ground between his knees. The kid was pitiful, but again, August knew it wasn't Otto's fault. Kids like him were pouring in every few hours, swarming the camp like a herd of lost goats, not knowing exactly where they should go or what they should do. Otto was just needing somebody to help him through his extreme anxiety, and August's help just might save his life. He would want somebody to help his little brother if he was ever in this ugly situation.

Otto sat down and followed August's instructions. August taught Otto not only how to load the gun but how to clean it and how to properly aim it with accuracy. "This gun is our biggest advantage, Otto. It's called a needle gun. Bismarck sent a group of Prussians to America a few years ago during their civil war. They learned how to move troops by train and lay telegraph wires to move the troops where they needed them, and they taught doctors new techniques in surgery and amputations."

"Amputations!" Otto interrupted. "Like arms and legs and things?" Otto's face turned pale as his jaw dropped. August didn't respond. He didn't have to. So he kept talking.

"But of everything we learned and acquired from their war, these guns were the most important."

Otto listened intently. "What makes this rifle so different, and how do you know all this?" Otto's background had not given him much of an education in warfare. Actually, since his father was a Lutheran pastor, his family didn't discuss war at all—ever.

"Otto, you know what a musket is?" asked August.

"Sure, I've seen pictures in history class of soldiers jamming that rod down into the barrel, then shooting at each other across fields. Why?" Otto responded.

"Then you know that when they have to reload, they have to

stand up," said August.

"Right, so?" asked Otto.

"Well, I just taught you how to load a cartridge in your rifle. Did you have to stand up?" August was leading Otto by the nose.

"No, August, we just sat here. So, you mean by not standing up, we aren't big targets like they are?" Otto was almost there.

"Not only can we sit. We can lie on our stomachs on hillsides and load. The needle rifle loads from the breech, up here near the trigger. And we can take three shots to every one of the enemies. And the Hanoverians and the Austrians don't have these, at least not yet. They have the old musket type. Gives us a lot of confidence in a battle, but I hope not too much." August was hoping he was making the boy feel better, but the gun was one thing, and these new inexperienced boys were another.

"I guess you've been in the army a long time then, August? But do you really think we're in danger?" Otto looked around in each direction, worrying the enemy was going to come at them from any direction at any time.

"In danger?" August blurted. "You're a soldier with a gun, kid, and both sides want to kill each other. That's how it works." August was blunt, and Otto knew he deserved an answer to his ridiculous question.

"But how many troops do we have? How many do they have? Are we attacking them or them us?" Otto was still naïve, not realizing that officers didn't take fondly to the foot soldiers talking about purposes or strategies. Nobody ever knew who was listening. And foot soldiers never knew for certain what was going on. August turned to Otto and shushed him with his finger to his lips as two soldiers passed close to them.

August could sense this boy was not much of a fighter. He looked like he came from a somewhat "soft" family. August guessed his mom or dad or both were teachers or professors of some sort, but he didn't go as far as to consider that Otto came from an entire family of clergy. August's father, on the other hand, had fought in the Napoleonic Wars, then learned the skill of making pottery, vases, bowls, jewelry and such. He was an artist of sorts, and they lived in a rough neighborhood. But Otto was now entering a world he had only read about in history books. He was terrified.

June 26, 1866

IN THE COUNTRYSIDE OF PRUSSIA THE DAY BEFORE THE BATTLE OF LANGENSALZA

"General Flies, I have a telegram, sir, from Field Marshal Moltke, sir." The corporal handed the telegram to Flies, saluted, then turned and left the tent as quickly as he had arrived. Flies opened the telegram from the head of the Prussian army. It read:

General Flies. We are moving troops to the north of Hanover. Hold your position. Do not attack until further orders. Destroy this telegram immediately.

"What is it, sir?" asked the lieutenant. "New orders?"

Flies walked slowly and confidently over to the candle sitting on his desk. He touched the corner of the telegram to the flame, setting the orders from his superior on fire. He watched it burn as long as he could hold it in his fingertips. He stood with arrogance in his eyes, gazing at the diminishing flames, then dropped the paper to the ground and smeared it into the dirt floor of his tent with the sole of his boot, leaving nothing but worthless ashes. Walking to his open tent flap, he stared out over the fog as the sun was setting behind the embankment. He saw nothing but imminent danger. At the same time, he envisioned another medal on his chest.

As he stared, he thought silently. *That old man's been in command way too long. We can kick their asses with our needle guns alone, not to mention our artillery and our horses. I don't want to sit here on this hillside while they move their troops into that valley, tonight perhaps, and fire on us at sunrise from that cloud down there. Nope, not going to happen. I won't allow it!*

"Send for my officers, lieutenant," Flies said with his quintessential conceit.

"Yes sir," and his top officers were all in Flies' tent within twenty minutes.

"Time to move, gentlemen," said Flies, deliberately defying the orders of the head of the Prussian army. "Get the men ready to march at three o'clock before daybreak." Yet Flies was the only one aware that this act was one of total disrespect and disobedience of the orders sent from the Chief Field Marshal himself.

• • •

It was in the infancy of Friday, June 27 at three A.M. when the squad leader stuck his head into August's tent, kicking the sleeping soldiers and whispering, "Get your things, men. Leave the tent where it stands. We're moving out, and be quiet. Unload your rifles for now." It didn't take long for August to realize what was happening. And Otto, who had moved into August's tent with a group of experienced soldiers (mainly because no one had told him where he was supposed to sleep), had a hunch of what was happening as well. It was time to attack.

"August, what's going on? Are we going into battle? Moving out where?" asked Otto, still only half awake, as most teenagers are at the first beckoning of their mothers in the morning.

"Keep your voice down, and only talk to me in a whisper directly into my ear. This is it, kid. Got your gun and ammo?" August directed Otto in a low murmur.

"Yes, s—I mean, August. I guess now is REALLY not the time to call you sir." Otto tried to fake a smile, but his fear was obvious. August ignored his comment. "August, why do we need to unload our rifles? You told me to always keep it loaded and by my side," asked Otto, making sure he had heard his squad leader and his mentor correctly.

"No, kid, this sounds like we're going to spring a surprise attack. If your gun goes off accidently, or anyone's, we may as well set an alarm clock for the Hanoverians."

• • •

In a long line, four abreast, the Prussian army marched as quietly as possible down the hillside and into the fog. Otto marched next to August, watching his every move and obeying August by not saying a word. Even though they had had no breakfast, Otto was so nervous, he vomited on the back of the boots of the soldier marching in front of him. The soldier instinctively glanced at Otto over his shoulder but kept marching as he turned his eyes forward. Otto peered over at August from the corner of his eye, expecting a frown. But August was smiling, still looking straight forward. The soiled soldier appeared even younger than Otto.

The infantry was quiet, with only the occasional broken branch in the darkness beneath its feet. And from the rear, an occasional whinny of a horse drawing a cannon or carrying a cavalry soldier. As the troops exited the fog of the first valley, they marched up and over three crests in total, about three miles.

Halfway up the third grassland to the wooded crest, they stopped. The officers ordered the first half of the foursomes to line the top of the crest on their stomachs and to keep their rifles empty until ordered to load. The second half of the foursomes were instructed to kneel behind the first row. The sun was just starting to rise in the east as a pinkish-purple glow crept onto the horizon. As light began to dominate the darkness, Otto, kneeling behind the first line of riflemen, could see the troops spanned at least a quarter mile along the crest and just back far enough from the top so the enemy guards could not see their position. Peacefully, Otto could hear the birds chirping, and a soft breeze caressed his cheeks. August could see small patches of smoke rising from over the next hilltop. The Prussians had positioned themselves perfectly for the

Hanoverians to charge up the hill while the Prussians shot down upon their musket-loading enemy.

Then it started. "Soldiers load your weapons and move to the top of the crest. Artillery—FIRE!" The artillery had been moved into place and fired from the hilltop in front of the foot soldiers, their shells cruising over the top of the next hill and into the enemy camped in the valley. In the distance, drums and bugles sounded the Hanoverian alarm as the explosions caused the whining of horses and the chaotic shouting of orders that could be heard over the silence of the morning.

"What now, August? Did we just win? What's next? Is it over?" Otto thought he could talk now that this was definitely no longer a surprise.

"Kid, that's just the first round." The cannons reloaded and fired again, and fired a third time. Otto thought the other army was just scrambling around on the other side of the hill and/or retreating already, but suddenly, cannon shells exploded behind them, even behind the Prussian cavalry. Tree limbs crashed to the ground; dirt and pebbles covered Otto's back as he covered his head and waited for August's next instructions.

"What's going on August? They're firing over our heads, not at us." Otto couldn't figure it out. But August knew precisely what they were doing. The Hanoverians were ready for them. Their spies had been quite thorough. They had been ready for days.

"They're shooting howitzers at us. This isn't good." It was the first time Otto saw fear in August's face.

"What's a howitzer, and why is that so bad, August" asked Otto.

"It's a cannon that shoots at a high trajectory, mainly for getting behind walls of castles and fortresses, or in our case, terrain. We've been shooting our cannons from up top here. We don't have howitzers. Our cannons shoot at a low trajectory, but since we're almost shooting straight across, the shells go over their embankment and into their camp. And our cannons would be great if they were charging us, but that's not what they're doing." August, not knowing Flies had disobeyed orders, figured the Field Marshal's spies had miscalculated and that he had marched his troops into a death trap. He was counting on the Hanoverians charging en masse over that crest on the other side, so the needle rifles and their artillery would desecrate the Hanoverian troops. But it was Flies who was wrong, not the Field Marshal.

"But I still don't understand, August. They're shooting way behind us. Why not right at us?" asked Otto.

"Listen close, kid. Can you hear? The explosions will keep getting closer behind us until they force us to charge down the hill in the open grassland. And look over there to our right. They have us flanked. I'm afraid we have no place to go but into the valley, then retreat towards Langensalza," said August. "Now just stay still and wait for the command."

"What command?" August was scared for himself, but he felt so responsible for the life of this young boy, who didn't have a chance without him. August thought, *I don't want to die, but this kid is so much like my little brother.*

"Just stay close to me, kid, and do exactly what I do," August said sternly.

As the cannon fire crept closer and closer from behind, the alarm rang, and the Prussian army stood and charged down the hill. But as they did, the Hanoverians appeared, one line at a time, kneeling at the top of their hill, firing down at them as the Prussians charged.

"What do we do, August?" cried Otto. "Should we lay on our stomachs and fire back with our needle rifles like you taught me?"

"We can't, kid. We lay on our stomachs on the downslope and we can't shoot up at them. We'll need to sit when we fire, which means we're sitting targets."

As the Prussians were trapped in between the howitzers behind and the musket fire from row after row of alternating Hanoverians, the thunder of hoofs came from their right: Hanoverian soldiers on horseback with swords and pistols. Flies knew he was about to be overrun, so he held his cavalry in place to limit his losses. The alarm for retreat was quickly sounded, and the Prussian troops ran down the valley to flee for Langensalza, their only seemingly obvious escape route. But as the Prussians began fleeing down the valley from the Hanoverian cavalry, unbeknownst to Flies, the Hanoverians had moved three battalions of about 3,000 men to the left, creating a musket barrier that with one round of shot wiped out all who had run the fastest in retreat, leaving nowhere but to scramble back up the hill and over the crest to escape.

As August and Otto ran back up the hill in the direction of the camp from which they had come, the Hanoverians aimed their howitzers down the valley. Right above them, a shell hit the top of a huge cedar and exploded, causing jagged branches to crash down on anyone in range. That was the same time the surrender flag was raised and the bugle sounded. All knew to drop their weapons and place their hands on their heads.

August looked around as the smoke from the gunpowder filled his lungs. His ears rang terribly, and he called out to Otto. "Drop your weapon kid, and put your hands on top of your head." But when August looked over, he saw Otto sprawled face down in the pine straw, blood running down his leg as a large broken branch from the cannon shell had fallen and penetrated the young boy's thigh.

Not thinking about anything but Otto, August didn't drop his gun in surrender but instinctively scrambled to the aid of his little friend. "No, kid, no. You're all right?" but as August rushed to the boy's side, another shell exploded into the trees and numerous splinters pierced his eyes. As he stopped and reached for them, a Hanoverian on horseback shot a bullet from his pistol directly through August's shoulder and out the front side, shattering August's collarbone. As the Hanoverian passed, he hit August squarely on top of the head with the butt of his pistol, knocking him to the ground, immediately unconscious. August's skull was bleeding profusely, blood pooling in the soil under his cheek.

The battle ended. The Hanoverians had won a quick victory over the soon to be court-martialed General Flies, who had arrogantly defied orders. Flies had taken his 9,000 untrained kids and pitted them against 19,000 well-trained and well-armed Hanoverians. In the end, due to the needle rifles and the surprise attack, the Prussians lost only 170 men, including eleven officers, while the Hanoverians lost 378 men. The Prussians had 643 wounded, including thirty more officers, while the Hanoverians had 1071 wounded. But with the surrender, the Hanoverians captured 907. But in the end, only a few days later, that battle stalled the Hanoverians from joining the Bavarians in time and allowed the Prussians to eventually win the Austro-Prussian War within a week, leading to the eventual unification of the German-speaking provinces under Prussia and the rule of King Wilhelm I. Germany was then a major world power.

June 23, 1866 — Cologne, Prussia

FOUR DAYS BEFORE THE BATTLE OF LANGENSALZA PRUSSIAN FAMILIES PREPARE FOR WAR

"Maria Rothert, my child, where have you been? You know we eat dinner at five o'clock sharp. You're an hour late," Maria's mother scolded as her father, Joseph, sat quietly at the head of a large wooden table draped with a white heirloom lace tablecloth. Joseph's tea sat steaming in front of him, his spoon clanking on the sides of his china teacup as he stirred in the sugar cube to dissolve. As the swirling came to rest, he could see his own frowning reflection in the cup. His wife, Ida, continued to stare intensely at her daughter as the interrogation began.

"I had something I had to do, Mother, and it couldn't wait," responded Maria. Joseph still sat quietly. Maria's four brothers and two sisters had already been excused from the table and gone outside to play, their chairs neatly positioned back under the table.

"Young lady, just because you graduated from high school three days ago, it doesn't mean you have the privilege of keeping your father and your siblings waiting. I'm sorry, but you will only receive cold scraps, if any remain. The leftovers are in the kitchen. Anna may be so kind as to fix you a plate if she is not finished with the dishes. Her work is finished for the day when the dishes are done." Ida's scolding was something the rest of the children took with no fear. But if Joseph got involved, whippings with a switch were in order.

Joseph blew gently on his steaming tea as he held the cup by the handle to his lips. "Daughter, tell Anna to prepare a plate for you, then come back in the room as she performs for you this undeserved task. Being tardy for dinner is not acceptable in this family, no matter how old you may think you have become." Joseph was calm, but Maria knew his tone was not being channeled through a tenor of acceptance.

"Yes, Father." Maria knew what she was about to tell her mother and father was to be either a proud moment for all or one to cause a clashing in their parent/child relationships.

Maria was raised in an intellectual and sophisticated environment. Her father was a well-respected physician in town, adapting the west wing of his inherited family mansion into three exam rooms and one small operating facility for the people of Cologne and the surrounding farmlands.

Although most of Joseph's practice consisted of caring for routine illness and stiches and setting an occasional broken bone, four years prior, Joseph had witnessed three horrific battles in the American Civil War, as Otto Von Bismarck had insisted Prussian surgeons and physicians learn from the American field physicians as he prepared his armies for the Austro-Prussian War imminent on the horizon. Bismarck and King Wilhelm I were preparing to dominate the German-speaking provinces, and not through diplomacy.

Joseph didn't speak much of his journey, except to those who could learn from his surgical and newly acquired amputation skills. His whole family was most proud of his bravery, but after his return home in 1863, his temperament had changed from gentle to somewhat intolerant of those who considered themselves in a position of high esteem. His enjoyment and thus his presence within the higher social circles of Cologne had diminished greatly.

Maria reentered the formal dining room and sat in her assigned seat, three chairs to the left of her father, as her father sat at the head and her mother sat at the end. "Okay, Father, I'm sorry I'm late for dinner, but there was something I found out today, and my immediate attention to the situation was mandatory." Maria sat with her hands folded in her lap, expressing perfectly her ladylike posture, looking down at the table and her food as it grew cold.

"Look at me, young one. What could be so important you could not perform this crucial task tomorrow? Your school days are over until your attendance at the university in the fall. Our family is strong because we respect each other's time and we meet to give thanks to the Lord every evening together as one." Ida was not settling down.

Maria began speaking, her voice trembling in the anticipation of the unknown reaction from her parents, especially her father. "Father, I must begin with my apology to you and Mother, and I understand and respect our family traditions to the highest, but allow me to explain." Joseph was quite impressed with the social skills and rhetoric of his oldest daughter.

"By all means, child, and I hope, for your sake, there is no falsification of your story," Joseph responded.

"Oh, no sir, those days of my youth are over. Let me begin by saying my last few days of school with Pastor Braun were quite stirring, and today an event happened that caused me to act upon his teachings." Although trembling, Maria was speaking in a most mature manner.

"Keep going, Maria, but there had better be a good reason why you're using a man of the cloth to excuse your tardiness," interjected her mother.

"Get on with it, child." Joseph was on the edge of becoming impatient.

Maria began. "Pastor Braun, as you know, teaches a class in our Lutheran High School. He teaches current events."

"Yes, and what?" interrupted Ida.

"Ida, let the girl speak. I'm most interested in why the pastor is involved in educating our children as to the situation of our world today. He should be teaching of our world beyond." Joseph was skeptical as to the clergy's opinions on politics.

Maria began again. "Thank you, Father. As I was saying, the pastor teaches us about what's happening in our current environment, and he told us that two years ago in 1864, in Geneva, an organization was founded to help soldiers injured in battle, to help the wounded as you did in America."

"Yes, Maria, I am quite aware of this organization, and I believe it is called the Red Cross. Our country has signed the agreement and joined this international group which protects those who display Red Crosses on their arms, dresses or shirts. However, at this point, they may only help those soldiers of their own country." Since his experience in America, he had become close to the powerful Otto Von Bismarck. Prussian government officials had been instructed to consult with Joseph as to his opinions and the organization of training manuals for volunteers. Joseph was a key figure in this organization, unbeknownst to his family.

"So what does this have to do with being late for dinner, child?" Ida snapped quickly and impatiently at Maria.

"Well, as you know, I and my friends graduated from high school three days ago, and we're almost all eighteen years of age now," Maria answered.

"Yes, and?" Ida snapped again.

"Well, the pastor's son, you both know my good friend Otto,

and five other boys were served letters at their homes this morning. They have been drafted into the Prussian army and must report for duty on Wednesday. Then they are to be trained and leave by rail to somewhere by week's end." Maria began to tear up.

"Oh my, that's awful. Those boys are too young to go into the army. What is wrong with Von Bismarck? He can't take our children from us. For God's sake, they are boys out of school for only one weekend. Tomorrow, Joseph, I insist we must go to the induction office and protest. That boy, Otto, is like one of our own. Joseph, he and Maria have spent many an hour in this house together." Ida was shocked. "So, Maria, you were late because you were saying goodbye to Otto? That is precious, and we so forgive you."

"Well Mother, that's not exactly the reason. When I heard, I did go to Otto's house, and we had lunch together and talked," said Maria.

Joseph sat quietly. He was beginning to put the puzzle together but was terribly afraid he was right. "Then why were you late? You're not making sense, child." Ida was losing her patience, while Joseph was regaining his composure but in deep concern.

"Say it, Maria. Just say it. You were late because you joined the Red Cross," he blurted. "Am I correct or not, child?"

"Yes sir," Maria answered as she looked down into her lap.

"No, no, no," said Ida. "You're too young, and you don't have the training to help them. War means death for anyone close to it. If you're not injured physically, you will be mentally. Look how your father—"

Ida was interrupted. "Ida, don't say it," said Joseph. "I know I'm not the same since I came back from America, but the Lord needed me to help. That's why I became a physician, then trained to be a surgeon. How can we blame our daughter for following in the footsteps of her father? I'm the one at fault here." Joseph sighed as he stared into a scene in which he had never imagined his daughter appearing.

"No, Joseph," Ida repeated herself. "That's different. You're a strong man. You're a smart man, and even though you're not the same since you returned, your skills will save many. What can this child do on a field of battle? She knows nothing."

"Ida, that's not exactly true. She has helped me many times in this house when patients come to visit. She has assisted me in stitching, and she has assisted me by bandaging and rebandaging many of my patients. I'm sure you know that. And she has a talent for it." Maria didn't expect this kind of response from her father at all. She had already decided she was going to continue as a volunteer for the Red Cross no matter what they said, even if it meant her father's switch.

"No, I'm going down there tomorrow morning and insist she not be allowed to volunteer in such a dangerous endeavor." Ida would have gotten the switch herself, but only Joseph was allowed to perform that kind of punishment.

"Mother, I'm eighteen and no longer a student, and I can choose my own future. You have no legal right to force them to refuse me. I don't need your permission." Ida was furious with that answer, but Joseph intervened.

"Ida, that's enough. I know you're scared to death you will lose your little girl, but she's not a little girl anymore. She's a young woman and a brave one. As frightened as I am for her to be in harm's way, not to mention the brutality of soldiers and their unspeakable acts towards women in these situations, I must admit that deep inside, I'm proud of our child." Maria lifted her humble face from her lap and saw a gentle smile on her father's face as well as tears welling in his eyes.

"Thank you, Father." Maria held her head high and turned it back and forth as she observed the expressions of both her mother and father. Then, finally, Ida laid her head on the table and began to weep.

As she did, Joseph spoke directly to Maria. "My daughter, I must tell you of one danger you may not have considered."

"Yes, Father, what is it? All I know right now is I'm going with my friends in the army to be a Red Cross nurse and help save the lives of the injured, as you have taught me. And I have proofread your government manuals for you many times. I'm ready."

"No, Maria, that's not it," her father answered. "You do realize the Red Cross has never been in a battle before? This will be the first time in history Red Cross volunteers will be anywhere near a fight. And Prussia and many other nations have sworn their support to the rules of the organization, and those countries will train their soldiers to protect you from both sides," Joseph said.

"Yes, I know that, Father. I read the entire enactment after Pastor Braun made me aware," replied Maria. "So what is it I don't know?"

"Prussia signed the agreement, but Austria did not. If you are shot on purpose by any of the Austrian state's soldiers, it will not be considered a war crime for them." Joseph finished, and Ida raised her head with a look of terror on her face.

"Father, what makes you think they won't sign it before a war breaks out? It will be maybe a year. They'll probably just be training me for a while. They already have forty-three volunteers. They wouldn't send us in to battle without training, would they?" This was new information for Maria.

"You told them you had worked with me, correct?" asked Joseph.

"Yes," said Maria.

"Then you're experienced as far as they are concerned. And the answer to your other question, and now something I have been wanting to say is, they would not be drafting all these young men and sending them away so quickly if we weren't going to war real soon, and I mean REAL soon. Like, the end of this week, perhaps. We have troops moving into Langensalza as we speak," Joseph answered, "including your young friends."

"How do you know that, Joseph?" asked Ida with deep curiosity.

"Because I received a visit from an army captain today. He asked me if I would please volunteer to leave in two days for Langensalza on the train with other medical personnel. I didn't go to America just to sight-see. Bismarck sent me there and told me that if Prussia goes to war, my services would be needed. No, actually, he said 'mandatory.'" Silence came over the table as Joseph finished.

Ida broke down crying again. She might not only lose her daughter but her husband as well. Maria and Joseph got up from their chairs and went to Ida. They hugged her and her grieving soul.

"Ida, we'll be fine, and we have God's work to do. Be proud of us and pray for us every night. We'll be back soon," said Joseph.

Then Joseph hugged Maria with an embrace Maria had never felt before. It was one of mutual love and respect. "We'll probably be on the same train and in the same car together with other medical providers. I'll help with your training and those of the others on our way. Plus, you've already read the training manual. I will need your help as much as you will need mine."

"I love you, Father," as Maria returned the hug.

"I love you too, daughter. Now let's get ready to save some brave soldiers. And you and your other nurses are about to make history."

June 24, 1866 — Cologne, Prussia

THE TRAIN FROM COLOGNE TO LANGENSALZA LEAVES TOMORROW. NO TIME TO REST AND NO TIME TO BE FRIGHTENED

Maria slept very lightly, so lightly she seemed to be floating poetically through an ethereal part of her mind, reviewing the events that had delivered her to this critical juncture of her life or to her death. She mentally leafed through the pages of her childhood:

teachers, her pastor, friends, and her immediate and extended family. Her decision to go off to battle so young didn't seem to stem from any emotional impulse. Every path on which her half-dream/half-reality thoughts led her throughout the night made her realize her life had progressed as destined, as if she had been walking down this narrow passageway, unable to exit until the end, where the sun gleamed brightly and the destination was clear. But as she peered into the wide-open spaces ahead, the sun was beginning to rise, and the grassy knolls seemed to roll endlessly from valley to valley. Her mind could only wonder what awaited her life over each of these mysterious hilltops and what waited in those valleys in front of her.

"Maria, Maria, are you awake?" her father whispered in her ear as he softly shook her shoulder and kissed her on the cheek. Joseph didn't want to awaken Maria's younger sister, the sister she had shared a room and a bed with for well over ten years now.

"Yes, Father, I'm awake. Is something wrong?" Maria sat up, rubbing her eyes, attempting to focus on Joseph's countenance in the early morning sunlight that crept through the small-paned windows.

"No dear. It's time for us to prepare for our departure. We leave tomorrow morning, and we must begin our process of gathering our needed supplies and instruments as soon as possible. We have no time to spare. I'd like for us to have the time to enjoy dinner as a family before we leave." Joseph was careful not to use the phrase "one last time," and he was no longer viewing his daughter as a child; he wouldn't treat her as one for the rest of her life, and she would give him no reason to do so.

"Father, give me a moment to brush my teeth, cleanse my face and dress. I'll come downstairs directly and join you for breakfast. I've been reviewing what you've taught me all night, but I want to learn more—and quickly." Joseph gently caressed Maria's hair with a look of such pride for his young lady who had just exploded unexpectedly into adulthood like a thunderbolt. But he also knew this was the end of her innocence, as it had been for him after viewing the world and its humanity, or inhumanity, in the American Civil War. Joseph knew he had changed dramatically on his return, and he knew she would never be able to view her family and friends as emotional peers. The sight of death and suffering does a lot to the fairytale world not only of a child but to any human with a heart that can feel compassion.

Maria pushed open the swinging door to the kitchen and entered as Anna had breakfast spread neatly across the worn wooden table. The celestial aroma of Anna's homemade loaves filled the room as if it were an invisible cloud. And the blackberry jam produced from the bushes in their garden, jarred and preserved by Maria and Anna together each year since she was a child, always brought a smile to Maria's face, except for this morning. Attempting to continue on her trail of denial, all in the room knew what the worst-case consequences could be to this beautiful family, what they all might need to endure in the very near future.

With tears swelling into both the eyes of Ida and Anna as they moved perpetually around the kitchen, Joseph and Maria sat across from each other on the long family benches. The other children had not yet awakened. "Maria, I'm going to make a list of medical supplies needed for our journey. You're to take this list to the army headquarters and ask for Captain Heil. You'll go with him and a few of his men to gather the supplies we will need in order to treat the wounded." Joseph's orders to Maria were given with no emotion, the same as if he were speaking to any assistant.

"If there are any wounded you mean, Joseph," Ida interjected, correcting her husband in a most curt fashion. Maria looked at her father to observe his reaction.

"Yes, dear. You're correct. We're assuming there will be some sort of altercation. But again, you are correct. There may not be." Joseph didn't argue with Ida. He was just as worried about his daughter's safety as she was. But Ida was the only one who had two loved ones to worry about. Joseph was not worried about himself; neither was Maria.

Maria came back to the topic of supplies, attempting to ignore her mother's interruption. "But Father, shouldn't the Red Cross personnel know what is necessary?" she asked. Joseph felt his daughter had asked a very logical but unfortunately very naïve question.

"My dear, from this point on, there are no secrets between us," replied Joseph.

"Okay, Father, I would hope not. But what are you saying?" asked Maria.

"I'll be wearing an army officer's uniform and be considered the leader of this Red Cross mission. The Red Cross has never been in a battle as of now in all of history. They have no field leaders. There's no one going, at least from our town, with the experience to do what I can do. And you are now my main assistant. You volunteered, and there's no turning back. I must be able to trust you completely; and you me."

"Yes, Father, I understand," said Maria. "But of these supplies, what might the quantities be that are needed? How can we know that?"

Ida turned towards Joseph with the question all wished to ask. The answer that came from Joseph would determine the expectations of the size of the battle and the amount of dead and wounded. It would determine the scope of the incursion.

"That's unknown to me at this point, Maria. Just tell Captain Heil that the amounts are dependent upon his estimated number of wounded. See this note on the bottom, Maria? The quantities necessary will be dependent upon each hundred men wounded in battle. Just multiply each supply by one hundred. Do you understand, Maria?" Joseph was very precise.

"Yes, sir, I understand. I'll leave now and report back as soon as the job is completed." Maria was no longer sounding like the shy schoolgirl at the dinner table the night before. Even her mother and Anna were emotionally affected by Maria's sophisticated response.

"Wait just a moment, there. I'm not done." Joseph was writing on a second page of his parchment with his quill. As he finished rather quickly, he pushed the parchment across the table at Maria. "Also tell him these instruments I have listed on this side of the page must be multiplied by the number of doctors capable of amputations and the other side of the page multiplied by those capable of removing musket balls and cannon shrapnel from the soldiers' tissues and inner organs." Maria began to feel ill from the thought but suppressed it and hid it courageously from her father as well as from Ida and Anna. The amputations her father had performed, and of which he rarely spoke, had been performed predominantly in America, but a few had been performed in the small operatory at the local hospital. Then suddenly, Ida, unable to control herself, vomited violently into the sink.

Thinking he would lighten the conversation, Joseph asked "Ida, are we expecting another child?" His attempt at humor was bluntly ignored.

"Come, Maria," said Joseph. "Let's finish this discussion in my office. Grab my instructions and your tea, and pack us a handful of those wonderful anise cookies your mother and Anna just made yesterday. Ladies, we love those cookies!" Joseph smiled, kissed Ida on the back of her head as she leaned over the sink. He then winked at Anna. Maria trotted quickly behind her father in order to keep up with the focused Dr. Rothert. But before they could exit through the swinging door, they were stopped. The reality of Maria's decision had finally overflowed in Ida's heart.

Ida cried out as she stomped her foot. "No, Joseph! You can't let her go with you. She isn't ready for that kind of horror. I forbid it!" Ida finally lost her composure, and her fear for her daughter could no longer be hidden. Panic had set in. The events to take place tomorrow were now absolute. In her wildest dreams, she thought her sons, maybe, but never did Ida imagine any of her daughters, especially her oldest, would ever be going off to war.

Joseph didn't respond to his wife. Maria looked over her shoulder at her mother's deep pain as she left the kitchen with her father. She didn't stop. She continued on, following the orders of her father, but knowing he was suddenly now more than that. He was her commanding officer, and lives now depended on both of them. The feelings in Maria's heart were mixed, but the overriding thoughts that drove her were those thoughts of her destiny. Something had pushed her into this abyss. It felt so right, she felt it must be God's calling.

Ida buried her face in Anna's bosom and sobbed as both women embraced, their hearts filled with maternal grief. "Your daughter is one strong woman already, Ida. She'll be protected by her spirit and the love of her family." Then Anna joined Ida with her tears dripping onto the top of Ida's beautiful blonde hair.

• • •

The day of preparation flew by like a flock of migrating geese as Joseph boxed his personal supplies and packed his surgical instruments in protective gauze. He then sat at his desk to prepare an agenda for the one-day train ride to Langensalza, a journey in which each hour must be planned with efficiency in order to teach his volunteers the fundamentals he would require from them on the battlefield, the pre-op, the operatory and the post-op. And while Joseph prepared his agenda in the safe and serene confines of his office, Maria bustled through Cologne with a band of soldiers, gathering the instruments and supplies needed.

Her plan was well-organized, since she had joined her father many times in the purchase of pharmaceuticals and other medical needs. She and her soldiers moved their wagons from pharmacy to pharmacy, gathering exactly what her father had instructed her to obtain in the quantities determined by the captain's estimate of the wounded to come. Her youth and inexperience as a leader were quickly forgotten by the team of soldiers placed under her direction. "Yes, Ma'am" and "No, Ma'am" were immediately found to be the appropriate salutation towards this young woman portraying such unexpected subliminal administrative skills.

Maria's competent intensity came naturally. She was introduced to all as the head nurse of the newly founded Red Cross team; therefore, all became aware she was responsible for the care of the wounded among both the soldiers who escorted her that day as well as all the sons of Cologne. And during this entire afternoon, Maria thought nothing of the danger she was about to encounter, only of the dire importance of her mission.

"Joseph," Ida shot in a curt manner at her husband as she stormed briskly into his office; her arms were folded, and a scowl was upon her face. "I told you dinner would be ready at five o'clock sharp, and now it's thirty minutes past that hour. And where is Maria?" The other children had been firmly told by Ida to be quiet as they sat in a perpendicular posture in their assigned chairs at the table.

"Ida, please, I promise you, Maria will be home at any time, and I just need ten more minutes. Please be understanding tonight, especially towards Maria." Joseph hadn't looked up as he continued to pack his last-minute surgical instruments.

Ida was having a hard time controlling her ghastly visions of the days to come. Just twenty-four hours prior, Maria was being scolded like a child for being late for dinner. Now, both her husband and daughter no longer seemed part of the family that, until yesterday, was so organized and so disciplined. "I'll instruct Anna to begin bringing the food from the kitchen. She has prepared hasenpfeffer and mashed potatoes, green beans and sauerkraut, Maria's favorite. Ten minutes, Joseph, but if Maria—"

Suddenly Maria, breathing heavily, burst into the room, interrupting her mother. "Sorry, Mother, Father, but I had to go to a few extra stores to get the quantity the captain required."

Ida knew what the "additional quantities" meant; so did Joseph, and from the tenseness in her tone, so did Maria. But that conversation was only acknowledged by each internally.

"What's that mouth-watering aroma, Mother? It's hasenpfeffer, isn't it? Oh, Mother, my favorite. Are we ready to eat? I have had nothing since breakfast." Maria was shaking slightly from the adrenaline pumping through her veins.

"Yes, Maria, dinner has been ready for a while, but you and your father have not. Joseph, come. You have all night to complete your preparations for tomorrow." But with that, Joseph and Maria could see Ida's eyes change from impatience to tears as she turned and left the room.

"Father," Maria began, "I have a few things I must tell you; but nothing bad. I went to—"

Joseph interrupted. "Not now, Maria, your mother is right. All have been waiting for us, and dinner is late. We'll talk after we eat." Joseph put his arm around Maria's shoulder, and they both strolled into the dining room to join the family. They took their seats. Anna had placed dinner beautifully on the table. The hasenpfeffer and its gravy smelled delectable.

"Oh, Anna, you made hasenpfeffer! You know that's my favorite. That's so sweet of you before Father and I—"

Joseph cleared his throat so Maria would not go on to make this a sad occasion.

"It was your mother's idea, child. She knows what you like and what you don't. You two may not get a great meal for a couple weeks, where you're going." Anna was trying to be optimistic, but everyone knew it could be a long time (if ever) before Joseph and Maria returned.

Dinner progressed, and nothing was said about what was about to happen at dawn the next day. As usual, the children didn't speak unless spoken to, and of course, the occasional reprimand by Ida to get an elbow off the table or to wipe one's mouth of errant food was expected. Then, as dinner ended, all the children except Maria were excused from the table. As they left, they all gave their oldest sister and their father a long and loving hug, but no tears.

Finishing their tea, Joseph, Ida and Maria were the only ones left at the table.

Joseph looked at Ida. "Excuse us, my dear, but Maria needs to debrief me on the events of her day. Maria, use the bathroom if you must, and join me in my office." Joseph and Maria left Ida alone at the table. She thought about how formal her husband was with Maria and how Maria was so respectful of the new position of her father in her life.

June 25, 1866 — Cologne, Prussia

DEPARTURE FROM HEAVEN TO HELL. "PEOPLE, CLASS IS IN SESSION"

Morning arrived before the sun had risen, and breakfast was re-peated with bread, homemade jam and tea. While Ida helped Anna, the children poked and prodded each other playfully around the kitchen table, waiting to depart for the train station. As the first signs of daylight peeked through the kitchen window, three large horse-drawn wagons and a carriage that sat six arrived in front of the house. At least a dozen soldiers, including Captain Heil, exited the wagons and knocked on the door, and Ida graciously showed then into the house. Joseph left his office and made his way through the back hallway straight to the kitchen. He opened the swing doors to the kitchen with staunch energy. "Come with me, Maria." Maria arose from the bench and followed her father immediately, with no hesitation.

Joseph said his good mornings to all in the vestibule and after doing so, addressed his wife as if she were a private in the army. "Ida, pack some breakfast for Maria and me? We'll need to load up our equipment and supplies into the wagons and check that all is present. We don't have time to eat. Thank you." Joseph went to his office with Captain Heil and Maria close behind.

The soldiers helped Joseph and Maria carry their gear to the wagon. Most of the supplies were in the wagons already from Maria's gatherings of the day before. As far as personal items, Joseph and Maria had very little. "Doctor, will you and your daughter please take a quick look inside the wagons and confirm we have all that you will need?"

"Captain, she is my daughter, but please refer to her as my head nurse, as she will need that respectful title when things get rough." Joseph was unemotional, but Ida heard it from the hallway. She wanted to stop her daughter from leaving Cologne. She felt Maria had already done enough for Prussia.

The supplies were confirmed by both Maria and Joseph. They both went back into the house with packages wrapped in paper under their arms. As they went upstairs to their bedrooms, Ida was puzzled. The captain entered the kitchen and instructed Ida and the children to follow him to the buggy that awaited outside. The buggy was supplied by the army to ride the Rotherts to the train station and send Joseph and Maria off on their journey to Langensalza. It was a cool morning, for June, and a slight mist caused Ida to cover herself and the children with two woolen blankets. The smell was like that of a wet animal. All were quiet, even the youngest of the children. They all found the soldiers intimidating.

"Where are Father and Maria?" asked the youngest. "They're going with us, right?"

Ida had a curious frown upon her face. "I'm not sure what they're doing, child, but I can assure you they will be riding with us to the station. The captain will decide when…" Suddenly Ida stopped in mid-sentence. The front door opened, and Joseph and Maria came out of the house, descending down the front marble stairway to the street. The children began to clap. Ida broke out in tears.

"Oh Joseph," Ida whimpered. "You look so handsome and strong, but please don't allow this to continue with our child." She buried her head in her hands as her oldest son hugged her.

Joseph was in a full officer's uniform with a captain's stripes, a hat, and a Red Cross banner wrapped around each arm. Maria was much more expressive. She was dressed all in white: shoes, stockings, full dress and nurse's cap. Sewn onto the front and back of her uniform was a Red Cross emblem as well as the banners on her arms. All the siblings as well as Joseph were stunned and so proud of her. And Ida was as well, but the thought of losing her child in battle continued to be too much to bear.

Maria and Joseph were instructed to sit in the covered supply wagon with the other soldiers, but Ida stood upright in the buggy, almost causing it to tip. "No, please, Captain, no. There is a spot in the buggy here next to me. Oh, please, sir, give us a few more minutes together before you take her from me. I beg of you."

Maria looked at her mother and could feel the pain she was enduring. "Mother," said Maria, "I love you and all of my family, and Anna, as much as anyone could love their family. But the captain is not taking me from you. This is my choice. This is God's will. If I'm ordered to ride with the soldiers, then that is what I must do." Joseph and Captain Heil looked at each other with smiles on their faces.

"Mrs. Rothert, there is a place in the buggy, and I think it would be most appropriate for you and all your children to escort the good doctor and our head nurse to the train station. Please, hold your daughter in your arms and let her siblings be proud of her. We need more loyal and dedicated Prussians like the two of them." The captain saluted the entire buggy.

"Thank you, sir," said Maria as she bowed her head in gratitude to the captain. The youngest of the boys stood and saluted in return.

Joseph squeezed the captain's arm and mouthed the words "Bless you" as he also saluted.

As the wagons and the family buggy began their short trek to the train station, Ida and Maria cuddled under the woolen blanket. As Ida looked ahead into the wagons of soldiers, she could barely endure the thought of her little girl in the midst of men fighting each other to the death. *No, this can't be real*, she thought.

The convoy arrived shortly at the train station. As steam was released from time to time from the train's engine and the mist began to change from a mild to a medium drizzle, the captain and his men emptied the supply wagons into one passenger car, while Joseph and Maria became intensely occupied checking off the list created by Joseph the day before. Both medical supplies and personnel would travel together.

As one of the wagons became empty, Captain Heil approached Ida. "Please, Mrs. Rothert, move your family into this covered wagon that is now empty. We still have to continue to load other soldiers and ammunition into the other cars you see down the tracks." With the sight of soldiers in uniforms with guns on their shoulders, the realization of what was happening swelled to even more and more tangibility to Ida. She began to weep profusely.

As Ida and the children were in the process of moving to the wagon and out of the rain, she watched the men in uniform being jammed into train cars with no seats. Then she heard someone crying out, "Mrs. Rothert, oh, Mrs. Rothert. Over here." As she looked closer, all the men's faces became those of little boys, and the one waving was Otto Braun, standing alongside his father, Pastor Braun, and his mother, Mrs. Braun.

She walked down one car and saw Otto's mother crying as well. They both embraced intently. "I'm so sorry, Mrs. Braun. Maria told us about Otto's draft letter Monday night. Oh dear. Not your son. Not Otto! He's too young. Way too young, Mrs. Braun."

"Oh, Ida, you're right. He is too young, and they just took him. They snatched him from my arms. They delivered the letter in person early Monday morning, then came to our house on Wednesday. They put him into a wagon filled with other boys, and off they went. We were told we could say our goodbyes this morning here at this platform." Mrs. Braun was heartbroken. "But Ida, your sons are too young to be drafted. Don't tell me the army broke the law and took one of them as well! Something is happening, and it's serious. I'm so frightened."

"No, they didn't take any of my sons, but they did somewhat force Joseph to be the head of the medical team and—" Ida choked up and couldn't speak.

"What is it, dear? I know it must be hard watching your husband leave again like he did a few years ago. But he came back unscathed. Those doctors stay behind the front lines." Mrs. Braun was trying to be delicate.

"No, Mrs. Braun, that's not it." Ida again hesitated as she watched Mrs. Braun dry her eyes. "After our daughter, Maria, found out about Otto, she came home Monday night late for dinner and informed us she had joined the Red Cross, that new international organization to help the wounded on the battlefields." Ida could barely finish her sentence.

Pastor Braun had overheard the women's conversation as well, but Otto had not. The boys were being pulled from their parents' embraces and forced onto the train. Hugs were given by all to Otto as the women wept. But Otto was actually excited. He felt like a man for the first time in his life. All three watched him board the train with his gun over his shoulder and backpack on his back. He disappeared into the ocean of young boys inside the stripped-down passenger car. It was "standing room only." Stretching her neck, looking into the car in a futile attempt to catch one last glimpse of her departing son, Mrs. Braun talked to Ida without turning her head. "Ida, I can't imagine how you must be feeling. Your husband's a doctor and has been trained in warfare medicine, but your daughter; that poor child. We'll pray for their safety every night and every Sunday. But I must tell you," as Mrs. Braun turned to Ida and held her by the shoulders, " I have known your little Maria since she was baptized in our church as an infant, and although I'm frightened for her, I must say, I never thought I'd be this overwhelmingly proud of her courage and her dedication to helping boys like our Otto. You and your family have ours and the Lord's deepest blessing."

They all hugged, and Ida heard out the window, "Goodbye Mrs. Rothert. We'll all be back soon! Give Maria my love when you get home." Otto was unaware that Joseph and Maria were just two cars in front of him. Looking out the window, Otto had such an innocent smile on his face. He would soon find out that war was the invention of Satan himself and that Satan would be visiting him from time to time for all eternity.

The train was ready to depart. The bell from the engine clanged, and "All aboard" was being yelled all down the track from engine to caboose. Joseph and Maria finished their inventory, and the whole family embraced, as they all knew this embrace might be their last. Except for Joseph and Maria, the family cried. Joseph made quick work of the goodbyes and told Maria to get on the train. Neither of them stood by the window and waved as the train moved slowly out of the station. Joseph and Maria knew it was time to get down to business.

• • •

With stops to pick up more soldiers and supplies, the train to Langensalza would arrive the following morning. During this period, Joseph took every moment possible to teach his three other doctors and some forty-three Red Cross nurses the art of warfare medicine. And Joseph didn't let up on Maria at any time. Her training was his main focus. It was she who needed to pass it on to the other nurses while he trained the doctors. Only a few times did Joseph allow himself to glance over at Maria as she worked diligently with her staff. And in those moments, he would become caught-up in his emotions of how much love and respect he had for his "little girl." Joseph knew, once the fighting started, there would be no room for love, only caring for the wounded.

June 26, 1866

LANGENSALZA'S COUNTRYSIDE SWARMS WITH CHAOS.

FOR JOSEPH, MARIA, AND THE RED CROSS, THEIR TIME HAS ARRIVED

It had been twenty-four hours since Joseph and Maria dramatically departed from their comfortable loving family life in the city of Cologne. The caravan pulled by the massive iron horse stopped at countryside train stations along the Prussian landscape in order to jam more young draftees into its claustrophobic passenger and box cars. The train arrived at its final destination by midmorning—the quaint farming town of Langensalza. As the sun rose, the air became denser, the heat already reaching the dehydration level for the young soldiers crammed inside the cars; nausea and fatigue were clear on the faces of the young soldiers. Joseph, now addressed as Dr. Rothert by all in the camp, and his crew were near exhaustion as well. He and Maria had spent almost the entire day and night of the trip training the inexperienced nurses in the art of stitching, bandaging, removing minor shrapnel and treating shallow bullet wounds. The car carried with it a pungent odor as the trainees practiced their new medical skills diligently on recently skinned pigs and slaughtered rabbits donated by the farmers of Cologne.

As the convoy arrived in Langensalza, the army had already set up three large tents filled with cots and lanterns to house the wounded and one large tent containing four operating tables and a canvas tarp protecting the entry; its purpose, to cover those waiting for surgery from the heat of the sun or the drenching of a thunderstorm.

Like cutter ants, the soldiers unloaded the medical supplies and stacked the crates in the corner of each tent. Maria logically directed the placement of supplies needed for triage and post-op care as Joseph set up those instruments and supplies needed for surgery in the operatory.

While preparation was underway for any unfortunate soldiers in the upcoming battle, chaos ruled the fields of tall grass surrounding the train station. Young soldiers descended the steps of the train cars like rats emptying a sinking ship. Many of the young men emptied directly to the far side of the train away from the station in order to relieve themselves by either pissing on the wheels of the train or defecating in the tall grass only a few yards away. Unable to clearly understand the barking of orders by sergeants and squad leaders above the heavy heaving of the steam engine and the talking and laughter of the young men glad to be out of that human fish tank, organizing the troops was near impossible. Very few of the officers had ever been commanders in true attack mode, and most of the young soldiers had no idea what made an officer an officer, other than that they were the ones attempting to yell over top of each other. Eventually, Otto Braun, lost in this sea of confusion and fear, had no choice but to drift inside a small group of men wandering towards what appeared to be an entire city of dirty canvas tents. As the edge of the tents was reached, the soldiers were instructed to stand in single file as the squad leader read off his list of names. When he finished, Otto raised his hand.

"Sir, you didn't call my name. It's Otto, Otto Braun. You sure you didn't miss it?" Otto was feeling anxiety climbing up from his stomach.

"Sorry, son, no Otto anything on this list." The squad leader stared coldly at Otto.

"What should I do, sir?" Most of the patrol laughed at Otto's innocent childlike plea for direction.

"What patrol were you assigned to, soldier?" asked the squad leader.

"The Ranger Patrol, sir, I think. Or maybe it was the Rhinehart patrol." Otto was beginning to panic.

"Go back to the train station kid, and hell, I don't know, ask somebody if you can spend the night with girls in town." Again, the patrol laughed. But Otto felt nauseous. He was both embarrassed and overwhelmed with a feeling of loneliness. He realized he had never been away from home, ever, not even to another city. And now he felt he was a lost puppy dodging horses in the street, unable to find his way home.

"Yes sir, thank you, sir, I'll find my way." Otto saluted the officer and walked off, wanting to run and cry all the way back to his bedroom in Cologne and bury his face in his pillow. But he didn't. Instead, he began to stroll through the camp, hoping someone else might be more understanding. He wandered the camp until he came across an older soldier sitting alone on the hillside. He approached the aloof infantryman, attempting to make friends with someone who perhaps could help him with his disorientation.

• • •

"Captain," asked Dr. Rothert. "Do we know how much time before we might be needed?" Joseph had some information unknown to everyone except him, but it was a secret between him and the higher-ups. And it wasn't a question that came from fear, simply one of necessity, so Joseph could determine his timeframe and the extent of his immediate preparation if the information shared with him was incorrect.

"Father—?" Maria began.

"Nurse Rothert, it's Dr. Rothert from here until we return home and once more we eat Anna's hasenpfeffer." That would be the last time for quite a while that Maria and her father would allow themselves to smile and hug. "Now, what can I help you with, Nurse Rothert?"

"When the fighting starts—"

"Or if, Maria, when or if. But a good medical team is always prepared, my good nurse. But what is it? What is your question?"

Joseph had a look that made Maria want to hurry with her inquiry.

"There are nurses that will need to stay here to help with bandaging, disinfecting, and stitching wounds. Also, others that are needed in surgery and post-op. But I feel skilled in triage and would like to go to the front to help with the evaluation of those in the field. I believe maybe ten of us should receive some additional training from you today in order to make decisions in the field as to the severity of their conditions."

It was with that request that Joseph suddenly felt a lump in his throat. He had never considered that his daughter could be on the front lines where she could be in mortal danger. He always saw her near him in the operatory or rebandaging wounds in the post-op, not near any sort of violence. This decision would certainly change his daughter's life forever or, God forbid, shorten it.

"Yes, Nurse Rothert. If that's what you wish, I can help you and a few others to evaluate severities. But I'll say this only once. As you are my daughter, I must warn you. A triage nurse must not only send the most severely wounded first, while others around you will be moaning in great pain from noncritical wounds such as broken bones or nonfatal gunshot wounds, but—" Joseph stopped and stared for the last time into the face of his wide-eyed innocent child. With what he was about to say, she would soon be a woman with tainted dreams and troubling memories forever. "You will also need to decide which men you must leave in the field to die."

Maria looked stunned. "Why would I leave someone to die?"

"Because if you look outside, it's a small town and you'll have a limited number of wagons and buckboards from the farmers and merchants who live here. And even though all will be forced by the army to volunteer their transportation—"

"Are you saying—?"

"Yes, Nurse Rothert. It'll be you and the other triage nurses to make decisions, decisions you will make many times in battlefields. I'll train your staff to recognize the signs of a man who has no chance of survival, even with surgery; the gurgling of their lungs filled with blood, the gray color of their skin, stomach wounds with the organs exposed and unrepairable, the smell of perforated organs unable to be repaired. You must send back only those we can save. You must leave those we cannot, and they will be gathered last, if they survive that long."

Joseph was as cold as Maria had ever seen a person. He was her father. He was loving and caring. He was a saint in her eyes. But now, this was not "Father." This was Dr. Rothert, who had witnessed a bloody, horrific civil war in America, and as she thought back on the days since he had returned, she realized he had never been quite the same. Maria began to fight back her tears.

"Don't you dare, Nurse Rothert. Your job is to save lives, period. As many as you can, as fast as you can. That's our job in wartime. Crying comes later when you're in your room at home with no one around, like I do when you all go to the market."

Maria held her head high and stared into Dr. Rothert's eyes. "Yes, sir, I understand completely. You are saying when all this is over, I'll be proud of the entire team for those lives we saved, but I will always be sad for those I had to leave behind."

"Not sad, Nurse, haunted. You will be haunted by faces from time to time in your nightmares. Meet me in the operatory tent in one hour with the triage candidates you feel can handle this emotionally. And you must explain to them what I just told you before you bring them. We don't have the time nor the place for the weak in that position."

"See you in an hour, Doctor." And Maria left the tent with a totally different attitude than when she had entered. She was scared. Not for herself, but for those poor boys she might have to leave suffering on the battlefield during their final hours on earth.

THE TIME TO WAIT HAS COME, BUT FOR HOW LONG?

AND WAIT FOR WHAT?

Joseph and his colleagues made their final inspection of the hospital to assure themselves that all supplies and instruments were in their proper places. Now came the grueling period of waiting for their skills to be used in an attempt to override the agony of pain and death. Meanwhile, soldiers across the way sat anxiously in the grass and on patches of bare earth, like ducks on the side of a riverbed. Throughout their worn encampment, an occasional muffled whimper would emanate from a homesick young boy, attempting relentlessly to be unheard as he buried his face in his khaki backpack.

"Dr. Rothert, do you feel you and your people are prepared and ready to take good care of our boys in case a battle begins?" asked the captain as he returned from inspecting his untrained and incompetent troops.

"How do they look, Captain? The troops I mean." Joseph knew the troops were young, but maybe not all had just been plucked from the arms of their nannies.

"They look like schoolboys on recess. Some think they're still playing soldier with toy guns, while others are hiding in bushes and tents, sobbing for their mothers. Doctor, if a battle ever does come to fruition, perhaps we should have brought some pediatricians with us." The captain removed his hat and ran his hand through his wet, greasy hair.

"A body's a body, Captain. We'll do everything we can to help your boys." Joseph was staying positive but was far from confident.

"Dr. Rothert, if you're prepared, get your team together and meet me by the road in back of your operatory. Dinner will be served shortly." Joseph frowned in perplexity. He had not even thought of dinner, but with that suggestion, now he was famished.

When the team had all assembled, the captain led them down the winding dirt road, about a mile, soon to arrive at a monumental gothic Lutheran church giving off an ancient stoic aura. They were greeted with handshakes, hugs and curtseys by the loving and peaceful people of Langensalza. As they were led inside, they were informed that an incredible meal was being prepared in their honor, a delicious meal of vegetables, sauerbraten with gingersnap gravy, and like every Prussian meal, sauerkraut.

"Allow us to show you to the rectory and a few more of our houses in close proximity, so you fine people may clean up from your long train ride, not to mention what must have been an exhausting day of training and preparation," said the pastor's wife. "Perhaps our parish can wash those beautiful white uniforms of yours overnight. We're expecting a quite breezy evening, and they should be dry by morning." The congregation was being most hospitable.

Joseph then addressed the pastor. "Sir, as much as I'm sure clean clothing would be a pleasure for my nurses, I'm afraid, from this moment on, we must be ready at any time to perform our services. We must prefer dirty over wet." All within hearing distance gave an understanding chuckle.

"But perhaps my people can take a broom to them and wipe them with a damp cloth, Dr. Rothert." Now that was a reasonable compromise accepted by all; however, Joseph did have to respond.

"Pastor, I'll be blunt. We so welcome your help and beautiful meal right now, but at some point, the stains on our uniforms will not be dirt and dust. I'm afraid the scrubbing of blood may be quite different and difficult for those that are faint of heart. Each nurse has two uniforms. We'll take you up on your offer, if need be." Joseph appreciated the naïve offer, but he always needed strength, not weakness.

"I thank you for your honesty, doctor. I do believe there will be some members of my parish unable to help with the cleaning, but they can cook, sir!" And Joseph and the pastor didn't laugh this time, knowing how important both tasks would become.

It was a quiet, solemn dinner, not one of frivolity in the least. The pastor blessed the food, and all prayed for the safety of all mankind on both sides. The townspeople knew from battles in their long history that their town might be under attack at any time if the Hanoverian troops broke through the Prussian lines.

Joseph rose to his feet. "Ladies and gentlemen, we all want to graciously thank you for your hospitality. And, as long as the days stay peaceful, we offer our medical services to your town free of charge during the day." The table of citizens clapped in appreciation. "But for now, it has been a stressful few days for all of us, and we need to return to our camp for a restful night of sleep. Again, thank you all, and bless you."

The group followed Dr. Rothert and the captain back up the road and to the tents set up for the wounded. The nurses took the cots in two of the tents and the doctors in one. The church people followed the team with buckboards filled with clean blankets and pillows. It was now reaching nine o'clock, and the medical team fell asleep as soon as their heads hit the pillows. Maria began to pray for courage and wisdom, but her eyes shut before her 'AMEN' arrived.

June 27, 1866 — Langensalza, Prussia

THE EARTH TREMBLED AS THE SKIES RUMBLED AND JUDGEMENT DAY CAME DOWN UPON MANY A YOUNG MAN

"Dr. Rothert, sir, wake up, please." Joseph opened his eyes to a softly lit kerosene lantern, unable to grasp where he might be or who this strange man was, lifting him from his deep, dreamless sleep.

"Who are you, sir, and where am I, may I ask?" Joseph inquired, believing he must be dreaming.

"I'm Corporal Schmidt; I was sent here by General Flies' staff," the corporal whispered closely in Joseph's ear.

Sudden reality entered Joseph's consciousness, and he grasped where he was. "What is it, soldier? Is it morning? It appears to be completely dark outside." Joseph sat up on the edge of his cot, stretched his arms and yawned. "Is someone sick?"

"No sir, it's time." The young corporal's voice was quivering as his hand touched Joseph's forearm. His touch felt as cold as that of a dead man.

"Come, kid, what do you mean 'it's time?' Spit it out!" Joseph was getting irritated with the vagueness being muttered in his ear, piercing the darkness.

"The troops are moving out, sir. It's three A.M., and they're starting to march to the Hanoverian camp. I think we're going to attack at daybreak. Their camp is less than three miles from here." The boy raised the wick of the lantern to emit more light.

"I'm assuming you're informing me to be ready for wounded soldiers by midmorning?" Joseph asked curiously. He had not told anyone how close he was with Von Bismarck. He had been the head surgeon for Bismarck and King Wilhelm I on the scouting expedition to the American Civil War. He had written textbooks on warfare medicine and spoken to Bismarck many times, both in person and by letter within the last year.

Still sitting on his cot, Joseph responded to the corporal. "Tell your general we'll be ready, and we'll have nurses and wagons following his troops, keeping about a mile from the front until the fighting ends. Then, when the firing ends, my people will go into action."

"Yes, sir, Captain Rothert," the young soldier said as he saluted Joseph and exited the tent.

"Oh, and Corporal, be sure to tell your general I'll not have any of my nurses enter the battlefield until the fighting ends. I'll not put them in harm's way." Joseph had never seen nurses in the field; no one had. He wasn't going to let any of them be hurt or captured. These women, especially his daughter, had volunteered their love and their services, not their lives.

"Yes, sir," the corporal repeated and sped off back to the command tent.

Joseph continued to position himself on the edge of his cot and thought, *This can't be. Bismarck told me we are a ploy to stall the Hanoverians from uniting with the Bavarians. He even leaked false troop counts to the Hanoverians about our numbers. General Flies is supposed to hold our position, not attack. Bismarck would never let these troops be slaughtered. And Ida, forgive me. I would never have let Maria come with me if I knew we would be in any real danger.*

• • •

Joseph woke the other doctors and succinctly explained the situation. He then went to the nurses' tents and, starting with Maria, instructed her to gently wake all the nurses, have them slip into their uniforms, then come into Maria's tent and sit on the cots without making a sound. Maria passed the word, and when all the nurses were dressed and assembled, Joseph and the other doctors reentered the tent. Dr. Rothert began his orders.

"Nurses, I've just been informed the army is moving out and will attack the Hanoverian camp at daybreak. That means that by midmorning, we'll be up to our bootstraps in blood. Some of you will go out with the triage nurses and buckboards onto the battlefield, but not until one of the officers tells you the fighting has ceased. Is that understood?"

The nurses were pondering, the mental atmosphere weighty. No one spoke a word. No one looked at each other. Maria's hands began to shake, so she sat on them so her father couldn't tell she was frightened.

"Once you're cleared to comb the battlefield, you'll bring back only Prussian infantrymen and cavalry, in accordance with the rules of the Red Cross, and you'll only bring us men who will, in your personal evaluations, survive with or without surgery. Next, if they need minor stitching and/or bandaging and they can walk back to our camp, let us do that here; point them toward our tents so as to save room for the others on the wagons. We have a few dozen pairs of crutches going with you. Then when the wagons return, repeat the triage." All the nurses sat staring at Dr. Rothert. "Do not, I repeat, do not send anyone back to us with a wound that you believe is fatal. By that, I mean a wound from which they won't survive no matter what we do. Those cases, if, in some way, they're still alive when we're gathering the dead, we'll do what we can."

Joseph was amazed at the lack of emotions among these women. They had volunteered for a reason, and this was it. They knew their purpose.

"And triage nurses, I know you're here to save lives, but you'll not save all of them. You've been given the power of God. You're going to make decisions over who lives and who dies out there. You'll never be the same after this day. But just remember, by passing over a mortally wounded soldier, your decision may just have saved someone's precious son from dying. God bless you all. I'm proud to be serving with each and every one of you and have total confidence in your souls."

As Joseph left the tent, he could see lanterns popping on like lightning bugs in the town. Word had been passed to the town's people. They were now diligently preparing their buckboards, wagons and horses for their part of the mission. Within an hour and a half, the supplies had been loaded along with stretchers, crutches and the medics and the strongest and most durable of all the soldiers. Anybody of any size could shoot a rifle or a cannon, but not everybody could carry and load grown men and boys on a stretcher made of two wooden poles and a piece of canvas.

The wagon drivers were instructed by the army's corporals to be as quiet as the bewitching hour that surrounded them. This was a surprise attack. They were briefed to move slowly so as not to stir up dust from the road. They were told they would be stopped by two soldiers on horseback about one mile from where the Prussian soldiers' front line was preparing to attack. All was in place, and General Flies was confident he would defeat his enemy, while Joseph was much more confident in his friend, Otto Van Bismarck's, overall strategy. This general was placing battalions of young Prussians in the path of death, and Joseph was furious. But his main concern, although he knew it was her choice, was the life of his innocent daughter, who was unaware of the danger this narcissistic general had put so many in on this needless path of destruction.

TIME TO MAKE DECISIONS.

TIME TO CHANGE ONE'S LIFE.

TIME TO CHANGE ONE'S DEATH.

Moving silently on the country road that snaked through the hills and valleys outside of Langensalza, two dozen makeshift ambulances driven by farm workers and their plow horses made their way to the unspeakable. Some nurses rode patiently in the backs of the wagons, while others marched more comfortably alongside. Twenty or so two-man medic teams marched alongside as well with their stretchers over their shoulders, prepared for the signal that would launch them like Greek track stars into action. And unexpectedly, a number of volunteers from the Lutheran church waited valiantly to supply water to both the patients and the medical team. All were about to make history, performing their first tasks on a battlefield as the newly founded International Red Cross.

Two Prussian cavalry members were instructed to stop the convoy precisely at a point on the road, preventing this mixture of people from being seen by the enemy and protecting them from cannon and gunfire. They would wait until the signal came that the fighting was over and they could proceed; but how protective those Red Cross badges would be was still unknown. The Austrians and their Hanoverian allies were still yet to sign the Red Cross treaty.

The two men on horseback could see the cannons and riflemen just below the crest of the next hill, as well as one hundred soldiers on horseback filling the valley behind the front line. Crystal-tinted sunlight gently and with peaceful elegance began to illuminate the very tops of the trees on the ridge in front of the convoy. As it did, a resounding discharge of multiple cannon fire broke the disquieting calm, followed by another round and then another. As prepared as the nurses had become and as courageous as they had been all through the last few days, gasps could be heard down the lines of wagons, and hugs sprung from the spontaneity of fear. Immediately, six town women retreated on foot for the city, while other townswomen grabbed the nurses in sheer panic. The plow horses needed to be restrained, as many reared, displaying their own form of panic.

Maria was perched on the seat of the front wagon. Her posture was one of strength and dignity, as if she were a pianist about to perform a concert. She was excited, scared and anxious all at the same time, but all the time, she remained focused and ready to go; no turning back. She stood and held up her arms, making the "stay where you are" signal to all behind her. "Be ready to move when I give the signal!" she yelled. As she said that, she saw gunpowder rise like a forest fire from the next valley, where the Prussian forces were positioned at the top of the ridge. The signalers on horseback moved backward down from the crest for protection. It was now enemy fire being returned; the howitzer shells exploded just out of the range where they could injure Maria and her corps.

Within minutes, continuous reports could be heard from the valley beyond, and the air became so saturated with gunpowder, the members of the convoy were forced to cover their noses in their sleeves to avoid burning their nostrils raw. Then more cannon fire, obviously from the Hanoverian camp, but this time, it was moving away from the convoy. Maria again motioned all to hold their positions, as they sat in bewilderment. The distinct and continuous sound of musket and needle rifles lasted for nearly twenty minutes, followed by the yelling of soldiers in the distance along with the stampeding of horses that could be felt a mile away.

Suddenly, over the crest to Maria's left, she heard one loud blast of musket fire, followed by Prussian soldiers pouring over the northern crest almost one-half mile down the valley, all running for safety in Langensalza. And to her immediate right, the Prussian cavalry raced over the southern crest and veered toward the road at the back of the convoy, retreating in haste towards the Prussian camp as well.

So within thirty minutes, almost as quickly as the battle had begun, there was silence once more—dead silence. The members of the convoy were unsure of what had just happened, but it didn't look good. Maria, watching the signalers without a break, saw one of them on top of the hill waving a white flag, motioning the convoy to begin moving up the road, as they raced down to lead them with their surrender flag. The battle was over, and the Prussians had quickly been defeated. The Hanoverians had been ready for their attack and had outnumbered them two to one. Maria and her team struck up the horses, and the wagons headed briskly to the battlefield. No one quite knew what they were about to encounter, but all knew they would need all their strength and courage to face something less than a mile away; they all were ready for something that had been described for generations to them as "the horrors of war."

Maria's wagon reached the top of the crest. All others stopped behind her. As she descended from her seat, she walked through the cannon-shattered tree branches. She reached the other side and gazed over the grassy slope. It was a sight so horrific, she could never have imagined it. It was sheer bedlam. And the sounds, the sounds of not only men and boys crying, groaning, rolling on the ground in pools of blood, but wounded horses with their final whinnies attempting to get to their feet but returning to the ground, helpless and dying.

In the distance, Prussian soldiers who were able to walk were being herded down the valley and forced most violently by the Hanoverians to move two abreast with their hands folded on top of their heads. Occasionally, the unique sound of a gun butt being smashed into a Prussian soldier's temple could be heard from across the valley. The Hanoverians were quite busy gathering over nine hundred prisoners of war. Maria wanted to run away and return to Anna's kitchen for milk and cookies. She wanted to vomit, but she knew she was the role model for everyone under her command. She was the leader and embraced that capacity entrusted to her by her father; she embraced it with all her heart. Within moments, she had evaluated the situation, and her courage soared like an eagle. It was time for her and her team to act. It was time for them to fire their own angelic cannons.

As Maria hurried back to the wagons, she yelled down the line. "It's not pretty folks. They need all of us. Just do your job, and let's see how many boys we can save." Those who had waited all of their lives for this moment clapped and cheered, even though that excitement was about to shrivel like a grape in the sunshine when they crossed that crest. "I need all triage nurses and medics to come up to the first three wagons as well as those carrying supplies. Medics, be prepared with your stretchers. Non-triage nurses, I need you all to stay by the wagons for when these big strong soldiers bring our boys back to you." How Maria ever knew how to make these competent commands in a situation never performed by anyone in the past was as strange to her as it was to all.

With Red Crosses on their arms and dresses, the first wave of nurses spread out like ants swarming on an anthill. None of them looked up at the Hanoverian, soldiers who were now all staring at this strange sight. The general watched from his horse as he saw his men ignoring their purpose of gathering POWs. Then he was approached by his field officers on horseback.

"General, who are those women, and what are they doing?"

asked one of the Hanoverian field officers. "Should we gather them up as POWs? They're not helping our wounded. Just the Prussians."

"No, we leave them alone. They aren't permitted to take care of our wounded, by treaty. And no army has ever taken care of the wounded of the enemy. I was briefed that they would be here. It's an organization called the Red Cross. They treat the wounded. Our government has not signed the pact, so in theory, we could capture them or even kill them if they aren't under a surrender flag." The general was being misunderstood by his officers.

"Good, let's do it. We can force them to take care of our boys instead, in a number of ways, if you know what I mean." The other officers smirked in a perverse fashion.

"Men, I agree with you. We certainly could sure use them, but no!" The general was adamant. "I'll report back to our Head Field Marshal about this. Maybe that'll knock some sense into their stubborn political heads, and they'll sign the pact. They have some brave women over there. If we abused them, the entire world would be up our ass." The officers didn't care; they just wanted to capture and abuse the women.

"Any of you that allows even one of your men to hurt any of those Prussian women will be in the stockade for a long, long time. Understood, gentlemen?" The general just stared across at the white dresses scurrying around the slaughterhouse of a hillside, wishing his army had a medical team of their own in that field. He returned the salutes from his officers as they galloped off to watch their men like prison guards watching their inmates. They knew the mentality of their troops, and none of them wanted to be thrown in the stockade for something one of their horny soldier-boys did.

As the medics brought the wounded, one by one, back to the loading area, their wounds were treated by the next skill level of nurses: minor stitching, attaching splints to broken limbs and removing shallow embedded musket balls. From there, the husky medics lifted onto the wagons the stretchers of those more severely injured. As each wagon was filled to its capacity, the farmers turned their horses and headed back as gently as they could to the operatory. Some soldiers said nothing, some cried and screamed in pain, some were brave and gave up their places on the wagons and attempted to walk back to camp via crutches.

Maria, again, observed the lines of captured Prussian soldiers with their hands folded on top of their heads, surrounded by musket-bearing Hanoverian soldiers. The POWs were extensive, most uninjured or injured only to a slight degree. The Hanoverians did not capture any soldiers even close to being severely wounded. They had enough of their own soldiers to treat, with an extremely limited number of caregivers. Maria soon felt safe for her team. The Hanoverians, it appeared, were allowing the women in white to complete their mission. Maria and the other triage nurses continued to wander down the crest, scouring the hillside and valley for those soldiers who were still alive and still treatable.

As Maria approached one wounded soldier, lying on his stomach in a grass-soaked pool of blood, she first felt for a pulse and rolled the soldier onto his back. "Medic, take one boot off this soldier and place it by his head," Maria instructed, "and hurry so we can move on to the next." Maria was stern, but she could hardly breathe after launching that command.

"But Ma'am, why would we do that? Aren't we taking him back to the wagons? I can see him breathing. Ma'am; he needs our help, or he'll die." The medic was totally confused and disrespectfully challenging Maria's instruction.

Maria stared with hostility into the young man's eyes. "I said take his boot off and put it by his head, medic, now! Are you questioning my authority as well as my judgement? I could have you court-martialed!" Maria didn't realize she was screaming and could be heard by the others close by. Both medics were stunned. No one had ever seen Maria react to anyone in such a fashion. But then Maria quickly regained her composure.

"I'm sorry, Ma'am." The medic immediately untied the soldier's left boot and placed it by his head." As he did, Maria addressed her helper as a few of the other nurses in close proximity listened in. All of the triage nurses had been trained in the "boot" protocol.

"Medic, I want you to kneel down and place your ear on that soldier's chest and tell me what you hear." The medic was scared, but he did it, avoiding the bloodstains on the soldier's shirt.

"It sounds like when my father snores real bad during his naptime at home." The medic looked up at Maria.

"And open the bottom two buttons of his shirt." Maria was sorry she had to do this, but she was doing it as much for herself as she was to teach the young medic and those around them. "What do you see, medic? And what do you smell?"

The young husky boy opened the two buttons, turned from the wounded soldier and gagged not only from the sight of the bloody, obliterated organs but from a smell he had never encountered before.

"That noise in his lungs is blood filling them quickly, and the smell is organ fluids seeping out of his thorax."

The medic almost came to tears. "Ma'am, he isn't going to live, is he?" he asked.

"No, soldier. He'll die before we get him onto a wagon. We put one boot by his head if he was still alive when we left him. Both boots mean he was dead when we found him. So if those with one boot are still alive after we clear the boys we can save, we'll see what we can do. If not, and they have died, all the dead soldiers will be loaded last, taken to the train station, and the few we can identify will be returned to their families as soon as possible. Those we cannot identify will be buried outside of Langensalza in a cemetery for unknown soldiers. But we have to move quickly gathering the dead as well."

"Why, Ma'am, if they're dead?" The medic wasn't paying attention to his surroundings.

"Look around, medic. Give it another couple of hours, and this field will be filled with more flies than you've ever encountered, and the turkey vultures will be having a feast. Get it? No one wants to see their son half-eaten by a bird, do they?" Maria was not talking like an eighteen-year old anymore. "Let's move, boys."

The soldier could see Maria holding back the tears and at the same time talking tough to try to straighten her mind. This was the first but not the last soldier she would have to leave behind to die. And the pungent smell of death was already beginning to fill the breeze as the sun rose to mid-day.

"Ma'am, I'm sorry. I'll never question you again," the medic apologized as he rose to his feet.

Maria, however, paid no attention to the apology. She turned, and the medics scampered to follow her. This was what her father had tried to explain to her when she had made the decision to be a triage nurse. Her personality had just been torn in two, and it would never completely heal. To add to that, this was just the initial battle of the war.

It had been hours since the surrender flag was raised, and Maria continued to make her way further down the crest, looking for more wounded soldiers on the outskirts of the battlefield. The huge bulk of the wounded had been taken back to the wagons, and she was about to return to the other nurses. But suddenly, she heard a soldier crying out in panic from just below the tree line on top of the crest.

"Otto! Where are you, Otto? Are you okay? Can you hear me, kid? Talk to me. Say something. I can't see, Otto, but I can hear."

No, thought Maria, *it's a common name. It's not my Otto. It's not Otto Braun. Please, Lord, let it not be him.* Maria ran to the man who was yelling. Blood was dripping slowly from his eyes as he crawled blindly on his hands and knees. A musket ball, as well, had passed cleanly through his shoulder from back to front, and it appeared he had been struck on the top of his head by a blunt object of some sort. His head wound was not actively bleeding but had dried, and without doubt he had a concussion.

"Medic, medic!" Maria yelled as she looked into August's face. "This man has tree splinters in his eyes and a minor bullet wound. He also has a wound on his skull and probably a concussion. Take him back and tell the nurses to—." Suddenly Maria looked over and saw a young soldier, alive but unconscious, about ten yards away. A tree branch had fallen from the cannon fire and pierced his thigh, pinning him to the ground. Maria ran over as fast as she could and dropped to her knees.

"Oh God, no. Oh God." Maria began to weep.

"What is it, Nurse Rothert. Is he dead?" asked one of the medics. "Are you okay? Why are you crying, Ma'am?" The medic was stunned at this woman who had shown little emotion all day but was now in tears.

"It's my best childhood friend. When he was drafted last week, he's why I joined the Red Cross." Maria needed to pull herself together for everyone's sake. This was not the time to lose it to human frailty.

"Who's there? Who's there? You sound like a woman? What's a woman doing here? Do you see my little friend Otto? He was hit by cannon fire just at the end of the battle as we were retreating. Otto! Can you hear me, Otto?" August was waiting to hear what was going on around him.

Maria yelled over to August. "I'm a nurse here to help you both. And Otto just so happens to be my best friend from home."

"Nurse, are you Maria from Cologne? He talked about you a lot. I can't see, Ma'am. How is he?" August wanted to help in some way, but his wounds kept him in a state of uselessness.

"I'm afraid Otto is in shock and unconscious. The tree branch has gone completely through his thigh and stuck into the earth. I need to put a tourniquet on his upper leg right here, medic. It can't wait to be done at the wagons." Maria knew how delicate this situation was for Otto, but none of the others knew what she knew. Her father had explained to her this type of injury in detail when it had happened to a local farmer in Cologne. The farmer was trimming a tree near his house when a branch broke loose. He bled out within minutes and died.

"Is he bleeding a lot, Nurse?" asked August. "How soon can you get him stitched up? Don't worry about me. I can walk. Just let me stay near Otto." August couldn't see, but Otto, to August, was his new little brother.

"Nurse," asked the medic. "Should we pull this limb from his leg and get him to the wagons? I think I can pull it out of the ground with little effort."

"No, no, no!" yelled Maria. "That branch has pierced his femoral artery. It's the branch that's keeping him alive. If it slips out of the artery, he'll bleed out in minutes. We need to lift him onto a stretcher without letting that branch move. Then he must be packed tight on his side on a wagon and that wagon must go ever so gently back to my father for surgery."

"But how do we get the branch from the ground without removing it?" asked the medic.

"We'll need to dig it free from under him, slowly, until we can lift him. I'm sure you all have pocketknives? If not, use your hands and claw the dirt from beneath him. Let's start…"

"Don't move. Nobody moves, or I'll blast this little girl's head off." As they looked up, they saw a Hanoverian soldier with the long barrel of his musket pressed firmly to the base of Maria's skull as she still knelt on the ground, continuing to evaluate Otto's situation.

"Soldier, I'm with the Red Cross, and according to the Geneva Treaty of—"

"Yea, yea, yea. Blah, blah, blah. My buddy has been blown up by one of your asshole cannon shells. You need to save him, or I swear I'll kill you, little girl. I'll splatter your brains all over this field." The Hanoverian was serious, and Maria knew it. They all knew it.

Maria was scared, like the first time she had seen the battlefield strewn with blood from the dead and wounded. But she also had to save Otto. She couldn't save him if she were dead. Her mind went around in circles, evaluating scenario after scenario.

"Why don't your own army's doctors take care of him, sir?" asked Maria.

"They said they'll be back for him later, but that's bullshit. He needs treatment now, or he'll bleed to death. Your soldier there's just got a big stick in his leg." The soldier was angry, and his hands were shaking. The medics and Maria knew his gun could go off accidently at any time.

"All right, soldier, stay calm. Take me to your friend, and I will take a look," Maria agreed with total insincerity.

"He's just over on that hillside, not far away. Most of my battalion's back at camp, and if anybody tries to hurt you while you're saving my friend, I'll cut their throats." That was not exactly a comforting compromise.

Maria and the medics approached the soldier's buddy, the gun now between Maria's shoulder blades. "Here he is. You have to save him. Take him to your wagons and back to your camp. If you don't save him, I swear to God, Nursie, I'll hunt you down and slice you up in little pieces."

"You aren't going with us, soldier?" asked Maria. "Somebody needs to bring him back here when he's healed." Maria knew what the answer was going to be before she asked it.

"Honey, they'd lock me up as a prisoner of war, and who knows what you crazy Prussians will do to me. We've heard stories. You're all savages. No, I'm staying here. So get him on that stretcher and get him to surgery, right now!" The soldier watched as they put his friend on the stretcher and departed for the wagons. The Hanoverian watched them as they went over the crest and out of sight, then he left and returned to his own camp.

As soon as Maria and the medics knew they were out of sight and out of danger, one of the medics looked at Maria, then looked down at the wounded soldier. "Nurse Rothert, what you taught me earlier, Ma'am?"

"What might that be, medic?" Maria's face was chilling. She didn't look like a teenager directly out of school. Her eyes pierced right through the medic like a she-wolf planning her next move of attack.

"I can hear this soldier's lungs gurgling and smell his organs like that boy we left behind earlier. You told me we have to leave those that won't live. Is it because we've gathered most of the boys that'll live, and we can now pick up those that have only a ghost of chance to survive?" The medic had learned well but wasn't taking everything into consideration.

"We must clear that stretcher, medic. We have a boy with a branch in his leg to save."

The medic was confused. "You mean put this one in a wagon without treatment, Nurse Rothert?" asked the medic.

Maria didn't say a word. With head and back bent towards the ground, she walked briskly to the two horsemen, one holding the surrender flag in a holster on his saddle. "One of you two soldiers, give me your rifle, please." The two looked at each other in a state of perplexity.

"Ma'am, why do you need my rifle?" asked the horseman.

"I need to put this Hanoverian boy out of his misery," responded Maria.

"Ma'am, we're under a surrender flag. It's against the rules of war to fire upon the enemy under this flag. The Hanoverians will hear it and come to investigate. I thought the Red Cross was about saving lives, not killing the enemy." The other medics and nurses overheard Maria's request. They looked up from their patients to try to contemplate why their head nurse needed a rifle.

"Soldier, then give me the sword on your side, and do it now. I have no time to waste." The two soldiers looked at each other, their eyes widened, and their shoulders shrugged. The one soldier dismounted, and as he stood by his horse, he spoke, "I'll escort you, Ma'am. I can help you with whatever you happen to need with my sword."

"No, soldier, I don't want you to assume any responsibility as to my actions. Just give me your sword, and no more talk. Get back on your horse and stay there." The soldier removed the sword from its sheath, and Maria hurried back to her medics.

"What is she going to do with my sword?" The one horseman asked the other.

"You know what she's going to do. Just turn your back and let her go," replied the other horseman.

Maria returned directly to her medics. "Put the stretcher on the ground and turn your backs, boys. Do it now! You don't need to see this." Maria was without emotion except for her passion to save her soldiers, especially Otto.

The medics put the Hanoverian on the ground, and no sooner did they turn their backs than they heard a thud and a gag. Then the medics quickly turned back around to see the end of the sword in the throat of the enemy soldier, all life draining from him and flowing onto the stretcher.

"Pick him up, medics," and as they did, she grabbed one of the boys by the shirt-sleeve, causing the stretcher and the other medic to follow. As they reached the side of the road only a minimal number of yards away, Maria looked at the medics. "Stand right next to this patch of thorn bushes." As they did, Maria said, "Clear the stretcher" while she grabbed the side and flipped the dead body into the bushes; wagon drivers, nurses, and other medics watched with intense horror.

"Nurse Rothert, I don't understand? Why did you—"

"Are you questioning me again, medic? I hope not. You know why. Now run this sword back over to the horseman and tell him I'm sorry I soiled it."

When the medic returned, Maria started her mission once more. "Pick up the stretcher and follow me." As they walked, Maria spoke as she led them back over the crest. "We only take our own soldiers, and we only take those we have a chance to save. He was neither. Let's go get the kid with the branch in his leg." The two medics stared at each other with quite respectful and satisfied grins on their faces. And before nightfall, that story had traveled through the camp. This little eighteen-year old girl would be called "Ma'am" everywhere she went, at least among the soldiers and her staff.

As Maria and the medics returned to Otto, they were startled. August, still bleeding from his eyes and unable to see, his shoulder throbbing in pain, had dug around the branch with his pocketknife and clawed the rest of the way with his fingernails, like an artist sculpturing a piece of pottery. The medics cut a hole in the stretcher and slid it ever so gently under the branch. As they lifted the stretcher upward, the branch protruded through the bottom, and Otto was on his way to a wagon. Due to the tourniquet, his leg was still bleeding, but fortunately, not hemorrhaging. If that were to happen, Otto would be dead within minutes.

Maria's nurses bandaged August's eyes and shoulder and cleaned the top of his head, placing three stiches in quickly, so they could begin their trek to return Otto to Dr. Rothert. The two medics who helped with Otto climbed in the wagon, holding him on his side to keep him as still as possible. August insisted he be allowed to remain with Otto, so Maria tore a strand of fabric from the bottom of her dress and tied it around August's wrist, tying the other end to the back of the wagon gate. August would be able to follow the wagon back to camp, but he would be stumbling like an old man attempting to find his way to the bathroom in the dead of night. "Thank you, Ma'am, for saving us from certain death," August said into the darkness around him.

"That's our job, soldier, and you're very welcome. And thank you for watching out for Otto." Maria finished attaching August to the wagon gate.

"I could hear what was going on with that Hanoverian, and I would have killed him myself to save all of you, but I couldn't see him. I thanked the Lord when I heard you return to us." Even with his eyes bleeding through the bandaging, Maria could tell this strong soldier was weeping tenderly in gratitude.

"My name is Nurse Rothert, soldier. My father is the head surgeon back in camp." Maria was being subtle enough to be sure he would know her when or if he could ever see again. "And what is your name, soldier?"

"August, Ma'am. August Wehmeyer. I was glad to do what I could. Will the boy be okay? He's a sweet kid! But way too young to be here." August had always been a hard, rather uncaring young man, but he cared about Otto with all his heart.

Maria didn't answer the first question, because had it been anyone else but Otto, she knew she would have left him with one boot at his head. "He is a sweet boy, and we both just graduated from high school together last week."

"Yes, he told me he did, but you? I can't see your face, but your bravery is way beyond your years." Maria felt an attraction to the kindness yet masculinity of this man., She had never been attracted to a man of August's age, only her adolescent school chums. It took her young breath away.

Otto was still unconscious. Being in shock, he was placed under a scratchy woolen blanket. As the wagon began to turn and head back to her father's operatory, one medic called to Maria from inside the wagon.

"Nurse Rothert?"

"Yes, soldier, what is it?"

"Why did we bring that Hanoverian back if you were going to kill him?"

"Medic, I had no intentions of treating him from the beginning. He wouldn't have lasted an hour. And I figured someone was going to die, and it wasn't going to be Otto, it wasn't going to be you, and I certainly wasn't going to take a musket ball to the brain on principal. Good job out there. Proud of you both. Now get going and keep that leg and branch from moving. If they do, it'll kill him!"

As the wagon pulled away, Maria and her triage nurses made one final round in the field to be sure no one was missed before the dead were gathered. The turkey vultures were now hopping from cadaver to cadaver on the grounds, flies were swarming the bodies, planting their eggs in the soldiers' open wounds, and the smell of blood and death regurgitated in the winds over the battlefield. It was now time to reexamine those with one boot and either return them to camp or leave the boots like tombstones at their heads. Not many one-boot soldiers were still alive, and those still breathing would certainly not survive the rapidly approaching sunset. The triage nurses had done a brilliant job. It was time to return to camp.

A few squadrons were sent back to the field under a surrender flag to flop the dead soldiers onto returning wagons, then unload those able to be identified in piles sorted by region, like sacks of grain to be callously dumped at grieving train stations throughout Prussia. The unidentified were thrown into mass graves dug by the townspeople outside of town.

General Flies waited in his tent, smoking his pipe and lacking any remorse for what he had done. But it would only be a few hours until his impending court-martial would be delivered, relieving him of his duties and stripping him of his rank.

Maria finally felt as if she had done all she could in the field, so she ordered the remaining nurses, medics and wagons back to Langensalza.

But Maria wanted to get back before her father started surgery on Otto. She approached the one horseman not carrying the surrender flag; the one whose sword she had use to kill the Hanoverian. "Soldier, ride me on the back of your horse as quickly as possible back to Langensalza. I need to help my father in surgery. That boy with the branch in his leg will require immediate attention, arriving at the camp. My father, Dr. Rothert, will need my help."

"Hop on, Ma'am. Let's go." The soldier grabbed Maria by the arm and pulled her onto the horse behind him. He galloped towards Langensalza and to the fate of her young friend.

ONLY GOD DECIDES WHEN THE EARTH MEETS THE SKY

Maria's face grimaced in pain as her buttocks pounded with brutality and her thighs stung from the chafing on the back of the chestnut colored stallion. With her arms wrapped tightly around the horseman's waist, the horse galloped steadily towards the operatory. Fifteen long minutes from camp, Maria overtook the wagon carting Otto's body heading towards surgery, followed by the bedraggled August Wehmeyer stumbling over the bumps and ruts in the dirt road. It was obvious by the rips and tears in the knees of his uniform that he had fallen many times on the road. However, he still held tight and with resolution to the rag from Maria's bloody skirt.

As the horse slowed down, Maria shouted to the medics. "What's his condition?" Her face was serious, but her gut burned, waiting for the answer.

"He's still unconscious, but alive. He's losing blood at a steady rate, and his face is becoming more and more cadaverous," responded the medic. "He needs help as soon as possible."

"I'm going to ride ahead and get my father to prepare a table for him. I'll see you in fifteen," and Maria clung tightly once more as the horseman kicked the stallion in the sides and off they went.

• • •

Maria rode into camp and directed the horseman directly to the operatory. Even before the horse stopped completely, Maria attempted to dismount, but the force of the inertia caused her to stumble backwards, falling violently on her backside. It hurt, but not enough to stop her from her mission. She made her way through the bodies on canvas blankets outside the operatory, waiting for their chance to survive their wounds. Nurses and medics scrambled and slipped on the bloody tarpaulins as they moved soldiers from outside to inside and onto operatory tables. Those that survived surgery were then taken to post-op. Those that did not would be carried to the train station and, if identified, sent back to their grieving families. Those unable to be identified were taken directly to the mass graves outside Langensalza.

"Bless this innocent soul, and may you accept him to live with you in eternity," Maria overheard one clergyman pray as he sprinkled a young boy with holy water, then pressed his cross on the departed boy's forehead. The men of God moved from stretcher to stretcher as the soldiers exited their successful or unsuccessful time with the surgeons.

Maria, panic pulsating from her face and without thinking, pulled back the tent flap of the operatory and yelled from the opening, "Father, Dr. Rothert, where are you? I need to talk to you right away!" The room became silent until a voice boomed from across the cramped space filled with people in aprons and the uncontrollable wailing of young men in agony.

"Nurse Rothert, remove yourself immediately from this room. If you wish to speak with me, do it after you have scrubbed your blood-stained body and removed your filthy clothing. Sterile attire is being boiled outside the tent." Joseph continued working, with his eyes directly invading the wound of his patient.

Maria's face turned red as she felt her body fill with the heat of embarrassment. Without hesitation, she exited the tent and did what she knew she should have done from the beginning. She scrubbed the dirt and dried blood from her face, arms and legs, as well as under her tightly trimmed fingernails. In haste, she darted through the screams and moans of the bleeding soldiers once again, boys awaiting their journey into the chilling unknown of the operatory. Twenty yards or so from the wounded, a small group of the townswomen boiled the bloody aprons of the surgical teams, then hung them on the clotheslines stretched between the trees.

Maria asked for an apron.

"Dearie, everything is either wet on the lines or still being cleansed," said one elderly woman with a sorrowful look on her wrinkled face.

"It's OK, Ma'am. I need to return to the OR now. I mean right now!" Maria could see the wagon approaching with Otto in the back and August stumbling like a prisoner behind it. She put a damp apron on her body overtop her long cotton underwear and went back into the operatory.

Without her ability to see her father's face amongst the other doctors working diligently on their patients, she could still tell her father by his tall stature and his hunchbacked posture. He was working on the insides of a young man's gut, removing a musket ball from his stomach. Joseph's cheeks were splattered in both fresh red and old brown blood. The pants of his uniform were saturated halfway up his shins, and his boots squished with blood as he walked from table to table.

"You and your nurses did a good job in the field today, my dear, and thank God you're safe. You're uninjured, are you not?" Joseph, just for a moment, allowed his focus to meander, realizing Maria was his daughter.

"I'm fine, Father," Maria answered, then they both went back to their purposes. "And thank you. We'll talk about that later. But I have brought Otto back, and I'm afraid…"

"You mean our little Otto Braun?"

"Yes."

"Let's not talk with emotions, Nurse Rothert. What's your diagnosis?" Joseph blurted.

"A tree branch severed by a cannon shell fell and punctured his inner thigh—"

"You didn't remove it? Tell me you didn't remove it."

"No, sir, I was afraid it would hemorrhage, so it's still in there. I placed a tourniquet above it, but I don't know if it's doing much good. He's lost a lot of blood, and he's in shock, the same as he was when I found him."

"Is he outside right now? Take me to see him when I'm finished with this boy." Joseph dropped the musket ball onto the floor and sewed the hole in the boy's stomach. "Someone 'close' this boy while I look at another boy in pre-op." A nurse immediately began suturing the outside of the torso, while the other nurse at the head of the table finished administering ether. As the anesthesia began to wear off, the boy began to squirm in pain. Two medics transferred him to a stretcher as another held him firmly all the way to post-op for bandaging.

As Joseph and Maria exited the OR together, the wagon had almost reached the pre-op mess of mangled bodies in waiting. "Over there, Father, he's on the wagon with the man with his eyes bandaged stumbling behind it."

"What's wrong with the man behind the wagon?" asked Joseph. "Is he a POW?"

"No, he's Prussian. He took splinters to his eyeballs at the same time Otto was pinned to the ground. He's unable to see. He was with Otto and dug him out of the ground with his bare hands, allowing us to get the stretcher under him."

"Why didn't your medics do that? They could see, couldn't they?" Joseph was puzzled.

"Long story, Father. You'll hear about it later around camp. You can be mad at me later and press charges if you must, but not now." Maria just kept her focus on Otto.

Joseph looked at Maria with his eyes and brows opening wide. "Press charges?"

"I said we'll talk later, Father," said Maria.

Joseph began to bark commands. "Get the man with the eye problem to the post-op. His life doesn't seem to be in danger yet, except for possible infection. Medic, take him to post-op and tell the nurses to clean his bandages and be careful not to break off any splinters. A doctor will examine him later." Joseph looked at Otto and could tell by the color of his face that the boy's chances were slim. His femoral artery had been punctured, and removal would cause him to bleed out within minutes. "Medics, bring him into the OR and be very careful not to move that branch." The two medics in the wagon and two others in somewhat sterile aprons delicately removed Otto from the wagon bed.

"Father, let me take the blind man to the post-op and change his bandages," Maria requested.

"No, Maria, I need you at the head of my table to administer ether. You observed my assistant do it at home when I removed the tumor from that old farmer's neck." Joseph needed Maria at his side as much for his own mental support as for his medical one.

"Oh, Father, that's Otto. I don't think I can..." Maria was about to crack but knew she couldn't, not now. She quickly changed her attitude. "Yes, Fa—"

"No, Nurse Rothert. It's back to Dr. Rothert for the rest of the day. Now let's go. You must be strong, nurse. Remember, you volunteered mainly due to Otto. And you brought him back here. Your choice, nobody else's. You'll follow my instructions to the tee. You're a Red Cross nurse now, are you not?" Both stared deeply into each other's eyes, then turned and went, again, to scrub their hands.

Joseph whispered in the ear of one of the medics as they were taking Otto to the table. The medic moved and waited by the door of the OR as Joseph had instructed. Two others took Otto to the table, the branch still through his leg and still through the hole in the modified stretcher.

"I need two more medics over here now!" Joseph yelled, and two came running. "Okay, here's what we need to do. Two of you hold the boy under his back, and two of you hold his legs. Keep his body parallel to the ground."

"We've got him, sir, now what?" asked one of the medics.

"Nurse Rothert, grab the head of the stretcher and I'll grab the foot. We're going to gently lower it without moving the branch. Boys, you have him secure?"

"Yes, sir, we've got him, doctor," said one of the medics.

"Maria, if we move that branch, Otto will hemorrhage and die within minutes. Ready? Okay, Maria, stay even with me; okay, slowly now." Joseph and Maria did so with precision as the four medics held Otto level with the ground. When the stretcher was clear of the branch, Joseph and Maria dropped it to the floor. "That's it, boys. Now, keep holding him flat; place his upper body only on the table. Don't let that branch touch anything." They did so, as Maria pulled the blood-soaked stretcher from under foot. "OK, now the two of you holding his legs, keep them straight and hold tight. I'll need you to hold the leg with the branch with all your might, so I can make the cut quickly."

"Dr. Rothert, no," said Maria. "You can't amputate. Not Otto. Plus, the wound is too close to his groin." Joseph ignored Maria, as did all the other persons following Joseph's strict orders.

"Nurse Rothert, when I pull the branch from his leg, if the femoral artery is severed, that branch is the only thing that has kept him alive this long. I'll need to saw quickly, and you boys have to give me that leverage. I must get to that femoral artery as quickly as I can if he has any chance at all." Maria wanted to run; so did the medics; so did the whole room.

"Maria, lean over and start the ether. We don't want him to wake up and squirm while I'm sawing. And don't get over the top of his face or the ether will take you down. OK, everyone ready?" Joseph looked at the medic at the door and nodded his head. The medic exited the tent.

"Here we go." Joseph, as gently as possible, pulled the branch from Otto's thigh, but as he did, he could see the blood beginning to pulsate and spurt from the wound. "Artery's been pierced. Nurse, saw!" And with that, the medics held tightly, Maria continued to administer the ether, and Joseph dropped to one knee and sawed quickly with all the force in his body. Both medics looked down at the floor, unable to watch until suddenly one of the medics tumbled backwards to the floor, Otto's severed leg grasped tightly in his arms.

"Nurse, quickly, sutures!" commanded Joseph. As Joseph began, he observed that a precarious splinter had dug its way deeply up into the artery's channel towards Otto's hip. Joseph was unable to tie it off. "Now, medic!" Joseph yelled across the room to the medic at the entrance, his body inside the tent but one arm outside.

"Make way, everyone, make way, move it!" The medic came into the OR with a burning log, one that had been in a fire pit boiling water for the cleansing of aprons. He handed Joseph the nonburning end of the log, the other end red hot. Joseph immediately jabbed it into the arterial cavity that was now squirting blood profusely. The log made a hissing sound from the blood attempting to extinguish it.

"Father, what are you doing?" Maria wasn't sick, only because she had nothing in her stomach to vomit.

"Cauterization, nurse, only option left." As Joseph rammed the end into Otto's stump of a leg, the smell of burning flesh filled the OR. Maria noticed that the bleeding was not spurting as badly as before. Otto began to move slightly. "Nurse Rothert, for God's sake, keep him asleep." Joseph began to sew some of the smaller arteries still seeping blood. When he was finished, he looked up. "Medics, get this boy back on the stretcher and to post-op to be bandaged quickly. Nurse Rothert, are you OK? Go take a moment outside then get back in here. We're not done yet. Lots of boys still need work."

Maria left the tent, walking through Otto's blood at the end of the table. As she exited the tent, she caught a glimpse of the medic carrying Otto's leg, now a color of pale blue she had never seen before and would never forget. He turned to his left, and Maria watched him as he threw the limb into a fire of burning gauze and limbs. As she scampered behind the OR tent, she dry-heaved a few times as she reflected on the day so far. *It was one thing to see boys injured or dead on the battlefield. I got used to that quickly. But Otto! And my father. This is my doing. I should have left Otto in peace with one boot at his head. I knew! I knew! Oh God, let him live! This is all my fault.*

Suddenly a nurse placed her hand on Maria's back, "Nurse Rothert, Dr. Rothert says he needs you inside, and I'm so sorry to tell you, but that boy with the leg amputation, he bled out before he reached post-op. I heard he was a friend of yours? Oh dear, I'm so sorry."

"Thank you, nurse, but time to cry later, I guess," said Maria as she took a deep breath.

"A lot, and for a long time," said the nurse. "Will you ever volunteer again?"

Maria just looked at her, walked through the moaning, groaning, living, dying soldiers on the bloody canvases as she rejoined her father at the head of his table.

THE SUN RISES OVER THE WEARY

The light of day was the only hint of relevance to time. Twenty-four hours had brutally passed since Maria's team had approached that peaceful lush valley with alien feelings of anxiety traveling through their bodies like a flash flood. From that first blast of cannon fire, then the first glimpse of the war-torn battlefield that followed, Maria was now finishing the day her father had presented to her, a day which would eventually become the gift of her adult wisdom. She remembered his response when she had asked to be a triage nurse: "You will never be the same."

When the final soldier was taken to the post-op, the train station or the grave, they both removed their aprons and left the tent of horror behind them. It took a few moments for them both to inhale and enjoy a morning breeze that didn't reek of death. It was only then they turned and peered into each other's eyes. With the sun beginning to quietly rise, the songs of birds rose in disharmony with the sounds of groans and cries coming from the marred and suffering unable to sleep in the post-op. Men and boys were crying, some screaming, as they realized they were missing a limb or they were strapped onto their cots painfully tightly, keeping them from reopening their wounds. The young soldiers who had survived being seriously wounded, killed or captured took inventory of the others still alive inside or outside of post-op. Then, with bandannas attempting to cover the stench of rotting flesh, they went through rows of corpses at the railroad station, looking for some sort of identification on the corpses' clothing or etched into their belt buckles.

"Can I call you Father now that we're alone?" Maria asked, looking up at her exhausted hero. He looked so different than he had just one week prior. He had aged considerably overnight, but then again, so had she.

Both still in bloody shoes and undergarments, they hugged each other, and Maria began to weep.

"No, no, my child. This is where you must be as strong as ever. You may cry when you're alone, but not now, not even in front of me. If you want to continue this line of work, this is the job. No emotions, or you'll be destroyed."

"Yes, sir, I understand." Maria let go of her father and stood as tall as her aching body and heart could endure. "You're an extremely brave man, Dr. Rothert. You saved many lives today."

"We both did. And the boys you sent back were in conditions that allowed us to save them. Your decisions must have been heartbreaking when leaving some of those soldiers behind. That's what a triage nurse must endure within her own conscience. You must harbor no guilt towards yourself. You are wise beyond your years." Joseph had had his doubts about Maria's fortitude, but no longer.

"Strangely, Father, I don't feel any guilt, except for Otto." Maria turned and looked towards the sunrise.

"Stop right there, Maria. You didn't cause his death. I did." Joseph stared at the sunrise with her as he thought back on his decisions in the OR.

"No, Father, don't try to make me feel better. It was me. I did it to both of you, and who knows, I may have caused some other boy to die while I had you waste your time on Otto. I knew what was going to happen when I saw him in the field. I knew his femoral would bleed out. I knew it was hopeless. But then I put you in a position to feel guilty about our young friend's death." Maria turned and hugged her father again." Oh Father, forgive me."

Joseph pushed her back and lifted her chin. "The only thing you did wrong was be human for a short time in the entire day. You mustn't feel bad about one questionable judgement, especially when it comes to personal attachments. We all do it."

"In my heart I know that. But Father, in order to attempt to save him, I killed an enemy soldier. I mean, I sliced his neck and dumped him into a patch of thorn bushes to make way for Otto." Maria pulled her chin from her father's hand and turned away. "I'll probably be let go. Father, do you hear me? I murdered a man. I mean, I brutally killed him, and I don't feel bad about it at all."

"I heard the story from one of the officers. The medics told me an enemy had a gun barrel to the base of your skull and was going to blow your head off if you didn't save his buddy. Is that true?" Joseph had faith in his daughter.

"Yes, that's true." Maria was cold.

"Would you have brought the Hanoverian back here to us if you thought we could have saved him? Was he treatable?" asked Joseph.

"No, Father, he would have bled out by the time he made it to the OR." Maria turned and again stared deeply into her father's eyes. "But it's one thing to leave one of our boys on the battlefield when you know he's not going to make it. It's another to slit a man's throat."

"It's war. You did the right thing. If you hadn't taken him on the stretcher, your brains would be all over that field. You know what that would have done to the infancy of the Red Cross? Why, women would become terrified to volunteer." Joseph sighed in relief. "And the way the story goes, you're a hero among the men, putting our soldiers before theirs."

"Really, Father? Someone said that?" Maria had a confused smile on her face, somewhere between pride and disgust.

"My daughter, the hero. That gave Otto the only chance possible. Let's not relay the details of the entire story to the Brauns when we return home. Let's just say he died fighting with valor, and during the battle, a cannon shell severed his femoral artery."

"Thank you, Father. I think I'll get cleaned up, and I need something to eat," said Maria.

"I'll join you, and then we can rest briefly," Joseph replied. "I'm famished."

"But first, I want to find the blind man who helped me with Otto. I want to thank him and assure him that he was in no way responsible for Otto's death. Digging him out to allow the stretcher under him, while he was blind and his eyes were bleeding, was a gallant act. He heard the Hanoverian take me, along with two medics, with the musket barrel on me. That's when he decided to crawl over and start digging. Now, that was heroic."

"Maria, I'll go with you to check on him, but not now. We all must rest, including him. We can only afford to have a few hours of sleep. When we awaken, we must check on all of the boys in post-op to do what we can to avoid infection. You know many of them are going to die by the week's end?"

"I know. Thanks for caring about me. You know, Father, there's something about that blind soldier. I must know why he was so loyal to Otto. Maybe he's from Cologne. I hope so." Maria sounded excited.

Joseph looked oddly at Maria. "Maria, be careful. It sounds like you're taking a fancy to this soldier, whom you know nothing about."

Maria blushed faintly. "Father, really, I'm a nurse and I just respect the man, that's all. Let's make him our first visit when we return. Now, however, let's eat."

• • •

Joseph and Maria were the last of the surgical team to head for town. It was only a slight downward incline on the dusty road leading to the Lutheran church in the middle of Langensalza, yet the fatigue of such a long day and night was agonizing on both of their knees and ankles. As they walked, their boots squished of blood; they were like two children who had been caught in a horrific thunderstorm.

To the side of the church, large pails of fresh cold well water were being filled by the townspeople from the pumps in their homes and businesses. Sheets were hung on clotheslines to give the nurses privacy as they scoured themselves frantically in the chilly water, exacerbated by the crisp morning breeze. The nurturing townspeople provided clean towels and strong lye soap to the caregivers in order for them to scrub the dried blood from their bodies. Small pointed utensils of any kind were gathered to clean the human cells, skin, and blood out from under their nails.

Maria, concentrating only on her own hygiene, heard the nurse next to her ask, "You think they'll let you slide for what you did?"

Maria looked up, at first not understanding the question. "I'm sorry, let me slide for what?"

"For murdering that soldier. I was there. I saw you slit his throat, but I won't say anything, I promise. After what I saw, I wanted to murder some of them Hanoverians as well. We aren't supposed to treat the wounds of the enemy, and we really aren't supposed to kill them under a flag of surrender." The nurse wasn't being condescending, she was being concerned. "You did breach the Red Cross articles, not to mention the international rules of war."

Maria had not really thought of it that way, not at all. But it was technically true. "Did what I had to do. Will you hand me your soap please?" Maria wanted to explain all the details surrounding the situation, but she was so tired. All the trauma in the last day had made her rather callous. This was something she needed to discuss with her father before she spoke to anyone. Up to this point, it had happened; period, end of story.

As she finished, a middle-aged woman resembling everyone's grandmother placed a woolen blanket over Maria's shoulders and gave her a damp but clean uniform. The uniform still exhibited shadows of bloodstains down the front. "Come, child, come inside and get something to eat, and then I'll take you to my house so you may rest."

Maria wanted to weep. This kind woman had just pulled Maria out of a world of violent rancor back into the world of human peace and love. "Thank you so much, Ma'am. The food and a place to lay my head for a few hours is so much appreciated. Dr. Rothert and I can only nap for a few hours. Then we must perform rounds in the post-op. Where might you live?"

"See that small wooden house down there with the thatched roof and the swing on the porch? That's mine. Just come there when you're done. My husband and I discussed it, and we aren't afraid to have you in our home." The woman gave a tender smile.

"Why would you be afraid to have me in your home, if I may ask?" Maria was again confused.

"We heard you're the one that killed that enemy soldier. Slit his throat wide open, ya did. You're the one, aren't ya missy? You certainly don't look like you could kill somebody. Pray often, and the Lord may someday forgive you for your mortal sin. People do funny things sometimes in crazy situations, I guess. Besides, others in the town have children that feel endangered by your presence, but our children are long grown and gone." The woman held Maria's hand in sympathy.

Maria went from confused to shocked. *Everyone had heard? Am I going to be prosecuted? I did what was right, and I thought everyone agreed. If it was wrong, I'd feel some sort of guilt, some sort of remorse. I must talk to Father.*

Nausea began to invade Maria's chest. She had just gone from feeling proud of what she and her father had just done to feeling as if everyone around her saw her as a war criminal. She entered the church where her father had just been served a plate of venison, sauerkraut and a hot cup of coffee.

"You look and smell a lot better, Maria. And this food is delicious. These country people know how to cook. Have a seat, come, sit." Joseph's weariness was pronounced by bags under his eyes and his haggard posture, his face chafed and rosy from the heavy scrubbing it had just been given. "Maria, is something wrong? It looks as if you've seen a ghost. My dear, you did everything you could for everyone, even Otto."

"I've just had two people, one nurse and one elderly townswoman, infer that I murdered that Hanoverian in the field. They think I'll be prosecuted, and the one woman told me the townspeople are afraid to have me in their houses and around their children. Father, I was forced at gunpoint to take him, and he was never going to live. It was either him or Otto on that stretcher. Father, I'm not a murderer, am I? I have no remorse; should I?" Maria sat on the bench and began to secretly cry behind the palms of her hands held to her face.

"Maria, I'm afraid there will be an inquiry. I told you, as far as the soldiers are concerned, you're a hero, not a criminal. You're one of them, as far as our boys are concerned." Joseph gave Maria a stern and proud look. "You killed one of the enemies that killed their friends. But the townspeople aren't soldiers. If you or any other triage nurses had made a decision to bring that Hanoverian soldier back here, even if he survived the journey, I would have maybe, and I say maybe, operated on him last."

"You mean, you would have just let him die on his own outside the OR?" Maria asked.

"Precisely, and no one would have questioned what I did at all. According to you, he wouldn't have survived. You did nothing wrong, but you may still may be required to explain your actions to the superiors." Joseph patted Maria on her knee under the table. "Let's go over exactly what happened one more time."

"Father, I slit his throat with a sword to put him out of his suffering and to make room for Otto on the next stretcher out. I didn't just refuse to treat him. I killed him." Maria was now questioning her own motives.

"Why did you pick that particular soldier off the battlefield to kill in the first place?" Joseph knew the answer.

"I had a Hanoverian soldier with a gun barrel in the back of my neck threatening to kill me if I didn't treat his buddy." It all started to turn in Maria's head.

"Anybody able to confirm that?" Joseph knew the whole story. One of the medics present had shared it with him as he was removing shrapnel from a boy's leg. But Joseph needed Maria to remember, so her guilt would fade.

"Yes, the two medics were with me the whole time. They know why I did it. That soldier was crazy. He was going to shoot me. That's why we faked it and carried his buddy over the ridge until we were out of sight."

"Then?" Joseph was leading Maria to tranquility.

"I saw, from the beginning, his entire stomach had been blown apart by a cannon shell. He would have died within the hour, and he was in deep pain." Maria still looked at her father with a questioning glance.

"There you go. You did the right thing. Had the Austrians joined the Red Cross, they would have had their own nurses and medics to save their own. Feel better, Maria?" Joseph could see she was still contemplating something coming from deep inside.

"Father, I graduated from high school last week, and the most violent thing up until then that I ever saw was a dog fight. In the last day, I've seen so much blood and death, pain, men crying and screaming in agony."

"Yes, Maria, and you have handled it well. What is it?" Joseph was not prepared for what Maria was about to say.

"Father, when I slit that man's throat, and the remainder of his blood gushed from his neck along with his life, I looked into his eyes. I felt nothing. He was just in my way of saving Otto. Yet now, when I relive that moment, I see his face vividly. He was young like most of us. I'm sure he has a family, and friends, and maybe even a pet. None of them will ever see him again, and I was the one—"

"No, stop. You weren't the one who killed him. Whoever fired the cannon killed him. But beyond that, it really was the governments of Prussia and Austria struggling for power over all of us that did it, and probably, when they unite someday as one nation, they'll go after the rest of Europe. These boys just do what they're told, or they are locked in the stockade or shot for treason."

"Father, I understand, but not only didn't I feel guilty about killing him, in a strange way, I liked it. I felt strong; I felt like a soldier. I wanted to get even for what they did to Otto. Am I dangerous like that old woman thinks I am?"

"Not at all, Nurse Rothert. You were performing your task so well, you enjoyed it. You felt good because you knew you had the guts to do what you needed to do. You needed to save Otto, one of our soldiers, not a dying enemy. Okay?" Joseph gave her a hug.

"Yes, sir."

"Now eat well and let's take a nap. Then we can make rounds and visit that man you're so interested in." Joseph continued to eat but with a slight smile on his face.

"Father, I'll tell you again." Joseph was enjoying Maria's reaction. "I'm only concerned about his recovery. He did so much for Otto, even with a bullet through his shoulder, a cracked skull, and blinded, bleeding eyes. How brave and dedicated he was to our Otto," said Maria.

Joseph didn't say a word this time. He just continued to eat with that faint smile on his face. He was reading his daughter perfectly.

AUGUST AND MARIA MEET WHILE JOSEPH HAS OTHER REASONS TO MAKE THE YOUNG MAN'S AQUANTANENCE

As the staff rested for a few hours, the morning progressed into early afternoon. Joseph and Maria, after splashing water onto their faces and having a strong cup of coffee, proceeded on their weary legs to perform their rounds in the post-op. The warm atmosphere accentuated the stuffy smell of the canvas tents. They entered the first tent, filled with the sounds of pain and fear as well as the aroma of dried blood and disinfectants. Nurses stumbled from patient to patient on their own exhausted legs, checking for fever or any sign of shock or infection. The clergymen from Langensalza prayed at bedsides for the men's recovery, or when suggested by nurses, delivered last rites.

"Where is this young man, Maria? Are you sure you can recognize him?" Joseph hoped she could, because he knew this man might be one of the few that could protect Maria from the legal charge of breaking the truce.

"His eyes will be bandaged, Father, he'll have a bandaged head wound, as well as a hole through his shoulder from a musket ball." Maria spoke anxiously as she scanned the dozens of wounded.

"You didn't tell me about his head and shoulder. You let that poor young man walk all the way back here like that? I don't understand, Maria!"

"He insisted on staying with Otto, and we didn't have room for him in the back of the wagon. The medics were taking up the platform making sure Otto was steadied. We explained that to him, but for some reason, he was clearly dedicated to our little friend. He insisted on walking behind the wagon." Maria stopped. "Wait, there he is over there in that dark corner." She urgently scampered through the maze of cots as Joseph slowly followed.

Maria couldn't tell if August was awake, asleep, or dead. Joseph felt August's wrist for a pulse as Maria placed the back of her hand on his cheek to feel if any undue heat was radiating from his body. His skin was blissfully the color of life. Then suddenly August's body jerked intensely, as if from a deep sleep. "Who's there. Where am I? Am I captured, or am I back in camp with my army?"

"You're back safely in your Prussian camp. Your injuries have you in our post-op. We have you protected, soldier," Maria said softly while Joseph said nothing.

"You're the nurse that saved Otto and led me to the wagons, are you not? I can tell by your voice. But it's much more serene. All I ever heard you do in the field was bark orders like a drill sergeant." Joseph smiled as Maria rolled her eyes. August was surprisingly alert.

"Yes, soldier, that was me. My name is Nurse Rothert. How are you feeling today? In much pain?" Maria knelt by his bedside and held August's hand.

"Who is the man with you? The one with the rough hands that just felt my pulse. Is he a doctor?" August, although taking a blow to the head, was mentally observant, his memory sharp.

"That's Doctor Rothert. He's the head surgeon in camp. We both came to check on you and to find out why you were so dedicated to our boy Otto." Maria didn't expect August's response.

"Are the two of you Otto's parents?" August was talking without hesitation, leaving no room for an answer. "I just met him yesterday. Fine young boy you have, but he was so lost and so untrained. He was wandering the camp like a lost puppy dog. He couldn't find his squadron. I took him under my wing. Actually, I had to teach him how to load and fire his weapon. He reminded me of my little brother back in Berlin."

Maria's heart dropped a notch, hearing "Berlin."

"So, soldier, you were both retreating when you were caught from behind and the cannon shells exploded. This was before the surrender." Joseph was gathering facts for what would inevitably be coming soon.

"No, sir, after we surrendered. The flag was up, and us experienced soldiers knew it was over. Shoot, sir, I knew we were going to lose before it started. Whoever gave that attack order was very uninformed. They were just waiting for us." August was stepping over the boundary of loyalty, but he didn't care. His head ached, his shoulder ached and he was blinded. His face periodically grimaced in pain.

"Son, you appear in pain. Have you received a morphine shot lately?" Joseph asked.

"No sir, I refused one. I heard I could become addicted, so I refused," August responded.

Joseph got the attention of a nurse nearby and ordered a syringe of morphine. She quickly returned and handed it to Joseph. "Son, your wounds will only cause you to need it for a short period. You'll be fine. But we need to talk just a bit more before I inject you and you fall asleep."

"Thank you, sir. What do you want to ask?" August needed someone to know what really happened yesterday.

"Okay, you say the surrender flag was up, and you and others knew it. So you were shot, and Otto was injured after the battle was over?" Joseph needed to know whether the Hanoverians had continued to attack against the rules of war.

"No sir, well, yes sir, but not exactly." August was beginning to sound confused. "I was running towards Otto to catch him and instruct him on the proper way to surrender, hands on top of his head, weapons dropped, you know, but he didn't do that. The flag had been raised and the alarm had already sounded. But he didn't understand what any of it meant."

"What do you mean he didn't understand what it meant?" Joseph scowled. But even though August couldn't see Joseph, he could pick up disgust in his voice.

"Sir, in the last three days, young boys, I mean really young boys, totally untrained, have flooded into this camp by train. I mean, they didn't even know how to use their weapons, let alone to drop them and put their hands on their heads. Many of them kept firing, but most just kept running in all different directions like schoolboys on a playground at recess."

"So what happened to Otto?" asked Joseph.

"With his rifle in his hand, he started running back up the hill. I chased after him, trying to stop him, but just then, since the boys all around kept firing and running, the Hanoverians kept attacking. A cannon shell exploded in the treetops above us. I had only that one glimpse of the branch falling through Otto's leg, then within a few seconds, another shell hit the treetop above me, and splinters flew into my eyes. Then I couldn't see anymore as, I could feel the pain and blood flowing from my eyes. Then I felt a bullet go through my shoulder, and I was knocked unconscious by a blow on top of my head. I can only assume it was a Hanoverian on horseback with his pistol."

"What do you remember next?" asked Joseph.

"I came to, but my hearing was faint. I remember hearing your wife's voice explaining, I assume to the medics, what needed to be done with your son. They needed to dig under Otto's leg to get him on the stretcher without removing the branch. But then, suddenly, a third voice came in, a voice threatening your wife's life if she and the medics didn't tend to another soldier first. Remembering the general direction of your wife's voice when she was observing Otto, I crawled in that direction until I could hear Otto breathing. I then began digging under Otto's body around the branch with my bare hands. The dirt was soft and muddy, due to his bleeding, I assumed."

"I see. You say a third rather angry man threatened our nurse. Was he one of our soldiers?" asked Joseph.

"I don't know sir, I couldn't see. I was blinded. But I can kind of remember he had a Hanoverian accent. But I'm not positive." August had finished telling Joseph all he could remember. "When can I visit my little buddy? Is he out of surgery?" August laid completely still as Maria injected August with the syringe of morphine.

Maria looked at her father; neither of them wanted to tell August the truth. Finally, Joseph spoke.

"Son, first off, Nurse Rothert is my daughter, not my wife. And Otto wasn't our son, he was our pastor's son in our hometown of Cologne." Joseph phrased his sentence carefully, but August still picked up the past tense.

"Was? Did you say Otto was your pastor's son? You mean he's dead. No, he was just a boy! He was a kind boy. Wilhelm and Bismarck had no right to pull all those little boys from their young lives and bring them here. We walked into a trap, sir. They were waiting for us. And because of that, Otto is gone?" Maria could see the bandages over August's eyes turning pink from the mixture of blood and tears.

Dr. Rothert spoke up. "August, I'll not repeat this, and I'll deny I ever said it, but General Flies was supposed to simply block the Hanoverians and force them into the huge part of our army. He disobeyed orders. And it cost Otto and many others their lives yesterday. It was senseless. He'll be treated harshly for that."

"Not harshly enough. I'll kill that son of a bitch myself when I get out of here. I swear I will." Maria held August down by the shoulders. He grimaced in pain.

"I would truly help you, son, if I thought we could get away with it, but I want you to live a long life, soldier."

Maria felt even more respect for August. His anger was justified. Flies had no justification to disobey orders except for his disgusting ego. "Now, let me take off your bandages and let my father study the damage to your eyes. We'll see if we can remove the splinters and debris surgically. Now, you need to settle down. We're still not sure you're without a concussion until we see your pupils."

Maria removed the bandages.

"Son, can you see how many fingers I have raised?" asked Joseph.

"No doctor, everything is just a blur, a faint blur." Maria could tell August was scared.

"Can you see colors?" asked Joseph.

"I can faintly distinguish browns and whites, but just faintly. What does that mean, sir?" asked August.

"First of all, son, it means those are the only colors in here, so it means nothing. It was a dumb question on my part." Joseph patted August on the forearm. "I need to take you to an operating table this afternoon outside in the bright light so I can get a good look at what is in your eyeballs."

"Will that help? Can you do something?" August voice began to quiver.

"I don't know yet, but I'll do all I can. You don't seem to have any brain damage or concussion from the bump on the head, and your shoulder was cleansed well by our nurses. Your shoulder will hurt for probably a few months until we start rehabilitation exercises, but it will be fine. Now get some rest, and Maria here will clean and redress your wounds." Joseph had never worked on eyes in the past and only knew of one eye surgeon; unfortunately, he resided in America.

"Thank you both." August said gently. The morphine was taking effect.

Joseph walked away as Maria began to rebandage. She touched August's face with a soft and caring palm. "No, August, thank you for doing everything you could for our friend Otto. I'll always respect and care about you for that." Maria smiled, but August couldn't make out her expression; still, he could feel it.

"And thank you. I understand you did something that put Otto and me in the front of the line. I'll always be grateful for that." Maria felt anxiety run through her body. She had a feeling she had not heard the last of the Hanoverian soldier.

"Soldier, I…"

"Please, call me August, August Wehmeyer from Berlin. Will you come back and talk to me from time to time and maybe write a letter to my parents for me?"

"And you must call me Nurse Rothert when others are around, but I would love for you to call me Maria when we are alone. And I'll tell you when that is." Maria squeezed August's forearm. August smiled as Maria placed him back in the darkness of a clean bandage.

MARIA CAN FEEL THE NOOSE TIGHTENING AROUND HER NECK

"Maria, wake up." Joseph was gently stroking Maria's soft messy hair. Maria's eyes fluttered as she attempted to regain her awareness.

"Uh, Father?" Maria asked. "What is it?"

"We've been summoned to the command tent by a committee headed by Lieutenant Otterbein. We're to come immediately." Maria could see concern on her father's face as well as hearing a nervousness in his voice that was very uncommon.

Maria still struggled to wake up completely as she had squeezed in a few more hours between rounds. She sat on the edge of her bed, not knowing where she was or what time it might be. Joseph opened the curtains to let the sunshine assist in her rise from sleep. "What time is it, Father, and we're to go where? Who's Lieutenant Otterbein?"

"Never mind for now. Just get dressed, comb your hair and look presentable. We'll find out what he wants when we get there." Joseph left Maria alone to get ready.

As they left the humble home of the two elderly townspeople, she noticed a hunting rifle leaning against the wall by the fireplace. They walked up the dirt road, past the post-op and towards the center of camp, where two guards with rifles intercepted them and escorted them into the command tent. Maria noticed a body covered by a sheet on a patch of barren ground only a short distance from the tent. The blood-spackled sheet was covered with flies, attempting to penetrate and obviously invade the dead body beneath. A waft of death floated across the breeze. As Maria and Joseph entered the tent, two officers and one of Joseph's surgeons sat at long table in the front. Sitting on benches to the rear of the tent were two medics, a nurse, and August Wehmeyer. It became obvious what this was about.

"Are you Maria Rothert of the Red Cross?" inquired the officer.

"Yes, sir," she answered nervously.

"And are you Dr. Joseph Rothert, head surgeon in this camp?" inquired the officer.

"Yes, sir," responded Joseph confidently.

The lieutenant came right to the point. "Nurse Rothert, we're here to determine whether you committed murder and if you are to be tried as a war criminal. Do you understand? If found guilty, the punishment for this offense will either be life in prison, or you could be hanged by the neck until dead."

A shock swept through Maria, her legs became weak and Joseph held her under her arm in order to steady her. But the contemplation of even the possibility of his daughter being executed was almost more than he could take as well; however, he retained his poise and strength.

"Lieutenant, I'm assuming you're speaking of the death of the Hanoverian soldier on the battlefield," Joseph began.

"No sir, I'm referring to the Hanoverian soldier who died after the flag of truce was raised, allegedly murdered by Nurse Rothert." The lieutenant made it very clear what direction this hearing was taking.

"Nurse Rothert was following my orders, sir, the same orders I gave all the other triage nurses when we arrived in Langensalza. They followed their orders perfectly and saved many lives while leaving many soldiers who were incapable of survival to die on the battlefield." The three committee members listened intently.

"But Dr. Rothert, did you instruct the nurses in the field to slit an enemy's throat whether the battle was being fought or whether it was under the flag of surrender?" The lieutenant was making a judgement before he had the facts, unaware he was putting himself in a dangerous situation he might soon regret.

"Of course not, Lieutenant. That is an illogical accusation. Sir, do you agree that a soldier that has no chance whatsoever to live with or without surgery should be brought back to our medical team and given priority over those we can save, enemy or not?" Joseph stared viciously at the lieutenant.

"Who gave you the authority, Doctor Rothert, to implement that policy? General Flies could be held responsible for a war crime due to your actions." The lieutenant had no idea what he was about to hear.

"First of all, General Flies will have much more to worry about than this hearing. The answer to your question, Lieutenant, is Otto Von Bismarck, sir. He was the villain that gave me the explicit authority." The lieutenant was puzzled by Joseph's answer. So puzzled his hand began to shake.

"Show me those orders and those procedures in writing, Doctor. Are you trying to tell me you have personally communicated with Von Bismarck?" The lieutenant wasn't buying it at all.

"Why do you think I'm here, soldier? I was sent to the American Civil War to study their battlefield medicine and tactics directly by Von Bismarck himself, and this is what we decided in Berlin."

The lieutenant knew he had to go in a different direction or be tried himself. "Doctor, I first must be sure this Hanoverian soldier was going to die despite the fact that your daughter slit his throat with a sword. The body is outside. Our soldiers pulled it from a hedge of thorns." The lieutenant looked at the doctor sitting next to him. "Would you and Dr. Rothert please go out and report back to me the status of the body?"

The two doctors left the tribunal and returned quite quickly. The doctor on the panel sat back down, and the lieutenant asked his opinion. "It appears the soldier was not shot in the stomach. It appears a shell exploded in close proximity to him. His stomach was completely open, and I could still smell the perforation of organs such as his stomach, liver and bowels. In other words, his organs from his rib cage and into his abdominal area looked like bloody ground beef."

"So you are saying that soldier was not savable? Do you agree, Doctor Rothert, that the soldier had no chance of survival whatsoever?" asked the lieutenant.

"Without a doubt, sir. I agree completely," answered Joseph.

"Then, Nurse Rothert, why did you and the medics pick him up in the first place? You left others to die who had no chance of survival. And why would you pick up an enemy soldier? That's against the Red Cross charter, if I'm correct. And then, if he was going to die anyway, why did you kill him?" The lieutenant had good points.

"Lieutenant, may we explain what happened, sir?" The two medics both stood up and waited for permission.

"Yes, please do. I must contend that Dr. Rothert possesses an extreme conflict of interest in this hearing." The medics came forward and told the story in detail. While they were testifying, a telegram was given to the lieutenant. It was short and to the point. He read it as he continued to listen to the two medics. When they finished, they were told to be seated.

"And why is this blind soldier here? Soldier, do you have anything to add?" asked the lieutenant anxiously, as if he had someplace else to be.

August was about to speak, but inside his head, a voice told him to stay silent and just agree. He figured all was going well and for him to even mention that Otto was a friend of Dr. and Nurse Rothert could complicate the committee's decision. "No, sir, I was just there when the Hanoverian threatened Nurse Rothert at gunpoint. I could hear it, but being blinded, I could not experience the entire thing as the medics did."

"Fine, soldier. Anybody else have anything to say? If not, I think we all find Nurse Rothert to have done her duty in saving our soldiers' lives by putting them first. The death of the Hanoverian was inevitable. But before we finish, Nurse Rothert, again, why did you kill the soldier if he was going to die anyway?"

Maria looked up at her father next to her, then back to the lieutenant. "Kindness, sir," and that was all she said.

"Case dismissed." The lieutenant stood and waited a moment.

Cheers were heard all the way back to the post-op. Joseph hugged Maria, and she couldn't help but cry on her father's chest. But that ended abruptly.

"Okay, Dr. Rothert," stated the lieutenant. "That telegram is telling me you and your staff must head to Bohemia the day after tomorrow. Compared to this, the battle there will seem like little boys fighting on a playground. We'll be responsible for returning the killed and wounded to their hometowns, and we'll be paying the townspeople to continue burying our unidentified dead. I'll give you more instructions, but Dr. Rothert, Von Bismarck wants you and your staff to train some new volunteers as soon as you arrive. Leave as few of your staff here as possible to take care of those unable to be transported. All right, people, let's move." The lieutenant was glad to be out of any controversy involving Von Bismarck, and Joseph and Maria were now treated as royalty.

"Father, I'm having second thoughts about this." Maria was confused.

"About what, Nurse?" asked Joseph.

"Father, in the last week since I've left home, I've seen death and blood and guts where I used to see beautiful pastoral landscapes. I slit a young man's throat, lost one of my best friends as I watched his leg being amputated, and now was almost hung by the neck for murder. I must say, I'm scared." Maria's lips tightened as she looked into her father's loving face.

"Nurse, you made this decision to come here all on your own. And you made the decision to become a triage nurse and go onto the battlefield, no one else. I warned you, you'd never be the same. You have been brave and courageous and learned to put life in high regard. Plus, I couldn't have saved half of those boys without you." Joseph was proud of his eighteen-year-old daughter. "But courage is bred from fear. Stay on this path, and you'll be an important influence on many people in your lifetime."

"Father, I have so many feelings I've never experienced before, and most are loving feelings, not ones of hate for the enemy. I want to continue, but I'm afraid of that court-martial trial. It could happen again." That was Maria's only reason for her second thoughts.

"Maria, you do as I instruct and follow those orders, and I assure you, Von Bismarck will never let any of these hot-shot officers challenge you or any of my people." Maria smiled. She'd had no idea her father had such power and was proud of his humility. "Now, let's determine who'll leave with us by determining which soldiers are ready to travel."

"Okay, Dr. Rothert. Is that all you need from me, sir?" Maria began to walk away, but Joseph grabbed her by the arm and whispered in her ear.

"One more thing. Be sure you get that blind soldier's full name and address, so you can write to him in Berlin when we get home." Maria blushed.

"Father, I don't really know him. What if he doesn't want to give it to me?" Maria looked down at the ground.

"Tell him I have some contacts that might be able to help his vision when this war is over. Will that make it easier?" Maria looked up and finally smiled.

"Do you really have contacts, Father? That would be wonderful. I'll give him ours as well." Maria's emotions in the last hour had been soaring and diving like a hawk over the mountains.

"Maria, I want to help him for what he did for Otto, and..." Joseph hesitated.

"And what Father?" Maria asked.

"I want him to see how beautiful you are, since both of you are already falling in love with each other. I like that boy, Maria. Don't know why, I just do." Joseph kissed his daughter on the forehead.

"Father, really," said Maria as she turned and walked away, hiding a little-girlish smirk on her face. After all, she was still only eighteen!

RETURNING TO THE SUMMER OF 1956

THE HOME OF THE ELDERLY WEHMEYER SISTERS IT'S PLAYTIME IN THE PARK ON A HOT SUMMER DAY

Alex was enthralled by the story of his ancestors in Prussia. Since Carrie could only finish parts between Mayme's naps, Alex learned a little bit of the story each day over the next week. He was becoming just as excited to hear the story as he was to play in the park.

"Have to stop for today, Alex. I believe Mayme's awake." They glanced at each other as they heard the floor creak and Alex saw his other aunt appear in the dining room ahead. "Why Aunt Mayme, did you have a good sleep?" asked Alex with an elated smile upon his face.

Mayme's eyes were bloodshot and blurry as she shuffled to the bathroom in her flimsy flowered robe. "Be with you in a jiffy, my little cubby. Let your Aunt Mayme get herself looking like a human. Carrie, can you make me some coffee along with some toast and jam, the grape jam we jarred last fall?"

Carrie went to the kitchen as Mayme brushed her thinning white hair and inserted her false teeth from the glass in the bathroom. Those teeth had grown a bit loose, and Alex, more than a couple of times, had seen them bounce across the floor, usually from a spontaneous sneeze. It was rare for him to see Mayme when she first awakened; however, he was finding it a pinch less frightening the older he became. While Mayme gathered herself together, Carrie prepared a modest breakfast for her sister. Alex sat on the couch and reviewed the interesting story of his great grand-parents in his head. Finally, Mayme, somewhat freshened from the grueling heat of the night, entered the dinette area. Alex, hearing Mayme slide her chair across the splintering wooden floor, left the couch and skipped to join her at the table.

"Okay, now it's time. Come here, my little pumpkin." Alex walked over to his aunt, and she squeezed him with as much force as she could muster; however, although the affection in her heart was exuberant, the arms that wrapped around him were lacking any muscle tone whatsoever. And her smell was the same as the odor he experienced when he was around his grandparents. Alex found it venerable. "We're going to the pool today, right, Alex? Brought your suit, did you? You're almost big enough to beat me in a water fight." Mayme stuck two fingers in her coffee cup and flicked coffee on Alex's face. "But not yet," she cackled.

Carrie came over with a towel to wipe Alex's face. "Mayme, behave. I mean it." Mayme continued to giggle like a schoolgirl. "Go ahead, Alex, get her back. You have your milk in front of you. Do it. She started it. It's okay."

"Aunt Carrie, I can't do that. If my mother ever found out..." Carrie interrupted and grabbed Alex by the hand. She then stuck his fingers in his milk and forced Alex's hand to flip milk on Mayme's face.

Mayme gave out another rather haunting giggle, wiped her face, then got up and made her way to Alex's chair. Alex knew what was coming. He tried to escape, but it was too late. She trapped him in his chair and started tickling him. He laughed and squirmed. But although Alex loved his aunt and he loved to play and giggle with her, tickling wasn't funny; it was painful. Alex broke free and was about to run.

"Okay, you two, that's enough. Mayme, finish your breakfast, and both of you put on your bathing suits. Let's go swimming at the park. It's noon already, and within an hour, all those little tadpoles from the neighborhood will swarm that place. Go on now, go get ready."

Both of them went to change. Carrie was the babysitter for both of them, in reality, and she had aged gracefully. Putting on a bathing suit at seventy-five and splashing in a kiddy pool was not her idea of what an ageing spinster would do, but it was Mayme's.

Alex came out of the bathroom with his chlorine-faded bathing suit covered with seashells, along with his clean white Mickey Mouse tee-shirt. His grin was ear to ear. He bounced around like popcorn popping in the pot. "Hold still now, little one." Carrie helped him restrap his sandals onto his young, unblemished feet. As she did, out came Mayme from the bedroom in what was probably the swimsuit she'd owned and worn since the 1920s. It resembled a navy-blue sailor's uniform, only with baggy feminine pants just down below her knees, then covered by her top, resembling a dress with no sleeves. White mesh lace around her neck completed her fashion statement. Along with the bathing suit, she wore a pink rubber bathing cap, a flower protruding over each ear. She was, without a doubt, the most interesting woman to be at any kiddy pool in the 1950s.

"Aunt Mayme, what are those scars on your arms? How did you get hurt?" asked Alex as he stared with curiosity.

With no hesitation, Carrie jumped in with the answer. "Alex, your Aunt Mayme used to grow roses and was cut many times by their thorns when she was young."

Without really hearing the question or the answer, since both had come out of nowhere, Mayme blurted, "What are we waiting for? Let's go have some fun. You ready, Alex? Hop on, and I'll give you one of my famous horsey rides to the pool." Mayme was more than ready, and so was Alex, but at that, Alex and Carrie glanced subtly at each other.

"Mayme, Alex isn't as little as he used to be. I don't think that's a good idea anymore." Alex agreed but stayed silent, even though he missed those horsey-ride days on Mayme's back. He especially missed the sounds she exuded, which sounded more like a donkey's hee-haw than the neighing of a horse.

"Nonsense, Carrie, Art's only three. What's the difference between last month and now?" Alex was always confused when she referred to him using the name of his grandfather. Carrie wasn't confused at all; she understood, as a shiver of sadness ran through her core.

"Mayme, this is Alex, not Art, and he's five now. You know how you used to pick him up? Give that a try now, and you'll hurt yourself." Carrie stayed close in case Mayme did pick him up. Carrie was not going to allow a tumble or injuries for either.

Mayme smiled, and as she got closer to Alex's face, she looked up at Carrie, then back at Alex. "You're not Art. Who are you? Art has a scar on his cheek. You're who, young man? Tell me right now!" Alex looked at Carrie, startled by Mayme's inability to recognize him.

"Aunt Mayme, it's me, Alex. Art's my grandfather, and he's old and really big." Mayme came even closer and held Alex's face in the palm of her hand.

"Mayme, Art's our sister Margaret's son. Yes, he's also our nephew as well. But this is Art's grandson. This is Mary's child, Alex. He's your youngest nephew, and you love him a lot, and he loves you." Carries hesitated and took a deep breath. "Mayme, slow yourself down. You know how you get when things start going quickly and you get excited."

"Carrie, Art, I mean Alex, I mean both of you, please give me a moment. I forgot something, and I'll be right back." Alex looked over at Carrie. He could see a tear running down one cheek and her hand quivering.

Mayme returned to the bedroom. The fan still oscillated, but the room had risen considerably in temperature and humidity, as the day was near high noon. She sat on her bed, her mind swirling like a tornado in her head. She attempted to grasp what, only a few minutes ago, had seemed clear to her. She reached for the bottle of Sambuca on the nightstand and poured herself a considerable belt. She slung it back like a cowboy in a saloon and thought deeply of Alex. As her mind settled, her memory of the current era returned, and her fondness for Alex again filled her heart. It was then, and only then, that she came out of the bedroom. "OK, Alex, Carrie, ready to go to the park and play. I'm ready, and I'm going to win our water fight today, Alex. Get your goggles, kid, cause you're going to need them."

"I have a brand-new pair, Aunt Mayme. Mom said my head was getting too fat for my old ones. Let's go." And Mayme knelt and gave Alex a loving hug and a scratchy kiss on the cheek.

"I love you, Alex."

"I love you too, Aunt Mayme," and Alex hugged her back. Then Alex and Carrie struggled helping Mayme back to her feet, and off went the trio, Mayme in her "Roaring twenties" swim-wear, Alex in his seashell speedo, and Carrie with two bath towels following a few paces behind. Mayme and Alex walked hand-in-hand down the block to the park.

Oh, what a fun afternoon they had! As usual, the pool was crowded with kids, mostly grade-schoolers. It was maybe the size of two big living rooms and without any filtration system; it was dosed with a high quantity of chlorine. Alex wasted no time jumping in off the side, while Mayme climbed down the steps slowly and feebly, with a big smile on her face. The kids and mothers watched the "Crazy old lady," as she was known to all in the neighborhood; however, she and Carrie commanded an odd amount of respect from all. They were what people called "good neighbors," always there to help if someone was in need. Only newcomers in the neighborhood were initially skeptical, but they quickly understood.

When Mayme finally completed her descent and established her feet firmly on the pool's bottom, Alex came towards her. "Put your goggles on, Art—I mean, Alex." As soon as he did, he was hit with a splash right in the face by the giggling Mayme. Alex splashed back. Then Mayme shoved a splash at another little boy and, after seeing Alex splash her, he splashed back as well.

The boy's mother came darting poolside. She was new to the surrounding streets. "No, no, no, Ben. We don't splash adults. Now apologize to this nice lady."

Suddenly, Mayme flung water at the mother, soaking her blouse. "C'mon, Momma, come join us and have some fun. He can splash me all he wants. I started it." Mayme turned towards Alex and the little boy with her cute little laugh, and pretty soon, the whole pool was in a water fight, laughing and smiling.

Carrie sat on the park bench with the towels, watching her sister, older by only one year, create chaos wherever she went, some good, some bad. Situations involving Mayme were getting worse, which meant Carrie's job was gaining in intensity; her job of protecting Mayme from harming herself or others was growing. Carrie spent times like this not knowing whether to be embarrassed for Mayme or to enjoy watching her play the same way she enjoyed watching Alex play. And it always brought back fond memories of when they had been little girls, at least up to one point in their lives.

After a couple hours, it was time. Carrie rose from the park bench and walked to the poolside. "Time to go, kids," she said to Mayme and Alex.

"No, Carrie. Can't we stay a little longer? Alex and I are having fun." Mayme was responding as any child having fun would. But it was Alex who was getting tired of the pool. He took Mayme's hand, and they both walked up the steps. Carrie placed towels around their shoulders.

"Can I play on the slide and the swings for just a little while, Aunt Carrie, please?" Of course, Carrie never could resist that face, and he asked so nicely. Mayme intervened.

"Art, I mean Alex, your Aunt Mayme needs to walk home,

but if Aunt Carrie wants to stay here with you, that's up to her." Mayme needed a little more Sambuca and then a nap. Her naps, as well as her memory lapses, were increasing day by day.

Carrie knew why Mayme wanted to mosey home, and she felt it best for her to do so. "Sure, Mayme, we'll meet you at home. We won't be long. Mary will be there soon. Just tell her where we are if we're not home."

"Okay." But as Mayme began to slowly walk away, she turned. "Carrie?"

"Yes, Mayme."

"Who's Mary?"

CARRIE CONTINUES THE STORY TO ALEX'S EXCITEMENT AS THEY BONCE BACK TO BERLIN, SEPTEMBER 16, 1866 IN THE COURTYARD OF THE WEHMEYER HOME

After the confrontation with August's little brother, Henry, and his mother, August sat silently on the concrete bench in the courtyard. With the latest letter from Maria gripped tightly in hand, August's mind regressed three months to that horrible day in Langensalza. His chest continued to heave in anger, and chills of adrenaline saturated his body. His anxiety was now at a peak over his actions towards his family, but they needed to respect his physical pain as well as his deep depression from losing Otto as well as his sight. He had found himself growing closer and closer to Maria as her intimate letters now arrived consistently from Cologne. But his reality always led him to envision himself as the blind man on the corner with a tin cup. The inner thought of *Why would any woman want that for a husband?* preyed upon his psyche.

"August, it's Katarina. Are you okay, my love?" She approached him and kissed him gently on the cheek. Her lips were soft, and her touch was caring.

"I know it's you, Katarina. I could hear you talking to Mother.

And you always wear that ambrosial perfume I gave you for your birthday." August's emotions were slowly settling like the light rain at the end of a summer downpour.

Katarina pulled August's bandaged head into her bosom and this time kissed him on top of the head. "Mother is quite upset, and so is Henry. But more with themselves and their lack of compassion for you than with you. What happened?"

"I don't want their sympathy." August handed the letter he held tightly in his hand to Katarina.

"Oh, another letter from Maria. You're afraid, aren't you?" asked Katarina.

"Wouldn't you be if you were me? I'm a blind man. I can never read again. I'll never be an educated aristocrat like her and her family. All I can do is throw pottery, or should I say, all I could do was throw pottery." August cried into Katerina's embrace. She was the only person to whom he would reveal his vulnerability.

"Have you tried yet, throwing pottery, I mean? Have you asked Father to let you give it a try down at his factory? Don't tell me my twin brother is afraid of something? You're the bravest man I know, August Wehmeyer. Don't do this to yourself. Pull yourself together and have faith! It appears this little nurse in Cologne has faith in you. She knows you're blind, and she keeps writing, doesn't she?" Katerina and her brother had always been close, but until now, she had always needed him more than he needed her, or anybody, for that matter.

"Perhaps I will. My shoulder is strengthening. Yes, perhaps next week." August was cooperating, but not with much confidence.

"Good. Now, shall we take a walk to the park and read that letter? Or we can do it here in your room. You decide, August." Katerina was the only one August wanted to know about his relationship with Maria. And if the letter came that told him what he was expecting—her goodbye—he wanted Katarina and no one else to be there for him.

"If we go to my room, Mother will know it's you reading the letters to me. But if we go to the park…"

"She knows, August, just not for sure. She asks me all the time if I know anything about the letters. I just say no. But she knows. Who else is closer to you than me? I love you, August."

"I love you too, my little clone. Let's go to the park. It feels wonderful out here, and the smell of the turning leaves is sweet." Katarina took August by the hand and began to lead him out the gate and to the park when he suddenly stopped.

"Katarina, run back in to Mother and tell her I'm sorry. And tell her not to tell Father about what Henry did this afternoon. I don't want him to be punished. He's just a kid and I forget that sometimes. He looks up to me like I'm some kind of war hero. He's hurting enough."

"You are August. You are a hero. We all look up to you!" Katarina ran to the kitchen and returned promptly. "Done!" She again took August by the hand and they left the courtyard for the park. August clenched the most recent letter tightly in his other hand. Katarina loved reading Maria's letters as much as August loved hearing them. She dreamed of the day when a man would be that in love with her.

PREVIOUS LETTERS FROM MARIA ROTHERT AFTER THE ENDOF THE AUSTRO-PRUSSIAN WAR

Letter received July 31,1866

Dear August,

I first must ask most sincerely for you to respond to this letter as soon as possible. I am unable to rest until I know your condition. Over half of the boys my father and I treated in the three major battles of that one-month war died of infection shortly after surgery. Father and I never forgot the day we met you, and Otto's family wishes to thank you for your dedication to their son. The funeral service was quite sad, but you were specifically named in the eulogy and prayed for by the entire parish.

I do not wish to continue, although I have a lot to tell you. First, could you send to me a telegram as to your health? Father and I will anxiously await.

My affections and respect,

Maria Rothert

Send to: The home of the Dr. Joseph Rothert Family

Letter received August 12, 1866

Dear August,

Father and I received your telegram, and we are so relieved you have healed and are slowly regaining your strength. I am so sorry about your sight; however, Father assures me a brave man such as yourself would never allow a handicap to keep him from love, success and a happy life.

When returning from the battlefield in late July, my family all wept in happiness for our safe return. We slept for three days straight and ate everything our housekeeper could prepare. However, my mind cannot rid itself of the sights and smells of war. It seems as if, no matter how hard I try, I cannot re-move all the blood from under my fingernails and toenails.

If you wish, please write back. I would love to hear about your family and your plans to restart your life. Again, I am so happy you are safe and healthy. I would be most pleased to see you again someday soon.

To our hero,

Maria Rothert

Letter received September 1, 1866

Dear August,

I so enjoy your letters and learning about your family and friends. I hope I have not overloaded you with information about mine. I am getting to a point where I believe I know you better than most of my friends here in Cologne. After my experiences, I find conversations with my young friends to be rather trite.

Father has been meeting with Von Bismarck recently in Berlin. He is being offered a position as a surgical professor, but our family is strongly rooted in Cologne; his practice is here as well as his dedication to the stability of our family.

However, he will be spending time teaching at Charite Medical College in Berlin from time to time, and Bismarck wants him to travel again to the United States to study the latest in techniques at the Harvard Medical School.

He says if he has time, he would like to visit and talk to you on his next journey to Berlin. Would you be so gracious as to welcome a visit from him, if nothing more than to have him thank you for your protection of Otto?

Write back soon. I live for your letters.

To my sweet friend. I adore you.

Maria Rothert

MARIA'S LAST LETTER TO AUGUST FOR MANY, MANY YEARS

Katarina and August made their way to the park with Maria's most recent correspondence in the hand of August. Surrounded by wilting flowers and beautiful multi-hued leaves he could not see, August could still feel the soft breeze on the legs of his trousers. He could hear the crackling of the crisp decaying leaves blowing into his shoe tops, and as Katarina sat him on the cold marble bench near the fountain, a soft mist occasionally touched August's cheek.

"All right, my love, are you ready for this most recent letter from your love? I've read all her letters to you, and I assure you, this one will not be telling you this is her last. She loves you, August. Any woman can hear that. But why she would ever love a man that put a dead mouse in his six-year old sister's slipper is beyond me." Katarina placed her other hand on top of August's and squeezed his in the middle. They could both hear the sound of their nervous giggles.

"Okay, funny girl. Now go ahead, read it to me. Thank goodness, if it is bad news, no one can see me cry through these bandages." August gave her the letter.

• • •

Letter received September 16, 1866
(The letter that caused the unfortunate confrontation with Henry in the courtyard.)

Dear August,

I have something I must tell you, and I so hope you will find this reasonable and not offensive. [Katrina looked at August and his hands were clenched tightly together between his knees. She continued.] I believe I alluded to my father becoming a part-time professor at Charite in Berlin. In order to do so, he must go to the United States to the Harvard School of Medicine for three months and train in a number of new surgical and sterilization technics. One of which is eye surgery in the removal of foreign bodies, such as yours. It is experimental; however, he has agreed to take you to Boston with him if you wish to take a chance. He is going to be in touch with you and your family in the next few days to discuss all of the facts and plans surrounding this opportunity. He is in Berlin now. By the time I receive your answer, he will be back.

That is all I am going to tell you in this letter, for I wish for him to discuss this with you and your family personally, so you understand all considerations and possible consequences.

My father has respected you and supported our friendship from the day he met you in the post-op. He is a good man. Please hear him out.

To my loving soldier,

Maria Rothert

Katarina and August sat in silence. The thought of someone cutting on his eyes was uncomfortable to August, to say the least. "Has this been a trick the entire time, Katarina, to use me as a research animal? I can't believe she would—"

"Stop it, August. You're just scared, and I don't blame you. But that girl and her father aren't just using you. They love and respect you. Perhaps this is God's way of rewarding you for your compassion to that young boy, Otto. Please, hear what the doctor has to say. We will all help you, but in the end, you must make this decision yourself."

Katarina was frightened and skeptical as well, not about Maria, but about Von Bismarck and Maria's father.

"Let's go home and let me think about this. It's almost dinnertime, and Father will be home."

Katarina kissed August on the forehead and took him by the hand. They returned home. Katarina changed the bandages on August's eyes, and before they joined the family table, she stopped before they reached the dining room.

"August, if a telegram comes from Dr. Rothert to set up a time to meet, just explain tonight that he's the doctor that helped you in Langensalza, at least for now." Katarina was always thinking steps ahead.

"That's what we'll do tonight at dinner. And I'll have Father give me a run at turning the pottery wheel once again, this time as a blind man." Katrina once again kissed August on the forehead and led him to his chair at the family's evening meal.

• • •

Dinner concluded, and the daughters along with Ida cleared the table. As the dishes were being washed in the kitchen by the women, the boys were excused to do their homework, leaving August and his father alone. "Father, I must make a request."

"No, son, I'm not going to take Henry to the shed, although I felt like it when I heard what he did to you. I know you didn't want me to know, but your mother and I don't keep secrets. Son, that's his way of wanting things to be as they were. He's quite hurt seeing his hero different from what he was before the war. He'll learn to respect your courage even more as time goes on."

"Thank you, Father."

"And I did tell your mother she needed to mind her own business. You're not a child anymore, August." James lit his pipe as he drank his coffee.

"No, Father, that's not it. I knew Mother was just scaring him, even though I wasn't. I'll knock him on his ass, though, if that's what it takes to teach him not to hit my shoulder, Father. It's getting stronger, but it's still painful to the touch."

James laughed "Agreed. Us men always have to know what the consequences can be. So what do you want to ask me, August?"

"Since I can't see anything other than a blur, and I don't know if I ever will, can you give me a shot at a turning wheel at your factory just to see if I can feel my way to competence, not needing my sight?" August didn't have to wait long for an answer.

"Without a doubt, son. I was waiting for you to want to become functional." James got up and gave his son a hug. But just as he did, a knock came at the front door. With the women unable to hear the knock in the kitchen over the clanking of dishware, James was forced to answer.

"Are you Mr. Wehmeyer, sir, father of August Wehmeyer? I'm Dr. Joseph Rothert. I assume I'm in the right place, sir." Joseph, dressed in tails and a top hat, stood on the stoop. James was confused. Katarina and August hadn't revealed any part of the content of the most recent letter from Maria to anyone.

"Doctor, you're in the right place, but I'm confused. We have no one hurt or ill in our home." James had still not invited Joseph in from the chilling autumn breeze.

"Mr. Wehmeyer, your son August was a patient of mine and my daughter's at Langensalza for a very brief period of time before we were shipped out for the next battle. He was quite influential in the unfortunately short life of Otto Braun. My daughter, a Red Cross nurse, and your son have stayed in contact via mail for the last two months. May I come in and speak with you and your family?"

James was startled. "Your daughter, then, is the one sending August those letters. He has kept the identity of the author from all of us, except his twin sister. Please, sir, we're honored. Join us for coffee, and I believe we have a piece of apple pie still available from dinner." James led Joseph to the dining room where August had faintly overheard the conversation.

As the creaks in the floor came closer, August spoke. "Dr. Rothert, sir, it's an honor to have you in our home." He stood up and extended his hand in the general direction of the doctor. "My sister just read Maria's most recent letter, and she said you were going to contact us to set up a consultation. I did not expect…"

"Son, I'm sorry to interrupt your family so spontaneously; however, I'm being called back to Cologne, as my mother has taken a turn for the worse. My apologies." Joseph was always gracious, and August could pick up the concern over his mother just from the intonation in his voice.

"Please, sir, have a seat, and I'll retrieve my wife with coffee and pie. You two can discuss the purpose for your visit preliminarily until we return." Dr. Rothert took a chair next to August and squeezed his forearm.

"Father, I need Katarina to join us in this discussion, but no one else. Just Mother, you, and her."

James turned and gave Joseph a look of curiosity.

In a few minutes, the parties were settled around the table, and James spoke. "For some reason, I don't feel this is a social call, doctor. You met my son for one day, and your daughter and my son have been writing ever since. Is your daughter in a 'family way' so to speak? Is my son…"

"Oh, no, no, Mr. Wehmeyer." August, Katerina and Joseph all chuckled softly. "I'm here because I am a professor of surgery at Chiate, and Von Bismarck is sending me to Boston to study new surgical skills."

"Why, that's impressive, sir, but why are you here? What do we have to do with it?" Ida and James looked at each other with total consternation.

"My daughter and your son have become close via the written word, and she has only seen him for less than forty-eight hours. And to be blunt, he has never physically seen her. But she witnessed his heroism, and I heard about it. I liked him from the beginning." Joseph hesitated while Ida and James' brows squinted.

"Go on, doctor," James said.

"I'm here to ask you if you would allow, with your son's permission first and foremost, of course, for me to take him and my daughter with me to Boston for about three months. There are some new techniques for removing foreign bodies like splinters and shrapnel from the eyes. I would like to give your son a chance to see again. I'm afraid, by our doing nothing, your son's eyesight will be a blur at best for the remainder of his lifetime." The entire Wehmeyer family listened with intensely mixed feelings. "I examined his eyes within hours after his injury, but there was nothing I could do without causing more damage or infection. This may, and I say *may*, allow August to see again. But I cannot impress upon you strongly enough that this is experimental. The worst that can happen is he remains blind."

The conversation continued for almost an hour, weighing the pros and cons. The trip would not cost the Wehmeyer family any money. It would be funded by the Prussian government. "Well, I'm not sure," said Ida, "He has been through a lot, and his father believes he can regain his pottery skills here at home even without his sight."

"I'm not sure either," said James, as he had no trust in modern medicine whatsoever.

"Well, I just thought I would present this—"

August interrupted and was short and to the point. "I'll go, sir, if you guarantee Maria will be going." Katarina squeezed August's hand under the table. "I can't be alone for three months without sight, and I want her there to help me with my recovery. And if it works, the first thing I want to see is her face. Sir, is your daughter as pretty as she is sweet in her letters?"

"More so, and she will give you a reason to live. I have never seen her so excited by anything as when your letters arrive. You helped her through a very mentally traumatic time after she worked with the dead and dying. And I'm so impressed with the respectfully romantic style in which you communicate with her. You're quite a writer, son."

It was everything Katarina could do not to take credit for her writing. She wrote what August told her to but added a few things she knew every woman wanted to hear from a man she adored. She squeezed August's hand even harder, with a smile on her face.

August smiled as well.

"My brother is tough on the outside, but what a lovely, elegant heart he has."

Joseph was shown out, and Ida and Katarina cried for different reasons; James and August said nothing. In two short months, August, Maria and Joseph landed in Boston Harbor.

December 17, 1866 – Boston City Hospital

THE DAY OF DETERMINATION FOR SO MANY PEOPLE IN SO MANY MANY WAYS

Snow fell softly in the vast New England city as the first sounds of Christmas could be heard in the streets, precipitated by the jingling of small bells attached to horse-drawn sleighs and carts belonging to the Bostonians. August's olfactory senses as well as his sense of hearing and touch had increased sharply after spending his last six months in darkness. The heady odor of bleach, to some small degree, irritated his nostrils as he lay quietly in one of the few private rooms of the Boston City Hospital, the hospital founded by the city to care for the poor. Most patient accommodations were wards containing eight to sixteen beds, but due to the voluntary and experimental surgery performed on this Prussian soldier and due to the patient's belonging to Dr. Joseph Rothert, August received most favorable treatment.

Two weeks had slowly passed since August's surgery. The emotions of those days were fueled by the memories of his last visions of the hills outside of Langensalza, rising gently up and down over the landscape. Except for the obscure sounds of pain floating down the hallway from the patient wards or the indistinguishable conversations of care providers outside his room, August was alone half of his waking hours. The other half was filled with bliss, as the voice of Maria filled his heart. Maria read to him and wrote letters to his family, and the soft touch of her hands and the gentle kisses on his forehead filled August's heart with euphoria. Maria shared parts of her day with her father, as he took her with him to attend lectures at Harvard and become more educated as to the science of medicine. But today was to be quite different. Today was the day the bandages would be unraveled and the surgery would be determined to be successful or unsuccessful.

Shortly after August finished his breakfast, Joseph and Maria entered the room along with the surgeon who had performed the surgery two weeks prior. August's and Maria's hearts pounded like hammers on an anvil.

Joseph began the conversation. "August, Dr. Murphy is going to remove your bandages. When he does, keep your eyelids shut until he tells you to open them. And when you do, open them very slowly. Do you understand?" Joseph was, as always, without emotion, showing the same temperament he exuded on battlefields.

"Yes, sir," responded August in such a calm and clear voice, all were surprised. The bandages were unwrapped and the pads of gauze peeled from August's eyes.

"All right, August, begin to open your eyes slowly, and be sure to look straight forward at my finger." August eyelids began to flutter as the first rays of light in months entered his pupils. "Well, son, what do you see?"

"The blur is a bit better. I can see colors; however, they are so faint. But no, I cannot see any detail." The room went silent.

"Do you feel pain?" asked Dr. Murphy.

"I did when I first opened my eyes, but it's waning." August's voice was still calm, as if he had not harbored any hope from the beginning. Quiet tears began to run down Maria's face. Joseph gripped her hand and placed his finger on his lips, suggesting she stay silent.

"I'm sorry, son, but I did have my doubts. Your wounds were deep into your iris area, causing your pupils to remain wide open. This is why you see a blur. Your pupils are incapable of dilating. In other words, you will be unable to focus."

"Not sure I get it, Doctor."

"What I'm saying is, your sight will always be a blur unless we discover a way to repair your iris. And as of now, we have no way to do that." Dr. Murphy was surprised at August's serenity and his acceptance of his condition.

"What now?" asked August.

"You'll be declared legally blind for the rest of your life. You'll need to wear dark glasses in bright light, but as of now, no normal glasses will help you. You can see light and faint colors. You'll be able to see objects directly in front of you, but I'm afraid you'll be unable to read or see anything clearly." Dr. Murphy had said all he needed to say. The surgery was a failure.

Maria approached August, clutched his hand and stroked his hair. Joseph spoke. "August, I'm so sorry I got your hopes up, but we all knew, including you, that this was experimental. But again, son, you amaze me with your bravery and courage, especially now that you know your future. I'll begin preparations to send you and Maria back to our families in Prussia."

"Sir, I thank all of you for your kind and competent treatment. I'm a victim of war. That was my choice. I enlisted. None of you must feel any remorse. We all did our best. I'll need to figure out my future." August became quiet and pensive. "But I thank the Lord I was able to spend time with your daughter, sir. It'll be a highlight of my life, and I've never felt these feelings for anyone and probably never will again. Maria, I will miss you."

Maria looked at her father and Dr. Murphy. "Can we have a moment, gentlemen?" And the room cleared.

"OK, August Wehmeyer. You don't get rid of me just like that. I've cared for you since I came back from killing that crazy Hanoverian in order to save Otto. Then I find this other crazy soldier bleeding from the eyeballs and digging underneath Otto with his fingernails. Then when you had me strap you to the wagon and you were literally towed back to camp. Nope, I'm here to stay by your side as long as you want me. Get it, soldier boy?"

August could do nothing but stare through his bloodshot eyes into the obscure world in which he would now exist. "Maria, I can't do that to you. You want to be a doctor, and I'm illiterate from here on. The only thing I can do is throw pottery. I don't want to be an invalid in Berlin being pitied by all my friends and relatives for the rest of my life. And I want a family someday, but who wants a blind man as a husband and father?"

"Then let's stay here, August," Maria blurted.

"'Let us', Maria? What do you mean by 'us?' Are you crazy? That's crazy, Maria. Why would you ever do that when you have a family and a great future in Prussia?" August wasn't going to helplessly get his hopes up until she came to her senses.

"I love you, August. I really mean it. I really do. I'm going to leave the room, but I'll be right back." Without hesitation, Maria went to find her father and inform him of her desires. After only a short time, she returned.

"August?" Maria said seriously but without hesitation. "I talked to Father, and he has a plan."

"I hope he is going to lock you in a crate and send you back to Cologne, right?" August was now scared.

"No, silly, he's all for it. He has, believe it or not, considered the idea of me studying here at Harvard and becoming a trainer for the American Red Cross." Maria was bubbling.

"What do we do for money? That can't be a big salary. And I refuse to be an invalid supported by his girlfriend." August almost said wife, but first things first.

"No, there's more. Here's the deal. Since I speak English, and I'm one of the few nurses in the world to ever be trained for the battlefield, Harvard really wants me. And I can teach you English as we go." Maria was getting more excited with every word she spoke.

"Maria, what if they decide they don't need you, since America is not in a war of any kind? Then you are stuck here with a poor blind man." August needed more convincing, as his hopes were slipping away.

"No, August, there's more. What I didn't know until just now is, one of Father's reasons for coming to America was to find a place to house Prussian medical students and hospital administrators. Then they and the Americans could share their expertise with each other." Maria was smiling, but August, of course, couldn't see that.

"Go on, Maria." August's eyes were beginning to feel pain from the light.

"The home will be purchased by the Prussian government. Your job will be to maintain it and feed and house these students during their stay." August was understanding, but still, one big question was on the table.

"Tell me again, Maria. What will I do while you're teaching and the students are learning?"

"You must learn English first, then you teach English to the students."

August was not going to accept that. "You mean, as well as stumble around, make beds, clean toilets and such." He was looking disheartened.

"What do you want to do, August? You're limited, you realize," returned Maria.

Reality struck August like that howitzer shell had done in Langensalza. Maria was feeling the wind leaving August's sails, but it only lasted momentarily.

"Maria, before I left Berlin, my father took me to the pottery kilns, and I attempted to throw a few earthenware. Even with bandages on my eyes, I could feel the faultlessness of the vase in my hands. The other potters cheered at my success, and I fogged up under the bandages. Maria, I'll help maintain the house the best I can, but I want to be a potter. I want to feel the clay within my grip. My lack of sight has enhanced my sense of touch."

Maria was even more excited than August. "Oh August, less than an hour after your hopes of a normal life are dashed, you are ready to be my hero again. What do you think? Is that a yes?" Maria kissed him on the lips for the first time. "I so love you!"

"Maria, can I speak with your father, please? Go get him."

Maria left the room and came back with Joseph in a matter of minutes.

"Yes, son, I assume you heard my proposal and you're open to it as well as being in the pottery business." As usual, Joseph was stoic.

"Sir, eventually I want my pottery to be classic works of art. And I did hear your proposal, and it is something that a blind man can only dream of." Joseph was pleased. "But I only have one more request, which may seem strange to you."

"Yes, son, what is it?" Joseph and Maria were scared to hear a question that might burst the deal.

"If she will have me, may I have your daughter's hand in marriage?" August was anxious, since he was unable to see any facial responses.

Joseph looked at Maria's smiling face as she shook her head up and down. "Yes you may, son, with my deepest blessing."

"Maria, will you marry me?" asked August.

"Yes!" And Maria kissed August again.

Within thirty days, Maria and August were married, as Joseph gave his daughter's hand to a blind Prussian soldier. Maria and August prepared their new home for Prussian visitors, and Joseph sailed back to Prussia with a thick stack of letters along with a briefcase full of wedding photographs.

Within a year, Maria would give birth to the first of her and August's eight children. They named him Otto.

• • •

"Well, Alex, there's the story of us Wehmeyers and your great-great grandparents. Like it?" Carrie could tell Alex loved it, because he had hung on every word for days.

"I want to be a writer someday, Aunt Carrie, and that will be one of the first stories I'm going to write." Alex put his arm around his aunt's neck and gave her a big hug. "Got any more stories you can tell me?"

Carrie sat quietly and smiled as she hugged him back. "Maybe someday, Alex. Maybe."

Late summer of 1960 — Cincinnati, Ohio

MAYME'S MEMORIES BEGIN THEIR UNCONTROLLABLE MARCH TO ETERNITY

"Mary, honey, this is Carrie. I'm sitting here at work at Dr. Ventress's front desk. I tried but couldn't get hold of you earlier, so I called your dad. Art and Ethel came over right away. Where are you now? I need you as soon as possible." Carrie's voice shivered with confusion; she was terrified. Something was happening to her sister, Mayme, that Carrie knew was way overdue.

"Carrie, I'm home right now. Why, what's wrong? Are you ill?" asked Mary.

"No, it's Mayme."

Mary was not surprised. She had been waiting for a call like this as she had observed Mayme's recent behavior.

"Is it a stroke or heart attack? Did you call the Life Squad? Why didn't you ride in the ambulance with her?" Mary had questions, lots of them.

"No, Mary, she's here at Dr. V.'s office. Art and Ethel will pick us up soon," answered Carrie.

"Carrie, slow down and tell me what happened." Mary's panic was subsiding, but her curiosity wasn't. She had her assumptions.

"Oh Mary, Mayme tried to get up this morning to go to the bathroom and collapsed on the floor. I heard a dining room chair fall over and strike the floor. I shuffled as fast as I could to see what happened." Carrie did not sound convincing, for some reason.

"Oh no, is she all right?" Mary was not going to sit Carrie under interrogation lights. It couldn't be too bad if she was at the ageing Dr. V.'s office. "I still don't know why you didn't call an ambulance. That's why they're there."

"No, Mary, that stubborn old bat wouldn't let me call them. She said it would wake the neighbors. I think she just didn't want anybody seeing her in her bra and panties, with no teeth." Mary could hear the frustration in Carrie's voice. "I helped her back to bed and called Art. Wow, that woman is like picking up a sack of flour. Art and Ethel came over right away. Ethel and I struggled to dress her. She was like a rag doll. Then she would go back and forth trying to decide what to wear. 'What would look appropriate?' she said. I could have bopped her on her stubborn noggin. Art then helped her gingerly down the steps to his car. He's a strong man, your dad is. Next, Ethel and I dropped Art at the factory on our way here. Dr. V. has called an ambulance. He wants to run some tests."

"So, she's at Dr. V.'s with you and Mom right now, and she's OK?" Mary felt she was missing something.

"Mary, she looks terrible, white as a ghost. Her fingernails are purple, and she's panting like a dog. This isn't good." Carrie knew Mayme's downhill spiral was reaching the bottom. Something had to be done soon.

"Carrie, does Dr. V. think it's a stroke? Can she speak? Can she smile? Is her face drooping? What can I do?" Mary was already thinking about what she needed to gather for her day at the hospital.

"Mary, I just need to know if you can cover Dr. Ventress's front desk for me today. Just until four o'clock. It's easy, and oh wait, I forgot, you've done it before. I need to go to the hospital with Mayme in the ambulance. She'd never be able to check herself in." Carrie had never been without Mayme or Mayme without Carrie in over fifty years. "Dr. Ventress says he thinks it's some kind of pneumonia , but I think it could be pleurisy from her heavy drinking, and her dementia's getting worse every day. I think it's because Francis would have been seventy-five in January this year. She's not been handling that well for months now."

"Carrie, who's Francis?" Mary had never heard the name before.

"Oh, Mary, please forget I said that, please; and don't ever ask Mayme, ever, ever, ever. Never say that name out loud." Mary's eyes opened wide. "Now, can you cover for me while I go to the hospital with Mayme? Dr. V. wants her to stay overnight." Carrie then remembered. "Oh dear, I forgot. What are you going to do with Alex?"

"He's at day camp until four. I just need to pick him up around then. Dr. V. must excuse me for that. I'm sorry, but I really can't stay late. And then I have to pick up the hubby from work." Mary felt guilty leaving her coverage, but she was insistent.

"The good doctor will be fine. We're all like family to him." Carrie had worked for the elderly doctor for years and was proud to be a nurse like her infamous mother.

"Okay, Carrie, let me get this all straight. My mom will pick up my dad from work, come to the hospital to visit Mayme for a while, then what, take you back to their house for dinner? Will you stay there, and do you need me to work for you tomorrow?" Mary was the planner for the entire family, had been since she was a teen.

"Mary, I need you!" Carrie was about to cry.

"I know, Carrie, I can cover your job, and it all depends on when Mayme comes home. Now don't cry, she'll be fine." Mary was helping her feeble aunt through her chaos.

"No, Mary, I've got all that covered. I need you in a different way. I need to share something with you that has now gotten to a point of no return, a point where someone is going to get hurt." Mary was assuming it was about Mayme's alcoholism and the rapid increase of her Alzheimer's. But Mary didn't realize Carrie's secret was about the cause of Mayme's state, not the effects.

Carrie continued. "What I'm going to share with you mustn't be shared with anyone in the family, not your husband, Alex, Art or Ethel; please, only you."

Mary was silent for a moment on the telephone. "Carrie, why me? What can this be that makes me the only trusted recipient? Are you sure I can really help?"

"Mary, I must tell someone, or I'll burst wide open. And Dr. V., you and I may be the only ones that can help Mayme. I love our family, but you're the only one that I trust. Please, honey, please help me."

"Carrie, what night this week would be good for you?" Mary asked.

"Oh no, honey, it must be tonight while Mayme's not here. I don't want her to know that anyone knows but her and me. She would never forgive me, and it would certainly make things worse. It must be tonight."

Mary had gone from curiosity to shock. "Carrie, tonight it is, for sure. Once I get the family fed and settled, I'll come to your house. You call me when you get home and are ready for me. I'll bring you dinner. Do you want wine? Blackberry?" Mary was all in.

"Mary, I love you, my sweet little niece. You are the only one I trust to hold this inside your heart. And what I'm going to tell you, you mustn't tell anyone until both Mayme and I have passed. And no, no wine, please. Now promise?" asked Carrie.

"I promise you with all my love. Now give me a few minutes to change my clothes and brush my hair. If the ambulance is there before I arrive, tell Dr. V. I'm on my way."

"Thanks honey…"

"Carrie, Carrie, wait. You know I'm there for both of you. I love my aunts; we all love you both! See you tonight. Bye, Carrie, and give my love to Mayme. I'll visit her tomorrow night."

"Bye, Mary. We love you too." And the phone call ended.

• • •

That night, Mary came to Mayme and Carrie's home with meat-loaf, mashed potatoes and green beans. They sat at the dinette table and discussed Mayme's condition. She would be able to come home in a couple days after the tests were finished. Both women cleared the table and retired to the living room. Carrie kissed Mary on the cheek. "Are you ready, honey? I must warn you, this is not a pleasant story, but it is one neither Mayme nor I should take to our graves. Perhaps someday, our story can be written and passed down. It may be of some value to understand the relationship between Mayme and me."

The look on Mary's face was pensive as well as disturbing. She thought, *What in the world am I about to discover about my ancestors?*

1887 — BOSTON, MASSACHUSETTS

THE HOME OF THE WEHEMEYER FAMILY
SUCCESSFUL AND LOVING

[Carrie began her story the same way she relayed to Alex the story of her parents' meeting. Mary would keep her promise and not reveal any of the following story of Mayme and Carrie until each of the aunts had passed on. And like both family epics relayed to Alex and Mary, the stories would become much more detailed, as Alex became a popular novelist and published his versions as they appear in this novel years later.]

The snow was blowing sideways, forced by the stiff breeze in the heart of the bustling city of Boston. The constant revolving flow of Prussian medical students began within months of the philanthropic agreement between Harvard and Von Bismarck. Bestowed upon the top Prussian medical student was the most charming of accommodations, provided by Dr. Rothert and the gracious new

Wehmeyer family. And to everyone's pleasant surprise, soon after the marriage of Maria and August, it was announced that their first child would be due near the date of the couple's initial anniversary. Maria had always spoken to her family about her desire to have a large family. So immediately upon the revelation of the coming child, Von Bismarck, out of respect for Joseph Rothert and Maria, approved a new wing of the house to be constructed, giving the Wehmeyer family a place of privacy. However, Dr. Rothert and Von Bismarck were just as concerned about any disruption by Joseph's future grandchildren; the necessity for silence was paramount for the Prussian students to concentrate on their studies.

While Maria taught English and nursing to the newly arriving students, August had taken a job as a potter in the manufacturing district of Boston, at a well-respected factory which not only created commercial flower vases and fruit bowls but also beautiful and expensive décor for the rich. As a matter of fact, some of their works were sent back with students to be given as gifts to King Wilhelm I. The pieces of Longworth Pottery created by August were proudly displayed in many of the Prussian palaces.

As the years passed, August became well-known, not because of his uniqueness as a blind potter but because his skill in creating almost any shape from clay was indeed heightened by his lack of clear vision. And although he was unable to paint or color his work himself, he found himself in high demand by artists who could decorate his works to perfection. The news of the partnerships between August and the artists began to spread, not only throughout Boston, but throughout other cities of midwest America. And as word spread, August's work increased, causing his royalties to increase; and as the royalties increased, the Wehmeyer family became quite financially comfortable.

One day, James Longworth, the owner of the pottery factory in which August worked, approached him with a proposition. As August was about to begin a new piece of work, Mr. Longworth gently gripped him by the forearm. "August, my friend, I wish to

request your presence in my office please. We must have a chat."
August was concerned. He felt that his popularity and craftsman-
ship, if not artistic prowess, was above reproach. Possibly the
company was being sold or cutting back on employees.

"Mr. Longworth, I hope there's not a problem with my work,
sir. I feel it's in demand, and the artists seemed most pleased with
my designs. And I feel I have created for them the requested tex-
ture of their visions." Although August could not see Mr. Longworth smile, the man's grin was one that applauded August's confidence as well as his humility. No one had more passion for their
work than August.

"No, no, August. Nothing's wrong, nothing at all; quite the opposite. I have an interesting proposition for you, and I don't want
an answer right now. I'm fully aware of the dedication you display
for your wife and family and them for you." Mr. Longworth stood
up from behind his desk and made his way around to sit in the side
chair next to August.

"Why, thank you, sir. My family's been most supportive of me
as well." August was smiling. He could sense this was leading into
a positive arena.

"August, not many men wounded and blinded in battle could
rise to success as an artist and a father, as you have. You're a true
hero." August was blushing but still curious. He had not been
called into Mr. Longworth's office just to be given compliments.
This was a business. "I realize you have a wife and six children to
whom you are quite dedicated. But just hear me out, please." Mr.
Longworth's voice sounded excited to August in a most puzzling
way.

"Yes, sir, I'm listening." August stared at the blur of his boss
in the chair beside him.

"August, my sister-in law, Maria Longworth, lives in Cincinnati, Ohio, and together we're opening a factory called Rookwood
Pottery."

"Congratulations, sir. Not sure where Cincinnati is, but I'm sure it must be nice if your brother and his wife live there." August felt he needed to respond somehow.

"August, my brother died of tuberculosis last year, and I wish to help his widow and her family support themselves." Mr. Longworth stared at the wall, reminded of his brother. "My brother was a wealthy and well-known individual, not only locally, but internationally."

"I'm sorry, sir, but I'm perplexed as to how all this involves me." August went silent.

"August, Rookwood Pottery will be much more than a pottery factory, much more." August continued to stay silent. "Let me explain before you begin asking questions, August. I know you must want to. The Longworth family in the midwest is quite well-known in the art circles of that region. My sister-in-law and I are funding the construction of the most incredible state-of-the-art kilns, and we're bringing people from all over the world into Cincinnati in an attempt to produce the most well-known pottery of all time."

"Okay, sir, but what does this have to do with me?" August had no idea what was about to come next.

"August, my sister-in-law already has some of the most prodigious artists in the world supporting her venture. They can paint beautifully, but they can't throw pottery. You're the most incredible potter I've ever had in all my years of production. I told her about you."

August had a strange look on his face. "Thank you, sir, but please get to the point." He was getting tired of the avoidance of the point.

"August, would you consider moving to Cincinnati with your family and working for Rookwood Pottery?" Mr. Longworth was sure he knew the answer but wanted to start his negotiation high.

"Mr. Longworth, sir, that's something I promised my wife when I proposed marriage to her years ago, and to her father. I promised them I would become an artistic potter someday and that she would be proud of me."

"August, I didn't expect a yes that quickly, but I'm so pleasantly stunned."

"No, sir, you didn't let me finish." Although August couldn't see his boss's reaction, he could sense it. "I couldn't possibly do that to my family. My wife loves teaching, and the intellectual stimulation from our students is not only part of our lives but the lives of our children. I'm sorry, sir." August already felt successful in his career, and a geographical move would be selfish and disruptive to his entire family at this point.

"August, I expected your overall rejection, but what if we compromise? I can arrange for you to be taken, with an escort, of course, to Cincinnati and back, let's say, every three months. Would you consider that? I can promise you a sizeable raise along with royalties by the artists for your collaboration."

August was being given an opportunity to reach his dream as well as bring pride to the hearts of Maria and his children.

"Sir, may I give you my answer tomorrow? I must discuss this with Maria." August was being flooded with the same adrenaline he had felt when he and Maria had become engaged.

"Of course. I think this can be something that will find its way to the pinnacle of the artistic history of pottery. Think it over carefully." August was led by the arm back to his workstation. As he sat, his grin was so strong, his cheeks began to cramp.

September 1887

BOSTON TO CINCINNATI THE FAMILY'S SEPARATION IS BITTERSWEET

Dear August, my beloved,

All is well here on the home front. The three months we spend apart seem so much longer than the those three we spend together as a family. Otto moved into the dorm at

Boston College last week. I wish you could have been here to experience his excitement. I was in tears as I watched him pack his clothes. He insisted on taking some of your pottery with him to decorate his room. All of us are so proud of you. Someday I pray we can visit you in Cincinnati. It would be such an educational trip for the children as well as myself.

The rest of the children are exceptional. The older four have been quite helpful to Mrs. Schmidt and myself in taking care of the students. They learn so much from discussions with the Prussians. Mayme and Carrie, at ten and nine, are still too young to care about conversation, and they certainly do not cheerfully accept any domestic responsibilities. And then there is Francis. At four, he's still the highest maintenance. It's all I can do to keep up with that little chipmunk. He's a mischievous one.

We all love when your letters arrive, but not near as much as when you walk in the front door. The house seems incomplete without you, my love. Please make time speed up to your return.

I so look forward to our season of holidays beginning when you return in October.

Write soon and often, my hero,

Maria

February 14, 1889 – Boston

THE DAY THE HEAVENS CAME CRASHING DOWN ON THE WEHMEYER SISTERS

Mayme and Carrie arrived home joyfully from school with their decorated Saint Valentine's Day boxes under their arms. Without hesitation, they scampered up the stairway to their bedroom. The anticipation of reading the young love notes and well wishes from all their friends bubbled inside them. But just as they removed their heavy winter coats and warm knitted mittens, they heard their mother calling from the first-floor hallway. "Mayme, can you come down here for a moment, please? I need your help, honey."

The two sisters peered at one another; their expressions and sighs exuded obvious disappointment. They had skipped, hand-in-hand, all the way home from school in order to read their Valentines together, especially the ones given to them by the little boys whose fancy they would cherish forever. "Yes, Mother, be right down," murmured Mayme in chagrin. Both of them bounced down the curved staircase together as Maria stood at the bottom with four-year-old Francis holding his mother's hand.

"Mayme, since you're the oldest, I'm going to give you this responsibility. Carrie, you may go back to your room if you wish." Carrie smiled but remained by Mayme's side. They were and always had been inseparable.

"What is it, Mother?" asked Mayme.

"Mrs. Schmidt's little boy was sick with a fever today, and he had to stay home from school," responded Maria in regard to her loyal housekeeper.

"I'm sorry to hear that, Mother," Mayme responded in a rather uninterested tone. She just wanted to get back to her Valentines with Carrie.

"Well, Mayme, that means I must run down to the market myself and pick up some dinner and breakfast supplies for the students. Your other siblings are doing their homework in the library of the far wing at the moment, so they can help me prepare and serve dinner later." Mayme and Carrie remained distracted by their curiosity as to which of their little beaus had crushes on them.

"So what do you need from me, Mother? I have homework as well." Mayme was trying to avoid her mother's coming request. Maria knew Mayme's homework was still minimal compared to the others.

"Mayme, I'll be gone for about an hour, and I need you to watch little Francis while I'm gone. Just play with him or read him a fairy tale or something. It'll only be an hour at the most." Maria transferred Francis' hand to Mayme's.

"Aww, Mother, I have a big test tomorrow. Yea, a real big one. Can't you take him with you?" Maria interrupted Mayme, rather perturbed.

"Mayme, you can study while the others are helping me with dinner. Now, be a big girl and watch your little brother." And with that, Maria put on her coat and woolen bonnet and left the house.

"Read me a book, Mayme, please. Read me the one about the witch that tries to eat the brother and sister and they push her in the stove and kill her. Come on Mayme, please. I want to kill a witch someday."

Mayme rolled her eyes. "Francis, you're already trouble compared to the rest of us. Why don't you take a nap, and I'll read to you when you wake up? Carrie and I have some important school-work to do." The thought of the Valentines sitting unread on the floor was weighing oh so heavily on the longings of the two little schoolgirls.

"I'm not tired, Mayme," Francis whined, "and I heard mother say you could do your homework later. She did. I heard her. Come on, Mayme, play with me." Being the youngest, Francis was so cute, and he had certainly learned how to use it to his advantage. The older children were possessed by this little sibling, but Mayme and Carrie were too close in age to see him as anything but competition for the love and affection of their mother and, especially, their father.

Suddenly, Carrie looked at Mayme with an interesting idea. "Francis, let's play hide and seek. Mayme and I will go to our room, and you go hide. Then we'll try to find you. But you must stay in the house; you can't go outside. Sound fun?" Mayme shook her head up and down with a huge grin, even though she didn't quite get Carrie's scheme as of yet.

"Okay, Carrie. I like that game. Let's start in your room." Francis was ready to romp through the house and hide like a monkey free from his cage.

Carrie took Mayme's hand as she climbed the stairs slowly. Francis had already scurried up the steps in front of them and into the two sisters' bedroom. Mayme stopped halfway to the top and turned to Carrie. "Carrie," asked Mayme, "I don't quite get it. How are we going to read our Valentines if we're searching all over the house for that little urchin?"

"Don't be silly; we aren't ever going to really look for him. He'll stay in his hiding place for a while, then when he gets tired of not being found, he'll come back and we'll just tell him we couldn't find him." Carrie's idea now made sense.

Mayme smiled again. "Brilliant, Carrie!" The girls went into their room and saw Francis already rummaging through their Valentines.

"How did you get so many Valentines? I only got one from Mother and Father." Carrie was about to scold Francis for invading their privacy, but then remembered that Francis was only four and couldn't read yet. Yet both sisters were still annoyed with this little human roadblock to their fun.

"Okay, Francis, you go hide while we count to ten. Then we'll come looking. Ready? Here we go; one, two, three…" Francis took off running.

Fifteen minutes later, Francis reentered the room with a cute little pouty face. The Valentines were spread all over the wooden floor. "You didn't look for me? I waited, but you didn't even look," Francis whined like every other four-year old.

"Yes we did, Francis. We looked everywhere, but you had such a great hiding place, we couldn't find you and gave up. You're a good hider." Mayme and Carrie were giggling over the gullibility of their little brother. "Okay, Francis, let's try it again." Carrie figured her mother would be home shortly anyway, and their chore would be over.

"Okay, Carrie, but I won't make it as hard for you to find me this time." Francis was again ready.

Mayme and Carrie continued to giggle. "Here we go; one, two, three…" And Francis skedaddled off once more. But after just a couple minutes, while both Mayme and Carrie were still enthralled by a few more of the little boys' "Roses are red" poems, they heard a horrific crash downstairs. It was a powerful thud that shook the house along with a simultaneous shattering of broken glass.

Both looked at each other with eyes wide open, then raced down the stairway. As they assumed the glass was from the kitchen, they raced through the pantry, but there it was. The ponderous oak china cabinet had tipped over with the top catching the opposite wall just before it hit the floor. Francis was trapped by the bottom drawers, the drawers he had pulled out like a ladder in order to climb on top and hide. Francis's chest was crushed, and his face and neck had been slashed severely by the glass door encasing the china.

"Oh Mayme, what do we do? He's bleeding so much, and he doesn't look conscious. I don't think he's breathing. I don't think he can breathe. Oh Mayme, Mayme!" Carrie was in a state of trepidation, unable to think or reason.

"Carrie, you grab that side and I'll get this side, and let's lift the cabinet off him." Both sisters lifted with all their strength, but Mayme's hand slipped, and her arm crashed through the glass that still remained unbroken on her side of the cabinet. The cabinet crashed back again onto Francis' chest. The glass slid down Mayme's forearm, slicing it like a vicious tiger claw from her wrist to her elbow, critically severing arteries all the way. Blood spewed from Mayme's wrist like a broken water line. She dropped onto the floor, gripping the wound that was rapidly draining the very life out of her.

Suddenly, the front door opened. "Kids, I'm home." With that, Mayme crawled frantically on her knees under the dining room table, whimpering in pain. She was frozen in terror as to what her mother was going to do to her after she saw Francis.

"Mayme, Carrie, Francis, are you kids upstairs?" Maria was being escorted by a couple of young boys from the market who had helped her home with the groceries. "Boys, just go through that pantry there and put the bags in the kitchen." But as they did, Maria heard one of the boys drop his groceries and scream, "Mrs. Wehmeyer, come quick! Hurry, hurry!"

Maria came running to the sight of Carrie weeping hysterically and her young precious Francis lying motionless under the pernicious china cabinet. She dropped to her knees and felt Francis's neck for a pulse. It was nonexistent. "Boys, help me get this cabinet upright." They did so. Maria pulled a shard of glass from Francis's bloody neck, but the blood didn't spurt, it just drizzled down his neck and onto the floor. There was no heartbeat. Maria lifted her little son's limp body and placed him on the dining room table. Blood had run out of his mouth and down his cheek as well. Maria knew his internal organs were mortally crushed. Francis was dead.

"Mrs. Wehmeyer, what can we do? Please, what can we do?" The boys were aghast at the sight of that much blood and the death of such a young child.

"Carrie, where's Mayme? She was supposed to be watching Francis. She knows how he loves to climb on everything in sight. She was to watch him!" Maria grabbed Carrie by the arm firmly. "Where is she, young lady?"

"I don't know, Mother. I was in my room by myself when I heard the crash. I don't know where she is." Carrie was so afraid of what her mother would do to her if she knew the truth, if she knew playing hide and seek was her idea. She lied, and it was a lie she would never forget. A lie she would always know Mayme had heard.

Suddenly, Maria heard a heavy sob under the table and saw a stream of blood coming out from under the lacey tablecloth at her feet. She dropped to her knees and saw Mayme, covered in blood, shivering, whimpering, and hugging herself into a little ball. Maria crawled under the table and dragged Mayme out. She quickly saw the main artery on her wrist deeply sliced and knew she needed care immediately.

"Mother, it's my fault. It's all my fault." Mayme was hysterical. "Don't save me. I don't want to live. I want to die, Mother. I want to die! Francis is dead because of me. Please let me die!"

"Hush, child. Boys, get our coats. I need you to give the three of us a ride to the hospital as quickly as possible, before this one bleeds to death. Carrie, go outside and get in the cart." Maria tied a tight tourniquet around Mayme's arm and somehow found the strength to carry her ten-year-old daughter to the street. But before she did, she put Mayme in the chair by the front door and returned to the dining room table where her precious son lay dead. She removed one of Francis's shoes and put it at the top of his head.

As she did, one of the boys asked Maria, "You're going to leave your little boy on the table like that? Shouldn't we take him with us, Mrs. Wehmeyer?" The boys and Carrie were stunned. Mayme was losing consciousness.

"I learned from my father many years ago, boys, on the battlefields in Prussia, you must leave those soldiers who won't survive behind to die and save those you can. Don't question me again, medic, do you understand me? I'm the head nurse here, and you'll do as I say, or you'll be court-martialed. We must get Mayme to Dr. Rothert's operatory as soon as possible." The delivery boys were stunned. It was as if Maria had totally changed personalities. She wasn't the sweet woman from the market. She was bossy and disturbing, not to mention unemotional.

The two boys helped Maria lay Mayme in the back of the delivery cart. They helped the hysterical sister, Carrie, into the cart as well. As the boys took their places on the bench in front, one boy flicked the reins, and the horse began its hurried trot to the hospital. As they made their way down the first block, the driver leaned over to his friend. "I'm confused. We aren't medics. And Mrs. Wehmeyer wasn't crying at all. Where has Mrs. Wehmeyer's mind gone? Who is Dr. Rothert? And what's with the shoe?"

Mayme was taken to the hospital, and her arm was stitched and bandaged. Those scars she would carry for the rest of her life, and they would remind the entire family of the day Francis had died. But for Mayme and Carrie, not only would those scars be about the death of their little brother, but they would be a reminder of their immature selfishness over those stupid Valentines, the concern of any boy caring about them, and something that would remain deep, deep inside forever. Between the two of them, denial would never be an option, but silence would be.

• • •

Within a year, Maria was unable to live in their home in Boston, and August was unable to tolerate his own grief alone in Cincinnati without Maria and the rest of his family. They packed up the children and their belongings and moved to Cincinnati, where August became an important staple of the distinguished Rookwood Pottery. However, his health fell steadily from his deep depression, and he died of grief ten years later at the age of fifty-five. And with the children nearly on their own, Maria Rothert Wehmeyer rejoined the Red Cross, teaching both nursing and the history of the very first battle. She died at age seventy-five, taking her own life by slicing her wrist with a shard of glass.

Late Summer 1960 — Cincinnati Ohio

ONE WEEK AFTER MAYME'S RELEASE FROM THE HOSPITAL CARRIE CRIES OUT FOR HELP BUT THE TIDE CONTINUES TO RISES QUICKLY

"Beckham residence, Alex speaking." Alex, now closing in on ten years old, had been trained by his father to answer the telephone professionally, always sporting a friendly smile on his face. His father was convinced people could hear the smile through the telephone. Alex's father had started his own business, and his mother, Mary, was working with him out of their small home. Business calls were not at all uncommon.

"Hi, Alex, it's Aunt Carrie. May I speak with your mother for a moment, please?" Carrie seemed to be in a hurry, with a strange cracking in her voice.

"Sure, Aunt Carrie. She's trimming the rose bushes outside. I'll get her." Alex accidently hung up the telephone and ran outside to retrieve his mother. "Mom, Aunt Carrie's on the telephone, well, I mean, she was, but I accidently hung up on her. Oops."

"Alex, you must be more careful. What if that was a business call, young man?" Mary wasn't happy with that mistake at all. But then again, he wasn't even quite ten yet.

"Sorry, Mom, really! But I always ask who's calling. This time I knew it was Aunt Carrie. Won't happen again, I promise. And Mom, she sounds weird, kind of out of breath." Alex stayed outside and threw his rubber ball against the garage wall. Mary rushed into the house, expecting to hear of a health emergency, perhaps a heart attack, as the reason for the recently infrequent calls.

Dialing the phone as fast as the rotor would recoil, Mary waited as her restless foot tapped the hardwood floor. She lit a cigarette. After two rings, the phone was answered, and Carrie picked up. "Carrie, I'm so sorry Alex hung up on you. Are you okay?"

"Well, I'm fine, but Mayme's getting worse, honey." Mary could hear a daunting tone quivering in Carrie's inflection.

"What do you mean by 'worse,' Carrie? I thought her medication was doing the trick, and her pneumonia was going away. I thought Mayme looked rather healthy when she returned from the hospital last week. I couldn't even tell she'd been sick. Quickest recovery from pneumonia I've ever seen, especially for her age." But Mary was sensing that something was not as it seemed. She waited for Carrie's answer, with confusion wrinkling her brow.

"Mary, Mayme's, well, let's just call it asleep at the moment," replied Carrie. She was trying to be subtly confessional.

"What exactly does 'call it asleep' mean, Carrie?" asked Mary. "Come Carrie, out with it. You're keeping something from me. This call isn't about your new batch of cookies, is it?" Mary was becoming impatient.

"Okay, Mary, you know our secret. The one about the death of our little brother and the death of our mother?" asked Carrie.

"Of course, Carrie. How can anyone forget that? Now, please, get on with it." Mary's brow frowned again but this time in deep concern.

"Well, I didn't tell you all of it. There's more." Mary didn't respond. "When we moved to Cincinnati, Mayme never did get quite right." Mary could sense that Carrie was about to weep.

"Keep going, Carrie," said Mary. "Talk through it, my sweet."

"Mary, our mother and father were devasted by the death of Francis, so when they moved to Cincinnati, Mother insisted on having another child right away to replace Francis. But Father was so hurt that he was totally against it. But Mother, as always, won out, and the child was born one year to the day after Francis's death." Mary could hear Carrie sniffle into a handkerchief.

"I'm still not picking up on the problem here, Carrie." Mary waited.

"Mary, I'll be blunt. Mother was so convinced Mayme was tragically irresponsible, she always blamed Mayme and her alone for the death of Francis. So much so, she would never let Mayme anywhere close to the new baby. Even when he became a toddler and beyond, Mayme was forbidden to be alone with the child. She was not allowed to hold him, hug him, kiss him, nothing. Mother would let me babysit, but Mayme had to stay away. Mother showed Mayme no forgiveness and no affection for the rest of her life." Carrie's crying was now obvious and intense.

"That's terrible, Carrie," said Mary. "Mayme's so loving and lovable to all of us; especially to Alex." Then the light bulb lit up her mind. "Oh, Carrie, you mean…"

"Precisely. She has loved Art and Alex so intensely because they are boys, and to her, they are Francis. Mother could keep Mayme away from her new child but had no power to keep Art and Alex away from her. Mayme needed to prove to all of us that she was not the horrible person our mother forced her to believe she was."

"Well, your mother had passed before Alex was born," Mary pointed out.

"True, but Art is our sister's child and the only sibling that stayed in Cincinnati. None of our siblings blamed Mayme. As a matter of fact, Mother's action put a spike through the heart of all our family relationships. I didn't want to tell you that story until Alex was older." Carrie wasn't sure how Mary was going to respond.

"Carrie, certainly you don't think if I knew I would be afraid to let Mayme be around Alex. Oh, Carrie, poor Mayme." Now Mary was about to cry.

"Mary, it gets worse. Mayme was so hurt and so ashamed of herself that she made several attempts on her own life. Mother and Father put her in an asylum a number of times to protect her from herself, but never from others. I promised my father on his death bed I would always be there to take care of her; and I have." Carrie stopped.

"Oh Carrie, I'm so sorry. What do you mean by 'it's getting worse'?" Mary's heart was beginning to race.

"Honey, she wasn't taken to the hospital for pneumonia. She took a whole bottle of aspirin trying to kill herself. Of course, that obviously wasn't enough to kill her instantly, so Ethel and I took her to Dr. Ventress. He gave her Ipecac in his office to flush her stomach. But Art insisted she be admitted so they could observe her behavior for a couple days." Mary was benumbed at what she was hearing. "Mary, hello, are you still there?"

"What can I do, Carrie? Has she threatened to hurt you?" Now Mary was scared.

"Mary, she put my favorite dress in the toilet and peed on it, giggling the whole time," Carrie blurted.

"Carrie, really?" said Mary "Mayme did that?"

"And she'll stick her tongue out at me during dinner with a mouth full of food, just like a little brat. She has even threatened to smother me in my sleep, and she belly-laughs about it." Mary could hear Carrie's voice shaking. She could almost feel the phone shake.

"Oh, Carrie, from what you've told me, it sounds like she's so pent up with rage, she's finally out of control. After all these years, she still blames you for Francis's death, doesn't she, or at least blames you for not standing beside her that day."

"And she's right. I should have taken half the blame or more. Art always calls her his 'Little Aunt Firecracker,' and she behaves exactly like a child around Alex. They are so absolutely adorable together. Now, however, I'm afraid she's reached the point where she's boiling over. Little Aunt Firecracker is exploding. She needs help more than ever. Mary, I'm really scared, scared for my life, scared for hers!"

"Carrie, a short while ago, you slipped and told me Francis would have been seventy-five this year. She turned worse on Valentine's Day this year, didn't she?" To Mary, it was all coming sadly together.

"Oh Mary, I've never seen her drink this much, ever. You have no idea what she's like when she drinks, and that's all she does these days, drink Sambuca and sleep. She's sleeping now. Mary, could you come over right away, before she wakes up? I'm afraid if she tries something, I won't be able to stop her." Carrie knew Mary was always there to help.

"Sure, Carrie, but I have to bring Alex. His father has a sales call tonight. The little one is visiting her grandmother. What if we make dinner at your place, and we'll both evaluate her to see how bad it is? Maybe she's just tired." Mary was concerned about Alex joining her, but she thought Alex's relationship with Mayme might actually be a calming influence.

"Oh, Mary, my beautiful little niece, thank you. I have food here, and we can all take Mayme's mind off of things." Mary could hear Carrie's sigh of relief through the phone.

"See you in an hour. Love you, Carrie."

"Love you too, Mary." And the phone disconnected.

• • •

The old Ford pulled up to the curb outside the home of two Wehmeyer spinsters' home exactly one hour after Carrie's call for support. Mary turned the car off, but before Alex was able to open his passenger door, Mary reached over and grasped his arm gently but firmly in her hand. "Alex, I need you to do something for me. You must promise to do exactly as I say, with no questions. Promise?"

"Sure, Mom, what is it?" Alex was excited to be visiting his two elderly aunts, who always treated him like a little prince. But as his age and size continued to increase, those good old days of horsey rides and swimming pool shenanigans with Mayme were gone forever. He knew he was changing. He also knew Mayme was not. She still made him laugh.

"When we go into the house, I want you to stay close behind me the whole time. Don't go running into the house to say hi like usual or go after cookies." Alex could see there was no playfulness in his mother's eyes. Something serious was happening inside her.

"Sure, Mom, but why?" Alex was puzzled.

"Alex, I said no questions, young man. And if I say 'run,' I want you to run to the car as fast as you can and lock yourself in. Do you understand me?"

Now Alex was really puzzled. "No, Mom, I don't understand. Why would I leave you and run to the car? Is there a robber or wild animal in the house or something?" Alex didn't want his mother to go in either if there was any danger. He thought this was more of a job for his grandfather, Art. "Dad left the baseball bats in the trunk. You want me to get one?"

"No, Alex, there's no robbers or wild animals inside, but I said no questions, and I mean it. Just do it. I'll explain someday." Mary squeezed Alex's arm tighter, and he knew she meant business.

Mary and Alex walked up the steps to the front door. Mary rang the bell. Suddenly, a face appeared quickly at the glass storm door, and instantaneously, the inside door was slammed so hard in Mary's face it shattered one of the panes of glass. Mary swirled around to protect Alex from the flying shards.

"Mom, was that Aunt Mayme that just did that? It didn't look like her, but it was her." Mary didn't respond except to reach for her keys and get the spare key to the house that she kept for emergencies. As they entered, Mary pushed Alex behind her with her arm, and they both crept in like mice entering a lion's den.

After slamming the door in Mary's face, Mayme had run from the door into the living room. "Carrie, Carrie, it's Mother, she's back from the market. Hurry, we must find Francis. Where could he be? We've searched everywhere. She's going to be so mad if she finds out we weren't really watching him." Carrie broke down, her face in her hands. Mary and Alex walked into the room, Alex peeking out from behind Mary's skirt.

"Carrie, are you okay? What was that all about? One of your front windowpanes is shattered." Mayme whisked away into the kitchen, her worn floor-length nightgown flowing and her gums devoid of her false teeth. Alex, even though he loved her, felt she resembled a ghoul in a Halloween haunted house.

"Mayme," Carrie called into the kitchen, "it's not Mother, it's Mary and Alex coming to visit. Everything is fine."

Mayme answered from the kitchen. "Carrie, you're just as responsible for Francis as I am. Now help me find him before he hurts himself." Mayme reentered the living room and looked over at Alex. "There you are, you little stinker. Now you sit down and don't move an inch while I make dinner. Not sure what Mother bought at the store." Alex was so perplexed. This was too weird for him to fathom.

Mayme went into the kitchen and poured herself a full glass of Sambuca. Carrie began crying on the sofa as Mary sat next to her and held her, rocking her back and forth. Alex sat on the far end of the sofa, staying close to Mary's side, as he'd been instructed. Mary learned over and whispered into Alex's ear, "And remember, if I say 'run,' then you run to the car like a jackrabbit." Alex didn't like this game. This wasn't fun at all. As a matter of fact, he realized this was not any sort of game at all. But what was happening?

Suddenly Mayme saw Carrie and Mary in an embrace. "What a minute. You're not Mother, and you're not Francis. What is this, some sort of trick? I'm supposed to be watching Francis."

"Mayme, go back in the kitchen and leave us alone for just a little while. I bet dinner is going to be fantastic." Mary was attempting to move Mayme's focus to the present.

"Leave you alone. You think Francis isn't safe around this disturbed little girl Mayme, don't you? You two are trying to keep me away from Francis, aren't you?" Then it all rushed back into her head. That horrific day seventy-one years ago that had changed her life. The day Carrie had taken no responsibility for Francis's death and never would, as far as she knew. Her mother always blamed her and her only: Mayme, the irresponsible one. Mayme marched back into the kitchen and immediately returned with a huge butcher knife. She pointed it straight at Carrie's face as if she were a matador ready to slay the bull.

"Mayme, what are you doing?" Mary stared directly into Mayme's eyes, stalling her attack.

"That crybaby ruined my entire life. She was as much to blame as I was that day, but no, she blamed it all on me. And now, instead of trying to kill myself all my life, I'm going to slice you up, Carrie. I'm going to slit your throat like Mother did that Hanoverian. She'll be proud of me when I tell her about your lies." Mayme looked to the ceiling. "Watch, Mother, watch what I do to that precious little Carrie of yours."

"I felt just as bad, Mayme, but I've taken care of you all my life. And it hasn't been easy. Go ahead, do it, do it. I can't stand to even look at you anymore, you old hag."

Out of nowhere, Alex left the sofa and stood between Mayme's knife and Carrie's life. "No Aunt Mayme, please. No, don't hurt Aunt Carrie. I love you both. Please put the knife down, please!" Alex had tears running down his cheeks, one from each eye.

Mary went into a panic but could see an odd look of serenity begin to flush over Mayme's face. Any quick moves, and Mayme might become disconnected from any reality whatsoever and attack. She looked at Alex. "Francis, is that you? You've grown so much. I haven't seen you in years; oh, my little sunshine."

"No, Aunt Mayme, I'm your nephew Alex, but you usually call me Art." Mayme was trying hard to put this ancestral puzzle together. "Remember, we go to the pool and splash and play dominoes together. Please Aunt Mayme, don't hurt Aunt Carrie, please." Alex and Mayme locked eyes.

Mayme took Alex by the chin and lifted his head. Mary thought she might be getting ready to slit Alex's throat. "No Mayme don't! It's Alex, he's my son. Look into his face. You love him, and he loves you." Mary and Carrie knew any physical assault on Mayme in her current state could cause a lot of injuries.

"I know who he is, and I would never hurt Art, I mean Alex." She kissed him on the forehead and grinned with a disturbing toothless smile. She returned to the kitchen and slammed another Sambuca.

Mary grabbed Alex by the arm and pulled her close to her bosom. "Don't ever do something like that again, Alex Beckham. I told you to stay behind me, didn't I?"

"Mom. It's just Aunt Mayme. She wouldn't hurt me. She's mad at Aunt Carrie for some reason. Mom, who is Francis?" Alex picked up on her anger but wanted to know more about this Francis kid.

They could all hear the butcher knife drop into the sink, and then Mayme was gone from the kitchen. Then as they looked ahead into the next room, they could see a faint object flow through the darkness; Mayme was heading to her bedroom. "I guess she needs time to settle herself down after that outburst," observed Mary. But it wasn't long before the three on the sofa got a gut-wrenching surprise.

"Oh dear, Mayme, what are you doing? Mayme, there's a little boy in the room. Mayme, back in the bedroom right now, do you hear me?" Carrie was standing in a face-off with Mayme, who was ten feet away in the doorway.

Shivers went through Alex's body. He was speechless. Mary didn't know what was best: tell Alex to run, pull Carrie back on the sofa, force Mayme back into the bedroom, or all three.

In that moment of bewilderment, there she stood. Alex's Aunt Mayme, age eighty, was completely naked in front of all of them. She bent halfway over, looked at her sister with one lip raised in disgust, put her thumb to her nose, waggling her fingers, and with an evil raspy voice blurted, "Kiss my ass, Carrie." Then, just as quickly as she had exposed herself, she ran back into her bedroom.

Carrie buried her face in her hands and sobbed uncontrollably. Mary held her head to her shoulder. "Alex, go to the bathroom and grab some tissues, please." But then she quickly reversed her instruction. "No Alex, I'm going to get Carrie some tissues, but you are coming with me." When reaching the doorway to the bathroom, Mary stopped and positioned herself so she could watch Mayme's bedroom door. "Alex, go into the bathroom and get some tissues for Aunt Carrie." Alex did what his mother asked. "Now take them to her but go through the kitchen. Then stay with her. I need to call someone."

Mary walked to the bedroom door and stacked three dining room chairs in front of it on the floor. Mayme was trapped in the bedroom, and though she would be able to eventually push hard enough to squeeze out, it would not be before Mary could return. Mary went to the music room, where she called Art.

"Hello" said Ethel.

"Mom, is Dad there? I need to talk to him right away," responded Mary.

"Honey, can he call you back? I'm making dinner, and he's napping," replied Ethel.

"No, Mom. It can't wait. I mean, this is a real emergency. Wake him now. I don't have a lot of time." It was obvious there was panic in her daughter's voice.

"It's not Alex, is it? Is he hurt?" Ethel was now panicked as well.

"No, Mom. It's Mayme. Get him now. No more questions." Mary was now stern, and her mother knew not to mess with her daughter when she heard that tone.

"Art, Mary's on the phone, and says she needs to talk to you. It's an emergency." Ethel knew his response.

"Ethel, I told you never to wake me up from my nap. It was terribly hot today in the factory. Did you tell her I—?" Art was angry.

"Art, she knows not to wake you, but she insists; it's an emergency with Mayme, Art, please. This must be really important." Art got up off the couch and shuffled to the telephone.

"This better be good, Ethel." Art picked the telephone off the phone stand. "Mary, I was sleeping. What do you want?" It was an ugly greeting.

"Dad, I need you here right now. Mayme has flipped out and tried to stab Carrie with a butcher knife. Alex and I are here, and I have her barricaded in the bedroom. You're the only one that can help us at this point." Art's response was without any questions.

"Oh Mary, I've seen this coming. My firecracker finally went off. I'll be there in less than ten. Keep Mayme confined." Art hung up the telephone and told Ethel to stay put. He put on his trousers and shirt and raced to the car.

Art arrived and joined the three of them in the living room. With Carrie sobbing on the sofa and Alex sitting totally befuddled, as any young boy would be, Mary relayed the events of the last couple hours. Then Carrie continued, describing other disturbing behavior from Mayme in the recent past.

From nowhere, Alex burst out with, "And can someone please tell me, who is Francis? Aunt Mayme said she was looking for Francis when we came in, and then she thought I was Francis. Usually she thinks I'm you, Grandpa."

"Alex, that's enough," Mary said as Carrie and Mary glanced at each other with a look of guilt.

Art looked at Carrie. "Carrie, didn't you tell me once you had a little brother that died of smallpox when he was young?"

Carrie looked at Mary. "Yes, Art, and Mayme loved our little brother so much. She was devasted, as we all were. That's probably why she adores all of her nephews—you, and now Alex. I would say that loss might have something to do with this issue." Mary stayed silent.

"Perhaps, but we need to have Dr. Ventress come over tonight and sedate her. And let's make sure he knows how much she has had to drink. As a matter of fact, I could use a cold beer right now, but your Sambuca out there will have to do." Art was now in charge.

Out of nowhere, Alex looked at his mother. "And can I have some blackberry wine? Aunt Mayme always lets me have some. She says it makes my tummy feel good." Alex had a smile on his face. All three glanced at each other.

MAYME LOSES HER WAY IN HER OWN LAND OF THE PAST THEN IS LOST TO THE FAMILY FOREVER

It was only a short period of time before Dr. Ventress made his way to the Wehmeyer home. Every so often, Art, Mary, Carrie and Alex could hear the chairs move as Mayme tried to open the bedroom door. But then it would stop.

Since it had been a couple of hours since her last Sambuca, the good doctor injected her with a sedative, and she slept through the night. Carrie went to stay with Ethel, and Art slept on the couch to protect his loving aunt from harming herself. For the next day, Dr. Ventress suggested that Art dilute the Sambuca, mixing it with water and a liquid sedative to keep Mayme quiet in the morning. By the following afternoon, a van arrived with men in white coats, and Dr. Ventress injected Mayme once more just before the men from the asylum helped Mayme down the steps and into the van at the curb. Art followed the van to help admit Mayme to her new home.

As the van drove away, Alex watched Mary embrace the broken-hearted sister, as she had wept for hours.

"Mary, this is all my fault. If only that day I had told Mother it was my idea to read those Valentines and not Mayme's, Mayme would not have felt so unloved. And in the end, if I wouldn't have convinced Mayme to let him go hide somewhere. Francis would still be alive." Carrie began to weep once more. Mary held her and patted her like a child.

"Aunt Carrie?"

"Yes, Alex."

"Who is Francis?"

Next and final episode of the series:
Alex comes to the harsh realization that is boyhood is coming to a close. It is time to move up to the first rung of the next ladder of life.

EPISODE VI

THE TIME HAS ARRIVED FOR ALEX TO CLIMB BEHIND THE WHEEL OF HIS LIFE

With our experiences continuing to intertwine with each other, coming incessantly on the heels of the last, we all have different ways to interpret them and react as we cross into our ever-changing stages of life. As toddlers are enthralled with walking, then running for the first time; the elderly prefers to sit in front of their TVs and watch game shows. As the young child craves the love and attention of their family members, the embarrassed teenager begins to walk six paces ahead or six behind their parents. As the young adult tempts fate and sometimes endangers life and limb for the pure fun of it, the parent discourages anything that may endanger their child's future. And as children prefer candy and soda pop, the adults and the elderly change their daily health habits to give themselves as many days on the planet as possible.

Alex had reached a harsh epiphany about what used to be his favorite day of the year—Christmas. Life had faded rapidly around him. His physical surroundings had changed rapidly. His feelings and priorities were leaving that little boy inside of him behind, replacing those feelings with heightened feelings of competition and an entirely different kind of need, the love and attention from the little girl sitting across the aisle. But on this Christmas Day, the change culminated from a slow simmering maturity to the absolute realization that his childhood was at an end. And with one terrible explosion, the philosophy that would develop so many varying parts of his life came into focus. It was time to begin his manhood with this small seed of wisdom germinated by the tears on his pillow.

CHRISTMAS NIGHT – 1966 – 10:12 p.m.

Alex retreated from his family, brushed his teeth, and climbed into his bed. He reclined on his back in a room that still felt foreign and distant, like the wooden cabins at summer camp. Unlike his room of less than a year ago, which he had shared with his younger sister for ten years, this one was dark and quiet. The roaring of trucks and the rattling of windows were not part of his new home. It was almost too quiet, and every creak caused by the settling of this structure or by the wind bashing into the aluminum awning over his windows caused a brief break in his sleep. With his hands folded behind his head, and staring at the smooth drywall ceiling, the thoughts of this very perplexing and emotional day brought forth the realization that the curtain had dropped on the drama based on the beginning of his life.

Unable to sleep, he found that those memories of years past would not leave him alone. They seemed to swarm through the room like ghosts in a condemned mansion. At age sixteen, unlike at age five, the days of cuddling between his parents for safety and tranquility in tough times were over. In the dark solitary shadows of his space, tears ran silently down his cheeks and onto his pillow. Sobbing to relieve his emotions was not necessary, but caring tears were. He now stood at the base of the next ladder. He knew that tomorrow, his feet would be standing on the first rung of the next stage of his life. The innocence of his youth would now be just memories from which to draw and grow.

THE SILENT MOVIE FLASHES BRIGHTLY INSIDE THE THEATRE OF ALEX BECKHAM

In the last few years, as Alex reached his adolescence, those endearing and often confusing relationships with his family members had drifted into the archives of his mind, as if the sun was setting gradually in his heart. It seemed so long ago when he had naively viewed his great-grandmother being placed in that bed and the men putting her in the back of a big black station wagon, then dropping her into a hole, like his parents did with his bird Pudgy. Anything prior to that day was simply a secondary memory passed on by the reminiscence of the storyteller, each time recounted with a different twist and supported by black-and-white photos or faded polaroids. Now they all seemed like fairy tales to Alex, while the pain and confusion of those incidents melted away, leaving only small emotional stains on the knees of his pants.

In the presence of his freshly blooming maturity and his struggling ability to control his new adult emotions, changes were exploding all around him. The hints of transition had begun with those disconcerting few days when he had witnessed his beloved playmate, his Aunt Mayme, being torn from the protection of her sister Carrie, placed in a drug-induced stupor, and escorted to the asylum. It was shortly after that when life had blasted Alex hard, as he learned of his Aunt Mayme's self-inflicted death. She was the first real family member he loved who had now left him behind with real feelings of deep mourning.

And to create more emotional trauma that would live inside Alex for years, Carrie had insisted on following their Prussian custom and having Mayme's funeral held in the dining room of what was now Alex's family's new home, the same place where they had displayed the bodies of Carrie's mother and two sisters. As Mayme was taken from her home on the journey to the family cemetery on that cold wintry day, Alex didn't realize what horrific memories had cursed Mayme, and now that family secret was protected only by Mary and Carrie.

Carrie's now being forced to accept the fact that her loving sister and lifelong friend would never return to her life meant that Alex's mother and his grandfather would bear the responsibility of fostering the life of the rapidly aging mind and body of their beautifully meek and gentle aunt. They became her transportation, her custodians, her very lifeline to the world. Alex was now old enough to mow Carrie's grass and trim her bushes and then after, to spend a bit of time playing gin rummy with her. He enjoyed it. But his one most difficult task was her insistence that he help her make her infamous anise cookies without Mayme, while she wept intermittently from her loneliness.

Within three years of Mayme's death and after Carrie had caught the kitchen curtains on fire for the second time as the wind blew them over the unattended burners on her stove, Art and Mary moved Carrie into a nursing home within close proximity, so all could visit. She survived and was protected, but her mind began to fade even more rapidly without her soulmate at her side. It was at that point that Alex's family, in order to help pay for her care, purchased the Wehmeyer home from Carrie, and the Beckhams moved in.

On this Christmas night, as Alex reflected on his bedroom ceiling, he heard his mother and father finally coming up the creaky steps, his father carrying the sleeping Melody in his arms. He tucked her in. Then Mary prepared herself for what Alex thought would be a very lonely night. He could hear a faint whimpering coming from his parents' bedroom. It was a sign of grief that soothed him. He had not seen that all day from his mother. He wanted to comfort her, but that was the job of his father in this moment of loss.

As the whimpering began to fade like a rain shower eases slowly from its trickling on the roof, Alex began his exploration of those childhood memories from before all this emotional transition had begun to empty into his life. He thought about his old house. He could see every room, their curtains, the scratches on the walls, their colors. He could see every tree and every crack in the driveway. He remembered the taste of the pears, the cherries, and the grapes. He remembered the smell of the roses and the irises bordering the driveway. He remembered the Christmas eves with his grandparents. The Christmas mornings opening the presents left under the tree by Santa. He remembered Easter mornings and the eventual repetitive hiding places of one noncreative rabbit. But from here to eternity, all of this would need to remain only in his head and in his heart, for the house had been demolished to build an interstate. Only a patch in the back corner of the yard was saved; that was where Pudgy was buried.

Alex was perplexed that all of this had changed within one short year, and now this afternoon as well. This was a new house, a new room, a new ceiling to use for contemplation, but it had no cracks, no streams, no lakes. This was the third Christmas without that special night before, with his Beckham grandparents. He realized at this point that that was the only time they had ever come to his home. But since Mayme's death, Grandpa Beckham had died of a heart attack while mowing his lawn, and Grandma Beckham died of a stroke in her bathtub. Johnny, the cousin he idolized, had joined the Air Force and left the area.

As Alex combed through the memories of his grandparents,

aunts, uncles, and cousins, he understood he would never see his grandparents again. He pictured them so sweetly in his heart and could even smell the lavender perfume from his grandmother that seemed to linger for hours on his shirt. But what he didn't realize that night was that he would see Johnny fewer than ten times over the rest of his life. The Beckhams' family Sundays had ended, and so had the tightness of that entire side of the family.

But nature has a way of protecting one's heart as it moves its younger generation into a position to assert their roles as parents and leaders, leaving only the conscious and subconscious influences of their elders to guide them through the coming stages. For Alex, acceptance of their passing would move from sadness to warm, fond memories to be cherished forever.

April 1966

ALEX OBSERVES THE MOUNTAIN AS THE AVALANCHE BEGINS

"Alex, wake up, listen to me." Mary shook her teenage son hard enough to piss him off. "I said wake up now!"

"Get off me, Mom, it's spring break. I'm off school this week. Leave me alone. I wanna go back to sleep, so get off me. Go away!" Alex rolled over, turning his angry back to his mother and curling into a fetal position. Not much had changed in this awakening process since Alex was a very young boy.

Mary grabbed him by the shoulder and jerked him back over. She pulled the covers off him and got in his face. "I need you today, boy. Your father and I and your uncle have all taken this day off to move your grandpa into the room downstairs. We need your help."

"All day!" Alex whined. "I'm too young to help."

"Right! You're fifteen and in better shape than any of us, including your father. And yes, all day. Stop acting like a child.

Those days are over, you know. But if you want to be treated like one, then—" Mary was flustered and wanted to smack him, but she knew it would hurt her hand more than it would ever hurt her son.

"No, no, I get it. You'll ground me and lock me in a playpen. Or your new one, 'I'm not mature enough for a driver's license.' I've heard them all before, Mom." Alex responded as many smart-ass teenagers do. But his parents were so thankful that this obnoxious attitude occurred only when he was being dragged out of bed.

"I expect you to be downstairs in fifteen minutes, Biddy-Buddie." She knew Alex hated to be called that, so she did it in lieu of smacking him. Mary turned and began to leave the room.

"Hey, hey. Where's Grandpa going to sleep? Not up here with me, right? I mean, I love him and all, but I've heard him snore, not to mention his beer farts. I'd rather go back to rooming with Melody and listen to her grind her freaky teeth all night." Alex wasn't thinking, and Mary didn't appreciate his tone of voice.

"Of course not. You're a goofball. I told you he was moving into the room downstairs. How do you think we'd get him up the steps in his wheelchair? We're getting the front room downstairs ready, where your Aunt Mayme and Aunt Carrie had their bedroom. He'll have a porch and some privacy. And yes, he does snore and fart, so your dad and I won't have to deal with that either. And we're putting in central air conditioning, so it'll be cool and quiet for him." Mary thought she had finished.

"But why now? Why are we moving him now? Is Grandma going to move in with us too when she gets out of the hospital?" Alex was confused.

The long silence began; at least, it seemed long to both Alex and Mary. But those types of silences always come with a price, a price that is actually known at the very first moment of the pause. "My mother isn't coming home, Alex. She'll be in the hospital for the rest of her life, which may only be a few more weeks." Tears filled Mary's eyes. Alex felt a chill run through his soul. "Your grandpa needs us. He's not handling this well, and he can't care for himself on South Jefferson since he lost his leg. He can't even drive yet. Probably never."

"Oh, Mom, I'm so sorry. I didn't know." Alex stood up and hugged his mother, returning all those loving embraces with which she had consoled him over the years. "Grandma's going to die? It's lung cancer, isn't it. It must be the way she's been coughing, and I've noticed blood on her handkerchief." Alex and Mary both began to weep as she placed her cheek on his shoulder, the shoulder high enough now to be that of a man. "I always said I didn't know what I'd do if Grandma died. I told her that a long time ago, Mom, when I was really little, right after Great-Grandma died. She lifted my chin, looked me in the eye, and promised me she would never die. I've never had anyone love me more than her."

Mary felt a twinge of pain inside with that last statement. She wanted that place in his heart for herself, but she was glad her son and her mother were always that close. She wished her mother would have loved her, as much as she did Alex, when she was a child.

"So Grandpa is coming to live with us full-time? He doesn't like me much, you know. He never has. He pretty much ignores me whenever I'm around, unless he needs a beer or a pack of cigarettes." Alex looked worried. "I can just steer clear, so he doesn't have to do any pretending."

"He likes you as much as he's able to like anybody, Alex. And as far as love goes, don't ever expect that. I never have. But I'm sorry to say, I'm going to need your help with him. It's been a rough year for him. so if you expect him to be happy, don't. He's had his leg amputated, and now, at fifty-eight, he's unable to work. He was a hard-working man, and he loved it. That alone is killing him. But now with your grandmother dying and being forced to leave and sell his house, he'll need to become reliant on us to take care of him. He'll be a mess for quite a while." Mary was comfortable in the upcoming role, as she had been the mother to both her alcoholic parents and her siblings for years.

"What do you want me to do, Mom? Do I need to give up basketball and baseball and hanging with my friends? Is that what you're saying?" Guilt swarmed through Alex's thoughts, as he was always taught to care for those in need. But now this was true sacrifice.

"No, no, Alex. Not at all. But this summer, try to be his friend and talk to him or play cards or something. Make him lunch or invite him to your baseball games. That's all. Now let's go. We have a long day ahead." Mary left the room, and Alex got ready to start another journey on his growth process. It was the first time he started to repay the favors and begin to care for those who had taken care of him all his childhood life.

Summer of 1966

THE ROLES REVERSE, AND NOT EQUALLY

The phone rang, and Alex answered. "Sure, but I can't be to the ballfield until about one o'clock. I'm making lunch for my grand-pa right now...Yeah, I have an extra baseball I can bring, but some of the stitches are tearing...All right, see you in about an hour."

From the living room, Art had heard Alex's conversation on the phone. As Alex went back into the kitchen, he stirred the veg-etable soup on the stove and continued to make two turkey sand-wiches. Art called out, "Alex, go to the ballfield now if you need to. I'm not that hungry." Art spent most of his time feeling as if he was a burden to his grandson and everyone else.

"Grandpa, I'm fine. I have to eat too. I would actually eat all day if I could." Art understood the appetite of a growing kid. "And my buddies never show up on time anyway. Want some tomato and pickles? I'm putting them on my sandwich."

"Sure, kid, that'd be nice."

"What do you want to drink, Grandpa?"

"A beer's fine."

Alex looked in the refrigerator. Then bounced down the basement steps to check the second refrigerator. As he ran back up, he stuck his head into the living room. "Sorry Grandpa, but we're out of beer. I'll call Mom and ask her to pick some up on her way home from work."

"Alex, can you run up the street to Mr. Thomas's and get me a six-pack of Hudy?" Art felt a little bad for asking, but not more than he would if he went the afternoon sober.

"Grandpa, I'm not old enough to buy beer or cigarettes," responded Alex with a chuckle. He assumed Art was kidding.

"I'll give you a note, Alex. Mr. Thomas knows you. He'll sell it to you. He did when you were five. There's some money in my dresser drawer."

Alex realized his grandfather was serious. He wasn't kidding. "Grandpa, those days are long gone. They'd put him out of business or put me in jail if they saw me carrying a six-pack down the street." Alex continued to make lunch.

"That's a bunch of crap. When did they start doing that? Hell, what am I supposed to do, wheel myself three blocks?" Art was angry, something that wasn't unusual since Ethel had died a month or so ago.

"It's a big ten years, Grandpa, and a five-year-old is one thing, but a fifteen-year-old who might drink it himself with his buddies is another."

"Getting to be too many rules, kid. Does your dad still have that bottle of scotch in the cabinet in the dinette?"

Alex went to check. "About half a fifth, Grandpa." He brought it into the living room and placed it on the end table with a glass. "Need ice?"

"Oh hell, no. A man don't drink liquor with ice. Straight-up puts hair on your chest." Alex smiled. He had not heard his grandpa say that in a long time. "Want to have a drink with me, kid? Lost all my old drinkin' buddies 'cause of this god damn stub of a leg." Art was upset.

"Grandpa, I wish I could, but I don't think Mom would be too happy with either one of us if I did that."

"Don't tell her, then. We can have a drink together here and there before your parents get home. I was already drinking at your age. Don't be a wimp."

Art was sadly desperate for a friend. So much so that he was attempting to embarrass his grandson to be one. Alex knew it would probably be a way to get closer to his grandfather, but it was certainly the wrong way.

He brought the soup and sandwiches from the kitchen and placed them on the TV tables. "Not much on television except those soap operas and game shows during the day. What do you want to watch?"

"Find a game show. That'll be fine." Alex and his grandfather sat quietly, eating lunch and watching television. When done, Alex cleaned up, called his mother, told her to bring home some beer and pick up a new bottle of scotch. He told her nothing of his grandfather's request, and Art knew Alex would keep it their secret.

"See you tonight, Grandpa. I have a ball game tomorrow night if you want to come." And with that, Alex grabbed his glove, his bat and ball, hopped on his bike and headed for the field.

This lunch routine went on all summer except for the request by Art for Alex to be his drinking buddy. Conversations were short and utilitarian. An occasional comment about the Reds or the weather, but the pain inside of Alex had faded from his early days around Art. He now observed Art as a quiet man, even to his son and daughters and any friends that came to visit. Alex felt better, realizing it was not a flaw in his own character or just his being that caused his grandfather not to love him. It was the way his grandfather treated everyone. But he would soon find out that Art's internal feelings were quite different from his external "tough guy" façade.

CHRISTMAS MORNING 1966
THE BREAKFAST TABLE

Christmas Day was no longer the internal and external fantasy that had germinated inside Alex each year, like flowers that fade every autumn, then push through their cold dark soil every spring to blossom into bright colors like God's smile. But at the age of sixteen, even the anticipation of the first day of school had surpassed that of Christmas morning. Now Alex's priorities were focused on his social world, which contained different types of gifts, like knowledge and friendships, and yes, even those beautiful youthful sparks of puppy love, like a piece of flint skipping off a rock, hoping to ignite a blaze.

This year, being in a new home and with the rapid maturity of Alex and Melody, Mary and Randall made the parental decision to postpone the immediate exchange of gifts under the tree and postpone the festivities until the afternoon, when Art's son, Jim, and Aunt Carrie would join them for Christmas dinner. But to begin this new tradition, Mary set the dinette table for breakfast for her new family of five, which now included her beloved father, Art, who she had taken into her benevolent nest. Since her mother Ethel had died a few months earlier and Carrie was at a point where she was even unable to take care of herself, Mary was now the matriarch of the Schaefer family. Sitting around the oval dinette table, Mary filled the house with the loving aroma of bacon, scrambled eggs, and everyone's favorite, banana pancakes.

As they all waited quietly, Mary poked her head around the kitchen stove, looking at everyone with a smile. "Well, Dad, I didn't get a chance to ask. Did you enjoy Alex's basketball game last week?"

Art's initial response was what Alex expected. "Sure, it was okay. I thought it would be harder to get me and my wheelchair into that gym, but that little hallway where you wheeled me was unexpectedly easy." Again, Alex had no supposition he would receive a compliment.

"Thanks for passing me the ball, Alex. Sorry I missed it." Art looked up at Alex with a sly grin, one of the few ever tossed to Alex in his lifetime by his grandfather.

Alex looked at Art with a smile. "Yep, Grandpa, that one kinda got away from me, didn't it? Sorry."

"Like when you hit me in the jaw with that roundhouse before the fight." Art smiled again, as Mary stuck her head around the corner once more, but with a startled look in her eyes.

"What fight? What do you mean, Dad? Alex, did you hit your grandfather, young man? You two never told me about an incident like that. When was this, last summer?" Mary and Randall looked concerned. But then Art and Alex both began to laugh at each other.

"Yep, the kid nailed me on my couch when he was five. I was teaching him how to box with those boxing gloves Jimmy used to have, right before we listened to the Sugar Ray Robinson bout on the radio. They were bigger than the kid's head. It was a stitch." Art was smiling.

"Grandpa, I was so scared you were mad at me when I did that. All these years, I've been sure that was why you never really liked me. You thought it was funny?" Alex wasn't sure whether that revelation was appropriate or not.

"Alex, I've always liked you. What makes you think I don't?" Art wasn't really puzzled. He knew why Alex surmised that. "You think because I don't say much or hug you or tell you I'm proud of you that I don't like you. Right?"

"Pretty much, Grandpa." Alex's heart began to pound. He didn't want to hear the answer. The grizzly bear was now out of his cage.

"First, kid, I must say that since your Uncle Jim has that same bleeding condition you have, I assumed you would grow up to be in a bubble like what your grandmother did to him. He's smart, but tough, not so much." Art had always been a bit disappointed that Jimmy was not a rough kid like he himself had been. "But I have to say, I was surprised when I saw you play basketball the other day."

Alex frowned, with a look of confusion. "Surprised? Why would you be surprised? At what?"

"When that kid tried to undercut you on that lay-up, you popped up off the floor and went after him. You grabbed him by the jersey and got in his face. I thought sure you were going to hit him. The referee had to pull you off. That kid could have punched you back." Art was proud of Alex in one way, but scared too, as he and Ethel always had been with Jim.

"Grandpa, that's part of the game. Somebody cheap-shots you, and you let him know not to do it again. I knew the referee was right there, and they always let that go for a moment to warn the other kid. I made the foul shots. At sixteen, I'm not six-foot, and I'm skinny. I have to play smart."

Melody giggled and looked at her brother. "You smart, Alex? You're right about being short and skinny, but definitely not smart. I think you're stupid." Alex had finally reached the age where he ignored his little sister's constant badgering. "When can we open presents, Mom, she whined." Melody was not in a happy place. She was only ten and wanted to open presents before breakfast like always, not sit and listen to grown-ups talk about stupid stuff.

Art was surprised at Alex's answer. "And I can see that nasty floor burn on your forearm. You dove for that ball like it was a fumble on the football field."

Alex came right back with an answer as he glanced over at his father. "As Dad says, whenever the ball's loose on the floor, it's mine, so go get it. I get some bruises here and there, but I'm alive and I play smart. I'm learning how far I can push it with this bleed-ing thing. Only thing is, I so want to play football, but I understand why that's going too far."

"Football was all I played, kid," Art said proudly. "There was a semi-pro team in Cincinnati in the twenties called the Bengals. I played center. We didn't wear facemasks. That's why my nose is crooked and smashed on my face."

"Mine too, Grandpa. Took an elbow on a rebound last year, but didn't stop. I dribbled all the way down the floor, made the basket. Then they stopped the game and had to wipe the blood off the floor and the ball. My jersey was a mess. I sat out the second half. I could have gone back in, but I saw Mom shake her head no to the coach. Didn't think I saw that did you, Mom?" Art and Alex were having a real discussion. "We won, anyway."

"Mine too," said Randall. "But I went over the handlebars of my bike and did a faceplant on the sidewalk," and they all started laughing.

"Kid, all I want to say to you is I never disliked you. You can ask your mother. I was quiet mostly because your grandmother did all the talking. You've seen it since I have been here. I don't say much to anybody. I'm just quiet, always have been. Actually, I never thought many people ever liked me. It's been a tough year for me. Thanks for all those summer lunches and for just hanging around. I always prayed it would rain so you'd stay home."

It was everything the people at the table could do to keep from crying except Melody, of course, who just wanted to open presents. Alex got up to give Art a hug. Art looked at him with a subtle smile. "Don't even think about doing what I think you're going to do. Don't push it. No hugging." Alex slapped his grandfather on the shoulder and with a warm grin, sat back in his chair. Mary brought breakfast to the table, and all exchanged stories of Christmases past. All except Art. He had said his piece.

CHRISTMAS DINNER TABLE – 4:00 p.m. – 1966

As all sat in the living room exchanging presents, the entire day lacked that joyous feeling of the past. There were ghosts swirling through each person like a swarm of bees, stinging each in a multitude of passion. Yet it was a bonding time for each, even if it was all unspoken. The recent sad memories were too fresh to turn into fun stories, and even the remodeled home of Mayme and Carrie, though filled with the energetic lives of the Beckham family, was not enough to overcome all three generations, with their quiet, swirling grief.

Last Christmas, on the eve of Christmas Day, the Beckhams had had their last dinner in the now demolished home, where bulldozers and wrecking balls had crashed and destroyed so many people's memories and family traditions involuntarily. It had been the third year of Christmas Eve without Alex's deceased grandparents; however, Mary had carried on the tradition for just the four of them, with a tomato juice appetizer and boiled lobster tails. This year, that banquet had remained the same, only in a new home and with the addition of Art.

And now, the Christmas morning opening of presents had moved to the afternoon in this new environment, and the excitement of opening gifts from Santa had evolved from the mania of ripping apart wrapped toys into fake smiles and "Oh, wow, a new pair of socks." Alex observed Melody, now age ten, as she opened a beautiful new dollhouse, the only fun gift under the tree. A sad thought went through his mind, a thought that was one of the first seeds of the soon-to-come adult stage of his life. He thought, through all the presents and all the changes in the past few years, my little sister has been young enough to escape most of it. Alex almost cried.

He thought, of all of us, Melody is the only one who truly has a new house. She had not been in this very living room to witness the end of his Aunt Mayme or the intense bereavement on his Aunt Carrie's face as she was taken away or the memories of a dead bird or playing hide-and-seek with the boys in the old neighborhood. She had a new house. One that she could decorate in her own way and make its life and the lives of her dolls happy in its new beginning. As Alex looked around the room, everyone watched her and smiled as their hearts were touched with their memories of those new and exciting days of their own youth.

But of all in the room, Art was the most somber as he fought back the tears. He missed his health. He missed his home and his dog. He missed his youngest daughter who, after he'd moved in with the Beckhams, had, without permission, taken his car and all his furniture and disappeared with her boyfriend to somewhere in Alabama. And his dear Aunt Mayme was not there next to Carrie's side, as she had been all his life. But way more intense, and something he couldn't accept, something that drove a spike through his heart all day, every day—he missed his dear little Ethel.

"Time to eat, everybody. Turkey's done. Alex, get everyone what they want to drink, and help me carry these dishes to the table. Dad, do you want to carve the turkey like always?" Jim had wheeled Art to the head of the table, where he certainly belonged.

"No, dear, that's Randall's job now. I'm just a guest in your home, honey. I'm a freeloader now." Art was having trouble talking.

"Don't be silly. We're all family. We love having you here. It's a new day, Dad."

Art stayed silent, but a bit of rage began to build. He thought, *I don't want a new day. I want the old ones.*

Alex helped his mother, and when the table was prepared, Randall finally entered from the kitchen with the succulent turkey and dressing, spread on a new artistic platter. "Okay, Dad, you want to say grace?"

"No, honey. Someone else." Art was having a terrible time getting his words out. He felt choked but refused to cry, as he had every year at the table. It was the only time, probably by permission of the alcohol, that he had told everyone how much he loved them, with Ethel tucked into his side.

Alex wasn't sure if everyone was thinking the same thing. He sat at the right hand of his grandfather. He looked around the table, and it seemed as vacant as the number of gifts under the tree. *Jim, Aunt Carrie, Mom, Dad, Melody, me and Grandpa, that's it.*

As Alex ate, his mind began to shuffle through those Schaefer Christmas dinners. There were a least a dozen every year around the table when he was still young but old enough to remember. The alcohol had flowed briskly, with no end. By dinnertime, his aunts, his grandma and her friends couldn't keep their hands off him, hugging and kissing and laughing. Art was laughing and kissing Ethel, the only time Alex ever saw Art being affectionate. Then came the year Grandma had forgotten to turn on the oven, and when Art made his first slice into the bird, it was raw, and blood ran down the side. Jim, age sixteen at the time, yelled at his mother, then he and Art started to argue, Ethel started crying, and within half an hour, all but Mary, who consoled her drunken mother, had left the house, including Art.

As Alex got older, he realized that other than that year, it was a fun and loving day had by all. But now, as they sat in the dining room, the same room in which his Aunt Mayme's body had been laid out for viewing at her death, the table was somber. Small talk was minimal, since no one really had anything in common any-more. And nobody wanted to reminisce. It was just all too sad.

"Help me clear the table, Alex, and we'll get desert on the table." Alex helped his mother, then sat back down as Randall poured coffee into the cups of Mary, Jim, and Carrie. They continued to finish quietly, all knowing it was close to the end, when they could all go back to their solitary lives, leaving this stressful occasion behind.

"Well, Dad, you've been so quiet," Mary said to Art. "We're thinking about going camping next summer. Want to go with us?" Art was silent. "Alex has a number of games starting right after New Year's if you want to join us. What do you think?"

Art looked at Mary and stayed silent. Alex glanced over and saw his grandfather's eyes watering and a tear run down his face.

He could hear short sobs being blocked from notice. Art looked at his daughter and said with a shaky voice, "Mary, I'm sorry I'm such a burden. I miss Ethel."

"Dad, stop it you're not…Dad?" Mary stood and peered down the table, eyes widened and her body tensed in horror.

Alex watched Art as his hand began to shake and his coffee rippled over the edge of his cup as he attempted to land it on his saucer. The cup and saucer began to clank helplessly together.

"Alex, Jim, wheel me to my bed," Art said with a slur. Jim's and Alex's eyes met in terror.

"Dad, what's wrong?" asked Jim. Alex saw drool coming from the right end of Art's mouth. Art's room was directly behind him at the table. Alex opened the two French doors, and Jim rolled his father to the bed. Then the two of them picked him up and placed him in his bed, his limbs drained of all strength. Only his eyes moved back and forth, connecting with those crowded in the room.

Jim removed Art's prosthesis, then slapped his good leg violently. "Feel that, Dad?"

Art's eyes fluttered in panic; his eyes were the only thing he could move. Then suddenly, his bowels released, with the smell of inevitable quietus. Mary ran to the phone and returned within moments.

"The ambulance is on its way, Dad. You're going to be fine." But he wasn't going to be fine; everyone knew it, even Art.

The ambulance came and rushed him to the emergency room. Jim and Mary followed, while Carrie, Randall, Melody, and Alex sat waiting in the living room, tears flowing down Carrie's weathered cheeks. Melody hugged her and cried in sympathy for her aunt as well as from the shock stirred by the deadly chaos that had just taken place in her new home. Randall and Alex quickly stripped the bed of its odiferous sheets, took them out the side door, placed them in an empty garbage can, then covered it tightly. During the entire process, Alex gritted his teeth to keep from vomiting. Then they both returned to the living room and sat in a numb silence.

It was less than an hour later when that silence was broken by the chilling ring of the telephone. Randall arose and answered, then returned quickly to the room. He wasted no time revealing the news from Mary.

"Art was dead on arrival. He was pronounced dead in the ambulance. The doctors said it was a massive cerebral hemorrhage. Mary said a vessel must have literally exploded in his brain." Randall was under control.

Alex spoke up with an obvious lump in his throat. "Wait, Mom and I just took Grandpa to the doctor last week. The doctor said Grandpa was fine. I don't get it." He felt angry; he had to blame someone.

"I don't know, Alex. That's all your mother said." With that, Alex finally began to cry. "Your mother said she and Jim have to complete some paperwork and will be home in a little while. Alex, help me clear the table and clean the kitchen before she gets home."

"Dad, can you give us all a minute please?" Alex was a bit disturbed at his father's lack of compassion. But the only time he had seen his father cry was at the death of his own mother.

After a few minutes, Alex got up without being asked and joined his father in straightening the house where Art had had his last Christmas dinner. Melody and Carrie continued to huddle on the living room sofa. Just as Alex and his father completed the cleanup and sat back down in the living room, Mary and Jim came into the room. Everyone stood and passed hugs of grief to each other. Carrie, Melody, and Alex began to cry once more. Mary and Jim seemed drained, but no tears.

Randall gave his wife a long hug. "You okay, honey? What can I get you? Anything for you, Jim? You both must be exhausted, but you both seem calm and at peace."

Mary sat in her favorite chair and looked at everyone in the room, showing no emotion. "We're fine. What should we do? It was what it was, a stroke, a cerebral hemorrhage. Nothing anybody could do about it. He went quick. No pain. I'm going to the phone to start spreading the news."

Mary went through the kitchen, grabbed a beer from the refrigerator, and sat down with her contact book in front of the phone. Jim stayed only a few more minutes, then took Carrie back to the nursing home, to be even more sad and alone than when the day began. Randall turned on the television just in time for the beginning of *The Wizard of Oz*. Melody fell asleep on the love seat shortly before the wicked witch appeared dead under the house.

Alex observed his father sitting comfortably on the sofa. "Dad, I don't really want to watch television. I'm think I want to just go to bed. You mind?"

"Not at all, son. Rough day for all of you. See you in the morning." Randall continued to stare at the movie.

Alex walked to his bedroom, but stopped to say good night to his mother. "Night, Mom. I love you." But as he went to give her a hug and kiss goodnight, she just gave a four-finger wave over her shoulder without looking at him at all, as she continued a conversation with someone on the telephone. Alex's eyes watered slightly as he climbed the stairs and made his way to his bed.

CHRISTMAS NIGHT – 11:00 P.M.

IN THE DARK MEMORIES OF THE MIND OF ALEX BECKHAM

For almost an hour, Alex had been lying in his bed connecting the puzzle pieces of his life that had brought him to this very moment. As he lay still, the house became dark and serene. His mother's whimpering had faded, and the assumption that all were asleep at the end of this unforgettable Christmas Day left him in a deep state of contemplation. It was then that Alex's mind hit on something, something he realized had been slowly embedded into his psyche in these early years of his life. Something that had been ingrained in him, something that needed to be slowly eradicated from his subconscious. Not the physical events. It was something that his mother had said that evening after returning from the hospital. Something she said that would haunt him for the rest of his life. It was something that would cause him to choose a different direction as he approached many crossroads to come.

His grandfather's death was not a "was what it was," as his mother had so calmly stated. It was caused by the repression of love and feelings taught to him from his very beginning. It was deep grief inside every cell of the man's body, causing intense pressure as it barricaded his emotions, until finally a series of powerful enough storms came along, and the flood waters from all those tributaries over the years that had fed into his imprisoned river exerted such pressure that the dam had burst, and along with it, inevitable death and destruction.

Art had appeared to be a tough man, a quiet man, a cold man. But as Alex had fortunately learned from Dr. Winston at an early stage of life, expressing one's feelings is okay. It's not expressing feelings at appropriate times that evolves into the source and growth of unbearable pain. His grandfather, without a doubt, had died of a broken heart. *That 'was what it was,' my dear mother,* thought Alex. Probably, the same deep-rooted torment that would eventually cause his mother to leave the earth at an early age.

Alex's eyes finally became heavy, and he fell asleep. He slept deeply, and the next morning was different. He loved his mother and father and sister as well as the rest of his family differently. It was okay to feel, and it was okay to tell them so. He coined a saying for himself: "It is never too soon to tell someone you love them, but it can be too late."

EPILOGUE

So those are a few tributaries from the perfectly imperfect ceiling of Alex Beckham's grandmother—those ever-growing rivers, streams, and lakes on her unavoidably aging ceiling. Over time, some of those tributaries would flow gently into Alex's life and make him stronger, while he found others needed to be damned and allowed to dry up forever. And others would fluctuate in times of storm from peaceful to raging rapids overflowing their banks, causing pain and destruction for everything in their path. Alex learned that life is in constant fluctuation, and even death has a way of continuing on from generation to generation.

Alex and I both wish to thank you for your respect and attention. We hope that we have given you a few small tales about what helped to form Alex's life, as in the end, we all end up emptying into the ocean with the droplets from all the tributaries that fed into our lives. Then as we evaporate into the empty sky, we fly high until we drop and become the tributaries themselves.

"It is one thing to be blessed, but it is better to be a blessing."

The End or the Beginning. You decide.

Made in the USA
Coppell, TX
31 January 2021

49280624R00218